The White Plumes Of Navarre

A Romance Of The Wars Of Religion

by

S. R. Crockett

Double 9
BOOKS

The White Plumes Of Navarre
A Romance Of The Wars Of Religion
by S. R. Crockett

ISBN: 978-93-63054-56-1

Published by

DOUBLE 9 BOOKS

2/13-B, Ansari Road
Daryaganj, New Delhi – 110002
info@double9books.com
www.double9books.com
Tel. 011-40042856

ABOUT THE AUTHOR

Samuel Rutherford Crockett was a Scottish novelist who published under the pen name "S. R. Crockett". He was born on September 24, 1859, in Little Duchrae, Balmaghie, Kirkcudbrightshire, Galloway, as the illegitimate son of dairymaid Annie Crocket. His Cameronian grandparents nurtured him on the tenanted farm until the family relocated to Cotton Street, Castle Douglas in 1867 (later fictionalized as Cairn Edward). In 1876, he obtained the Galloway bursary at Edinburgh University, where he earned an MA. He began his journalistic career in 1877 to support his bursary by writing for journals. He left the university in April 1879 without receiving a diploma. From 1879 to 1881, he traveled throughout Europe as a tutor before returning to Edinburgh's New College to prepare for the ministry. The Crocketts had four children: Maisie Rutherford, Philip Hugh Barbour, George Milner, and Margaret Douglas, all of whom appeared in his children's stories. In 1906, the family relocated from Bank House in Penicuik to Torwood House in Peebles, but Crockett spent much of the year overseas and made frequent trips back to Galloway. In 1886, he released a volume of poetry under the alias Ford Brereton, titled Dulce Cor (Latin for Sweet Heart). Dulce Cor is a ruined abbey in Galloway. In the late 1880s, he was a regular contributor to The Christian Leader magazine, edited by W.H. Wylie.

CONTENTS

BEFORE THE CURTAIN RISES

The night was hot in Paris. Breathless heat had brooded over the city all Saturday, the 23rd of August, 1572. It was the eve of Saint Bartholomew. The bell of Saint Germain l'Auxerrois had just clashed out the signal. The Louvre was one blaze of lights. Men with lanterns and poleaxes, as if going to the shambles to kill oxen, hurried along the streets.

Only in the houses in which were lodged the great Huguenot gentlemen, come to the city for the marriage of the King's sister Marguerite to the King of Navarre, there were darkness and silence. None had warned them—or, at least, they had taken no warning. If any suspected, the word of a King, his sworn oaths and multitudinous safe-conducts, lulled them back again into security.

In one chamber, high above the courtyard, a light burned faint and steady. It was that beside the bed of the great Admiral—Coligny. He had been treacherously wounded by the arquebuse of one of the guard of the King's brother—Monsieur de France, Henry Duke of Anjou, afterwards to be known to history as Henry III., the favourite son of Catherine de Medici, the cunningest, and the most ungrateful.

There watched by that bedside many grave men, holding grave discourse with each other and with the sick man, concerning the high mysteries of the religion, pure and reformed, of the state of France, and their hopes of better days for the Faith as it had been delivered to the saints.

And at the bed-foot, with towels, bandages, and water in a silver salver ready for service, one young lad, a student of Geneva, fresh from Calvin and Beza, held his tongue and opened wide his ears.

"Pray, Merlin de Vaux," said the wounded Admiral to his aged pastor, "pray for life if such be God's will, that we may use it better—for death (the which He will give us in any case), that the messenger may not find us unprepared."

And Merlin prayed, the rest standing up, stern, grave, prepared men, with bowed and reverent heads. And the Genevan Scot thought most of his dead master Calvin, whom, in the last year of his life, he had often seen so stand, while his own power rocked under him in the city of his adoption, and the kingdoms of the earth stormed about him like hateful waves of the sea.

And somewhat thus-wise prayed good Merlin.

"Thou, O Lord, hast put down the mighty from their seats and has exalted them of low degree! Clay are all men in Thy hands—potter's clay, broken shards or vessels fit for altar-service. Yet Thou has sent us, Thy servants, into the wild, where we have seen things, and thought things, and given us many warnings, so that when Thou standest at the door and knockest, we may be ready for Thy coming!"

Then at these words, prompt as an echo, the house leaped under the heavy noise of blows delivered upon the outer door. And the Admiral of France, sitting up in his bed, yet corpse-pale from his recent wound, lifted his hand and said, "Hush, be still—my Lord standeth without! For dogs and murderers, false kings and queens forsworn, are but instruments in His hand. It is God who calls us to His holy rest. For me, I have long been ready. I go with no more thought than if my chariot waited me at the door."

Then he turned to the Huguenot gentlemen who were grouped about his bed. This one and that other had tried to catch a glimpse of the assailants from the windows. But in vain. For the door was in a recess which hid all but the last of the guard which the King had set about the house.

"It is only Cosseins and his men," said one; "they will hold us safe. We have the King's word. He placed the guard himself."

"The hearts of Kings are unsearchable," said the Admiral. "Put not your trust in princes, but haste ye to the garret, where is a window that gives upon the roof. There is no need that young and valiant men should perish with a wounded man and an old. Go and fight for the remnant that shall be preserved. If it be the Lord's will, He shall yet take vengence by your arms!"

"Ay, go," said Merlin the pastor, casting back his white hair; "for me, I am old, and I stay. Only yester-night I saw an angel stand in the sun, crying to all souls that did fly through the midst of heaven, 'Come, gather yourselves to the Supper of the Great God.' But when, thinking myself called, I would have drawn nearer, lo! between me and the table spread, on which was the wine ready poured out, I saw the Beast, the kings of the earth, and their warriors gathered together to make war against the Lamb. And I heard a voice that said, 'Nay, but first thou must pass through the portal of death ere it be given thee to eat of the marriage supper of the Lamb.' So to me it spake. The message was not for you—ye heard not the Voice. I will stay, for I am weary, and am minded to fall on sleep—to find rest after many years."

And to this Paré, the wise and skilled surgeon, who was ever beloved by Admiral Coligny, likewise adhered, saying, "I have not heard the voice of the angel. But I hear well enough that of false Cosseins who is sent by the King to murder us. I have looked from the window, and though I saw no vision of Beast, I saw clearly my Lord Duke of Guise stand without calling to them to slay and make an end! So I also will remain for the love I bear to my lord, and because it is my duty as a good physician so to do."

And the lad John Stirling, the Scot from Geneva, the pupil of Calvin, ventured no word, being young. But, though the others would have carried him with them, he shook them off, and abode where he was. For his vision, and the purpose of it, were yet to be.

And so it came to pass that this young man from Geneva saw the killing of the great Admiral, and heard the words in which he forgave his assassins, telling them how that he was ready to die, and that at the most they had but shortened his life by some short count of days or hours!

And ever through the brief turmoil of the killing, the voice of the Duke of Guise mounted impatiently up the stairway asking if the Admiral were not yet dead, and hounding on his dogs to make an end of that noble quarry.

And even when they assured him he would not believe, but desired to look on the face of his own and his father's enemy.

"Open the window and throw him down!" he cried.

So they cast him out. But the aged prince, with the life still in his body, clutched by instinct at the sill of the window as he fell. The young Duke, first ordering up a couple of flambeaux, deliberately wiped the blood from the face of his enemy with his kerchief, and cried out, "It is even he—I know him well. So perish all the enemies of the King and of the Catholic League!"

Then, as his men still called from the window, the Duke looked up, angry to be disturbed in his gloating over his arch-foe.

"There is also a lad here," they cried, "one from Geneva, who says he is of the Admiral's opinion. What shall we do with him?"

"What is that to me?" said the Duke of Guise haughtily; "throw him after his master."

And that is the reason why a certain John Stirling, a Scot of Geneva, went through life lame, wearing a countenance twisted like a mask at a fair, and—loved not the Duke Henry of Guise.

Moreover, though he saw the Duke spurn his dead enemy with his foot, the boy felt not at the time the kicks with which the scullions imitated their master, but lay in a swoon on the body of Coligny. He came to himself, however, being cast aside as of no account, when they came to drag the Admiral's body to the gallows. After a while the spray of a fountain that played in the courtyard roused him. The lad washed his hands and crawled forth. He had lain all the terrible Sunday in the bloody court of Coligny's lodgings, under the shadow of the trembling acacias, which cast flecks of light and dark on the broad irregular stains of the pavement. But when the evening had come again, and the angry voices shouting "Kill! kill!" had died away, the lame boy hobbled painfully out. Somehow or other he passed through an unguarded gate, to find himself sustained by a fellow-countryman carrying a child, a little maid of four years. He must have been a strong man, that chance-met Scot, for he had an arm to spare for John Stirling. He spoke, also, words of hope and comfort to the boy. But these fell on deaf ears. For through the dull ache of his bones and the sharp nip of his wounds, undressed save for the blood that had dried upon them, the heart of the cripple remained with Henry of Guise.

"No," he said over and over to himself, repeating the Duke's words, "the work is not yet finished!" It had, indeed, scarce begun.

And he registered a vow.

CHAPTER I
THE DAY OF BARRICADES

"The good Duke! The sweet Prince! The Church's pillar! Guise! The good Guise!"

Through the open window the shouts, near and far, invaded the quiet class-room of the Sorbonne. It was empty, save for the Professor of Eloquence, one Dr. Anatole Long, and a certain vagrant bluebottle which, with the native perversity of its tribe, sought out the only shut square of glass (bottle-green, by way of distinction) and buzzed loudly all over it.

The Professor thumbed the discourse of the day on "Peace as the Characteristic Virtue of the Christian Faith." It was a favourite lecture with him. He had used it as exposition, homily, exhortation; and had even on one occasion ventured to deliver it before the Venerable the Conclave of the Sorbonne itself.

Professor Anatole sighed as he listened to the ringing shouts outside, the clatter of steel on peaceful educational stairways, and when through the open windows, by which the early roses ought to have been sending up their good smell, there came a whiff of the reek of gunpowder, the excellent Anatole felt that the devil was loose indeed.

It was the great Day of Barricades, and all Paris was in arms against the King, royal, long-descended, legitimate—and worthless.

"Rebellion—rank rebellion," groaned the Professor; "no good will come of it. Balafré, the Scarred One, will get a dagger in his throat one day. And then—then—there will be a great killing! The King is too ignorant to forgive!"

"Ah, what is that?"

A noise of guns crashed, spat, and roared beneath the window which gave on to the narrow street. Professor Anatole rose hastily and went to the casement, worried a moment with the bar-fastening (for the window on that side was never unhasped), opened it, and looked forth. Little darting, shifting groups of lads in their dingy student cloaks, were defending themselves as best they might against a detachment of the King's Royal

Swiss, who, on the march from one part of the city to another, had been surprised at the head of the narrow Street of the University.

An old man had somehow been knocked down. His companion, a slim youth in a long, black cape, knelt and tried to hold up the failing head. The white beard, streaked with dark stains, lay across his knees. Now the Professor of Eloquence, though he lectured by preference concerning the virtues of peace, thought that there were limits even to these; so, grasping his staff, which had a sword concealed in the handle, of cunning Venice work, ran downstairs, and so found himself out on the street.

In that short period all was changed. The Royal Swiss had moved on. The battling clerks had also vanished. The narrow Street of the University was blank save for the old man who lay there wounded on the little, knobbed cobble-stones, and the slim, cloaked youth bending over him.

Professor Anatole does not remember clearly what followed. Certain it is that he and the lad must have carried the wounded man up the narrow stair. For when Anatole came a little to himself they were, all the three of them, in his wide, bare attiring-chamber, from which it was his custom to issue forth, gowned and solemn, in the midst of an admiring hush, with the roll of his daily lecture clasped in his right hand, while he upheld the long and troublesome academic skirts with the other.

But now, all suddenly, among these familiar cupboards and books of reference, he found himself with a dying man—or rather, as it seemed, a man already dead. And, what troubled him far more, with a lad whose long hair, becoming loosened, floated down upon his shoulders, while he wept long and continuously, "Oh—oh—oh—my father!" sobbing from the top of his throat.

Now Professor Anatole was a wise man, a philosopher even. It was the day of *mignons*. The word was invented then. King Henry III. had always half-a-dozen or so, not counting D'Epernon and La Joyeuse. That might account for the long hair. But even a *mignon* would not have cried "Ah—ah—ah!" in quick, rending sobs from the chest and diaphragm.

He, Anatole Long, Professor of Eloquence at the Sorbonne, was in presence of a great difficulty—the greatest of his life. There was a dead man in his robing-room, and a girl with long hair, who wept in tremulous contralto.

What if some of his students were minded to come back! A terrible thought! But there was small fear of that. The rascals were all out shouting for the Duke of Guise and helping to build the great barricades which shut in the Swiss like rats in a trap. They were Leaguers to a man, these Sorbonne students—for fun, however, not from devotion.

Yet when he went back to the big empty class-room to bethink himself a little (it was a good twenty years since he had been accustomed to this sort of thing), lo! there were two young fellows rooting about among the coats and cloaks, from the midst of which he had taken his sword-cane when he ran downstairs.

"What are you doing there?" he cried, with a sudden quick anger, as if students of eloquence had no right in the class-room of their own Professor. "Answer me, you, Guy Launay, and you, John d'Albret!"

"We are looking for——" began Guy Launay, the son of the ex-provost of the merchants, a dour, dark clod of a lad, with the fingers of a swordsman and the muscles of a wrestler. He was going to say (what was the truth) that they had come up to look for the Professor's sword-cane, which they judged might be useful against the King's folk, when, of instinct far more fine, his companion, called the Abbé John, nephew of the great Leaguer Cardinal, stopped him with a swift sidelong drive of the elbow in the ribs, which winded him completely.

"We have come to listen to your lecture, master!" he said, bowing low. "We are sorry indeed to be a little late. But getting entangled in the press, it was impossible for us to arrive sooner. We ask your pardon, dear master!"

Under his breath the Abbé John confided to his companion, "Evidently old Blessings-of-Peace has carried that sword-stick off into his retiring-room for safety. Let him begin his lecture. Then in five minutes he will forget about everything else, and you or I will sneak in and bag it!"

"You—you mean," said Launay; "I should move about as silently as a bullock on a pontoon bridge!"

With his eye ever on the carefully-shut door of his private chamber, and his ear cocked for the sound of sobbing, the Professor moved slowly to his reading-desk. For the first time in his life he regretted the presence of students in the class-room. Why—why could they not have stayed away and dethroned anointed kings, and set up most Catholic princes, and fought for the Holy League and the pleasure of clouting heads? That was what students of the Sorbonne seemed to be for in these latter days. But to come here, at the proper hour, to take notes of a lecture on the Blessings of Peace, with the gun-shots popping outside, and dead men—no, somehow he did not care to think of dead men, nor of weeping girls either! So at this point he walked solemnly across the uneven floor and turned the key in the door of his robing-room.

Instantly the elbow of Guy Launay sought the side of the Abbé John, called alternatively the Spaniard, and made him gasp.

"D'ye see that?" whispered Guy, "the old rascal has locked the door. He suspects. Come, we may as well trip it. We shan't get either the sword-cane nor yet the pistols and bullets on the top of the guard-robe. My milk-brother, Stephen, saw them there when he took his week of chamber-valeting Old Peace-with-Honour!"

"Screw up your mouth—tight!" said the Abbé John politely; "a deal of nonsense will get spread about otherwise. I will attend to everything in the room of Old Blessings-of-Peace!"

"You!"

"Yes, I—wait and see. Get out your tablets and take notes—spread your elbows, man! Do as I do, and the blessing of Saint Nicholas of Padua be upon all thieves and rascals—of whom we are two choice specimens!"

"Speak for yourself, Spaniard!" spluttered the other, having accidentally sucked the wrong end of his pen; "my uncle is not a cardinal, and as to my father——"

"He sells hanks of yarn, and cheats in the measurement!"

"I dare you to say so, you left-hand prince, you grease-spot on the cardinal's purple—you——"

"That will do," said the Abbé John calmly; "to-morrow I will give you thwacks when and where you like. But now listen, mark, learn, and in any case keep our good Master Anatole from so frequently glancing at that door. One would think he had the devil shut up within!"

"Impossible—quite impossible; he is loose and exceedingly busy outside there! Listen to the shots," said Guy, inclining an ear to the window.

Crack—crack! Bang!

The windows rattled.

"Hurrah for the People's Duke! Down with the King! Death to the Huguenots!—to the Barbets!—to the English! Death! Death! Death!"

"Lively down there—I wish we were up and away!" mourned the son of the ex-provost of the merchants, "but without arms and ammunition, what can fellows do?"

"As sayeth the Wise Man"—the voice of the Professor of Eloquence began to quicken into its stride—"'all her main roads are pleasant roads; and her very by-paths, her *sentiers*, lead to peace!'"

"If we could only get at those pistols and things!" murmured Guy Launay. "I wager you a groat that the old man is mistaken! Oh, just hearken to them outside there, will you? Peace is a chafing-dish. War is the great sport!"

"Down with the King! Bring along those chains for the barricade! Students to the rescue!"

Then came up to their ears the blithe marching song, the time strongly marked:

"The Guises are good men, good men,
The Cardinal, and Henry, and Mayenne, Mayenne!
And we'll fight till all be grey—
The Valois at our feet to-day,
And in his grave the Bearnais—
Our chief has come—the Balafré!"

"Keys of Sainted Peter!" moaned Guy Launay, "I cannot stand this. I am going down, though I have no better weapon than a barrel-stave."

And he hummed, rapping on the inscribed and whittled bench with his fingers, the refrain of the famous League song:

"For we'll fight till all be grey—
The Valois at our feet to-day,
In his deep grave the Bearnais—
Our chief has come—the Balafré!"

But Professor Anatole did not hear. He was in the whirl of his exposition of the blessings of universal peace. The Church had always brought a sword, and would to the end. But Philosophy, Divine Philosophy, which was what Solomon meant—peace was within her walls, prosperity, etc.

And by this time the Spaniard, otherwise the Abbé John, was crawling stealthily towards the locked door. Guy Launay, on the contrary, was breathing hard, rustling leaves, taking notes for two, both elbows working. The Master was in the full rush of his discourse. He saw nothing, knew nothing. He had forgotten the robing-room in the affirmation that, "In the midst of turmoil, the truly philosophic may, and often does, preserve the true peace—the truest of all, peace of mind, peace of conscience."

Bang!

There was a tremendous explosion immediately under the window.

"The King's men blowing up a barricade!" thought the Abbé John, with his hand on the great flat key, but drawing back a little. "If that does not wake him up, nothing will."

But the gentle, even voice went on, triumphing—the periods so familiar to the lecturer ringing out more clearly than ever. "Wars shall cease only when Wisdom, which is God, shall prevail. Philosophy is at one with Religion. The Thousand Years shall come a thousand times over and on the earth shall reign— —"

The key gritted in the lock. The Abbé John disappeared behind the heavy curtain which hid the door of the robing-room.

The next moment he found himself in the presence of a man, lying rigidly on the Professor's table, all among the books and papers, and of the fairest young girl the Abbé John had ever seen, gently closing eyes which would never more look out upon the world.

Within, the Professor's voice droned on, discoursing of peace, righteousness, and eternal law. The great Day of the Barricades rattled and thundered without. Acrid blasts of sulphurous reek drove into the quiet room, and the Abbé John, speechless with amazement, looked into the wet eyes of this wonderful vision—the purest, the loveliest, the most forlorn maid in France.

CHAPTER II
CLAIRE AGNEW

A long moment they stood gazing at each other, the girl and the Abbé John. They might have been sister and brother. There was the same dark clustering hair, close-gripped in love-locks to the head. The same large, dark, wide-pupilled eyes looked each into each as they stood and gazed across the dead man.

For a moment nothing was said, but the Abbé John recovered himself first.

"He knows you are here?" he questioned, jerking his thumb over his shoulder.

"Who?" The girl flung the question back.

"Our Professor of Eloquence, the Doctor Anatole Long?"

"Aye, surely," said the girl; "he it was brought us hither."

He pointed to the dead man.

"Your father?"

The girl put her hand to her breast and sighed a strange piteous affirmative, yet with a certain reserve in it also.

"What was he, and how came you here?"

She looked at him. He wore the semi-churchly dress of a scholar of the University. But youth and truth vouched for him, shining from his eyes. So, at least, she thought. Besides, the girl was in a great perplexity.

"I am Claire," she said, "the daughter of him who was Francis Agnew, secret agent from the King of Scots to his brother of Navarre!"

"A heretic, then!" He fell back a step. "An agent of the Bearnais!"

The girl said nothing. She had not even heard him. She was bending over her father and sobbing quietly.

"A Huguenot," muttered the young Leaguer, "an agent of the Accursed!"

He kept on watching her. There was a soft delicate turn of the chin, childish, almost babyish, which made the heart within him like water.

"Chut!" he said, "what I have now to do is to get rid of that ramping steer of a Launay out there. He and his blanket-vending father must not hear of this!"

He went out quietly, sinking noiselessly to the ground behind the arras of the door, and emerging again, as into another world, amid the hum and mutter of professorial argument.

"All this," remarked Doctor Anatole, flapping his little green-covered pulpit with his left hand, "is temporary, passing. The clouds in the sky are not more fleeting than——"

"Guise! Guise! The good Guise! Our prince has come, and all will now be well!"

The street below spoke, and from afar, mingling with scattered shots which told the fate of some doomed Swiss, he heard the chorus of the Leaguers' song:

"The Cardinal, and Henry, and Mayenne, Mayenne!
We will fight till all be grey—
Put Valois 'neath our feet to-day,
Deep in his grave the Bearnais—
Our chief has come—the Balafré!"

Abbé John recovered his place, unseen by the Professor. He was pale, his cloak dusty with the wriggling he had done under the benches. He was different also. He had been a furious Leaguer. He had shouted for Guise. He had come up the stairs to seek for weapons wherewith to fight for that Sole Pillar of Holy Church.

"Well?" said Guy Launay, looking sideways at him.

"Well, what?" growled the Abbé John, most unclerically. He had indeed no right to the title, save that his uncle was a cardinal, and he looked to be one himself some day—that is, if the influence of his family held. But in these times credit was such a brittle article.

"Did you get the weapons?" snapped his friend—"the pistol, the sword-cane? You have been long enough about it. I have worn my pencil to a stub!"

The Abbé John had intended to lie. But somehow, when he thought of the clear dark eyes wet with tears, and the dead Huguenot, within there—somehow he could not.

Instead he blurted out the truth.

"I forgot all about them!" he said.

The son of the ex-provost of the merchants looked at him once, furiously.

"I think you are mad!" he said.

"So do I!" said the Abbé John, nodding blandly.

"Well, what is the reason of it?" grumbled the other. "What has Old Blessings-of-Peace got in there—a hidden treasure or a pretty wench? By the milk-pails o' Mary, I will go and see for myself!"

"Stop," said the Abbé John, with sudden heat, "no more spying! I am sick of it. Let us go and get weapons at the Hotel of the Duke of Guise, if you like—but respect the privacy of our master—our good and kind master!"

Guy Launay eyed his companion a moment murkily.

He gritted his teeth viciously, as if he could gladly have bitten a piece out of his arm. He showed large flat teeth when angry, for all the world like a bad-tempered horse.

"Stop and take notes on the comforts of philosophy by yourself," he said; "I am off to do my duty like a man. You have turned soft at the moment of action, like all Spaniards—all the breed are alike, you and your master, the Demon of the South!"

"You lie!"

"And you! But wait till to-morrow!"

"Ah," cried the Abbé John, "like all Frenchmen, you would put off a fight till to-morrow. Come out now, and I will break your head with a quarter-staff!"

"Pshaw!" quoth Guy Launay, "quarter-staffs indeed, on the Day of Barricades. I am off to kill a King's man, or to help spit a Huguenot!"

And the next moment the Professor of Eloquence had but one auditor.

CHAPTER III
THE PROFESSOR OF ELOQUENCE

"My name," she said, "is Claire Agnew. But since we lived long in Provence and Spanish Roussillon, my father, being learned in that speech, called me most often Euphrasia or Euphra, being, as he said, 'the light of his eyes'"!

"Then you are English, and a heretic?" said the young man, while the Professor, having discharged his papers into the drawer of a cabinet, already full and running over, bent his ear to the breast of the old man.

"I am Scottish, and you are the heretic!" said the girl, with spirit.

"I am no heretic—I am of the Faith!" said the young man.

"The Faith of treaty-breakers and murderers!"

She knit her fingers and looked at him defiantly—perhaps, if the truth must be told, more in anger than in sorrow.

The voice of the Professor of Eloquence broke in upon them.

"Young man," he said, "you have surprised a secret which is not mine—much less yours. Be off at once to your uncle, the Cardinal d'Albret, and to your friend's father Launay, the ex-provost of the merchants. Get three passports—for me, for my daughter Claire, and—for my nephew——"

"What nephew?" said the youth, rubbing the ear which the Professor had pulled.

"One I have adopted recently!" said the Professor gravely, "a certain worthless loon, who came up hither seeking what was not his—a sword-cane and a pistol, and who found that which, God knows, belongs to neither of us—an uncomfortable possession in these days, a Huguenot maiden with eyes like a flame of fire!"

"They are more like pansies!" said the young man doggedly.

"How do you know? How dare you? Is she not my daughter?"

"Aye, master, she is, of course, your daughter if you say so"—the voice of the Abbé John was uncertain. He did not like the Professor claiming so much—and he beginning to be bald too. What have bald pates to do with pretty young girls? Even thus he growled low to himself.

"Eh, what's that?" the Professor caught him up. "Be off—it is to save her life, and you are a young blade who should never refuse an adventure, specially when at last it gives you a chance to be taken for the relative of a respectable man——"

"And the cousin of this fair maid, your—daughter?"

"Well, and have I not a good right to a daughter of my own? Once on a day I was married, bonds and bands, parchments and paperings. For ten years I endured my pain. Well might I have had a daughter, and of her age too, had it not been my hard lot to wed a woman without bowels—flint-heart—double-tongue——"

"I wager it was these ten years that taught him his eloquence!" said the young man under his breath. But aloud he answered otherwise, for the young girl had withdrawn into the small adjacent piece, leaving the men to talk.

"And this?" said the Abbé John, indicating the dead man—"what are we to do with this?"

The face of the Professor of Eloquence cleared.

"Luckily we are in a place where such accidents can easily be accounted for. In a twinkle I will summon the servitors. They will find League emblems and holy crosses all about him, candles burning at his head and feet. The fight still rumbles without. It is but one more good Guisard gone to his account, whom I brought hither out of my love for the Cause, and that the Sorbonne might not be compromised."

Almost for the first time the student looked at his master with admiration.

"Your love for the Cause——" he said. "Why, all the world knows that you alone voted against the resolution of the assembled Sorbonne that it was lawful to depose a king who refused to do his duty in persecuting heretics!"

"I have repented," said the Professor of Eloquence—"deeply and sorely repented. Surely, even in the theology of the Sorbonne, there is place for repentance?"

"Place indeed," answered the young man boldly, "but the time is, perhaps, a little ill-chosen."

However the Professor of Eloquence went on without heeding him.

"And in so far as this girl's goodwill is concerned, let that be your part of the work. Her father, though a heretic, must be interred as a son of the Church. It is the only course which will explain a dead man among the themes in my robing-room. He has been in rebellion against the King—but there is none to say against which king! It does not need great wisdom to know that in Paris to-day, and especially in the Sorbonne, to die fighting against the Lord's Anointed, and for the Duke of Guise, is to receive the saint's aureole without ever a devil's advocate to say you nay!"

"It is well known," commented the youth, "that you were ever of the King's party—a Politique! It was even spoken of in the Council of the Sixteen."

"Do you go seek your cousin, sirrah," said the Professor of Eloquence, "and with her be very politic indeed!"

The Abbé John accepted the duty indicated with brisk alertness.

"Mind you, no love-making," said Dr. Anatole. "That would be not only misplaced, but also exceedingly ill-suited to your ecclesiastical pretensions."

"Hear me before we go farther," cried the Abbé John; "I am a good Leaguer and a good Catholic, but I will not have it said that I am a churchman just because my uncle is!"

The Professor paid no heed. Instead, he went to a corner cupboard of ornate Spanish mahogany carved into dragons and gargoyles, and from it he took the medal of the League, the portraits of the Duke of Guise and of the King of Spain. Then, tying a white armlet of Alençon lace about the dead man's wrist, he bade the Abbé John summon the servants.

The Abbé John stood opened-mouthed watching the preparations.

"I had always thought— —" he began.

"Of course you had—of course you did. You all do, you half-baked babies! You always take your instructors for ancient innocents, purblind, adder-deaf mumblers of platitudes. But you are wrong—you and Guy Launay, and all your like. A good professor is a man who has been a good student, who remembers the tricks of the animal, and is all ready fixed for them before the whisper has run along Bench One! I will conduct this necessary funeral in person. Please do you, since you can be of no other use, make it your business to explain matters to your cousin!"

The servants of the Sorbonne, Leaguers to a man, at last appeared, trickling upstairs half reluctantly. The Professor of Eloquence met them at the door with a grave face.

"This man has been slain—accidentally," he began, "I believe by the King's Swiss. I have brought him here myself. It will be as well for the Sorbonne that these matters go no further—good for you, as well as for myself, and for all the college of the Doctors, after the resolution of which we know. Let Father Gontier be called, and the dead man interred with all due ceremony in the private sepulchre of the faculty."

When the servitors of the Sorbonne had seen the half-hidden wristlet of the good Leaguer, the medals of the two great chiefs, they understood. After all, the King might win—and then—men might stay or flee, Guises rise and set, but it was clearly the destiny of the Sorbonne to go on for ever, if only to afford them a means of livelihood.

They were men with families, and the advantage of keeping a still tongue in each several head had often been pointed out to them. It was, indeed, a condition of their service at Sorbonne.

So the funeral of Francis the Scot took place in the strictest secrecy. As a mourner, close beside the bier, knelt the niece of good Dr. Anatole, the Professor of Eloquence. It was not thought unusual, either that Doctors of the Sorbonne should have nieces, or that they should be overcome at the sight of war and dead men. Grave doctors' nieces were almost proverbially tender-hearted. The Abbé John, a cousin by the mother's side, and near relative of the great Leaguer Cardinal, ordered, explained, and comforted, according as he had to do with Sorbonne servitors, Jesuit fathers, or weeping girls.

He found himself in his element, this Abbé John.

CHAPTER IV
LITTLE COLETTE OF COLLIOURE

While the Abbé John was gone to seek the passports from his uncle, and from what remained of royal authority in a city now wholly given over to the League, Anatole Long, college professor, explained matters to his new charge.

"You saw but little of your father, I take it?" he began gently. The Sorbonnist was a large-framed, upstanding man, with an easy-going face, and manners which could be velvet soft or trampling, according to circumstances. They were generally the former.

"There is no use in wasting good anger," he would say, "at least, on a pack of cublings."

He was referring to the young men of his class, who thought themselves Platos for wisdom and Kings of Navarre in experience. For though they cursed "the Bearnais" in their songs and causeway-side shoutings, in their hearts they thought that there was none like him in the world—at once soldier, lover, and man.

"My father," said Claire Agnew, looking the Professor in the face, "was a brave gentleman. He owed that to his race. But he had long been in this service of politics, which makes a man's life like a precious glass in the hands of a paralytic. One day or another, as he takes his medicine, it will drop, and there is an end."

"You speak bitterly?"

The Professor's voice was very soft. It was a wonder that he had never married again, for all knew that his youth had been severely accidented.

"Bitterly," said the girl; "indeed, I may speak truly and yet without honey under my tongue. For my father made himself a hunted hare for the cause that was dear to him. Yet the King he served left him often without a penny or a crust. When he asked for his own, he was put off with fair words. He spent his own estate, which was all my portion, like water. Yet neither from King James of Scots, nor from Elizabeth of the English, did he get so much as a 'thank you' for the travail of years!"

"And from Henry of Navarre?" said the Professor of the Sorbonne.

"Why," said Claire Agnew, "I am shamed to own it. But though never a man needed money more than the King of Navarre, it is on his bounty that we have been living these four years. He is great and generous!"

"I have heard something less than that said of the Bearnais," answered the Professor; "yet he is a true Frenchman of the Gascon breed, great to men, generous to women, hail-fellow-well-met with all the world. But he loves the world to know it! And now, little lady," said Professor Anatole, "I must conduct you elsewhere. It is not seemly that a pretty one like you should be found in this dingy parchment den, counting the sparrows under the dome of the Sorbonne. Have you any friends in Paris to whose care I can commit you for the time being?"

"Not one!" cried the girl fiercely; "it is a city of murderers—Leaguers— our enemies!"

"Gently—fairly, little one," the Professor spoke soothingly; "there are good men and bad in Paris, as elsewhere; but since you have no friends here, I must conduct you to Havre de Grace, where we will surely find a captain biding for a fair wind to take him through Queen Bess's Sleeve into the North Sea, far on the way for Scotland."

The girl began to cry bitterly, for the first time.

"I have no friends in Scotland, not any more than in France," she said. "My father was a true man, but of a quick high temper, and such friends as he had he quarrelled with long ago. It began about his marrying my mother, who was a little maid out of Roussillon, come to Paris in the suite of the wife of some Governor of Catalonia who had been made Spanish ambassador. It was in the Emperor's time, when men were men—not fighting machines— and priests. My father, Francis Agnew, was stiff-necked and not given to pardon-asking, save of his Maker. And though little Colette Llorient softened him to all the world else, she died too soon to soften him towards his kinsfolk."

The Professor meditated gravely, like one solving a difficult problem.

"What?" he said—"no, it cannot be. Your mother was never little Colette of the Llorients of Collioure?"

"I have indeed always believed so," said the girl; "but doubtless in my father's papers——"

"But they are Catholics of the biggest grain, those Llorients of Collioure, deep-dyed Leaguers, as fierce as if Collioure were in the heart of Lorraine!"

Claire bent her head and nodded sadly.

"Yes," she said, "for my father's sake my mother embroiled herself with her relatives. She became a Huguenot, a Calvinist like him. Then they had a family meeting about her. All the black brothers, mailed and gauntleted, they say, sat round a table and swore that my poor mother should be no more of their family!"

"Yes, I can fancy it—I see them; there was huge Bernard, weasel-faced Giles, subtle Philippe——"

"How," cried the girl, surprised in her turn; "you know them—my mother's people?"

"Well, I ought," said the Professor of the Sorbonne, with a young look flushing back into his face, "seeing that my mother has held a 'mas' from the family of Llorient of Collioure for more years than I can remember. When I was a lad going to the collegiate school at Elne, I remember your mother, Mademoiselle Colette, as a little maid, playing by herself among the sand-dunes. I looked up from my Greek grammar to watch her, till the nurse in the flat Limousin cap shook her fist at me, stopping her nursing to do it."

Here the Professor seemed to rouse himself as from a dream.

"That rascal John should be getting back by now," he said, "unless he has elbowed a way into the crowd to fight or fall for his great Duke!"

"You do not love the Duke of Guise?" said the girl.

"I have not your reasons for hating him," the Professor of Eloquence answered. "I am no Huguenot, by family or feeling. But I think it is a poor day for France when the valet chases the master out of house and home. The King is the King, and all the Guises in the world cannot alter that. Also, since the King has departed, and I have been left, alone loyal of all the faculty of the Sorbonne, it is time that I too made my way to see my mother among the sand-hills of Collioure. Ah, John, you rascal, what has kept you so long?"

"The porter at my uncle's would give me no satisfaction—swore I had come again to borrow money. A manifest falsehood! As, indeed, I proved on the spot by pulling him out of his lodge and thumping him well. A varlet— to dare to suppose, because a gentleman comes twice to borrow money from a rich and loving relative, that he has returned a third time upon the same errand! But I got the passports, and they are countersigned and stamped by Merlan at the Secretary's office, which will do no harm if we come across King's men!"

"As for the Bearnais and his folk," said the Professor to Claire, "I suppose you have your father's papers safe enough?"

The girl blushed and murmured something indefinite. As a matter of fact, she had made sure of these while he yet lay on the ground, and the Royal Swiss were firing over her head. It was the instinct of her hunted life.

They left the Sorbonne together, all cloaked and hooded "like three carrion crows," said the Abbé John. None who saw them would have supposed that a young maid's face lurked beneath the sombre muffling. Indeed, beneath that of the Abbé John, curls of the same hue clustered just as tightly and almost as abundantly.

The street were silent all about the quarter of the University. But every hundred yards great barricades of barrels and paving-stones, earth and iron chains, had to be passed. Narrow alleys, the breadth of a man and no more, were generally left, zig-zagging among the defences. But almost as often the barricades had to be surmounted, after discovery of identity, by the aid of friendly pushes and hauls. In all cases, however, the examination was strict.

At every barricade they were stopped and called upon to declare their mission. However, the Doctor Anatole was generally recognised by some scapegrace runaway student, at scrambling horse-play among the pavement cobbles. At any rate, the Abbé John, who had been conspicuous at the meetings of the Elect Leaguers as the nephew of the great Cardinal d'Albret, was universally hailed with favour.

He was also constantly asked who the lady in the hood might be, whom he was convoying away so secretly. He had but one reply to gentle and simple.

"Give me a sword, come down hither, and I will afford any three men of you satisfaction on the spot!"

For, in spite of the Abbé John's peaceful cognomen, his credit as a pusher of the unbuttoned foil was too good for any to accept his proposition. They laughed instead.

One of the Duke Guise's "mud-porters" called the pair an ugly name. But it was (happily) in the Latin quarter, and a score of eager hands propelled him down into the gutter, where, after having his nose rubbed in the mire, he was permitted (and even assisted) to retire to the rear. He rubbed himself as he went and regretted mournfully that these things had not happened near the street of Saint Antoine.

Altogether they escaped well. The Sorbonne, a difficult place to get into, is easy to get out of—for those who know how. And so the three, guided by the Abbé John, slipped into the great Rue St. Jacques by the little port St. Benoit, which the students and even the professors found so necessary, whenever their errands were of such a private nature as to disqualify them from crossing the square of the Sorbonne, with its rows on rows of enfilading windows.

It was up the narrow stair of the Abbé John's lodgings that they found a temporary shelter while the final arrangements were being made. Horses and a serving-man (provided for in the passports) were the most pressing of these.

It was in connection with the serving-man that Claire Agnew first found a tongue.

"I know a lad," she said, "a Scot, seemingly stupid, but cunning as a fox, who may be of service to us. His apparent simplicity will be a protection. For it will be evident that none bent on escaping would burden themselves with such a 'Cabbage Jock.' He is of my father's country and they were ofttimes in close places together. His name is— —"

"No matter for his name—we will call him Cabbage Jock," cried the Abbé John. "Where is this marvel to be found?"

"Not far away, as I judge," said the girl, taking a silver whistle, such as ladies wore at that time to call their waiting-maids, from about her neck. She blew lightly upon it, first two long and then two short notes. And from the street corner, prompt as if he had been watching (which, indeed, he had been), came running the strangest object ever seen in a civilised land. He gave one glance at the window at which Claire's head appeared. Then, diving under the low door like a rat making for a hole, he easily evaded the shouting concierge, and in a moment more stood before them.

CHAPTER V
THE SPROUTING OF CABBAGE JOCK

Cabbage Jock was immensely broad at the shoulders. He stooped slightly, so that his long arms fell below his knees when he stood erect. His mouth was slightly open, but so large in itself that a banana could easily have been inserted sideways without touching the wicks. There was a look of droll simplicity on the lad's face (he was apparently about twenty) which reminded one of the pictures of Lob-Lie-by-the-Fire, or the Brownie of Scottish fireside tales.

Yet for one so simple he had answered with strange readiness. There was a quick flash of the eye as he took in the two men before him.

"What may you be?" demanded the Professor of Eloquence.

"A he-goat upon the mountains, comely in the going!" said the lout, in very good French. The learned man of the Sorbonne noted at once that he quoted (and mixed) words of the Genevan Version common among the Huguenots.

"He speaks French, this good lad?" he asked, turning to Claire.

"Yes, when it pleases him, which is not always—though indeed he always obeys me. Is it not so, Jock?"

"My name is not Jock! Nowise—as you well do know. I am called Blastus of the Zamzummims! Against all Armenians, Hussites, Papishers, Anabaptists, Leaguers, and followers of the high, the low, and the middle way, I lift up my heel. I am a bird of fair plumage on the mountains of Zepher. I fly—I mount—I soar——"

"Go and find four horses," said his mistress; "two of them good and strong, one Spanish jennet for me, one Flanders mare for yourself and the saddle-bags."

The Bird of Fair Plumage scratched his long reddish locks in a sort of comic perplexity.

"Am I to steal them or pay for them?" he said.

"Pay, of course," said his mistress, scandalised.

"That will leave our purse very light—the purse that was your father's. It were easier these days, and also more just to spoil the Egyptians. The lion-like man of Moab, which is the Duke of Guise, walketh about like the devil roaring (as sayeth Peter), and because of the barricades there are many good horses tied by their bridles at the gates of the city—masterless, all of them."

"Pay for them, do you hear?" said Claire; "do not stand arguing with your master's daughter. I thought you had learned that long ago."

Blastus of the Zamzummims went out grumbling to himself.

"At least she said nothing about cheating—or clipped money, or bad money—or money from the Pope's mint. I will buy, and I will pay for all. Yes—yes—but——"

It was obvious that Jock of the Cabbage's hope of spoiling Egypt had not been properly rooted out of his mind even by his mistress's commands.

A strange soul dwelt in this Jock of the Cabbage. He was the son of a reputable Scottish refugee at Geneva, from whom he had sucked in, as a frog does the autumn rains, the strongest and purest Calvinistic doctrine. He had, however, early perceived that his ludicrous personal appearance prevented him from obtaining eminence as a preacher.

He had therefore chosen another way of being useful.

John Stirling had deliberately made himself Cabbage Jock—which is to say, "Jean-aux-Choux," and by that name was famous alike in the camps of Henri of Navarre, and in making sport for the "mignons" of the King of France. But it was not known to many alive that a mind clear and logical, a heart full of the highest determinations, were hidden away under the fool's motley and the tattered cloak of the gangrel man.

Only to Francis Agnew had the Fool talked equally and with unbound heart. Even Claire did not guess what lay beneath this folly of misapplied texts and mirth-provoking preachments. There can be no better mask for real fanaticism than the pretence of it. And whereas Francis Agnew had been a gentleman and a diplomat always, his henchman, Jock the Fool, was a fanatic of the purest strain, adding thereto a sense of humour and probably a strain of real madness as well.

"Come up hither, Jean-aux-Choux!" cried the lads on the barricades. "Turn a somersault for us, Cabbage Jock!" shouted a fellow-countryman, on his way to preferment in the Scots Guard, who in the meanwhile was filling up his time by fighting manfully against the King's troops.

"Lick the tip of your nose, Jock!" roared yet a third; "waggle your ears! Ah, well done! Now jest for us, and we will give you a good drink—

Macon of the fourth year—as much as you can take down at a draught. This Guisarding is dry work."

The streets were full of excited men, cheering for Holy Faith and the Duke of Guise. They cried that they were going to kill the King, and make that most Catholic Prince, the Head of the League, King in his stead.

The Protestants in Paris had fled or hidden. There were great fears of a second St. Bartholomew. But those who remembered the first, said that if that had been intended, there would be a deal less noise and a deal more private whetting of daggers and sword-blades.

Once the Professor of Eloquence left them for a moment in order to run upstairs to tell his housekeeper and her husband that they were to hold his house against all authority save that of the King, and not yield too soon even to that. He might be away some time, he said.

The Abbé John, whose housekeeping was of a desultory sort—consisting chiefly in going to see his uncle, the Cardinal d'Albret, when he was in need of money or of the ghostly counsel of a prince of the Church—made no preparations for flight, save to feel in his breeches pocket to make sure that he had his gold safely there.

"My creditors can wait, or importune my uncle, who will have them thrown in the Seine for their pains," said the young student of the Sorbonne easily; "and as for my dear gossips, they will easily enough console themselves. Women are like cats. As often as they fall, they fall upon their feet!"

It was a strange Paris which they passed through that day—these four. The Professor of Eloquence went first, wearing the great green cloak of his learned faculty, with its official golden collar and cuffs of dark fur.

That day Paris was not only making the history of the present, but was unconsciously prophesying the future—her own future. Whenever, after that, the executive grew weak and the people strong, up came the paving-stones, and down in a heap went the barrels, *charettes*, scaffoldings, street-doors. It was not only the Day of the Barricades, but the first day of many barricades. Indeed, Paris learned the lesson of power so well, that it became her settled conviction that what she did to-day France would homologate to-morrow. It was only the victory of the "rurals" in the late May of 1871 which taught Paris her due place, as indeed the capital of France, but not France itself.

Dr. Anatole's cloak was certainly a protection to them as they went. Caps were doffed as to one of the Sixteen—that great council of nine from each of the sixteen districts of Paris, whose power over the people made the real Catholic League.

Dr. Anatole explained matters to Claire as they went.

"They have long wanted a figure-head, these shop-keepers and booth-hucksters," he said bitterly. "The Cardinal leads them cunningly, and between guile and noise they have so intoxicated Guise that he will put his head in the noose, jump off, and hang himself. This King Henry of Valois is a contemptible dog enough, as all the world knows. But he is a dog which bites without barking, and that is a dangerous breed. If I were Guise, instead of promenading Paris between the Queen-Mother's chamber and the King's palace of the Louvre, I would get me to my castle of Soissons with all speed, and there arm and drill all the gentlemen-varlets and varlet-gentlemen that ever came out of Lorraine. There would I wait, with twenty eyes looking out every way across the meadows, and a hundred at least in the direction of Paris. I would have cannons primed and matches burning. I would lay in provisions to serve a year in case of siege. That is what I should do, were I Duke of Guise and Henry of Valois' enemy!"

At the Orleans gate Jean-aux-Choux, in waiting with the horses (bought, stolen, or strayed), heard the conclusion of the Professor's exposition.

"Let Wolf Guise eat Wolf Valois, or Wolf Valois dine off Wolf Guise—so much the better for the Sheep of the Fold," he commented freely, as became his cap-and-bells, which in these days had more liberty of prophecy than the wisdom of the wisest.

CHAPTER VI
THE ARCHER'S CLOAK

As they left Paris behind and rode down the Orleans road, it soon became evident that they had changed their surroundings. Men-at-arms, Scots Guards, with great white crosses on their blue tabards, glared at the four suspiciously. Cavaliers glanced suspiciously as they galloped past. Some halted, as if only prevented from investigating the circumstances by the haste of their mission. Gay young men, on passaging horses, half drew their swords and growled unintelligible remarks, desisting only at the sight of Claire Agnew's pale face underneath her hood.

"What can be the matter?" they asked each other. "Why do we, who passed through swarming Paris in the flood-tide of rebellion, who scrambled on barricades and were given drink by the King's enemies—why should we now be looked askance at, riding peaceably Orleans-ward on our own hired beasts?"

None found an answer, but deep in every heart there was the conviction, universal in such a case, that somehow it was the other fellow's fault. It was Cabbage Jock who solved the mystery.

"In Rome you must do as the Romans," he said; "in Babylon's cursed city, though an abomination to do obeisance to the great whore (as sayeth the Scripture), I have found it of remarkable service to don her uniform occasionally—even as Paul did when he took shelter behind his Roman citizenship. It is that green furred gown of yours, Sir Professor! These be King's men, hasting after the Master of the Mignons. I'll wager the nest is empty and the bird flown from under the pents of the Louvre."

"And what shall I do?" said the Professor of the Sorbonne, looking regretfully at the fine Spanish cloth and rich fur. "Am I to cast away a matter of twenty good golden Henries?"

"By no means," said Cabbage Jock; "I came away somewhat hastily, to do you service. I have no saddle saving these two millers' bags. I will fold the good gown beneath the two, and so sit comfortable as on an ale-house couch, while you will ride safe— —"

"And plumeless as a docked parrot," said the Abbé John, who was now sufficiently far from Paris to begin to laugh at his master—at least a little, and in an affectionate way.

The Professor looked disconsolate enough as he suffered his fine cloak to be stripped from his back.

"Ne'er mind," quoth Jean-aux-Choux, "we will soon right that. I know these King's men, and 'tis the Pope's own purgatory of a warm day. There are inns by the wayside, and wherever one is held by a well-made hostess, who lets poor puss come to the cream without so much 'Hist-a-cat-ing,' I'll wager they will leave their cloaks in the hall. So we will come by a coat of the King's colours, all scallops and Breton ermines in memory of poor Queen Anne."

"I will not have you steal a cloak, sirrah," said the Professor; "indeed, I am nowise satisfied in my mind concerning these horses we are riding."

"Steal—not I," cried the Fool; "not likely, and the Montfaçon gibbet at one's elbow yonder, with the crows a-swirling and pecking about it as in the time of naughty Clerk Francis. Nay, I thank you. I have money here to pay for a gross of cloaks!"

And Cabbage Jock slapped his pocket as he spoke—which indeed, thus interrogated, gave back a most satisfactory jingle of coin.

The Professor had first of all meant to point out to Jean-aux-Choux that to have the money in his pocket, and to pay it out, were two things entirely different, when it came to borrowing other men's cloaks, but something else leaped up in his mind, sudden as a trout in a pool. He turned upon Jean-aux-Choux.

"How do you know about Clerk Francis and the gallows at Montfaçon?" he demanded. For at first, with the ear of a man accustomed to talk only to men who pick up allusions as pigeons do scattered grain, he had accepted the words without question.

"How am I to know?" retorted Jean-aux-Choux. "One hears so many things. I do not know."

"But," said the Professor of Eloquence, pursuing his idea, "there are not many even at the Sorbonne, which is the grave of wisdom whence is no resurrection (I am of the Sadducean faction), who have heard tell of one Clerk François Villon, Master of Arts, and once an ornament of our University. How came you to know of him? Come now, out with it! You are hiding something!"

"Sir," said the Fool, "I have made sport for Kings of the Louvre and Kings of Bedlam; for Henry of yesterday, who is Henry of Valois; for Henry of to-day, who is Henry of Guise; and for Henry of to-morrow, who is— —"

But the Professor of the Sorbonne was a man of sense, and he knew that the place for discussing such things was by no means on the Orleans highway.

So he commanded Jean-aux-Choux to trouble no more about royal Henries past, present, and especially Henries to come, but to be off and find him a cloak.

Then Cabbage Jock, in no haste, simply glanced at the ale-house doors as they came near Bourg-la-Reine, and at last with a wave of his hand signalled his three companions to ride on.

When he overtook them an hour afterwards, Bourg-la-Reine was hidden far behind among the wayside trees. Jean-aux-Choux saluted, and asked in a quiet man-servant's voice if the honourable Doctor would be pleased to put on his coat.

"Then, you gallows' rascal," said the Professor of the Sorbonne, "it was true, after all. You have stolen the cloak, and you would have me, a respectable citizen, reset the theft!"

Jean-aux-Choux held up his hand.

"Sir," he said, "I have often heard from my masters that it is the special function of a cook to make ready the soup, and of the Sorbonne to resolve cases of conscience?"

"Well, then," he went on, as Doctor Anatole did not answer, "here is one."

"In an ale-house were certain sons of Belial, whose very jesting was inconvenient, and their words not once to be named among us, as sayeth the apostle. Well, there came a certain braggart out of this foul poison-box. He had seen an honest man pass by, fleeing from Paris, with all his goods laden on a mule. Now this knave would have taken all and slain the honest merchant as well, had I not passed by, and so belaboured him that he will not rise from his bed for a fortnight. Then the good merchant (he was a Jew from the Quartier Saint Jacques) bade me choose what I would for my recompense. And so from his packages I chose this fine cloak, fit for the Provost of the Merchants himself, and with that he thanked me and went his way."

"And what," cried the Abbé John, hugely interested, "became of that rascal's companions? It is strange that, hearing the racket, they did not hive out to his assistance! Yesterday they hamstrung a man for less—an archer of the King's!"

"It would indeed have been somewhat strange," agreed Cabbage Jock, "if, before our little interview, I had not taken the liberty of locking both the outer and inner doors of the inn. But they have nothing to complain about, these good lads. They have a kindly hostess and a full cellar. E'en let them be content!"

And with no more words he took out of his pouch two keys, one large and rusty, the other small and glittering. These he tossed carefully, one after the other, into the Orge. They were just upon the famous bridge across which the postillion of Longjumeau so often took his way. The keys flashed a moment on the water as the drops rose and fell. Then Cabbage Jock turned on his companions and smiled his broad simpleton's smile as he waved his hand in the direction of the inn.

"Let there be peace," he said solemnly—"peace between Jew and Gentile. Will it please you to put on your coat now, Sir Professor?"

And as the air bit shrewdly, it pleased the Professor well enough.

CHAPTER VII
THE GREAT NAME OF GUISE

Claire had indeed seen little of her father. All her life she had been accustomed to be left in the charge of strangers while Francis Agnew went about his business of hole-and-corner diplomacy. Claire was therefore no whit astonished to find herself with two men, almost strangers to her, alone upon the crowded road to Orleans.

She mourned sincerely for her father, but after all she was hardly more than a child, and for years she had seen little of Francis Agnew. He had, it is true, always managed to take care of her, always in his way loved her. But it was most often from a distance, and as yet she did not realise the difference.

She might therefore be thought more cheerful than most maids of a quieter day in the expression of her grief. Then, indeed, was a man's life on his lip, and girls of twenty had often seen more killing than modern generals of three-score and ten. It was not that Claire felt less, but that an adventurous present so filled her life with things to do, that she had no time for thought.

Also, was there not Jean-aux-Choux, otherwise Cabbage Jock, but with an excellent right to the name of John Stirling, armiger, jester to three kings, and licentiate in theology in the Reformed (and only true) Church of Geneva? Jean-aux-Choux was a fatalist and a Calvinist. Things which were ordained to happen would happen, and if any insulted his master's daughter, it was obviously ordained that he, Jean-aux-Choux, should set a dagger between the shoulder-blades of the insulter. This in itself was no slight protection. For the fool's sinews were reputed so strong that he could take two vigorous men of the King's Guard, pin them with his arms like trussed fowls, and, if so it pleased him, knock their heads together.

So through the press the four made their way into Orleans, where they found the bearing of the people again changed, and that for the worse.

"It behoves your learned and professional shoulders to be decorated once more with the green cloth and fur trimmings of the Sorbonne," said Jean-aux-Choux. "I can smell a Leaguer a mile off, and this city is full of them. Our Scots Guards have turned off on the road to Blois. There are too many bishops and clergy here for honest men. Besides which, the King has a château at Blois. We had better change my saddle-cloth—though 'twill be to my disadvantage—inasmuch as an archer's tabard, all gold embroidering, makes noways so easy sitting as fox fur and Angoulême green."

So it chanced that when they rode up to the low door of the Hostelry of the Golden Lark, in the market-place of Orleans, the Professor of Eloquence was again clad in his official attire, and led the way as became a Doctor of the Sorbonne in a Leaguer town.

It was a pretty pink-and-white woman who welcomed them with many courtesies and smiles to the Golden Lark—that is, so far as the men were concerned, while preserving a severe and doubtful demeanour towards the niece of the learned Professor of the Sorbonne. Madame Gillifleur loved single men, unaccompanied men, at her hostelry. She found that thus there was much less careful examination of accounts when it came to the hour of departure.

Still, all the same, it was a great thing to have in her house so learned a man, and in an hour, as was the custom of the town, she had sent his name and style to the Bishop's palace. Within two hours the Bishop's secretary, a smart young cleric dressed in the Italian fashion, with many frills to his soutane, was bearing the invitation of his master to the gentlemen to visit him in his study. This, of course, involved leaving Claire behind, for Anatole Long ordered the Abbé John to accompany him, while the girl declared that, with Jean-aux-Choux to keep her company, she had fear of nothing and nobody.

She had not, however, taken her account with the curiosity of Madame Celeste Gillifleur, who, as soon as the men were gone to the episcopal palace, entered the room where Claire was seated at her knitting, while Jean-aux-Choux read aloud the French Genevan Bible.

Cabbage Jock deftly covered the small quarto volume with a collection of songs published (as usual) at the Hague.

"The fairer the hostess the fouler the soup!" muttered Jean, as he retired into a corner, humming the refrain of a Leaguer song.

Madame Gillifleur saluted her enemy with the duck of a hen which has finished drinking. To her Claire bowed the slightest of acknowledgments.

"To what do I owe this honour?" she inquired, with dryness.

"I thought my lady, the Professor's niece, might be in need of some service—a tiring-maid perhaps?" began the landlady. "My own you would be heartily welcome to, but she is a fresh, foolish wench from the Sologne, and would sooner groom a nag of Beauce than pin aright a lady's stomacher! But I can obtain one from the town—not too respectable, I fear. But for my lady, and for one night, I suppose that does not matter."

"Ha, from the town!" grumbled Jean-aux-Choux out of his window-seat. Then he hummed, nodding his head and wagging his finger as if he had just found the words in his song-book:

"Eyes and ears, ears and eyes—
Who hires maids, lacks never spies!"

The landlady darted a furious look at the interrupter.

"Who may this rude fellow be, that is not afraid to give his tongue such liberty in my house?"

Jean-aux-Choux answered for himself, as indeed he was well able to do.

"I am philosopher-in-chief to the League; and as for that, when I am at home with his Grace of Guise, he and I wear motley day about!"

The face of the landlady changed. Remembering the learned Professor of the Sorbonne, who had gone to visit the bishop, she turned quickly to Claire and asked, "Does the fellow speak truth? Is he really the jester to the great Duke, the good Prince, the glory of the League?"

"I have reason to believe it," said Claire calmly; "but, for your complete satisfaction, you can ask my uncle the Professor upon his return."

"I trust they will not be long gone," grumbled Jean-aux-Choux. "I have an infallible clock here under the third button of my tunic, which tells me it is long past dinner-time. And if it be not a good worthy meal, I shall by no means advise His Grace to dismount at the Golden Lark when next he passes through Orleans!"

"Holy Saint Marthe!" cried the landlady; "I will go this minute, and see what they are doing in the kitchen. I will warm their scullion backs——"

"I think I smell burned meat!" continued Jean-aux-Choux.

"Faith, but is it true that the Duke of Guise is indeed coming this way?" Madame Celeste Gillifleur asked anxiously.

"True, indeed," affirmed Jean, with his nose in the air, "and before the year is out, too. But, Madame, my good hostess, there is nothing he dislikes so much as the smell of good meat spoiled in the basting."

"I will attend to the basting myself, and that forthwith!" cried the lady of the Golden Lark, darting kitchen-wards at full speed, and forgetting all the questions she had come up to ask of Claire in the absence of her legitimate protectors.

Jean-aux-Choux laughed as she went out, and inclined his ear. Sounds which indicated the basting of not yet inanimate flesh, arrived from the kitchen.

"Mistress, mistress," cried a voice, "I am dead, bruised, scalded—have pity on me!"

"Pity is it, you rascal?"—the sharp tones of Madame Celeste rose high—"have you not wasted my good dripping, burnt my meat, offended these gentlemen, spoiled their dinner, so that they will report ill things of the Golden Lark to his most noble Grace of Guise?"

"Pity—oh, pity!"

Followed a rapid rushing of feet to and fro in the kitchen. Furniture was overturned. Something of the nature of a basting-ladle struck sonorously on tables and scattered patty-pans on the floor. A door slammed, shaking the house, and a blue-clad kitchen boy fled down the narrow street, while Madame Celeste, basting-ladle in hand, fumed and gesticulated in his wake.

CHAPTER VIII
THE GOLDEN LARK IN ORLEANS TOWN

"Now," said Jean-aux-Choux, "unless I go down and help at the turning-spit myself, we are further off dinner than ever. I will also pump the lady dry of information in a quarter of an hour, which, in such a Leaguer town, is always a useful thing. But stay where you are, my lady Claire, and keep the door open. You will smell burnt fat, but the Fool of the Three Henries will be with you in as many jumps of a grasshopper whenever you want him. You have only to call, and lo, you have me!"

When Jean had disappeared to do double duty as spy and kitchen-drudge beneath, Claire went to the window which looked out upon the market-place. From beneath in the kitchen she could hear shouts of laughter climb up and die away. She knew that Jean-aux-Choux was at his tricks, and that, with five minutes' grace, he could get to windward of any landlady that ever lived, let alone such a merry plump one as Madame Celeste.

That dame indeed disliked all pretty women on principle. But she was never quite sure whether she preferred an ugly witty man who made her laugh, or a handsome dull man who only treated her as a gentleman ought. But women—young women and pretty women—pah, she could not abide them! And by this we can guess her age, for not so long ago she had been young and even pretty herself.

The tide that comes in the affairs of men is not nearly so marked as the ebb which comes in the affairs of women.

Claire stood a long while meditating, her eyes following the movement of the market-place vaguely, but without any real care for what was happening. She truly mourned her father, but she possessed much of that almost exclusively masculine temperament which says after any catastrophe, "Well, what is the next thing to be done?"

"I care nothing about my mother's people," she meditated to herself, "but I would see her home, her land, her country."

She had never seen her father's. But when he had spoken to her of the fresh winds, lashing rains, and driving snows, with nevertheless the rose blooming in the sheltered corners about the old house on Christmas Day, she had somehow known it all. But Collioure and its sand-dunes, the deep sapphire of the southern sea, cut across by the paler blue line of the sky—she could not imagine that, even when the Professor and the Abbé John, with tears glittering in their eyes, spoke together in the strange pathetic speech of *la petite patrie.*

But she would like to see it—the strand where the little Colette had played, the dunes down which she had slidden, and the gold and rose of the towers of Château Collioure, within which her mother was born.

A noise without attracted her attention. A procession was entering the square. In the midst was a huge coach with six mules, imported, equipage and all, from Spain. An outrider in the episcopal livery was mounted on each mule, while running footmen scattered the market-stalls and salad-barrows like the passage of a sudden strong wind.

There was also great excitement down below in the Golden Lark. The kitchen emptied itself, and Madame Celeste stopped hastily to pin a bow of ribbons to her cap, unconscious that a long smear of sooty grease decorated one side of her nose. The Bishop's carriage was coming in state to the Golden Lark! There could not be the least doubt of it. And the Bishop himself was within, that holy man who so much more willingly handled the sword-hilt than the crozier—Bishop Pierrefonds of Orleans, certain archbishop and possible cardinal, a stoop of the League in all the centre of France.

Yes, he was conveying home his guests in state. He stepped out and stood on the pavement in front of the house, a right proper prelate, giving them in turn his hand as they stooped to kiss his amethyst ring. Then, seeing over the Abbé John's bowed head the lady of the house, he called out heartily to her (for he was too great to be haughty with any), "Mistress Celeste, mind you treat these gentlemen well. It is not every day that our good town of Orleans holds at once the light of the Sorbonne, its mirror of eloquence, and also the nephew of my Lord Cardinal of the Holy League, John d'Albret, claimant at only twenty removes to the crown of France."

"Pshaw," muttered the Abbé John wearily, "I wish the old fool would go away and let us get to dinner!"

For, indeed, at the Palace he had listened to much of this.

The hostess of the Golden Lark conducted her two guests upstairs as if to the sound of trumpets. She gathered her skirts and rustled like the poplar leaves of an entire winter whisking about the little Place Royale of Orleans. The Professor of the Sorbonne had suddenly sunk into the background. Even the almighty Duke of Guise was no better than a bird in the bush.

While here—well in hand, and hungry for an honest Golden Lark dinner—was a real, hall-marked, royal personage, vouched for by a bishop, and still more by the bishop's carriage and outriders! It was enough to turn the head of a wiser woman than Madame Celeste Gillifleur.

"And is it really true?" demanded Claire Agnew.

"Is what true, my dear lady?" said the Abbé John, very ungraciously for him. For he thought he would have to explain it all over again.

"That you are a near heir to the throne of France?"

The Abbé John clapped his hands together with a gesture of despair.

"Just as much as I am the Abbé John and a holy man," he cried; "it pleases them to call me so. Thank God, I am no priest, nor ever will be. And as for the crown of France—Henry of Valois is not dead, that ever I heard of. And if he were, I warrant his next heir and my valiant cousin, Henry of Navarre, would have a word to say before he were passed over!"

"But," said the Professor of Eloquence, smiling, "the Pope and our wise Sorbonne have loosed all French subjects from paying any allegiance to a heretic!"

"By your favour, sir," said the young man, "I think both made a mistake for which they will be sorry. Also I heard of a certain professor who voted boldly for the Bearnais in that Leaguer assembly, and who found it convenient to go see his mother next day, lest he should find himself one fine morning shortened by a head, all for the glory of God and the Holy League!"

Doctor Anatole laughed at his pupil's boldness.

"You are out of disciplinary bounds now," he said, "and as you are too old to birch, I must e'en let you chatter. But what is the meaning of the Bishop's sudden cordiality?"

"Oh," said the Abbé John, with a sigh of resignation, "these Leaguers are always getting maggots in their brains. If my mother had been my father—if I had been a Bourbon instead of a d'Albret—if Henry the Bearnais had been in my shoes and I in his—if—if—any number of 'ifs'—then there might be something in this heir-to-the-crown business. But the truth is, they are at their wits' end (which is no long distance to travel). The Demon of the South, our good, steady-going King of Spain, drives them hard. They dare not have him to rule over them, with his inquisitors, his blazing heretic fires, and the rest of it. Yet it is a choice between him and the Huguenot, unless they can find a true Catholic king. The Cardinal Bourbon is manifestly too old, though one day even he may serve to stop a gap. The Duke of Guise may be descended from the Merovingians or from Adam, but in either case his family-tree is not convincing. It has too many branches—too few roots! So the plotters—my good uncle among them—are looking about for some one—any one—that is, not a Guise nor yet a Huguenot, who may serve their turn. His Grace of Orleans thinks I may do as well as another. That is all—only one Leaguer maggot the more."

"And must we, then, always say 'Your Royal Highness' or 'Your Serenity' when we kiss your hand—which shall it be?" Claire asked the question gravely.

"I had much rather kiss yours," said the heir to a throne, bowing with equal gravity; "and as for a name—why, I am plain John d'Albret, at your service!"

He doffed his cap as he spoke, and the Professor noted for the first time, with a touch of jealousy, that he was a comely lad enough—that is, if he had not been so ludicrously young. The Professor (who was not a philosopher for nothing) noted the passing twinge of jealousy as a sign that he was growing old. Twenty years ago he might have been tempted to break his pupil's head for a presumptuous jackanapes, or challenge him to a bout at the small swords, but jealousy—pah, Anatole Long thought himself as good as any man—always excepting the Bearnais—where the sex was concerned.

It was a good and substantial supper to which they sat down. The cookery did credit to the handicraft of Madame Celeste, especially the salmon steaks done in parsley sauce, and the roast capon stuffed with butter, mint, and bread-crumbs. The wine, a white Côte Rotie, went admirably with the viands. The Professor and Claire had but little appetite, but the eyes of the landlady were now upon the Abbé John alone. His plate was scarce empty before it was mysteriously refilled. His wine-glass found itself regularly replenished by the fair plump hands of Madame Celeste herself. All went merry as a marriage-bell, and Jean-aux-Choux, seated a little way below the salt, and using his dagger as an entire table equipment, worked his way steadily through everything within his reach. For though the Fool of the Three Henries held nothing in heaven or earth sacred from his bitter tongue when in the exercise of his profession, he equally let nothing in heaven or earth (or even under the earth) interfere with his appetite. He explained the matter thus:

"I have heard of men living from hand to mouth," he told Claire; "for twenty years I have lived from table to mouth—always the same mouth, seldom twice the same table. There was you, my little lady, to be served first. And a hundred times your father and I went hungry that you might eat your milk-sop hot-a-nights. While, if I could, I would cheat my master as to what remained, his being the greater need."

"Good Jean!" said Claire, gently reaching out to pat his shaggy head. The long-armed jester shook a little and went pale under her touch, which was the stranger, seeing that with a twist of his shoulders he could throw off the clutch of a strong man.

Such were the three with whom Claire travelled southward, in an exceeding safety, considering the disturbed time. For any of them would have given his life to shield her from harm, though as yet Jean-aux-Choux was the only one of the three who knew it. And with him it was a matter of course.

CHAPTER IX
THE REBELLION OF HERODIAS' DAUGHTER

"And I suppose I am to bait the trap, as usual?"

"You forget, Valentine, that I am your uncle and a grandee of Spain."

It was the usual beginning of their quarrels, of which they had had many as they posted along the Bordeaux road Pariswards. The Marquis Osorio was travelling on a secret mission to Paris, a mission which had nothing to do with the crowned and anointed King of France, now in uncertain refuge at Blois.

King Philip had sent for him, and the Demon of the South had been in good humour when he gave the stout Leonese gentleman his instructions. He had just heard of the Day of the Barricades, and the success of the Duke of Guise.

The Marquis had stood up before the master of two worlds, bronzed, hale and bearded: not too clever, but just shrewd enough to please the King, and certainly indomitable in doing what he was told. He had very much the air of a free man and good subject, with his flat travelling cap in one hand and the fingers of the other gripped staunchly about his sword-hilt.

"The iron is hot on the anvil," said the King, "strike, Osorio! It is a good job that the Duke of Err is out of the way. The pressure of the times was too much for him. His poor old brain rocked. His Duchess has taken him off somewhere to feed with spoon-meat. Olivarez, whom I have sent to follow him, will give you no trouble. He will occupy himself with King Henri and the Medici woman. The League and Guise—these are your game—especially Guise. I suspect him to be a wind-bag, but put him under your arm, and the wind in him will bravely play our music, like a pair of Savoyard bagpipes. And hark ye, Osorio, listen to the Jesuit fathers, especially Mariana—a very subtle man, Mariana, after mine own heart. And also (here he sank his voice to something mysterious), above all take with you your—your niece— Valentine?"

"Valentine la Niña!" ejaculated the King's representative, with a quick, startled look at his master.

"Even so," said Philip, casting his eyes through the slit behind the high altar of the Escorial to see what the priests were doing; "even so; our Holy Mother Church is in danger, and if any love father or mother, son or daughter more than her, he is not worthy of her!"

So by royal command Valentine la Niña rode northward with her uncle, and though these two loved one another, they wrangled much by the way.

Claire and her cavalcade were reaching Blois, when the uncle and niece entered Angers by the Long Bridges of Cé.

The cause of the girl's outbreak of petulance had been a harangue of the envoy, in which he had explained, amongst other things, the reasons for keeping their mission a secret. The King of France must not hear of it, because their Philip did not want to show his hand. Henry of Navarre must not hear of it, or he might send men to harry the Cerdagne and Aran. Besides, what was the use of making a show in Paris, when the very shop-tenders and scullions there played King Philip's game? Was not the Sorbonne packed with wise doctors all arguing for Spain? Wild monks and fanatic priests proclaimed her as the only possible saviour of the Faith. At the back of Guise stood King Philip. Remained therefore (according to the envoy) to push Guise forward, to use him, to empty him, and then—let the Valois and the Medici have their will of him. There was no reason for Spain to appear in the matter at all. Guise must be induced to go to Blois, and—his enemies would do the rest.

It was then that Valentine la Niña burst forth in indignation.

She would not be the lure, she said, even for a king—a bait dangled before an honest man's eyes—no, not even for her uncle!

"I am an Osorio," the envoy answered her sternly, "the head of the family, you can surely trust me that nothing shall be asked of you which might cast a stain on the name——"

"Not more than was asked of my mother!" she retorted scornfully, "only to sacrifice herself and her children—a little thing for so good a king— his people's father!"

"And for the Faith!" said the Marquis, hastily, as if to escape discussion. "Listen, Valentine! The famous Father of the Gesù, Mariana, will be in Paris before us. He has been reporting to the King, and he it is who has asked for your presence. None can serve the Church so well as you."

"I know—I know," cried the girl, "fear not, I have been well drilled. My mother taught me that the whims of men were to be called either high policy or holy necessity. It little matters which; women have to be sacrificed in either case. Let us ride on to Paris, Uncle Osorio, and say no more about it!"

They lighted down in the empty courtyard of the Spanish ambassador's house, which was next to the hotel of the Duke of Guise. A shouting crowd had pursued them to their lodging. For the Spaniards were popular in the city, and the arrival of so fine a cavalcade had rightly enough been interpreted to mean the adherence of Philip of Spain to the new order of things.

"Had Spain been for the King, this envoy would have hied him to Blois," said De Launay, the old provost of the merchants. "But since Philip sends his ambassador direct to the good city of Paris, why, then, it follows that he is of the mind to put down Valois, to set aside Navarre, and to help us to crown our only true king, the King of Paris and of France, the King of the Faith, and of his people's hearts—Guise, the good Guise!"

Because, even thus early, the habit of municipal eloquence had been formed and its pattern set for all the ages. De Launay was considered a good practitioner.

The windows of Valentine Osorio's chambers looked on the garden of the Hotel of Guise—a shady orchard close where in the evening the Duke often walked with his gentlemen, and specially with his handsome young brother, the Duke of Bar.

On an evening of mackerel cloud, pearl-grey and flaky gold vaulting so high overhead that the sky above the small smokeless Paris of 1588 seemed infinite, Valentine sat gossiping with her maid Salome.

To them, with the slightest preface of knocking, light as a bird, entered a priestly figure in the sombre robes of the Society of Jesus—a little rosy-cheeked man, plump and dimpled with good living, and, as it seemed, good nature.

But at the sight of him a nervous shudder passed through the body of the young girl. So in a school, when the master returns before his time, playing scholars draw unwillingly with downcast, discontented eyes to sterner tasks. Yet the Jesuit was kindly and tolerant in manner, prodigal of smile and compliment. There was nothing of the Inquisitor about the famous father Mariana, historian and secret politician.

"Fairer than ever, Mistress Valentine," he murmured, after he had exchanged a glance with the maid Salome, "ah, the blessed thing which is beauty when used for sanctified ends! Seldom is it thus used in this world of foolish women! But you are wise. The Gesù are under deep obligations, and the King—the King—ah, he will not forget. He has sent you hither, and has commissioned me to speak with you. Your good, your excellent uncle, Osorio, knows some part of King Philip's plans, but not all—no, not all. He is too blunt an instrument for such fine work. But *you* can understand, and shall!"

The girl struck her hands together angrily and turned upon him.

"Again—again!" she said, "is it to be treachery again?"

"Not treachery, dear lady," cooed the father; "but when you go to tickle trout, you do not stand on the bank and throw in great stones. You work softly underneath, and so guide the fish to a place from which they cannot escape."

"Is it Guise?" demanded the girl, breaking fiercely through these dulcet explanations.

"As you say," smiled the Jesuit; "himself and no other."

"And what is to be my particular infamy?"

"Child, beware of your speech," said the Jesuit; "there is no infamy in the service of Holy Church, of the Society, and of your King."

"To a well-known air!" said the girl, sneeringly; "well, I will sing the song. I know the music."

And she went and placed herself by the window which overlooked the pleasaunce of the Duke of Guise.

"Salome," she said, "come hither and comb out my tresses!"

And with the graceful ease of strong young arms, she pulled out a tortoise-shell pin here and a mother-of-pearl fastening there till a flood of hair escaped, falling down her back, with dark, coppery lights striking out of the duskier coils, and the lingering sunset illuminating the ripples of fine-spun gold.

"Thus goes the exercise," she said with a cold anger, "the Holy Society trains us well. But for this, and all else, God will enter into judgment with you and your like!"

But, heedless of her words, the priest was already stooping and peering behind the curtain.

"There they go," he whispered eagerly, "Guise and Mayenne together, Bar and the Cardinal behind—ah, there, it takes! Gripped—netted—what did I tell the King? He has his kerchief out. Quick, Valentine, yours! What, you have left it behind? Here is mine. Twice—I tell you, twice—and your hand upon your heart. Ah, he salutes! He will soon call upon the envoy of the King of Spain now. I wager we shall have him here in the morning before breakfast! Ah, what news this will be to send by the courier to-night to your—to King Philip! He will sleep sound, I warrant. And remember, to-morrow, speak him fair when he comes. All depends on that. I shall not be far away. I shall know and report to the King. It shall not be well with you otherwise. Guise must go to Blois—to the King of France. He must take his gentlemen with him. No sulking in his own territories. To Blois, and face it out—like a man."

The girl rose from the window and came back into the chamber. She opened the door, and with a gesture of proud weariness indicated the dark corridor without.

"Your turn is served," she said, "now go!"

But Mariana, a cunning smile on his face, held out his hand.

"Give me first my kerchief!" he said.

The girl crushed the embroidered linen into a ball in her hand, holding it at her side and slightly behind. Then she threw it out of the window with a gesture of contempt. The next moment the door slammed unceremoniously in Father Mariana's face. But the church historian was not in the least put out. He laid his finger slowly to the side of his nose and smiled stilly.

He descended the stairs to the entresol, and there from a window which overhung the court he looked forth in time to see the Duke of Guise stooping to pick up something white from the ground.

He saw him kiss it and thrust it into the breast of his black velvet doublet.

And the worthy Jesuit chuckled softly, saying to himself, "There are things in this world which are cheap even at the loss of my best broidered kerchief!"

As Mariana had foretold, the Duke of Guise and his brother the young De Bar called upon the Marquis Osorio the following day. That morning the Duke had made the life of his valet a burden to him while dressing, and he now appeared gorgeous in a suit of dark blue velvet trimmed with gold lace. A cape of silk was over one arm, and he carried Mariana's embroidered kerchief carefully in his hand.

In his most stately fashion the Marquis Osorio received the head of the League. He presented his credentials as to a reigning monarch, and began to talk of revolutions of Holy Church, concerning the culpable laxness of the Pope in his own interests, and the fidelity of the King of Spain to his ideals and to his allies. It was evident, however, that Guise paid but scant heed. His ears were elsewhere. As for De Bar, he stared insolently about him, now at the ambassador, now at the tapestry on the walls, and again and most often out at the window. But his brother listened, almost without disguise, to a slight noise, which came occasionally into the room from without. There was, for instance, the rustling of a woman's silken robe in the passage. Voices also, that sounded faint, pleading, expostulatory, cut into the even rise and fall of Castilian diplomacy.

"For these reasons my royal master judged it expedient to send me as his representative, charged with— —"

Guise twisted impatiently this way and that in his black oaken chair, in vain efforts to catch what was going on outside. De Bar observed his brother's uneasiness, and as the Lorraine princes went at that time in constant fear of assassination, it did not cost him two thoughts, even in the house of the Spanish ambassador, to rise and throw the door wide open.

Then through the wide Romanesque arch of the audience chamber Valentine Osorio entered, as a queen comes into a throne room.

At sight of her the envoy stayed his speech to make the presentation in form. Guise instantly dropped all interest in the goodwill of King Philip and his views upon state policy. He crossed over to the window-seat, where Valentine had seated herself.

Mariana had followed, and the next moment the Marquis resumed his interrupted speech, addressing himself to the Jesuit and De Bar, whose ears were rigid with listening to what was going on in the window, but who feared his brother so much that he dared not follow his movements with a single lift of his eyelids.

"My lady," said Guise, as he stood before Valentine, "I judge that I have the privilege of restoring to you a kerchief which you dropped by accident last night into my garden—we are neighbours, you know."

Valentine la Niña did not flush in the least. She said only, "It is none of mine. If you will throw it behind the curtain there, my maid Salome will see that it goes to the wash."

Guise stood staring at her, internally fuming at his own stupidity in thus attempting to force the situation.

Valentine la Niña was dressed in a vaporous greenish lawn, which added value to the clearness of her skin, the coiled wealth of her fair hair, and the honey-coloured eyes which looked past the great Duke as if he were no more than a pillar between her and the landscape.

Manifestly Guise was piqued. He was a man of good fortunes, and of late the Parisians had spoiled him. He was quite unaccustomed to be treated in this fashion.

"Countess," he said at last, after long searching for a topic, "I am from the north and you from the south. Yet to look at us, it is I who am the Spaniard and you the Frank!"

"My father was a Flamand!" said Valentine la Niña calmly.

"And, may I ask, of what degree?"

"Of a degree higher than your own!" said Valentine, turning her great eyes indolently upon him.

Guise looked staggered. He had not supposed that the world held any such.

"Then he must have been a reigning prince!" he stammered.

"Well?" said Valentine, looking at him with direct inquiry.

"I had not understood that even so ancient a house as the Osorios——"

"I never said that my father was an Osorio!"

"Ah!" said the Duke, "then I ask your pardon. I was indeed ignorant."

He scented mystery, and being a plain, hard-hearted, cruel man of the time, thrust into a commanding position by circumstances, he resented being puzzled, like a very justice of the peace.

"If you do not believe me——" Valentine began.

"Most noble princess," he protested, bending nearer to her as she sat on the low seat looking straight up at him; "not once have I dreamed——"

"Go to my native country of Leon and ask the first gentleman you meet whether Valentine la Niña be not the honest daughter of a king. Only do not, if you value your life, express such disbelief as you did just now, or the chances are that you will never again see fair Lorraine!"

She looked about her. What she had expected all along had happened. They were alone. By some art of the Jesuit father, subtly piloting the course of events, Osorio had gone to the private parlour to find certain papers. Mariana and De Bar had followed him.

Instantly the girl's demeanour changed. Half rising, she reached out her hand and clutched the astonished Guise by the cuff of his black velvet sleeve.

"Do not trust the King of France," she whispered, "do not put yourself in the power of the King of Spain. Do not listen to my uncle, Osorio, who does his bidding. Keep away from Blois. Make yourself strong in your own territories—I, who speak, warn you. There is but a hair's breadth between you and death. Above all, do not listen to Mariana the Jesuit. Do not believe him on his sworn oath. His Order seeks your death now that you have served their turn, and—I do not wish harm to come to a brave man."

Had Valentine's eyes been upon the door she would have seen it open slightly as if a breeze were pushing it.

"And pray, princess," said Guise, smiling, well content, "would it be the act of a brave man thus to shun danger?"

"The lion is not the braver for leaping into the prepared pit with his eyes open. He is only foolish!"

Guise laughed easily.

"If I were to take you at your word, princess," he said, "I should hear no more of you in my dull Lorraine. I could not carry you off to cheer me at Soissons. But here in Paris I may at least see you daily—hear your voice, or if no better, see you at the window as I walk in my garden——"

"Ah," cried Valentine, thrusting out her hand hastily, palm outward, "do not think of me. I am but the snare set, the trap baited. I am not my own. I can love no man—choose no man. I belong to Those Unseen——"

She cast her hand backward towards Spain, as if to indicate infinite malign forces at work there. "But I warn you—get hence quickly, avoid Blois. Do not trust the King, nor any king. Do not listen to my uncle Osorio, and, above all, do not listen to Mariana the Jesuit."

And with a rapid rustle of light garments she was gone. Guise attempted to take her hand in passing, but it easily evaded him. Valentine vanished behind the arras, where was a door which led directly to the women's apartments.

A moment Guise stood pulling at his moustache sourly enough, ruminating on the warning he had received and, in the sudden disappointment, half inclined to profit by it. To him entered the Jesuit, smiling and dimpled as ever.

"My Lord Duke, I find you alone," he began courteously, "this is ill treatment for an honoured guest. Permit me——"

"That lady," demanded Guise, brusquely, "who is she?"

"The niece of the Marquis Osorio," murmured the Jesuit, "my old scholar, dear to me as the apple of mine eye, almost a daughter."

"Is she of royal blood?" said Guise, who, though he had to be upon his manners with Valentine herself, saw no reason for mincing matters with a mere Jesuit scribbler.

"As to that it were well to consult her uncle," said Mariana, very softly, "we of the Society do not concern ourselves with matters purely secular. In any case, be assured that the family honour is quite safe in the Marquis's hands!"

"I did not doubt it," said Guise, tossing his silken cape over his arm and evidently about to take flight. Mariana accompanied him to the foot of the stairs, murmuring commonplaces, how that there would likely be a thunderstorm which would clear the air, and that he would take it upon him to make the adieux of his Grace of Guise to the Marquis Osorio, his good friend and kinsman.

But just at the last he glided in his dart.

"And by the way, we may not see you again, unless you too are going south. We start to-morrow for the Blois, where the Queen Mother holds her court. She has written most graciously to the Countess Valentine offering her hospitality, and the gaiety which young folk love, among her maids of honour!"

And as he tucked up his soutane in order to remount the stairs, the Jesuit chuckled to himself. "And that, I think, will do—if so be I know the blood of the breed of Guise!"

CHAPTER X
THE GOLDEN DUKE

The river flowed at their right hand, the water blue, the pebbly banks chased silver, green walls of wood framing the picture, and noble châteaux looking out here and there.

Almost audibly Claire's heart beat. She had seen the court of the King of Navarre, what time Margaret of Valois made Nerac gay for a whole year, as ever was Paris under the first Francis. But even there, betwixt the old grey château on the hill and the new summer pavilion in the valley, something of the warriors' camp had ever lingered about that Capua of the "Bearnais."

Besides, Claire had been young then, and many things she had not understood—which was perhaps the better for her and the happier. But now, she doubted not. The child was a woman, and all would now be made clear. Not Eve, looking up at the Eden apple-tree in the reserved corner of the orchard, had more of certainty that all happiness lay in the tasting of the first of these golden pippins.

Presently they began to mingle with the crowd, and from under his shaggy brows the Professor watched the gay young courtiers with unconcealed displeasure.

As he listened to the quick give-and-take of wit from this galliard to the other, he murmured to himself the words of the Wise Man, even the words of Jesus the son of Sirach, "There is a certain subtlety that is fine, but it is unrighteous."

And to his pupil he said, "Answer not these fools according to their folly. Your sword's point will make a better answer! Even I myself——"

But here he checked himself, as if he would have said something that became not a grave Professor of the Sorbonne in the habit of his order.

And even while saying so—lo! in a moment, the swords were out and flickering, his own first of all, the same little, thin, snaky sword-cane made in Toledo, supple as a reed, which the Abbé John and Guy Launay had returned to appropriate on the Day of the Barricades. John d'Albret stood on his defence with an Italian blade, having a small cup to protect the over-guard, which was just coming into fashion among the young bloods. While from the rear Jean-aux-Choux spurred his Flanders mare into the riot, waving over his head a huge two-handed sword of Italian pattern, like those with which the Swiss had harvested the armoured knights like ripe corn at Granson and at Morat.

And the reason of the pother was this.

A couple of gentlemen-cavaliers had approached from behind, and descending as suddenly as hawks into a courtyard full of doves fluttering and pacing each in his innocence, had deftly cut out the little jennet of Arab blood on which Claire was riding.

Her dark student's over-mantle, descending low as her spurs, had not concealed from these faithful stewards of their master that the younger and more delicately featured of the two clerks was no other than a pretty maiden.

"Our great Duke would speak with you, Mistress," was all the explanation they deigned to give. And in such troubled times even so much was frequently omitted.

But the hawks soon found out their mistake. Though the Professor's sword-cane might have been safely disregarded by the breast-plate wearers, it was otherwise with the huge bell-mouthed pistol which he carried in his left hand. It was also far otherwise with the snaky blade of the Abbé John, the daintiest sworder of all the *Pré des Clercs*. The man at the left of Claire's bridle-rein felt something sting him just at the coming together of the head-piece and shoulder-plates. Even less could the two captors afford to disregard Claire's last defender, when, all unexpectedly, with a shrill war-cry of "Stirling Brig an' doon wi' the Papishers," Jean-aux-Choux whirled two-handed into the fray.

The first blow fell on the right-hand man. Fair on the boss of his shoulder-plate, heavy as a mace, fell that huge six foot of blade.

The armour was of proof, or that head would have been shorn from his body. As it was, the man fell senseless from his horse. Promptly his companion let go the rein of Claire's pony, crying, "Help there, my Lord Duke!" And so, wheeling his horse about, put speed to it, and rode in the direction of a group of gay knights and gentlemen who, as it now appeared, had been watching the fray with some amusement without caring to meddle with it.

Then from the midst of the little crowd there came one forth, the finest and properest man Claire had ever seen. He was tall and magnificently arrayed. The cloak over his light chain-armour was of dark crimson and gold, and the six enamelled lilies on his helmet marked him as next in rank to the princes of the blood.

The cavaliers about him drew their swords, and after saluting, asked if it were the will of their Lord Duke that they should punish these caitiffs who had so battered Goulard and Moulinet.

But "My Lord" put them aside with an impatient gesture of his glove.

"It would have served Goulard and Moulinet right if they had gotten twice as much!" he said. "They meddled in what did not concern them."

All the same, as he rode forward, his eyebrows, which were thick and barred across, twitched threateningly. He threw off his crimson cloak with an impatient gesture, and suddenly shone forth in a dazzling array of steel breast-plate and chain armour, all worked and damascened with gold.

"Epernon—Epernon—for my life, Epernon!" muttered the Abbé John under his breath to the Professor of Eloquence; "we could not have fallen on worse!"

The King's reigning favourite and boldest soldier rode straight up to them, with the careless ease which became the handsomest man in the kingdoms of France and Navarre.

"What have we here?" he demanded. "A pretty girl, two holy men, and a scarecrow! You are Genevists—Calvin's folk—Huguenots! This will not do; a fair maid's place is in a king's court. I will escort her thither. My wife will have great pleasure in her society, and will make her one of her own or of the Queen's maids-of-honour. From what I hear, her elder Majesty hath great need of such!"

"Not more than His Majesty has need of men of honour about him," cried the Abbé John fiercely—"aye, and has had all his life!"

"Hola, young cock-sparrow, clad in the habit of the hoodie-crow!" said D'Epernon, turning upon him, "from what stable-heap do you come that you chirp so loud?"

"From that same heap on which you serve as stable-boy, my Lord Duke!" said the Abbé John.

The Duke's brow darkened. He put his hand quickly to his gold-hilted rapier.

"Ah, pray do," sneered the Abbé John; "follow your inclination. Let the bright steel out. Get a man to hold our horses, and—have at you, my good Gascon!"

By this time the Duke d'Epernon's gentlemen were spurring angrily forward, but he halted them with a wave of his hand, without turning round in his saddle or taking his eyes off John's face.

"What is your name?" he demanded, his brows twitching so quickly that the eye could scarce follow their movements.

"I am John d'Albret, nephew of the Cardinal Bourbon and — —"

"Cousin of the Bearnais?" sneered the Duke, his eye glittering.

"Student at the Sorbonne!" said the Abbé John firmly. "All the same, if clerk I am, I am no poor clerk, and so you will find me—if, waiving my royal blood, I consent to put my steel to yours upon the sward. Come, down with you—and fall on!"

Now the Duke d'Epernon was anything rather than a coward. He made a motion as if to dismount, and there is little doubt but that his intention was to match his long-trained skill and success as a swordsman against the Abbé John's mastery of the latest science of sword-play learned in the Paris *salles*.

But suddenly D'Epernon checked himself. Then he laughed.

"No," he said; "after all, why should we fight? We may need each other one day, and there is no honour in killing a bantam, even if he hath a left-hand strain of kingly blood in him!"

"Left-hand!" cried the Abbé John: "you lie in your throat. My blood is infinitely more dexter than your own, and I make a better use of it! I am no mignon, at least."

Now this was a bitter taunt indeed, and even the tanned face of the King's warlike favourite flushed.

"As to mignons," he said, "you look much more like one yourself, young cockerel. I have overly many scars on my cheeks for the trade. And this is, I presume, your sister—to judge by the resemblance?" The Duke turned to Claire, who had been looking at him with a certain involuntary admiration. "What, no? Your niece, you say, my good Sorbonnist? I am not sure but that, as a strict Catholic, I must object. The age is scarce canonical!"

"I am no priest," said Doctor Anatole, roughly, for this touched him on the raw. "I am only the Professor of Eloquence attached to the faculty of philosophy. And I have the honour to inform you that I travel with my niece, to put her under the care of my mother at her house near to Collioure, in Roussillon."

"What!" cried the Duke, "now here is another of the suspicions which awake in the mind of the most guileless of men. Here we have a Bourbon, next-of-kin to the Cardinal himself, together with a Professor of the Sorbonne (that hotbed of sedition), travelling towards the dominions of the Demon of the South—of Philip of Spain! As a good subject, how am I to know that you are not on your way to stir up another rebellion against the King my master?"

It was then that Claire spoke for the first time.

"Sir," she said quietly, but looking full at the Duke with her eyes—dark green eyes the colour of jade, with little golden flashlets floating about in them, "I vouch for my friends. They are loyal and peaceful; I who speak am the only Huguenot. You can take and burn me if you like!"

The great Duke d'Epernon stood a moment aghast, as if the hunted hare had turned upon him in defiance. Then he slid off his helmet, and saluted, bareheaded.

"*Ma belle damoselle*," he said, "you may be the niece of a Doctor of the Sorbonne and at the same time a Huguenot. These are good reasons enough for carrying you to the castle of His Majesty. But be comforted—we are not as Philip of Spain, our enemy. We do not burn pretty brave maids such as you!"

It was then that Jean-aux-Choux forced himself forward on his big, blundering Spanish mare, driving between a couple of cavaliers, and sending them right and left like ninepins.

"Great Duke," he said, "you would do well to let us go on our way. You talk much of His Majesty—I ask you which. You have served the 'Bearnais'—you will serve him again. Even now you have cast an anchor to windward. It sticks firmly in the camp of the Bearnais, not far from that King's tent."

Duke d'Epernon turned on Jean-aux-Choux his fierce, dark eyes.

"It seems to me that I have seen you before, my churl of the carroty locks," he said; "were you not at the King's last fooling in the Louvre?"

"Aye," said Jean, "that I was, and in a certain window-seat behind a certain curtain I gave your Dukeship a certain letter——"

"It is enough," muttered the Duke, waving his hand hastily. "I am on my way to Angoulême, which is my government. Come all of you with me to Blois, and there abide quietly in a house till I return to salute the King.

The Estates meet in the late autumn, and if things go as it seems likely after this Day of the Barricades, we may need your blood royal, my excellent Clerk d'Albret—your best wisdom, my good and eloquent Professor—your rarest quips, my merry scarecrow—and, as for you, little lady, my newly-wed wife Marguerite will not be sorry to have a companion so frank and charming among the fading blossoms and over-ripe fruit of the court of the Queen-mother!"

"My lord," said the Professor, "I fear that I have not time to wait upon the King. I must go to visit my mother, and carry this maid with me!"

The Duke smiled.

"I am not demanding your learned preferences, most eloquent Professor," he said; "I am taking you into safe keeping in the name of the King. After all, I am not an ignorant man, and I know well that it was a certain Doctor Anatole Long who, in the full concourse of the Sorbonne, voted alone for the rights of the Valois. Give the King, therefore, a chance of voicing his thanks. Also, since the King is at Chartres and I must speed to Angoulême, I will leave you at Blois in good and comfortable keeping with the young damsel, your niece, taking with me only this young man, that he may see some good Leaguer fighting. He hath been, I dare say, on the Barricades himself. It is permitted to his age to be foolish. But he has never yet seen a full-grown, raw-hide, unwashed Catholic Leaguer. Let him come to Angoulême with me, and I will warrant to improve his sword-play for him! Close up, gentlemen of my guard! To Blois! Ride, accommodating your pace to mine, as I shall do mine to that of the palfrey of the new lady companion of Marguerite of Foix, whom I have the honour to love!"

He lifted his gloved hand, and from the fingers blew a kiss in the direction of the north, daintily as a girl upon a high terrace to a lover over the sea.

And so by the river-side, in the golden light of the afternoon, they rode forward to Blois.

In the rear Jean-aux-Choux continued to mutter to himself, trudging heavily along on his Flanders mare, laden with cloaks and provend, "'Tis all very well—very well—but what does his golden dukeship propose to do with me? I will not leave my little mistress alone in a strange city, and with a man who, though ten times a professor at the Sorbonne, is no more kin to her than I am to this fat-fetlocked Flemish brute."

He pondered a little, dropping gradually behind. But as soon as they had passed the gates of the city, he guided his beast into the first little alley, letting the cavalcade go on, amid much craning of necks from the windows, towards the royal pavilion where D'Epernon was to lodge.

"I will seek out Anthony Arpajon, that good man of the Faith," he said. "He has a stable down by the water-side, and being a lover of the learned, he will give me bite and sup for teaching him some scraps of Greek wherewith to puzzle the wandering Lutheran pastors. For a Calvinist stark is Anthony, and only wants a head-piece like mine to be a clever man. But he hath an arm and a purse. And for the rest, I will load him up with the best of Greek, and also teach him to read the *Institutions of John Calvin*, my first and greatest master!"

So through the narrow streets of Blois he made his great mare push herself lumberingly, crying out whenever there was a crowd or a busy street to cross, "Hoo! hoo! hoo! Make way for the King's fool—for Jean-aux-Choux—for the fool—the King's fool!"

CHAPTER XI
THE BEST-KNOWN FACE IN THE WORLD

Jean-aux-Choux dismounted from his Flanders mare at the entrance of a wide courtyard, littered with coaches and carriages, the best of these being backed under a sort of penthouse, but the commoner sort set out in the yard to take the bitter weather with the sweet. Some had their "trams" pitifully uplifted to heaven in wooden protestation against such ill-treatment; some wept tears of cracked pitch because the sun had been too much with them. Leathern aprons of ancient diligences split and seamed with alternate rain and drought. Everywhere there was a musty smell of old cushion-stuffing. A keen whiff of stables wandered past. Not far off one heard the restless nosing of horses in their mangers, and from yet another side came the warm breath of kine.

For Master Anthony Arpajon was a *bien* man, a man of property, and so far the Leaguers of Blois had not been able to prevail against him. In the courtyard, stretched at length on sacks of chaff, their heads on their corn-bags, with which, doubtless, on the morrow they would entertain their beasts by the way, many carters and drivers of high-piled wine-chariots were asleep.

The lower part of Master Anthony's house was a sort of free hostel, like the caravanserai of the East. The upper, into which no stranger was permitted to enter on any pretext, was like a fortified town.

To the left of the entrance, a narrow oblong break in the wall made a sort of rude buffet. Sections of white-aproned, square-capped cooks could be seen moving about within. Through the gap they served the simpler hot meats, bottles of wine, bread, omelettes, and salads to the arriving guests. It was curious that each, on going first to the barrier, threw the end of his blue Pyrenean waist-band over his shoulder. A little silver cow-bell, tied like a tassel to the silk, tinkled as he did so.

For this was the chosen sign of the men of Bearn. All the warring Protestants, and especially the Calvinists of the south, had adopted it, because it was the symbol of the arms of Bearn. And wherever it was unsafe to wear the White Plume of the hero on the cap, as in the town of Blois, it was easy to tuck the silver cow-bell of King Henry under the silken sash, where its tinkling told no tales.

But among these wine-carriers and free folk of the roads there was scarcely one who did not know Jean-aux-Choux. Yet they did not laugh as he entered, but rather greeted him respectfully, as one who plays well his part, though he came in shouting at the top of his voice, "Way for the fool of fools—the fool of three kings—and not so great a fool as any one of them!"

One man came forward, speaking the drawling speech of Burgundy, all liquid "l's" and slurred "r's," and with a clumsy salute took the Jester's beast. Many of the others rose to their feet and made their reverences according to their kind, clumsy or clever. Others whispered quietly, passing round the news of his arrival.

For the fool had come to his own. He was no more Jean-aux-Choux, the King's fool, but Master John Stirling, a Benjamin of the Benjaminites, and pupil of John Calvin himself.

The white-capped man behind the bar opened carefully a little door, and as instantly closed it behind Jean.

He pointed up a narrow stair which turned and was lost to sight in the thickness of the wall.

"You will find them at prayers," he muttered. "He is there."

"Kings are in His hand," responded Jean-aux-Choux, setting a foot on the first worn step of the narrow stair-case; "the Lord of Battles preserve him from the curs that yelp about his feet."

There came to Jean a sound of singing—sweet, far away, wistful, a singing not made for the chanting of choirs or the clamour of organs, but for folk hiding on housetops, in dens and caves of the earth—soft singing, with the enemy deadly and near at hand. The burden of their melody was that thirty-seventh Psalm which once on a time Clement Marot had risked his life to print.

"Wait on the Lord! Meekly thy burden bear;
Commit to Him thyself and thine affair!
In Him trust thou, and He will bring to pass
All that thou wouldst accomplish and compass.
Thy loss is gain—such is His equity,
Each of His own He guards eternally.
This lesson also learn—
He clasps thee closer as the days grow stern."

Jean opened the door. It was a long, black, oak-ceiled room into which he looked. There were perhaps a score of Huguenots present, all standing up, with Marot's little volume of the *Trente Psaumes* in their hands. A pastor in Geneva gown and bands stood at a table head, upon which a few great folios had been heaped to form a rude pulpit.

Beside him, not singing, but holding his psalter with a certain weary reverence, was a man with a face the best-known in all the world. And certainly Henry of Navarre never looked handsomer than in the days when pretty Gabrielle of the house of D'Estrees played with fire, calling her Huguenot warrior, "His Majesty of the Frosty Beard."

Such a mingling of kindliness, of humour bland and finely tolerant, of temper quick and high, of glorious angers, of swift, proud sinnings and repentances as swift, of great eternal destinies and human frailties, never was seen on any man's face save this.

It was "The Bearnais" — it was Henry of Navarre himself.

So long as the singing went on Jean-aux-Choux stood erect like the rest. Then all knelt at the prayer — the King also with them — on the hard floor under that low, black pent-roof, while the pastor prayed to the God of Sabaoth for the long-hoped-for victory of "His Own."

Beside "His Own" knelt Jean-aux-Choux, a look of infinite solemnity on his face, while the grave Genevan "cult" went quietly on, as if there had not been a Catholic or an enemy within fifty miles. The minister ceased. The King, without lingering on his knees as did the others, rose rapidly, mechanically dusting his black cloth breeches and even the rough carter's stockings which covered his shapely calves.

He sighed sadly, as his keen, quick-glancing eyes passed over the kneeling forms of the Huguenots. He did not take very kindly to the lengthy services and plain-song ritual of those whom he led as never soldiers had been led before.

"Hal Guise hath the Religion,
While I need absolution."

The Bearnais hummed one of the camp songs made against himself by his familiar Gascons, which always afforded him the most amusement — next, that is, to that celebrated one which recounted his successes on other fields than those of war. They were bold rascals, those Gascons of his, but they followed him well, and, after all, their idea of humour was his own.

"Ha, long red-man," he called out presently, when all had risen decently from their knees, "you made sport for us at Nerac, I remember, and then went to my good brother-in-law's court in the suite of Queen Marguerite. What has brought you here?"

A tall man, dark and slim, leaned over and whispered in the King's ear.

"Ah," said the Bearnais, nodding his head, "I remember the reports. They were most useful. But the fellow is a scholar, then?"

"He is of Geneva," said the man at the King's ear, "and is learned in Latin and Greek, also in Hebrew!"

"No wonder he does his business with credit"—the King smiled as he spoke; "there is no fool like a learned fool!"

With his constant good humour and easy ways with all and sundry, Henry of Navarre stepped forward and clapped Jean-aux-Choux on the shoulder.

"Go and talk to the pastor, D'Aubigné," said the King to his tall, dark companion; "I and this good fellow will chat awhile. Sit down, man. I am not Harry of Navarre to-night, but Waggoner Henri in from Coutras with some barrels of Normandy cider. Do you happen to know a customer?"

"Ay, that do I," answered Jean-aux-Choux, fixing his eyes on the strong, soldierly face of the Bearnais, "one who has just arrived in this town, and may have some customs' dues to levy on his own liquor."

"And who may that be?" demanded the King.

"The Governor of Normandy," Jean answered—"he and no other!"

"What—D'Epernon?" cried the Bearnais, really taken by surprise this time.

"I have just left his company," said Jean; "he has with him many gentlemen, the Professor of Eloquence at the Sorbonne, the nephew of the Cardinal Bourbon——"

"What, my cousin John the pretty clerk?" laughed Henry.

"He drives a good steel point," said Jean-aux-Choux; "it were a pity to make him a holy water sprinkler. I was too ugly to be a pastor. He is too handsome for a priest!"

"We will save him," said the Bearnais; "when our poor old Uncle of the Red Hat dies, they will doubtless try to make a king of this springald."

"He vows he would much rather carry a pike in your levies," said Jean-aux-Choux. "It is a brave lad. He loves good hard knocks, and from what I have seen, also to be observed of ladies!"

The Bearnais laughed a short, self-contemptuous laugh. "I fear we shall quarrel then, Cousin John and I," he said; "one Bourbon is enough in a camp where one must ride twenty miles to wave a kerchief beneath a balcony!"

"Also," continued Jean-aux-Choux, "there is with them my dear master's daughter, Mistress Claire——"

"What, Francis Agnew's daughter?" The King's voice grew suddenly kingly.

Jean nodded.

"Then he is dead—my Scot—my friend? When? How? Out with it, man!"

"The Leaguers or the King's Swiss shot him dead the Day of the Barricades—I know not which, but one or the other!"

The fine gracious lines of the King's face hardened. The Bearnais lifted his "boina," or flat white cap, which he had resumed at the close of worship, as was his right.

"They shall pay for this one day," he said; "Valois, King, and Duke of Guise—what is it they sing? Something about

'The Cardinal and Henry and Mayenne, Mayenne!'

If I read the signs of the times aright, the King of France will do Henry of Guise's business one of these days, while I shall have Mayenne on my hands. At any rate, poor Francis Agnew shall not go unavenged, wag the world as it will."

These were not the highest ideals of the Nazarene. But they suited a warring Church, and Henry of Navarre only voiced what was the feeling of all, from D'Aubigné the warrior to the pastor who sat in a corner by himself, thumbing his little Geneva Bible. There was no truce in this war. The League or the Bearnais! Either of the two must rule France. The present king, Henry of Valois, was a merry, sulky, careless, deceitful, kindly, cruel cipher—the "man-woman," as they named him, the "gamin"-king. He laughed and jested—till he could safely thrust his dagger into his enemy's back. But as for his country, he could no more govern it than a puppet worked by strings.

"And this girl?" said the King, "is she of her father's brood, strong for the religion, and so forth?"

"She is young and innocent—and very fair!"

The eyes of the Fool of the Three Henries met those of the Bearnais boldly, and the outlooking black eyes flinched before them.

"These Scottish maids are not as ours," said the King, perhaps in order to say something, "yet I think she was with her father in my camp, and shared his dangers."

"To the last she held up his dying head!" said Jean-aux-Choux. And quite unexpectedly to himself, his eyes were moist.

"And where at this moment is Francis Agnew's daughter?" said the King. Then he added, without apparent connexion, "He was my friend!"

But his intimates understood the word, and so, though a poor fool, did Jean-aux-Choux. Instinctively he held out his hand, as he would have done to a brother-Scot of his degree.

The King clasped it heartily, and those who were nearest noticed that his eyes also had a shine in them.

"What a man!" whispered D'Aubigné to his nearest neighbour. "Sometimes we of the Faith are angry with him, and then, with a pat on the cheek, or a laugh, we are his children again. Or he is ours, I know not which! Guise shakes hands all day long to make his dukeship popular, but in spite of himself his lip curls as if he touched a loathsome thing. Valois presents his hand to be kissed as if it belonged to some one else. But our Bearnais— one would think he never had but one friend in the world, and— —"

"That this Scots fool is the man!"

"Hush," whispered D'Aubigné, "he is no fool, this fellow. He was of my acquaintance at Geneva. In his youth he knew John Calvin, and learned in the school of Beza. The King does well to attach him! Listen!"

Jean-aux-Choux was certainly giving the King his money's-worth. Henry was pacing up and down, his fingers busily and unconsciously arranging his beard.

"I have not enough men to take him prisoner," he said; "this ex-mignon D'Epernon is a slippery fish. He will deal with me, and with another. But if he could sell my head to my Lord of Guise and these furious wool-staplers of Paris, he would think it better worth his while than the off-chance of the Bearnais coming out on top!"

He pondered a while, with the deep niche of thought running downward from mid-brow to the bridge of his nose, which they called "the King's council of war."

"The girl is to be left in Blois," he muttered, as if to sum up the situation, "with this Professor of the Sorbonne—an old man, I suppose, and a priest. Very proper, very proper! My cousin, John Jackanapes, the young ex-Leaguer, goes to Court. They will make a Politique of him, a Valois-divine-right man—good again, for after this Valois-by-right-divine (save the mark!) comes not Master John d'Albret, but—the Bearnais! Yet—I do not know—

perhaps, after all, he had better come with me. Then I shall hold one hostage the more! Let me see—let me see!"

Here Jean-aux-Choux, who had at that time no great love for the Abbé John, but was an honest man, protested.

"The time for crowning and seeking crowns is not yet," he said; "but the lad they call the Abbé John, though he fought a little on the Barricades, as young dogs do in a fray general, means no harm to Your Majesty, and will fight for you better than many who protest more!"

"I believe you—I believe you!" said Henry. "If there is aught but eyes-making and laying-on of blows in him, I shall soon find it out, and he shall not trail a pike for long. He shall have his company, and that of the choicest of my army."

Suddenly the pastor sprang up. He had a message to deliver, and being of the prevailing school of the mystics, he put it in the shape of a vision, as, indeed, it had appeared to him.

"I see the earth dissolved," he cried, "the elements going up in a flaming fire, the inhabitants tormented and destroyed——"

"Thank God! Thank God!" responded the deep, dominating voice of Jean-aux-Choux.

The King requested to know the meaning of this unexpected thankfulness for universal destruction.

"Anything to settle the League!" said Jean-aux-Choux.

CHAPTER XII
THE WAKING OF THE BEARNAIS

Jean-aux-Choux's deflection from his course created little remark and no sensation in the brilliant company which entered Blois in the wake of the royal favourite. D'Epernon had dismissed him from his mind. The Abbé John and—oh, shame!—the doctor of the Sorbonne were both thinking of Claire. So it came to pass, in revenge, that only Claire of all that almost royal cavalcade spared a thought to poor Jean-aux-Choux.

As, however, Claire was the only one concerning whom Jean cared an apple-pip, he would have been perfectly content had he known.

As it was, he waited till the Bearnais had betaken himself to his slumbers in Anthony Arpajon's best green-tapestried chamber, and then sailed out, hooded and robed like a Benedictine friar, to make his observations. In the town of Blois, as almost anywhere else in central and southern France, the ex-student of Geneva knew his way blindfold. He skirted the bare rocky side of the castle, whereon now stands the huge pavilion of Gaston of Orleans.

"They will not come and go by the great door," he said, "but there is the small postern, by which it is the custom to make exits and entrances when Court secrets are in the wind."

Accordingly, Jean placed himself behind a great hedge which marked the limits of the royal domain. The city hummed beneath him like a hive of bees aroused untimeously. He could hear now and then the voice of some Leaguer raised in curses of the Valois King and all his favourites. The voice was usually a little indistinct because of the owner's having too frequently considered the redness of the Blesois wine.

Anon the curses would arrive home to roost, and that promptly. For some good royalist, crying "*Vive D'Epernon*," would bear down upon the Guisard. Then dull smitings of combat would alternate with war-cries and over-words of faction songs. Once came a single deadly scream, way for which had evidently been opened by a knife, and then, after that, only the dull pad-pad of running feet—and silence!

In the palace wall the postern door opened and someone looked out. It was closed again immediately.

Jean's eyes strove in vain to see more clearly. But the windows above, being brilliantly lighted, threw the postern into the darkest shadow.

A moment after, however, four persons came out—first two men, then a slender figure wrapped in a cloak, which Jean knew in a moment for that of his mistress.

"He is keeping his word, after all," muttered Jean; "it may be just as well!"

He who stepped out last was tall and dark, and turned the key in the lock of the low door with the air of a man shutting up his own mansion for the night.

They went closely past Jean's hiding-place and, to his amazement, took the very way by the water-side, down the Street of the Butchery, by which he had come. More wonderful still, they turned aside without hesitation—or rather, their leader did—into the yard of Anthony Arpajon. Silently Jean-aux-Choux stalked them. How could they know? Was it treachery? Was it an ambush? At any rate, it was his duty to warn the Bearnais—that was evident.

But how? The blue-bloused carters and teamsters, wearing the silken sashes fringed so quaintly with silver bells, were asleep all about. But Jean-aux-Choux darted from sack to sack, dived beneath waggons, ran up stairways of rough wood. And presently, before the leader of the four had done parleying with the white-capped man behind the bar, the intruders were surrounded by thirty veterans of Henry of Navarre's most trusted guards. The chain mail showed under the trussed blouses of the wine-carriers. And D'Epernon, looking round, saw himself the centre of a ring of armed men.

"Ah," he said, with superb and even insolent coolness, "is it thus you keep your watch, you of the old Huguenot phalanx, you who, from father to son, have made your famous family compact with death? Here I find you asleep in a hostile city, where Guise could rouse a thousand men in an hour! Or I myself, if so minded— —"

"I think, my Lord Duke," said D'Aubigné, putting his sword to the Duke's breast, "that long before your clarion sounded its first blast, one fine gentleman might chance to find himself in the Loire with as many holes in him as a nutmeg-grater!"

"It might indeed be so, sir," said the Duke, still haughtily, "but on this occasion I shall literally go scot-free. Wake your master, the King of Navarre. Tell him that the Duke of Epernon craves leave to speak with him immediately. He is alone, and has come far and risked much to meet His Majesty. Also, I bid you say that I come on the part of Francis Agnew the Scot, whom he knows!"

"You bid!" cried D'Aubigné, whose temper was not over long in the grain. "Learn, then, that none bids me save my master, and he is neither King's minister nor King's minion."

"Sir," said the Duke, "I do not need to prove my courage, any more than the gentlemen of my Lord of Navarre. At another time and in another place I am at your service. In the meantime, will you have the goodness to do as I request of you? I must see the King, and swiftly, lest I be missed—up yonder!"

"The King is asleep!" said Anthony Arpajon—"asleep in my best tapestried chamber. He must not be waked."

"Harry of Bearn will always wake to win a battle or a lady's favour," said D'Epernon. "I can help him to both, if he will!"

"Then I will go," said Anthony. "Come with me, Jean-aux-Choux. Take bare blade in hand, that there be no treachery. I have known you some time now, Jean. For these others there is no saying!"

So these two went up together to the King's sleeping-chamber. Anthony knocked softly, but there was no answer, though they could hear the soft, regular breathing of the sleeper. He opened the door a little. Jean-aux-Choux stood looking over his shoulder. A night-light burned on the table, shaded from the eyes of the sleeping man on the canopied couch. But a soft circle of illumination fell on the miniature of a lady, painted in delicate colours, set immediately beneath it.

"His mother—the famous Jeanne d'Albret," whispered Anthony; "he loved her greatly. She was even as a saint!"

Queen Jeanne was certainly a most attractive person, but somehow Jean-aux-Choux remained a little incredulous. "How shall we wake him?" asked Anthony, under his breath.

"Sing a psalm," suggested Jean-aux-Choux.

"Alas, that I should say so concerning his mother's son, but from what I have seen in this my house, I judge that were more likely to send him into deeper sleep."

"Nay," said Jean, "I know him better—he is an old acquaintance of mine. Only keep well behind the door when he wakes. For the Bearnais rises ever with his sword in his hand—unless he is in his own house, where the servants are at pains to place all weapons out of his reach. Sing the Gloria, Anthony, and then he will rise very cross and angry, demanding to know if we have not sung enough for one night."

"Ay, the Gloria. It is well thought on," quoth Anthony; "I have heard them tell in our country how it was his mother's favourite. He will love the strains. As I have said, she was a woman sainted—Jeanne the Queen!"

"Hum," said Jean-aux-Choux, "that's as may be. At all events, her son, the Bearnais, was born without any halo to speak of."

"The prayers of a good mother are never wholly lost," said Anthony sententiously.

"Then they are sometimes a long while mislaid," muttered Jean.

"Shame on you, that have known John Calvin in your youth," said Anthony, "to speak as the unbelieving. Have you forgotten that God works slowly, and that with Him one day is as a thousand years?"

"Aye," said the incorrigible Jean, arguing the matter with Scots persistency, "but the Bearnais takes a good deal out of himself. He is little likely to last so long as that. However, let us do the best we can—sing!"

So they sang the famous Huguenot verses made in the desert by Louis-of-the-Hermitage.

"Or soit au Père tout puissant,
Qui règne au ciel resplendissant,
Gloire et magnificence!"

The Bearnais turned in his sleep, muttering restlessly.

"Why cannot they sing their psalms at proper hours," he grumbled, "as before a battle or on Sunday, leaving me to sleep now when I am weary and must ride far on the morrow?"

The psalm went on. Sleepily, the King searched for a boot to throw in the direction of the disturbance, possibly under the impression that his sentinels were chanting at their posts—a habit which, though laudable in itself, he had been compelled to forbid from a military point of view. The Bearnais discovered, by means of a spur which scratched him sharply, that his boots were on his feet. He muttered yet more loudly.

"His morning prayers," said Anthony in Jean's ear; "his mother, Jeanne the Queen, was ever like that. She waked with blessing on her lip—so also her son."

"I doubt," said Jean-aux-Choux.

"Sing—gabble less concerning the Anointed of God," commanded Anthony Arpajon.

And they sang the second time.
"In Sion's city God is known,
For her defence He holds Him ready,
Though banded kings attack at dawn,
God's rock-bound fortress standeth steady."

This time the Bearnais stood up on his feet, broadly awake. He did not, as Jean-aux-Choux had foretold, thrust a sword behind the arras. Instead, he picked up the painted miniature on which the little circle of light was falling. He pressed it a moment to his lips, and then, with the click of a small chain clasping, it was about his neck and over his heart, hidden by his mailed shirt.

"His mother's picture—even from here methinks I recognise the features," asserted the faithful Anthony.

"Most touching!" interjected Jean-aux-Choux.

"It astonishes you," said Anthony Arpajon, "but that is because you are a stranger——"

"And ye would take me in," muttered Jean under his breath.

"But in our country of Bearn we all worship our mothers—with us it is a cult."

"I have noticed it," said Jean-aux-Choux. "In my country we have it also, with this difference—in Scotland it is for our children's mothers, chiefly before marriage."

But at this moment they heard the voice of the King within.

"Where is D'Aubigné? Why does he not insure quiet in the house? I have ridden far and would sleep! Surely even a king may sleep sometimes?"

"Your Majesty, it is I—Anthony Arpajon, the Calvinist, and with me is John Stirling, the Scot, called Jean-aux-Choux, the Fool of the Three Henries."

"And what does he want with this Henry—does he jest by day and sing psalms by night?"

"I have to inform Your Majesty," said Jean-aux-Choux, "that the Duke d'Epernon is below, and would see the King of Navarre."

Now there was neither blessing nor cursing. The Bearnais did not kiss the picture of his mother. A scabbard clattered on the stone floor, was caught deftly, and snapped into its place on his belt.

"Where is my other pistol? Ah, I remember—D'Aubigné took it to clean. Lend me one of yours, Jean-aux-Choux. Is it primed and loaded?"

"He is with my lady mistress, the daughter of Francis the Scot, and with him are only the Sorbonne doctor and your cousin D'Albret for all retinue."

"Oh, ho," said Henry of Navarre, "a lady—more dangerous still. Hold the candle there, Jean-aux-Choux. I must look less like a hodman and more like a king."

And he drew from his inner pocket a little glass that fitted a frame, and a pocket-comb, with which he arranged his locks and the curls of his beard with a care at which the stout Calvinist, Anthony Arpajon, chafed and fumed.

"It is for the sake of his mother," whispered Jean in his ear, to comfort him, after the King had finished at last and signified that he was ready to descend. "She taught him that cleanliness is next to godliness," said Jean, "and now, when he is a man, the habit clings to him still."

"If he were somewhat less of a man," said the Calvinist, in the same whisper, "he would be the better king."

"Ah, wait," said Jean-aux-Choux—"wait till you have seen him on a battle-front, and you will be sure that, for all his faults, there never was a more manly man or a kinglier king!"

CHAPTER XIII
A MIDNIGHT COUNCIL

The Bearnais met D'Epernon in the inner dining-room of Master Anthony's house. His servants had hastily lighted a few wax candles. In the waggon-littered courtyard without, a torch or two flamed murkily. With a quick burst of anger, Henry leaned from a window and bade them be extinguished. So, with a jetting of sparks on the hard-beaten earth of the courtyard, the darkness suddenly re-established itself.

There was, on the side of the Duke, some attempt at a battle of eyes. But, after all, he had only been the little scion of a Languedocean squire when the Bearnais was already—the Bearnais.

The Duke bowed himself as if to set knee to the ground, but Henry caught him up.

"Caumont," he said, using the old boyish name by which they had known each other in their wild Paris youth, "you have never liked me. You have never been truly my friend. Why do you come to seek me now?"

The busy scheming brain behind the Valois favourite's brow was working. He had a bluff subject to deal with, therefore he would be bluff.

"Your Majesty," he said, "there is no one in all France who wishes better to your cause, or more ill to the League than I. When you are King, you shall have no more faithful or obedient subject. But friendship, like love, is born of friendship; it comes not by command. When the King of Navarre makes me his friend, I shall be his!"

"Spoken like a man, and no courtier," cried the Bearnais, slapping his strong hand into the white palm of D'Epernon with a report like a pistol; "I swear I shall be your friend till the day I die!"

And the Bearnais kept his word, and gave his friendship all his life to the dark, scheming, handsome man, who had served many masters in his time, but had never loved any man save himself, any woman except his wife, and any interest outside of his own pocket.

The soldiers of the Guard Royal made a rhyme which went not ill in the patois of the camp, but which goes lamely enough translated into English. Somewhat thus it ran:

"Duke Epernon and his wife,
Jean Caumont and his wife,
Cadet Valette and his Cadette,
Louis Nogaret and *his* wife—
If ever I wagered I would bet
My pipe, my lass, and eke my life,
That this brave world was made and set
For Duke Epernon and his wife—
Jean Caumont and his wife,
Louis Nogaret and his wife,
Cadet Valette and his Cadette!"

And so *Da Capo*—to any tune which happened to occur to them in their semi-regal license of King's free guardsmen.

Which was only the barrack and guard-room way of saying that Jean Louis de Nogaret, Cadet de la Valette, Duc d'Epernon and royal favourite, looked after the interests of a certain important numeral with some care.

"Caumont," said the King of Navarre, "how came you to know I was in this town? I arrived but an hour ago, and in disguise."

"Our spies are better than Your Majesty's," smiled the Duke. "Your true Calvinist is something too stiff in the backbone to make a capable informer. You ought to employ a few supple Politiques, accustomed to palace backstairs. But, on this occasion, I acknowledge I was favoured by circumstances. For I have with me the daughter of Francis the Scot, called Francis d'Agneau, born, I believe, of a Norman house long established in Scotland near to the Gulf of Solway. Among the saddle-bags of the damsel's pony, hastily concealed by other hands than her own (I suspect a certain red-haired fool), there was found a series of letters written by Your Majesty, which, in case they might fall into worse hands, I have the honour of returning to you. Also we found an appointment for this very night, to meet with Francis the Scot at the town of Blois in the house of Anthony Arpajon! Your Majesty has, as the Leaguers know, a habit of uncomfortable punctuality in the keeping of your trysts. So I have availed me of that to confide the letters and the maid to you, together with a good Doctor of the Sorbonne, one who has done you no mean service to the honest cause in that wasps' nest—so good, indeed, that if he went back, the Leaguers of his own hive would sting him to death. Therefore I commit them all to you! Only the young man I would gladly keep by me. But that shall be as Your Majesty judges."

"No, no," cried the King. "I must have my cousin, if only to look after. If the Leaguers get hold of him, he might gain a throne, indeed, but assuredly he would lose his head. He is a fine lad, and will do very well in the fighting line when Rosny has licked him a little into shape! But I am truly grateful to you, D'Epernon. And in the good times to come, I shall have better ways of proving my gratitude than here, in the house of Anthony Arpajon and in the guise of a carter."

This was all that D'Epernon had been waiting for, and he promptly bowed himself out. The instant the Duke was through the door, the Bearnais turned to the little circle of his immediate followers.

"Who of you knows the town and Château of Blois? It might be worth while following the fellow, just to see if any treachery be in the wind. It may be I do him wrong. If so, I shall do him the greater right hereafter. No, not you, D'Aubigné. I could not risk you. You are my father-confessor, and task me soundly with my faults. Indeed, I might as well be a Leaguer— they say the Cardinal sets more easy penances. Brother Guise is the true Churchman—he and the King of Spain!"

The King looked about from one to another doubtfully, seeking a fit envoy.

"No, nor you, Rosny; you can fight all day, and figure all night. But for spying we want a lad of another build. Let me see—let me see!"

As the King was speaking, Jean-aux-Choux put on his brown Capuchin robe, and covered his red furze brush with the hood.

"I tracked my Lord of Epernon this night once before," he said, "and by the grace of God I can do as much again. I know his trail, and will be at the orchard gate of the Château before he has time to blow the dust out of his key!"

"How do you come to know so much?" demanded the Bearnais.

"By this token," said Jean carelessly; "that I saw my lady here and the three men come out of the Château, I followed them hither, and had your men roused and ready, so that if there had been any treachery, his Dukeship, at least, would have been the first to fall!"

The King looked about him inquiringly.

"Rosny and D'Aubigné," he said, "what do you know of this—does the man speak true?"

"A pupil of John Calvin speaks no lie," said Jean bravely. The King laughed, whereupon Jean added, "If I do act a lie, it is to save Your Majesty — the hope of the Faith!"

"That is rather like the old heresy of doing evil that good may come," said Henry; "but off with you! If I can accommodate my conscience to a waggoner's blouse, I do not see why you should not reconcile yours to a monk's hood!"

Jean-aux-Choux departed, muttering to himself that the Bearnais was becoming as learned as a pupil of Beza or a Sorbonne Doctor, but consoling himself for his dialectical defeat by the thought that, at least, in the Capuchin's robe he was fairly safe. For even if caught, after all, it was only another trick of the Fool of the Three Henries.

It was, indeed, the only thing concerning which Leaguers, Royalists, and Huguenots were agreed — that Jean-aux-Choux was a good, simple fool!

CHAPTER XIV
EYES OF JADE

Claire Agnew was left alone among a world of men. But as she had known few women all her life, that made the less matter. Her dark, densely ringleted hair, something between raven-black and the colour of bog-oak, was crisped about a fine forehead, which in his hours of ease her father had been wont to call "Ailsa Craig."

"Oh, cover up Ailsa!" he would say often to tease her, "no girl can have brains enough for a brow such as that!" And so, to please him, she had trained her hair to lie low on her forehead, and then to ripple and twist away gracefully to the nape of her neck, looking, as she turned her head, like a charming young Medusa with deep green eyes of mystic jade.

Such was Claire Agnew in the year of grace 1588, when she found herself fatherless in that famous town of Blois, soon to be the terror, the joy, and the hope of the world. Not that any description can do much to make the personality of a fair woman leap from the printed page. Slowly and only in part, it must disengage itself in word and thought and deed.

Like almost all lonely girls, Claire Agnew kept, in her father's tongue, often in his very dialect, a journal of events and feelings and imaginings—her "I-book," as she used to name it to herself.

That night as she curled herself up to sleep—it was almost morning—she arranged in her mind how she would begin the very next day to write down "all that happened, as well as" (because she was a girl) "all that she hoped would happen."

The closely-packed script has come down to us, the writing fine, like Greek cursive. The paper has been preserved marvellously, but the ink is browned with time, and the letters so small and serried that they can only be made out with a magnifying-glass.

"This is my I-Book, and I mean to be more faithful with myself in writing it out; from this time forward—I shall write it every night, no matter how tired I may be. Or—at least, the next day, without the least failure. This shall have the force of a vow!"

(Poor Claire—even thus have all diaries opened, since the first Cave-man began to scratch the details of his Twelfth of August "bag" on a mammoth-tusk! What a feeble proportion of these diaries have survived even one fortnight!)

"Yes, I like him," Claire wrote, without prelude or the formality of naming the him—"I like him, but I am glad he is gone. Somehow, till I have thought and rested a while, I shall feel safer with just our excellent Doctor Long, who preaches at me much as Pastor Gras used to do at Geneva. Indeed, I see little difference, except that the pastor was older, and did not hold my hand as he talked. But no doubt he does that because I have lost my father."

Doubtless it was so; nevertheless it needs some little explanation to make it clear why, after having been committed by D'Epernon to the care of the King of Navarre, Claire and the Professor should still be in the little town of Blois, with the young girl busily writing her journal, and lifting her eyes at the end of every sentence to look across the broad blue river at the squares and oblongs of ripening vintages which went clambering irregularly over the low hills opposite.

"The Loire here in this place" (so she wrote) "is broad and calm, not swift and treacherous like the Rhone, or sleepy like the Seine, nor yet fierce like the Rhine as I saw it long ago, lashing green as sea-water about the old bridge at Basel. I love the Loire—a wide river, still and unrippled, not a leaping fish, not a stooping bird, a water of silver flowing on and on in a dream. And though my father is dead and I greatly alone (save for old Madame Granier in her widow's crape) I cannot feel that I am very unhappy. Perhaps it is wicked to say so. I reproach myself that I lack feeling—that if I had loved my father more, surely I would now have been more unhappy. I do not know. One is as one is made.

"Yet I did love him—God knows I did! But here—it is so peaceful. Sadness falls away."

And peaceful it certainly was. The Bearnais had gone back to his camp, taking the Abbé John with him, where, in the incessant advance and retreat of the Huguenot army, there was little room for fair maids.

Before he went away, the King had had a talk with Jean-aux-Choux and with his host, Anthony Arpajon. They reminded him that for some months at least, no one would be more welcome in Blois than this learned Professor of the Sorbonne. Was not the Parliament of the King—the loyal

States-General—to be gathered there in a few weeks? And, meantime, the provident Blesois were employed in making their rooms fit and proper for the reception of the rich and noble out of all France, excepting only the Leaguer provinces of the north and the Huguenot south-east from the Loire to the Pyrenees.

"I would willingly keep the maid and the Professor," said Anthony, "but it is of the nature of my business that there should be at times a bustle and a noise of rough lads coming and going. And though none of them would harm the daughter of Francis the Scot—having me to deal with, as well as wearing, for the most part, the silver cow-bell at their girdles—yet a hostelry is no place for a well-favoured Calvinist maid, and the daughter of Master Francis Agnew!"

"What, then, would you do with her?"

The brow of the King was frowning a little. After all, he thought, had the girl not followed her father, and been accustomed to the rough side of the blanket? He had not found women so nice about their accommodation when a king catered for them.

But a well-timed jest of Jean-aux-Choux concerning the young blades which the mere sight of Claire would set bickering, caused the Bearnais to smile, and with a sigh he gave way.

"Well, Anthony the Calvinist, you are an obstinate varlet. Have it as you will. I am an easy man. But tell me your plans. For, after all, the girl has been committed to my charge."

The Calvinist innkeeper had his answer ready.

"There dwells," he said, "by the water-side yonder a wise and prudent wife, whose husband was long at the wars, a sergeant in your Cevenol levies. She will care for the maid. And if there be need, Madame Granier knows a door in her back-yard by which, at all times, she can have such help or shelter as the house of Anthony Arpajon can give her."

"And the Professor of Eloquence?" said Henry, with a quick glance.

"Is he not her uncle—in a way, her guardian?" said Anthony, with an impenetrable countenance. "She could not be in safer hands. Leave us also the fool, Jean-aux-Choux, and, by my word, you shall have the first and the best intelligence of that the King and his wise Parliamenters may devise. They say my Lord of Guise is soon to be here with a thousand gentlemen, and such a tail of the commonalty as will eat up all the decent folk in Blois like a swarm of locusts!"

"Good," said the King of Navarre. "Guise has long been tickling the adder's tail; he will find what the head holds some fine day, when he least expects it!"

These were quiet days in the little white house, with only the narrow quay underneath, and the changing groups of washerwomen, bare-armed, lilac-bloused, laving and lifting in the tremulous heat-haze of the afternoon. But somehow they were very dear days to Claire Agnew, and she clung to the memory of them long afterwards.

She was near enough for safety to the hostelry of the Silver Cow-bell (presently held by Anthony Arpajon), yet far enough from it to be quite apart from its throng and bustle. All day Madame Granier gathered up the gossip of the quarter, and passing it through a kind of moral sieve, retailed it at intervals to her guest.

Furthermore, Claire had time to bethink herself. She had long, long thoughts of the Abbé John. She remembered how bright and willing he had ever been in her service, how he had respected her grief, and never breathed word her father might not have heard.

And her good Professor of Eloquence—Doctor Anatole Long? What of him? He was there close under her hand, always willing to stroll with her along the river's bank. Or in Dame Granier's little living-room, he would explain the universe to Claire Agnew to the accompaniment of Madame Granier's clattering platters and her rhyme of King Francis.

"Brave Francis went the devil's way,
Bold sprang the hawk, laughed maidens gay!
Yet he learned to eat from an Emperor's tray,
Sans hawk, sans hound, sans maiden gay.
A-lack-a-day! A-lack-a-day!
From Pavia's steeple struck Doomsday!"

After all, it was best by the river-side. You saw things there, and if the Professor were in good humour, he would talk on and on, while you could—that is, Claire could—throw stones in the water without disturbing the even flow of the big, fine words. Not too large stones, but only pebbles, else he would rise and march on, with a frown at being interrupted, but without at all perceiving the cause. For at such times Claire always looked especially demure.

"You are indeed my dear Uncle Anatole," she said one day, when they had been longer by the water-side than usual; "you were just made for it. If you had not been—I declare I should have adopted you!"

There was something teasing about Claire's accent, at once girlish and light, which fell pleasantly on the Professor's ear. But the words—he was not so sure that he liked the words.

"I am not so old," he said, the deep furrow which dinted downwards between his thick eyebrows smoothing itself out as he looked, or rather peered at her with his short-sighted blue eyes; "my mother is active still. I long for you to see her; and I have two brothers, one of whom was thinking of marrying last year, but after all it came to nothing!"

"I should think so, indeed," said Claire suddenly.

"And pray why?" The Professor swung about and faced her. "What was there to prevent it?"

"The girl, of course!" said Claire, smiling simply.

"Umph!" said the Professor, and for half a mile spoke no more.

Then he nodded his head sagely, and communed to himself without speech.

"She is right," he said; "she is warning me. What have I to do with young maids?—I who might have had maids of my own, fool that I was! Hey, what's that? Stand back there, or I will spit any two of you—dogs!"

A laughing, dancing convoy of gold-laced pages from the Château, now rapidly filling up for the momentous meeting of the States-General, swirled out of the willow-copses by the Loire side. Claire was caught into the turmoil of the dance, as a flight of wild pigeons might envelop a tame dove wandering from the Basse Cour.

"Go up, bald-head!" they cried, "grey beards and young maids go not well together!"

The Professor of Eloquence, stung by the affront, lifted his only weapon, a stout oaken cudgel. And with such a pack of beardless loons, the mere threat was enough. They scattered, screaming and laughing.

"I will report you to the Provost-Marshal, to the Major-domo of the palace, and your backs shall pay for this insolence to my niece!"

"I think they meant no harm, sir," said Claire breathlessly, taking the arm of the Professor of the Sorbonne. She was astonished at his heat.

"The whipping-bench and a good dozen spare rods are what they want!" growled the Professor. "These are ill times. 'Train up a child in the way he should go,' saith the Book. But in these days the young see only evil all their days, and when they are old they depart not from that!"

CHAPTER XV
MISTRESS CATHERINE

Upon the return of the Professor and Claire from the river-side to the little walled garden and white house of Dame Granier, they found Anthony Arpajon waiting for them. With him was a lady—no, a girl of thirty; the expression is right. For through the girlish brightness of her complexion, and in spite of the quick smile that went and came upon her lips, there pierced the sure determination and settled convictions of the adult of a strong race.

"I am Catherine d'Albret and a cousin of your friend," said the girl; "I have a number of followers—brave gentlemen all of them, who have ridden with me from the south. They are lodging with our friend Anthony here. But I am come to abide with you—if I may. We shall share the same room and, if you like me, we shall talk the moon across the sky!"

She held out both her hands, but Claire's shy Scottish blood still held off. The Professor came to their assistance.

"As my lady is a D'Albret," he said, "she must be a cousin-germain to our good Abbé John!"

The girl smiled, and gave her head a little uplift, half of amusement, half of contempt.

"Ay, truly," she said, "but we are of different religions. I love not to see a man waste his life on the benches of the Sorbonne; and all for what—only to wear a red hat when all is done, like my Uncle of Bourbon!"

The Professor sighed, and thoughtfully rubbed his brow. Then he smiled, as he answered the girl.

"Ah," he said, "it is always so with you young people. Here am I who have spent the best part of my life on these very Sorbonne benches, teaching Eloquence to a party of young jackanapes who had far better hold their tongues till they have something to say. And for me, no cardinal's hat at the end of all!"

He sighed a second time, as he added, "Indeed, I know not very well what, after all, is at the end—certainly not their monkish dreams of hell, purgatory, paradise!"

The newcomer stepped eagerly forward and laid her hand on his lips. "Hush," she said, "you have lost your way. You have wandered in your own mazes of subtlety, and arrived nowhere. Now we of the Faith will lead you in the green pastures, beside still but living waters, which your soul shall love!"

The Professor watched the maiden before him a little sadly. Her face was all aglow with enthusiasm. There was a brilliant light in her eyes.

"Yes, I shall teach you—I, Catherine of Navarre——"

There was a noise outside on the quay.

She turned towards the window to look out. At the first step, a little halt in her gait betrayed her. The Professor of Eloquence sank on one knee.

"You are Jeanne d'Albret's own daughter," he said, "her very self, as I saw her a month before the Bartholomew. Even so she spoke—even so she walked. The Bearnais hath no philosophy other than his sword and the ready quip on his tongue. He cares no more for one religion or the other than the white plume he carries in the front of battle. But not so you."

"Henry of Bourbon-Vendôme is my brother," said Catherine, "all king, all brave man. His faults are not mine—nor mine his. I am, as I said, a manifest D'Albret. But Henry holds of Bourbon!"

The two young maids mounted to their chamber. Madame Granier was already there, ordering the bed-linen for the new guest. The girls stood looking a long while into each other's faces.

"You are prettier than I," said Mistress Catherine; "but they tell me that, for all that (and it is saying much), your father made you a good daughter of the Religion!"

"He was indeed all of good and brave and in instruction wise—I fear me I have profited but little!"

"Ah," said the Princess, "that is as I would expect your father's daughter to speak. For the present, I cannot offer you much. I have a great and serious work to do. But one day you shall be my maid-of-honour!"

It is the way of princesses, even of the wisest. But the daughter of Francis the Scot was free-born. She only smiled a little, and answered, with her father's quiet dignity of manner, "Then or now, I will do anything for the daughter of Queen Jeanne!"

"By-and-by, perhaps, you will be willing to do a little for myself," said the Princess gently, putting out her arms and taking Claire's head upon her shoulder. "We shall love one another well, little one."

The "little one" was at least four inches taller than the speaker, but something must be forgiven to a princess.

Meantime, Madame Granier had arranged all Mistress Catherine's simple linen and travelling necessities—the linen strong, white, and country-spun, smelling of far-off Navarre, bleached on the meadows by the brooks that prattle down from the snows. The brushes and combs were of plain material—no gold or silver about them anywhere. Only in a little shagreen case rested a silver spoon, a knife, and a two-pronged fork, with a gilt crown upon each. Otherwise the camp-equipment of a simple soldier of the Bearnais could not have been commoner.

When the hostess had betaken her downstairs, Mistress Catherine drew her new friend down on a low settle, and holding her hand, began to open out her heart gladly, as if she had long wished for a confidante.

"I have come to seek my brother," she said; "I expected him here in this house. There is a plot to take his life. Guise and D'Epernon both hate him. And, indeed, both have cause. He is too brave for one—too subtle for the other. You heard how, at the beginning of this war, he sent messengers to the Duke of Guise saying, 'I am first prince of the blood—you also claim the throne. Now, to prevent the spilling of much brave blood, let us two fight it out to the death!' But Guise merely answered that he had no quarrel with his cousin of Navarre, having only taken up arms to defend from heresy the Catholic faith—what a coward!"

"It seems to me," said Claire, "that no man can be a coward who ventures himself with an angry treacherous king as freely as in his own house."

"Ah"—the Princess smiled scornfully—"our cousin Guise does not lack courage of the insolent sort. Witness how on the day of the Barricades he extended his kind protection to King Henry III. of Valois in his own city of Paris, where he had dwelt fourteen years. Nay, he even rode in from Soissons that he might do it!"

"You do not love my Lord of Guise?" said Claire. "Yet my father used to call him the best Huguenot in France, and swear that neither Rosny, nor D'Aubigné, nor yet he himself did one half so much service to the Bearnais as the Duke of Guise!"

The King's sister pondered a while upon this.

"That is perhaps true," she said at last; "Guise is vain, and venturesome because he is vain. He cannot do without shouting crowds, and hands held out to him by every scavenger and pewterer's apprentice—'Guise—the good Guise!' Pah! The man is no better than a posturer before a booth at a fair!"

"I have heard almost as much from my father," Claire answered; "he used to say that Mayenne led the armies, the priests collected the pennies, and as for Guise, he was only the big man who beat the Leaguers' drum!"

"Your father is dead, they say," murmured the Princess softly; "but in his time he must have been a man of wit."

"He taught me all I know," Claire assented, "and he died in the service of the Faith and of the King of Navarre."

"It is strange that I should never have met him," said Catherine. "I have heard say he was on mission to my brother."

"On secret mission," said Claire; "we came often to the camp by night, and were gone in the morning."

The Princess looked at her junior in great astonishment.

"Then you have seen camps, and men, and cities?" she asked eagerly.

"And you, courts!" answered Claire, on her part not a little wistfully.

A shudder traversed the slender body of the Princess. Her lip curled with disgust.

"You speak like a child," she answered hotly. "Why, I tell you, on the head of my mother, you are safer and better in a camp of German *reiters* than in any court in Europe. But I forgot—you, at least, can pick and choose. You were not born to be only a pawn in the chess-play. If you do not wish to marry a man, you have only to say him nay. You are not a princess. I would to God I were not!"

"What is the plot against your brother?" said Claire, willing to turn her companion from black ideas; "perhaps I can help. At least, I have with me one who, though they name him 'fool,' is yet wiser than all the men I have met, excepting only my father."

"And they name this marvel—what?" demanded the Princess.

"Jean-aux-Choux—the Fool of the Three Henries."

Mistress Catherine clapped her hands almost girlishly, forgetting her accustomed dignity.

"I have seen him," she cried; "once he came to Nerac, where he pleased the Reine Margot greatly. She is a judge of fools!"

"Our Jean is no fool, really," said Claire, "but born of my nation, and a learned man, very zealous for the Faith."

"I know—I know," said the Princess; "I have heard D'Aubigné say of him, that folly made the best cloak for unsafe wisdom. As to the design against the King, it is this. Before the Duke of Guise comes to the Parliament, the Valois will first invite my brother to a conference—not here in Blois, but nearer his own lines—at Poitiers, perhaps, or at Loches. The Queen-Mother, the Medici woman, though sick and old, has gathered many of her maids-of-honour. She will strive to work upon my easy brother with fair words and fair faces, in the hope that, like Judas, he will betray his Master with a kiss!"

"I had not thought there could be in all the world such—women!" said Claire. "After all, our Scottish way is fairer—and that is foot to foot and blade to blade!"

"Even the Valois dagger in the back is better," said the Princess; "but this Italian woman is cunning, like all her fox-brood of Florentine money-lenders! How shall we foil her? It is useless speaking to my brother. He would only laugh, and bid me get to my sampler till he had found a goodman of my own for me to knit hose for!"

"Let me ask counsel of the Doctor of the Sorbonne who is with me," Claire urged; "he is very wise, and——"

"A Doctor of the Sorbonne!" cried Mistress Catherine—"impossible! Why, have they not cursed my brother, excommunicated him? They have even turned against their own King!"

"Ay, but," said Claire, now eager to do her friend justice, "*my* Doctor they have excommunicated also, because he withstood them in full Senatus. If he went back to Paris just now, they would hang him in his gown from the windows of his own class-room!"

So in this way Doctor Anatole of the Sorbonne entered into the heretic councils of the Bearnais. Indeed, his was the idea which came like a lightning-flash of illumination upon the councils of Claire and the Princess Catherine.

"What of La Reine Margot?" murmured the Professor, as if he had been speaking to himself; "is she of her husband's enemies?"

"Nay—but," began the Princess, "that would be pouring oil upon fire!"

"Where one fire has burned, there is little fuel for a second," suggested the Professor sententiously.

"It is not the highest wisdom," said the careful Princess, "I fear it would not bring a blessing."

"It is wisdom—if not the highest, my Lady Catherine," said the learned Doctor, "and if the matter succeeds—that, for your Cause, will be blessing enough!"

"Then our Cause is not yours?" Catherine demanded sharply of him. The Professor smiled.

"I am old, or you children think so. I have at least seen the vanity of persecuting any man for the thought that is in his heart. I was bred a Catholic, yet have been persecuted by my brethren for differing from them. But I agree that most honest folk of the realm are of your brother's party— the brave, the wise, the single of eye and heart. There never will be a king in France till the Bearnais reigns."

The Professor spoke with a certain antique freedom, and the Princess, moved with a sudden impulse, laid her hand on his arm.

"You are with us, then, if not of us?" she said.

"I am of this young lady's party," smiled the Professor, turning to Claire, who had been listening quietly. There was a look of great love in his eyes.

"Then I must needs make sure of her!" said the princess, putting her arm about Claire's waist. "Mistress Claire, vow that you will recruit for our army!"

"Long ago one made me vow that vow!" said Claire. "I am not likely to betray the Cause for which my father died!"

The face of the Princess Catherine grew grave. She was thinking of her own father. Anthony of Bourbon had not made so good an end.

"I vowed my vow night and morning at my mother's knee," she said. "Thus it was she bade me promise, in these very words—'As I hope for Christ's dear mercy, I will live and I will die in the Faith given to the fishermen of Galilee. I will cleave to it, despising all other. Every believer, rich or poor, shall be my brother or my sister—they all princes and princesses in Jesus Christ, I only a poor sinner hoping in His mercy!'"

The Professor bowed his head, crossed himself instinctively, and said, "Amen to so good a prayer! At the end, it is ever our mother's religion which is ours!"

CHAPTER XVI
LA REINE MARGOT

The Bearnais was too wise to venture so near the wolf's den as Loches or Tours. The conference, therefore, took place in the little town of Argenton, perched along either side of the Creuse, a huddle of wooden-fronted houses cascading down to a clear blue river, every balcony filled with flowers and fluttering that day with banners.

Catherine, the Queen-Mother, was to travel from Chartres to represent her son King Henry III. of Valois, of Poland, and of France. Henry the Bearnais rode over from his entrenched camp at Beauregard with a retinue of Huguenot gentlemen, whose plain dark armour and weather-beaten features showed more acquaintance with camp than with court.

The Bearnais, as usual, proved himself gay, kindly, debonnaire. The Queen-Mother (also as usual) was ambassador for her slothful son, conscious that her last summer was waning, mostly doing her travelling in a litter. Catherine de Medici never forgot for a moment that she was the centre round which forty years of intrigue had revolved. The wife of one king of France, the mother of three others, she played her part as in her youngest days. With death grappling at her heart, she surrounded herself with the flower of the youth and beauty of Italy and France, laughing with the gayest and ready with smile and gracious word for king or knave.

The deportment of the Bearnais was in strong contrast with that of his Huguenot suite. The King of Navarre made merry with all the world. He was ever the centre of a bright and changeful group of maids-of-honour to the Queen-Mother, with whom he jested and laughed freely, till Rosny whispered behind his hand to D'Aubigné, "If this goes on, we shall make but a poor treaty of it!"

And to him D'Aubigné replied grimly, "I will wager that my Lord Duke d'Epernon looks well to that."

"No," said Rosny shortly, "the old vixen is the sly renard."

Soon the festival ran its blithest. The Queen-Mother had withdrawn herself, possibly to repose, certainly to plot. With D'Epernon and the maids-of-honour the Bearnais remained, our Abbé John by his side, laughing with the merriest. Turenne and the other Huguenot veterans brooded sullenly in the background, seeing matters go badly, but not able to help it. Afterwards—well, they had a way all their own of speaking their minds. And the brave, good-humoured king would heed them too, in nowise growing angry with their freedoms. But, alas! by that time the steed would be stolen, the treaty signed, and the Medici and her maids-of-dishonour well on the way to Chartres.

The question was, whether or not Henry III. would throw himself wholly into the hands of the League at the forthcoming Parliament of Blois, or if, by a secret compact with the Bearnais, the gentlemen of the Huguenot Gascon provinces would attend to support the royal authority.

"I shall go, if our Bearnais commands me," said Turenne; "but I wager they will dye the Loire as red as ever they did the Seine on Bartholomew's Day—aye, and fringe the Château with us, as they did at Amboise. These Guises do not forget their ancient tricks."

"And right pretty you would look, my good Lord Turenne, your frosty beard wagging in the wind and a raven perched on your bald pate!"

"If I were in your shoes, I would not talk so freely either of beards or of baldness, D'Aubigné," growled Turenne. "I mind well when a certain clever lad had no more than the beard of a rabbit, which only comes out at night for fear of the dogs!"

"It is strange," said D'Aubigné, not in the least offended with his comrade, "that he who has no fear of the swords, should grow weak at the fluttering of a kerchief or before the artful carelessness of a neck-ribbon."

"Not strange at all," said Turenne; "is he not a man and a Bearnais? Besides, being a Bourbon, he will pay those the best to whom he owes least. And we, who have loved him as we never loved father or mother, wife or child, will be sent back to the chimney-corner with our thumbs to suck!"

"Aye, because he is sure of us!" retorted D'Aubigné gloomily, unconsciously prefiguring a day when he should sit, an exile in a foreign town, eating his heart out, and writing a great book to the praise of an ungrateful, or perhaps forgetful master.

"The most curious thing of all," said Rosny, "is that we shall always love him—put down his fickleness to the account of others, cherish him as a deceived woman does the man from whom she cannot wholly tear her heart!"

"Yes," cried a new voice, as a red hassock of hair showed itself over the brown Capuchin's robe, "these things will we do—some of us in exile, all in sorrow, some in rags, and some in motley——"

He opened the robe wider, and under the stained brown the jester's motley met their eyes.

"Who is this fool who mixes so freely in the councils of his betters?" cried Turenne. "Is there never a wooden horse and a provost-marshal in this—this ball-room?"

But Rosny, whose business it was to know all things, had had dealings with Jean-aux-Choux.

"It is the Fool of the Three Henries!" he whispered, "a wise man, they say—bachelor of Geneva, a deacon at the trade of theology, and all that!"

"I see nothing for it," D'Aubigné interrupted drily, "but that we should agree to put all three Henries into motley, and set Jean-aux-Choux on the throne!"

"Speak your mind plainly, Jean-aux-Choux," cried Turenne peremptorily; "we are none of us of the Three Henries. And we will bear no fooling. What is your message to us—Sir Fool with the Death's Head? Out with it, and briefly."

Jean-aux-Choux waved his hand in the direction of the bridge of Gargilesse.

"Yonder—yonder," he said, "is your answer coming to you!"

Beyond the crowded roofs of the old town, thatched and tiled, the white track to Gargilesse and Croizant meandered amid the sparse and sunburnt vegetation of autumn. Sparks of light, stars seen at noonday, began to dance behind the little broomy knolls, where the pods were cracking open merrily in the heat of the sun.

"They are spears," cried the well-advised veterans of the south, men of the old Huguenot guard. "Who comes? None from that direction to do us any good!"

Then Rosny, who, in moments of action, could make every one afraid of him, with his fair skin and the false air of innocence on his face, in which two blue eyes strange and stern were set, rode up to the King and, bidding him leave ribbons and sashes to give his mind for a moment to sword-points, he indicated, without an unnecessary word, the cavalcade which approached from the south.

Henry of Navarre, who was never angered by a just rebuke, instantly left the ladies with whom he had been jesting, and jumping on horseback, rode right up to the top of a steep bank, which commanded the bridge by which the horsemen must cross.

There he remained for a long while, none daring to speak further to him. For again, in a moment, he had become the war-captain. Though not very tall when on foot, the Bearnais sat his horse like a centaur, and it was said of him, that the fiercer the fray, the closer Henry gripped his knees, and the looser the rein with which he rode into the smother.

"Why," he cried, setting his gloved hands on either hip, "it is Margot— my wife Margot, with another retinue of silks and furbelows!"

And the Bearnais laughed aloud.

"Check and checkmate for the old apothecary's daughter," he chuckled. "After all, our little Margot is *spirituelle*, though she and I do not get on together."

And setting spurs to his charger, he rode on far ahead of all his gentlemen to welcome the Queen of Navarre at the bridge-head of Argenton. There he dismounted, and throwing the reins to the nearest groom, he walked to the bridle of a lady, who, fair, fresh, and smiling, came ambling easily up on a white Arab.

It was Marguerite of Valois, his wife, who five years ago had possessed herself of the strong castle of Usson in Auvergne. Sole daughter of one king of France, sole sister of three others, and wife of the King of Navarre, Marguerite of Valois had been a spoiled beauty from her earliest years. The division of blame is no easy matter, but certainly the Bearnais was not the right man to tame and keep a butterfly-spirit like that of "La Reine Margot."

The marriage had been made and finished in the terrible days which preceded the Saint Bartholomew. The two Queens of France and Navarre had the business in hand. It had been baptised in torrents of Protestant blood on that fatal night when the Guise ladies watched at their windows, while beneath the Leaguers silently bound the white crosses on their brows. Indeed, from the side of Catherine de Medici, the marriage of Henry of Navarre and Marguerite of Valois had been arranged with the single proper intent of bringing Coligny, Condé, and the other great Huguenots to the shambles prepared for them.

It served its purpose well; but when her mother, Catherine de Medici, and her royal brothers would gladly have broken off the marriage, Margot's will was the firmest of any. But though there was little of good in the life of the Queen Margot, there was ever something good in her heart.

She refused to be separated from her husband, merely to serve the intrigues of the Queen-Mother and the Guises.

"Once already I have been sacrificed to your plots," she said. "Because of that, I have a husband who will never love me. A night of blood stands between us. Yet will I do nothing against him, because he is my husband. Nor yet for you, my kinsfolk, because ye paid me away like the thirty pieces of silver which Judas scattered in the potter's field. I was the price of blood," so she taunted her mother, "and for that my husband will never love me!"

No, it was not for that, as history and legend tell all too plainly; but she was a woman, and had the woman's right to explain the matter so.

Rather, it was the root-difference of all lack of common interest and mutual love. Two young people, with different upbringings, with mothers wide apart as the heaven of Jeanne d'Albret and the inferno of the Medici, were suddenly thrown together with no bond save that of years to unite them. Each went a several way—neither the right way—and there is small wonder that the result of such a marriage was only unhappiness.

Said Henry of Navarre to Rosny, his best confidant, when there was question of his own wedding:

"Seven things are needed in the woman I ought to marry."

"Seven is a great number, Your Majesty," answered the Right Hand of the Bearnais; "but tell them to me, and I will at least cause search to be made. I will make proclamation for the lady who can put her foot into seven glass slippers, each one smaller than the other!"

"First, then," said the King of Navarre, posing a forefinger on the palm of his other hand, and speaking sagely, as a master setting out the steps of a proposition, "she must have beauty of person!"

"Good," said Rosny; "Your Majesty has doubtless satisfied himself that there are such to be found in the land—once or twice!"

"Wait, Rosny—let me finish!" said the King. And so continued his enumeration of wifely necessities, as they appeared to a great prince of the sixteenth century.

"*Item*, she must be modest in her life, of a happy humour, vivid in spirit, ready in affection, eminent in extraction, and possessed of great estates in her own right!"

For all answer Rosny held up his hands.

"I know—I know," smiled the Bearnais, "you would say to me that this marvel of womankind has been dead some time. I would rather say to you that she has never been born!"

So it came about that Marguerite, the pretty, foolish butterfly of the Valois courts, and her Bearnais husband, rough, soldierly, far-seeing, politic, had not seen each other for five years. Marguerite had shut herself up in the castle of Usson, one of the dread prison fortresses built by "that fox," Louis the Eleventh.

Though sent almost as a prisoner there, or at least under observation, she had speedily possessed herself of castle and castellan, guard and officers, kitchen scullions and gardener varlets. For she had the open hand, especially when the money was not her own, the ready wit, and above all, the charming smile, though even that meant nothing. At least, Margot the Queen was not malicious; and so it was without any fear, but rather with the sort of silent amusement with which we applaud a child's new trick, that the King dismounted, kissed his wife's hand, answered her gay greetings, and even cast a critic's eye on the array of beauties who followed in her train.

Many gallant gentlemen of the south also accompanied her. Raimonds and Castellanes were there, Princes of Baux and Seigneurs de la Tour—all willing at once to visit the camp of the Bearnais, and to testify their loyalty to the Court of France. For in the south, the League and the Guises had made but little progress.

"Why, Margot, what brings you hither?" said the Bearnais, as he paced along by his wife's side, while the suite had dropped far enough behind for them to speak freely.

"Well, husband mine," said the Queen Margot, "you have been a bad boy to me, and if I had not been mine own sweet self, you and my brother (peace to his ashes, as soon as he is dead!) would have shut me up in a big, dull castle to do needlework alone with a cat and a duenna. But I was too clever for you. And, after that, they poisoned your mind against little Margot—oh, I know. So I do not blame you greatly, Henry. Also, I have a temper that is trying at short range—I admit it. So I am come to make up—at least, if you will. And further, if by chance my good, simple mother and that gallant, crafty Epernon lad have any tricks to try upon you—why, then I have brought a bag of them too, and can play them, trick for trick, till we win—you and I, Harry!"

Margot the Queen waved her hand to the covey of beauties who rode behind her.

"I would say that they are all queens of beauty," she said, smiling down at him; "but do you know (I am speaking humbly because I know well that you do not agree) I am the only really pretty queen in the world?"

"As to that I do most heartily take oath," said the Bearnais.

"Ah, but," said Margot, touching him gently on the cheek with the lash of her riding-whip, "I mind well how you swore you would wed the Queen of England, provided she brought you that rich land—aye, though she had as many wrinkles on her brow as the sea that surrounds her isle, or even the Infanta of Spain, old and wizened as a last year's pippin, if only she brought you in dower the Low Countries!"

"Ah, Margot," said Henry, smiling up at his wife, "and I thought it was your sole boast that you never cast up old stories! You always found new ones—or made them!"

"I did but tease," she said; "but indeed, for all my mother is so ill, this is no time for jesting. I have come to see that you get fair play among them all, my little friend Henry. Though you love me not greatly, and I did sometimes throw the table-equipage at your head, yet Margot of France and Navarre is not the woman to see her husband wronged—least of all by her own mother and that good, excellent, mignon-loving brother of mine, the King-titular of some small remnant of France."

CHAPTER XVII
MATE AND CHECKMATE

At this moment, the litter of Catherine de Medici was seen approaching. D'Epernon had hastened to tell her of the unexpected arrival of her daughter, the Queen of Navarre.

"No, it cannot be—she is safe at Usson, entertaining all the Jackass-erie of Auvergne!" cried the Queen-Mother, hastily wrapping herself in a bundle of dark cloaks, with the ermine sleeves and sable collars, which the thinness of her blood caused her to wear even in the heat of the dog-days. Scoffers declared she was getting ready for the hereafter by accustoming herself gradually to the climate. But those who knew better were aware that the vital heat was at long and last slowly oozing from that once tireless body, though the brain above remained clear and subtle to the end.

D'Epernon helped the Queen-Mother into the litter of ebony and gold in which she journeyed. She called for her maids-of-honour, but was informed that they were all busied with welcoming the new arrivals.

Then the face of Catherine took on a hard and bitter expression.

"This is not the first, nor the second time that Margot has outwitted me"—she almost hissed the words, yet not so low but D'Epernon caught them. "Has ever a woman who has given all, done all for her family, been cursed with sons who will do nothing even to save themselves, and a daughter whose pleasure it is to thwart the mother who bore her? But— patience, all is not yet lost! Wait a while. Little Margot of the Large Heart may not be so clever as she thinks!"

Yet so artful was the dissimulation of both women, that when at last they approached each other, Margot, the Queen of Navarre, threw herself into her mother's arms, and hid her face (possibly, also, her emotion) on her shoulder, while Catherine wept real, visible, globular tears over her one daughter, whom she embraced after so many years.

Only D'Epernon knew that they were tears of rage and mortification.

It was when husband and wife were left alone on the broad balcony of the Mansion of the Palmer, by the southern river-front of Argenton—the

Creuse, sweetest and daintiest of streams in a land all given over to such, slipping dreamily by—that Margot told the Bearnais why she had come.

"Do not thank me," she said; "you have that Huguenot sister of yours to thank—a good, brave girl, too good to be married as I was (and as you were, my poor Henry!) for politics' sake, and a few more acres of land. Also, you owe it to the good counsels of yonder Scottish maid, called Claire Agnew, who——"

Henry rose from the low chair on which he had been carelessly resting his thigh.

"Why, I remember the girl"—he threw up his hands in humorous despair. "Oh, you women, a man never knows when he will have you! I thought that you, Margot, my wife, would have been at Usson flying your hawks, and gathering snails for the Friday's *pot-au-feu*; that Catherine, my admirable sister, had been safe at her prayers in the Castle of Pau, where I left her in good charge and keeping; and of my carefulness I had even provided that this Scots maiden, the daughter of my good friend Francis Agnew, should abide in douce tranquillity with her Professor of the Sorbonne, within ear-shot, not to say pistol-shot of a certain Anthony Arpajon, a sure henchman of mine, in the town of Blois. But here be all three of you gadding at my heels, Margaret from Auvergne, Catherine from Pau, and even the Scots maid from Blois, all blown inward like so many seagulls on the front of a westerly storm!"

"Harry," cried Margot the Queen, "your beard is frosting, and there are white hairs on my coif at thirty-eight. Yes, there are; you need not look, for, of course, I have the wit to hide them. We have not agreed well, you and I. But I like you, great lumping swash-buckler of Bearn. Even as the husband I was not allowed to choose, I like you. If you had been any one else, I might even have loved you!"

"Thanks—it is indeed quite possible!" said the King quietly.

"But since they wrote it in a catechism, learned it me by rote, made me swallow love and obedience willy-nilly before half-a-dozen cardinals and archbishops glorious, why then, of course, it was 'nilly' and not 'willy.' So things have gone crosswise with us. But there's my hand on't, Henry. In all save love, I will serve you true. Not even your beloved Rosny and dour D'Aubigné will help you better, or expect less for it than I, Margot, your Majesty's humble prisoner!"

"So be it," said the King, kissing her hand, and passing over all that was not expressed in this very sketchy view of the case; "I have found many to betray me who owed me more than you, Margot. But never you, my little Queen!"

"Thank you, Henry," quoth La Reine Margot, smiling demurely, with something of the subtle Italian irony of her mother. "Perhaps, after all, I do not help you so much because I like you, as because I love to spite some other people who are plotting against you."

"Are they seeking my life, Margot?" said the King. "Well, there is nothing new in that. I always keep a man or two on the look-out for assassins. I have quite a collection of knives—some Guisard, and some Italian, but mostly of Toledo make. There are four gates to my camp, and the men of my guard kick the varlets south if the knife smells of our brother Philip, north to cousin Guise, if 'Lorraine' is marked on the blade—and as for Italy——"

"Do not say any evil of Italy," smiled Margot; "pray remember that I am half an Italian—therefore I am fair, therefore I am cunning, therefore I am rich—at least, in expedients."

The Bearnais said nothing, for having so many war charges, he had more than once refused to pay Madame Margot's debts!

"I have come," she continued, after the King had sat some time silent on the tapestried couch beside her, looking out on the sleeping Creuse, "first of all, to see that you sign no treaty that I do not approve. Well do I know that a woman has only to smile upon you to make you say 'Yes.' It is your weakness. The Queen, my mother, knows it also, and she has brought hither many fair women in her train. But none so fair as I, your wife—your wife Margot, whom camps, and wars, and kingdoms have made you sometime forget!"

"There is, indeed, no one so fair as you, little Margot!" said her husband. And, for the moment, he meant it.

Margot the Queen entered her tiring-room that night clapping her hands, and dancing little skipping "tarantellas" all to herself, after the Italian fashion.

"I have done this all by myself at eight-and-thirty," she cried. "I thought I was no longer Parisian, after so many years of hiding my head in Auvergne. But Henry never moved from my side all the evening, and as for D'Epernon, he was as close as might be on the other. Come in, girls! I have much to tell you."

She rose, and threw her arms about the neck of her sister-in-law, Catherine of Navarre. She had entered, flushed, walking so fast that her slight D'Albret limp was not noticeable.

"Oh, we three," cried the Queen Margot—"we three were as Juno, Minerva, and Venus. The men stood round, and gazed and listened, and listened and gazed, each like a stupid Paris with a golden apple in his hand, a prize of beauty which he wanted to give to all three at once. You, Katrin my sister, were the grey-eyed Minerva; you, Claire, must be Juno—though, my faith, you are more of the mould of Dian; but as for me—of course, that is obvious! And the defeated enemy—the maids of honour! Ha! Did you see how the Queen, my mother, called them in to heel, like so many useless hounds of the chase, to receive their whipping? How they cowered and cringed! Truly, the game was carried off by another pack—a buck—a buck royal of ten tines is the Bearnais. We had a plot indeed—but no treaty. Pricked like a wind-bladder it was. If I am a feeble house-wife, I am at least a true ambassador, and they shall not cheat my husband—not while little Margot lives, last of the Valois and half Medici though she be! To bed, girls, and get your beauty-sleep. You will need it to-morrow!"

CHAPTER XVIII
THE APOSTLE OF PEACE

"She may be a witch, and the daughter of Jezebel," murmured D'Aubigné low to Rosny, "but this time, of a verity, she has snatched the chestnuts out of the fire for us!"

"I would she were safe back again in Auvergne," said Rosny; "our Henry is never himself when he gets among that crew."

The two Huguenot chiefs spoke truly. There was no doubt that the Queen of Navarre had outwitted her mother, and strengthened the warlike resolutions of the Bearnais, so that he refused all art or part in the gathering of the States-General at Blois.

Catherine, the Queen-Mother, had to depart ill-satisfied enough. The little town of Argenton dropped back again into its year-long quiet. Gallantly Henry escorted his wife part of the way to her castle of Usson, and so far, at least, husband and wife were reconciled. As for the Princess Catherine, she was sent off with a guard of gentlemen to Nerac, while once more in Blois the house of Madame Granier, close to the hostelry of Anthony Arpajon, was occupied by its trio of guests. At least, Claire and the Professor abode continually there, and took their pleasant walks in the quickly-shortening days of autumn. The willows began to drop their narrow flame-shaped leaves into the current of the Loire after every gust. And in the windless dawns, as soon as the sun struck the long alignment of ashes, these dainty trees proceeded to denude themselves of their greenery with sharp little reports like toy pistols.

As for Jean-aux-Choux, he had great business on hand. Every day he invented some new folly at the Château. He laughed with the pages, who told their masters, who in turn told their ladies. And so all the world soon knew that the Fool of the Three Henries was to be present at the meeting of Parliament. Well, so much the better. In such times they needed some diversion.

Jean came little to Anthony the Calvinist's hostel. That was too dangerous. Yet often by night he would slip through the little river-door which opened into the courtyard of Madame Granier's house, to talk a while with his dead master's daughter and her Professor—also to observe, with his small twinkling grey eyes, the lie of the land.

Indeed, it was a time in which to be mightily circumspect. The town of Blois was filled to overflowing with all the hot-heads of the League. The demagogues of Paris, the full Council of the Sixteen, led by Chapelle Marteau and Launay, cheered on the princes of Lorraine to execute their firm intention of coercing Henry III., and compelling him to deliver the crown into the hands of the Duke of Guise and his brothers—the princes of the House of Lorraine.

By permission of the Bearnais, to whom, as his cousin and chieftain, the Abbé John had now made solemn offer of his allegiance, that youth was permitted to remain as an additional pair of eyes in the Château itself—and also, he told himself, as a good sword, not too far away, in case any harm should threaten Claire in her river-side lodging.

The green robe of the Professor of Eloquence, with its fur sleeves and golden collar now wholly repaired by the clever fingers of Claire, whose care for her father's wardrobe had given her skill in needlework, passed to and fro in all the stairways and corridors of the Château. He was welcome to the King, who knew the classic orators, and had devoted much time to the cultivation of a ready and fluent mode of address. And it was, indeed, no other than our excellent Professor Anatole who prepared and set in order, with sounding words and cunning allusions, the famous opening speech of the King to his nobles on the 18th of October, 1588.

Altogether, the privileges of our friends at this time were many, and the Leaguers did not seriously incommode them. D'Epernon, who was thoroughly loyal to Henry III., and for the time being, at least, meant to keep the agreements made on his master's behalf with the Bearnais, stood ready in Angoulême, with all the Royalists he could muster.

As far as Blois itself was concerned, however, the Guisards and the champions of the League would have swamped all, save for the threat of a strong Huguenot force hovering in the neighbourhood. This restless army was occasionally reported from Tours, again from Loches, from Limoges, so that the Leaguers, though of incomparable insolence, dared not, at that time, push the King of France directly into the arms of the Bearnais.

But we may as well hear the thing reported by eye-witnesses.

Cautiously, as was her custom, Madame Granier had peered through the thick *grille* of the water-door before admitting the Professor and the Abbé John. Silent as a spectre Anthony Arpajon had entered from the other side by his own private passage, locking the iron port behind him. They sat together in Dame Granier's wide kitchen, without any lighting of lamps or candles. But the wood burned red on the hearth, above which Dame Granier kept deftly shifting the *pot-au-feu*, so that none of its contents might be burned.

Each time she did so she thrust in underneath smaller branches, gleaned from last year's willow-pollarding. The light flared up sharply with little spitting, crackling noises, so that all in the kitchen saw each other clearly.

Now they discussed matters from the standpoint of the Château. That was the Professor, with a little assistance from John d'Albret, a poor prince of the blood some-few-times-removed. They talked it over from the point of view of the town. It was Anthony Arpajon who led, the widow Granier adding a word or two. They heard, in a low whisper, the most private states of mind of the King, seen only by those who had the right to penetrate into his cabinet. It was a red-haired, keen-eyed fanatic who spoke of this, with the accent and Biblical phraseology of Geneva—namely, one Johannus Stirling, Doctor in Theology, commonly denominated Jean-aux-Choux, the Fool of the Three Henries.

As for Claire Agnew, she gazed steadily into the fire, elbow on knee, her rounded chin set in the palm of her hand, and her dark curls pushing themselves in dusky confusion about her cheek. The Abbé John was the only person at all uneasy. Yet it was not the distant dubious sounds from the town which troubled him, nor yet the cries of the boatmen of St. Victor dropping down under the bridge of Vienne, the premier arch of which sprang immediately out by the gable of Dame Granier's house.

No, the Abbé John was uneasy because he wished to move his little three-legged stool nearer to the black oaken settle at the corner of which sat Claire Agnew.

The Leaguers might seize his person to make him a king—in default of better. Well, he would keep out of their way. His cousin, the Bearnais, would certainly give him a company in the best-ordered army in the world. His other yet more distant cousin, Philip of Spain, would, if he caught him, present him with a neat arrangement in yellow, with flames and devils painted in red all over it. Then, all for the glory of God, he would burn him alive because of consorting with the heretic.

Many careers were thus opening to the young man. But just at present, and, indeed, ever since he had looked at her across the dead man, stretched so starkly out among the themes and lectures on Professor Anatole's Sorbonne table, John d'Albret had felt that his true call in life was to minister to the happiness of Mistress Claire Agnew. And incidentally, in so doing, to his own.

Of this purpose, of course, Mistress Claire was profoundly unconscious. That was why she looked so steadily at the fire, and appeared to be revolving great problems of state. But it is certain, all the same, that no one else of all that company was deceived, not even sturdy Anthony Arpajon, who so far forgot himself, being a widower and a Calvinist, as to wink behind backs at Dame Granier when she was bringing up a new armful of dried orchard prunings to help boil the pot.

"I for one would not sleep comfortably in the Duke of Guise's bed at night," said the Professor sententiously. "I spoke to-day with that brigand D'O, whose name is as short as his sword is long, also with Guast, the man who goes about with his hand on the hilt of his dagger, familiarly, as if it were a whistle to call his scent-dogs to heel. No, I thank God I am but a poor professor of the Sorbonne—and even so, displaced. Not for ten thousand shields would I sleep in the Duke's bed."

"Perhaps that is the reason," suggested Jean-aux-Choux darkly, "why he prefers so often that of his friend Monsieur de Noirmoutier. He is afraid of seeing the curtains put suddenly back and, through the mists of his last sleep, the dark faces of the assassins and the gleaming of their daggers! Yet why should either you or he be afraid—a gurgle, a sigh, and all would be over!"

A shudder moved the shoulders of Claire as she drew nearer to the blaze, and, by consequence, further from the restless encroachments of the Abbé John's three-legged stool.

"He is a brave man, though he has done such ill," she said, sighing. "I love brave men!"

The Abbé John instantly resolved to demand the captaincy of a forlorn hope from the Bearnais, and so charge single-handed upon the ramparts of Paris.

But the Professor of the Sorbonne would listen to no praise whatsoever of the Guises. "The Duke," he averred, "spins his courage out of the weakness of others. He takes the King of France for a coward. 'He does not dare slay me,' he boasts; 'I am safe in his castle as in mine own house. If Henry of Valois slew me, he would have three-quarters of his realm about his ears in a week! And what is better, he knows it!'"

"Yes," said the Abbé John, speaking for the first time, "and I heard his sister, Madame de Montpensier, say only to-day, that she and her brother Henry were going to give the King the third of the three crowns on his scutcheon. He has been King of Poland, he is King of France, and the third crown represents the heavenly crown which will soon be his. Alternatively, she exhibits to all comers, even in the antechamber of the King, the golden scissors with which she is going to cut a tonsure for 'Brother Henry,' as she calls him—the Monk Henry of that order of the Penitents which he organised in one of his fits of piety!"

Jean-aux-Choux shook his shaggy head like a huge water-spaniel.

"They flatter themselves, these dogs of Guise," he said; "they fill themselves with costly wine, that the flower of life pass them not by. They hasten to crown themselves with rosebuds, ere they be withered. 'Let us leave the husks of our pleasures in every place,' they say. 'For this is our lot. We alone are the great of the earth. The earth belongeth to Lorraine, and the goodliness thereof. Before us, kings twice-born, cradled in purple, are as naught. A good man is an insult to us. Let us slay and make an end, even as we did on the Eve of Bartholomew, that we may pass in and enjoy the land'—such is their insolence—'from Dan to Beer-sheba, and from Zidon even to the sunny slopes of Engedi—lest we be too late, lest we also pass away, as in the summer sky the trace of a cloud. For the Sea of Death is beneath—the Sea of Death is beneath!' Aha, aha! The mouth of the Lord hath spoken by Guise, even as by the mouth of Balaam his ass, in the strait-walled path betwixt the two vineyards, as thou comest unto Arnon!"

At the voice of the Fool turned Prophet, all sound ceased in the wide kitchen-place of good Dame Granier. Anthony Arpajon stood rapt, not daring to move hand or foot. For he believed that the word of the Lord had entered into Jean-aux-Choux, and that he was predicting the fall of the Guises.

"Verily, the bloody and deceitful man shall not live out half his days!" he muttered.

"It were truer, perhaps, to say," the Professor interjected, "that they who take the sword shall perish by the sword, and that those who arouse in King Henry of Valois the blackness of his gall, shall perish by the sword held under the cloak—suddenly, secretly, with none to help, and with the sins of a lifetime as lead upon their souls!"

"Amen!" cried Jean-aux-Choux; "stamp on the serpent's eggs! Cut the Guisards off, root and branch — —"

"Is not that only your own Saint Bartholomew turned upside down?" demanded the Professor of Eloquence sharply. "You have read the Book of the Wisdom, I hear. I would remind you of the better way which you will find written therein. For, if prudence worketh, what is there that worketh better than she? You, who are a learned theologue, answer me that!"

"Prudence," cried the Genevan fiercely. "Have not I made myself a fool for the Kingdom of Heaven's sake? This is no time for prudence, but for fewer soft answers and more sharp swords! Ha, wait till the Bearnais comes to his own. Then there will be a day when the butchers of Paris shall cry to their shambles to fall on them and hide them. We of the Faith will track them with bloodhounds, and trap them like rats!"

"Then," retorted the Professor, "if that be so, I solemnly declare that you of the Huguenots are no whit better than the Leaguers and Guisards, who are even now seeking my life. I stand in the middle way. May God (such is your cry) give you victory or give you death. Well, I am sure that victory would be the worst present He could give you, if such were the use you would make of it."

But Jean-aux-Choux, pupil of Calvin, was not to be put down.

"Have ye never read in the Psalms," he cried, "how David said that the Lord would arise in judgment to help all the meek of the earth, and how that surely even the wrath of man God would turn to His praise?"

"I have also read in the same place," retorted the Professor of Eloquence, "that 'the remainder of the wrath He will restrain.' You Huguenots are not quite of the meek of the earth. When one cheek is smitten, doth the Bearnais turn the other? I, for one, should not like to try. Nay, not even with good Master Johannus here, Doctor in Theology, late of Geneva, commonly known as Jean-aux-Choux!"

"If, indeed, you know a better way, my good Doctor of the Sorbonne," said Jean, "pray show it forthwith! I am open to conviction, even as was my master, John Calvin!"

"That I will," quoth the Professor; "if you will have none of prudence, then seek wisdom. Ask of God. He will not refuse you. Is it not written in the Book that 'Wisdom, the worker of all things, hath taught me? For in her is the spirit of understanding—holy, only begotten, manifold, subtle, clear, undefined, loving the good and doing it, courteous, stable, sure, without care, having all power, yet circumspect in all things—and so, passing into all intellectual, pure, and subtle spirits.' So, indeed, it is written."

"Ah, that is part of your lecture on the blessings of peace," said the Abbé John, disgusted that he could arrive no nearer to the goal of his desirings. A three-legged stool makes a courser both slow and noisy.

"Eh," said the Professor, "it may be—it may be. I have often read these words with delight and, I grant you, I may have used them in another connexion."

"I have the notes of the lecture in my pocket!" said the Abbé John.

"Hum," commented Professor Anatole, looking sidelong at his pupil, "it is well to find you so attentive once in a way. At the Sorbonne the thing did not happen too often."

There was a short, uncomfortable period of silence, for the tone of the Professor of Eloquence had been somewhat rasping. He was annoyed, as perhaps John d'Albret had expected.

But he resumed again after awhile, his anger having as quickly fallen.

"I do not deny it. I am by nature a man urbane. I hold with him who said that the worst peace that ever was made is better than the best war that ever was waged. I am of Paul's faction, when he counselled 'Follow peace with all men'!"

There came a sudden loud knocking at the river-gate. A hush and an awe fell upon all. Instinctively hands drew to sword-hilts. John and Anthony leaned forward, listening intently, hardly daring to breathe. But the man who flung the door wide open was the Apostle of Peace himself— even Professor Anatole Long, Doctor of the Sorbonne.

Having done so, he found himself with his sword-stick bare in one hand, and a loaded pistol in the other.

CHAPTER XIX
DEATH WARNINGS

D'Epernon stood at the door.

The splendid favourite of the King of France was attired in a plain, close-fitting black dress, while a cloak of the like material dropped from his shoulders. A broad-brimmed hat, high-crowned, and with a sweeping black feather, was on his head. He held out both hands.

"See, my good Professor," he began, "I am at your martial mercy. I have come without arms, clothed only with my sole innocence, into this haunt of heretics. Let me enter. I am, at least, a well-wisher of the white *panache*, and an old friend of Monsieur Anthony Arpajon there!"

The Professor of Eloquence, though in his heart he liked not the bold favourite, knew him for a keeper of his word. He stood back and let him pass within. D'Epernon carefully barred the door behind him, and with a grand salute strode masterfully into the kitchen of Dame Granier, which seemed to shrink in size at his entrance.

"Fairer waters than those we are now crossing be to us and to France!" said the Duke, who loved a sounding phrase. There was a silence in the kitchen, all wondering what this sudden interruption might mean. "You are all strangely speechless," continued the Duke.

"We would be glad to know what is your Grace's will with us," said Jean-aux-Choux; "after that, we will speak as plain as men may!"

"You are, I take it, for the King of France so long as he may live, and for the Bearnais afterwards?"

"We are of different schools and habits of thought," said Doctor Anatole, with a certain professional sententiousness, "but you may take it that on these points we are agreed with my Lord Duke of Epernon!"

"We are all against the League!" said Jean-aux-Choux brusquely.

"I stand by my cousin Henry," said the Abbé John.

"And I keep an open hostelry and a shut mouth!" added Anthony Arpajon.

As for Claire, she said nothing, but only moved a little further into the shadow. For Dame Granier had thrown a handful of resinous chips on the fire, which blazed up brightly, at which D'Epernon muttered a curse and trampled the clear light into dim embers with the heel of his cavalier's boot.

"To be seen here does not mean much to most of you," he said, with sudden unexpected fierceness, "but with the city full of the spies of Guise, it would be death and destruction to me! In a word then—for this I have come. The King has resolved to bear no longer the insolence of Guise and his brothers. There is to be an end. It will be a bitter day and a worse night in Blois. Women are better out of it. I have taken measures to keep safely mine own wife—though there is no braver lass in France, as the burghers of Angoulême do know—what I have to ask is, how many of you gentlemen I can count upon?"

"There is a difference," said the Professor. "I am an advocate for peace. But then Duke Guise and the Princes of Lorraine will not leave us in peace. So, against my judgment and conscience, I am with you so far as fighting goes."

"And I," said the Abbé John eagerly; "but I will have no hand in the assassination. It smells of Saint Bartholomew!"

"It is going to smell of that," answered D'Epernon coolly; "you are of Crillon's party, my friend—and truly, I do not wonder. There are butchers enough about the King to do his killings featly. Of what use else are swaggerers like D'O, Guast, Ornano, and Lognac? For me, I am happily supposed to be in my government of Angoulême. I am banished, disgraced, shamed, all to pleasure the League. But just the same, the King sends me daily proof of his kindness, under his own hand and seal. So I, in turn, endeavour to serve him as best I may."

"You can count on me, Duke d'Epernon," said Jean-aux-Choux suddenly, "aye, if it were to do again the deed of Ehud, which he did in the summer parlour by the quarries of Gilgal, that day when the sun was hot in the sky."

"Good," said D'Epernon, "it is a bargain. To-morrow, then, do you seek out Hamilton, a lieutenant in the Scots Guards, and say to him 'The Man in the Black Cloak sent me to you'!"

"When—at what hour?"

"At six—seven—as soon as may be, what care I?"

"Aye," said Jean-aux-Choux, "that is good speaking. Is it not written, 'What thou doest, do quickly'?"

"It is indeed so written," said the Professor of Eloquence gravely, "but not of the Duke of Guise."

"Fear not," said Jean-aux-Choux, taking the reference, "I shall meet him face to face. There shall be no Judas kiss betwixt me and Henry of Guise."

"No," murmured the Professor, "there is more likely to be a good half-dozen of your countrymen of the Scottish Guard, each with a dagger in his right hand."

As it happened, there was a round dozen, but not of the Scottish archers.

D'Epernon—than whom no one could be more courteous, in a large, deft, half-scornful way—stooped to kiss Claire's hand under the spitting anger of the Abbé John's eyes.

"A good evening and a better daybreak," said D'Epernon. "I would escort you to Angoulême, my pretty maiden, to bide under the care of my wife, were it not that you might be worse off there. The last time my Lady Duchess went for a walk, our good Leaguers of the town held a knife to her throat under the battlements for half-a-day, bidding her call upon me to surrender the castle on pain of instant death. What, think you, said Margaret of Foix? 'Kill me if you like,' says she, 'and much good may it do you and your League. But tell Jean Louis, my husband, that if he yields one jot to such rascals as you, to save my life twenty times over—I—will never kiss him again'!"

"I should like to know your wife, my lord," said Claire; "she must be a brave woman."

"I know another!" D'Epernon answered, bowing courteously.

Then, after the great man was gone, the party about Dame Granier's fire sat silent, looking uncertainly at one another in the dull red glow, which gave the strange face of Jean-aux-Choux, bordered by its tussock of orange-saffron hair, the look of having been dipped in blood.

Then, without a word, the Fool of the Three Henries took down his wallet, stuck the long sheath of a dagger under his black-and-white baldrick, and strode out into the night.

His vow was upon him.

"I will betake me to my chamber," said the Professor of Eloquence, "and pray to be forgiven for the thought of blood which leaped up in my heart when this proud man came to the door."

"And I," said Claire, "because I am very sleepy."

She said good-night a little coldly to John d'Albret. At least, so he thought, and was indeed ill-content thereat.

"I am not permitted to fight in a good hard-stricken battle," he murmured. "I cannot bring my mind to rank assassination—for this, however my Lord of Epernon may wrap it up, means no less. And yonder vixen of a girl will not even let me hold her coloured threads when she broiders a petticoat!"

But without a doubt or a qualm Jean-aux-Choux went to find Hamilton of the Scots Guard and to perform his vow.

As for the Duke, he spent his days with the Queen-Mother, and his nights at the lodgings of Monsieur de Noirmoutiers. Catherine de Medici was ill and old, but she kept all her charm of manner, her Italian courtesy. Personally she liked Guise, and he had a soft side to the wizened old woman who had done and plotted so many things—among others the night of Saint Bartholomew. When Guise came to any town where Catherine was, he always rode directly to her quarters. There she sermonised him on his latest sins, representing how unseemly these were in the avowed champion of the Church.

"But they make the people love me," he would cry, with a careless laugh. And perhaps also, who knows, the perverse indurated heart of the ancient Queen! For the Queen-Mother, though relentless to all heretics and rebels, was kindly within doors and to those she loved—who indeed generally repaid her with the blackest ingratitude.

But at Blois Guise had a new reason for frequenting his old ally. Valentine la Niña had become indispensable to Catherine. She was, it seemed, far more to her than her own daughter. The Queen-Mother would spend long days of convalescence—as often, indeed, as she was fairly free from pain—in devising and arranging robes for her favourite.

And amid the flurry Guise came and went with the familiarity of a house friend. His scarred face shone with pleasure as he picked a way to his old ally's bedside. Arrived there, after steering his course through the wilderness of silks and chiffons which cumbered the chairs and made even sitting down a matter of warlike strategy, Guise would remain and watch the busy maids bending over their needlework, and especially Valentine la Niña seated at the other side of the great state bed, which had been specially brought from Paris for the Queen to die upon. There was a quaint delight in his eyes, not unmingled with amusement, but now and then a flush would mount to his face and the great scar on his cheek would glow scarlet.

Once he betrayed himself.

"What a queen—what a queen she would have made!"

But the sharp-witted old woman on the bed, catching the murmured words, turned them off with Italian quickness.

"Too late, my good Henry," she said, reaching out her hand; "you were born quite thirty years too late. Had you been King and I Queen—well, the world would have had news!"

She thought a little while, and then added:

"For one thing all men would have known—how stupid a man is the Fleming who calls himself King of Spain. We should have avenged Pavia, you and I, my Balafré, and Philip's ransom would have bought the children each a gown!"

But Valentine la Niña knew well of what the Duke of Guise had been thinking. She understood his words, but she gave him no chance of private speech. Nor did she send him any further warning. Once at Paris she had warned him fully, and he had chosen to disobey her. It was at his peril. And now, in Blois itself, she treated the popular idol and all-powerful captain with a chilling disdain that secretly stung him.

Only once did they exchange words. It was on the stairway, as Valentine gathered her riding-skirt in her fingers in order to mount to the Queen-Mother's room. The Duke was coming down slowly, a disappointed look on his face, but he brightened at sight of her, and taking her gloved hand quickly, he put it to his lips.

"Now I have lived to-day!" he said gently.

"If you do not get hence," she answered him with bitterness, "it is one of the last days that you will!"

"Then I would spend these last here in Blois," he said, smiling at her.

"You would do better for the Cause you pretend to serve if you took my grey alezan out there, and rode him at gallop through the North Gate. I give him to you if you will!"

"I should only bring him back by the South Gate," he said, smiling. "While you remain here, I am no better than a poor moth fluttering about the candle!"

"But the Cause?" she cried, with an angry clap of her hands.

"That for the Cause!" said Guise, snapping his fingers lightly; "a man has but one life to live, and few privileges therein. But surely he may be allowed to lay that one at a fair lady's feet!"

Without answering, Valentine la Niña swept up the stairs of the Queen's lodging, her heart within her like lead.

"After all," she murmured, as she shut herself in her room, "I have done my best. I have warned him time and again. I cannot save a man against his will. Paugh!" (she turned hastily from the window), "there he is again on the other side of the way, pacing the street as if it were the poop of an amiral!"

The little walled garden at Madame Granier's, with its trellised vines, the wind-swept wintry shore of the Loire, and the bleached shell-pink of the shingle, all went back to their ancient quiet. The whole world was in, at, and about the Château. Men, women, and both sorts of angels were busy around the Castle of Blois in these short grey days of mid-most winter.

Now and then, however, would come a heavenly morning, when Claire, left alone, looked out upon the clear, clean, zenith-blue sweep of the river, and on the misty opal and ultramarine ash of the distance, ridge fading behind ridge as drowsy thought fades into sleep.

"It is a Paradise of beauty, but"—here she hesitated a while—"there is no Adam, that I can see!"

In spite of the winter day she opened her window to the slightly sun-warmed air.

"I declare I am somewhat in Eve's mood to-day," she continued, smiling to herself as she laid down her embroidery; "even an affable serpent would be better than nothing."

But it could not be. For all the powers of good and evil—the Old Serpent among them—were full of business in the Château of Blois during these days of the King's last parliament. And so, while Claire read her Amyot's *Plutarch* and John Knox's *Reformation*, the single stroke which changed all history hung unseen in the blue.

CHAPTER XX
THE BLOOD ON THE KERCHIEF

The most familiar servants of my Lord of Guise dared not awake their master. He had cast himself down on the great bed in his chamber when he came in late, or rather early—no man cared to ask which—from the lodging of Monsieur de Noirmoutier. Even his bravest gentlemen feared to disturb him, though the King's messenger had come twice to summon him to a council meeting at the Château.

"Early—very early? Well, what is that to me?" said the herald. "Bid your master come to the King!"

"The King! Who is he?" cried insolently the young De Bar. "Brother Henry the Monk may be your master—he is not ours."

"Hush!" said the aged Raincy, Guise's privileged major-domo and confidant, the only man from whom the Duke took advice, "it were wiser to send a message that my Lord of Guise is ill, but that he will be informed of the King's command and will be at the Château as soon as possible."

Guise finally awoke at eight, and looking out, shivered a little at the sight of as dismal a dawning as ever broke over green Touraine. It had been raining all night, and, indeed, when the Duke had come in from his supper-party he had thrown himself down with but little ceremony of undressing. This carelessness and his damp clothes had told upon him.

"A villain rheum," he cried, as he opened his eyes, to listen ill-humouredly enough to Raincy's grave communication of the King's demand. "And what do you tell me? A villain day? Draw aside the curtains that I may see the better. What—snow? It was rain when I came in."

He sneezed twice, on which Raincy wished him a long life.

"'Tis more than the King of all the Penitent Monks wishes me," said the Duke, shovelling notes and letters of all shapes and sizes out of his pockets. Some had been crumpled in the palm of the hand scornfully, some refolded meditatively, some twisted between the fingers into nervous spills, but by far the greater number had never been opened at all.

"See what they say, Raincy," cried the Duke. "I can dress myself—one does not need to go brave only to see the King of France playing monkey tricks in a turban and woman's dressing-gown, scented of musk and flounced in the fashion! Pah! But, Raincy, what a cold I have taken! 'Tis well enough for a man when he is young to go out supping in December, but for me, at eight-and-thirty—I am raucous as a gallows' crow! Give me my cloak, Raincy, and order my horse!"

"But, Your Grace," gasped the alarmed Raincy, "you have had no breakfast! Your Grace would not go thus to the council—you who are more powerful than the King—nay, whom all France, save a few heretics and blusterers, wish to be king indeed!"

"Aye—aye—perhaps!" said Guise, not ill-pleased, "that may be very true. But the Bearnais does not pay these rogues and blusterers of his. That is his strength. See what an army he has, and never a sou do they see from year's end to year's end! As for me"—here he took a paper out of his pocket-book, and made a rapid calculation—"to entertain a war in France, it were necessary to spend seven hundred thousand livres a month. For our Leaguers cry 'vivas' with their mouths, but they will not lift a pike unless we pay them well for it!"

He folded the paper carefully, as if for future reference.

"What money have I, Raincy?" he said, flapping his empty purse on the table; "not much, I fear. It is time I was leaving Blois, Raincy, if I wish to go with decent credit!"

Now was the valet's chance, which he had been waiting for.

"Ay, it is indeed time—and high time," said Raincy, "if these letters speak true. Let us mount and ride to Soissons—only Your Grace and I, if so it please you. But in an hour it may be too late."

The Duke of Guise laughed, and clapped his major-domo on the shoulder. "Do not you also become a croaker," he cried; "leave me at least Raincy, who sees that the League holds the King in a cleft stick. My good man, he dare not—this Henry of the Fox's Heart. I have the clergy, the Church, the people, most of the lords. The Parliament itself is filled with our people. Blois, all except the Château, is crammed with our men, as a bladder is with lard!"

"Ah, except the Château," groaned Raincy; "but that is the point. You are going to the Château, and the Fox is cunning—he has teeth as well as another!"

"But he dares not trap the lion, Raincy," laughed Guise. "Why, you are as bad as Madame de Noirmoutier, who made me promise to ride off to-day like a whipped cur—I, the Guise. There, no more, Raincy! I tell you I will dethrone the King. Then I will beat the Bearnais and take him about the land as a show in a cage, for he will be the only Huguenot left in all the realm of France. Then you, Raincy, shall be my grand almoner. Be my little one now! Quick, give me twelve golden crowns—that my purse, when I go among my foes, be not like that of my cousin of Navarre!"

As the major-domo went to seek the gold, Guise stretched his feet out to the blaze and, with a smile on his face, hummed the chorus of the Leaguers' marching-song.

"I would I were a little less *balafré* on such a cold morning," grumbled the Duke; "scars honourable are all very well, but—give me a handkerchief, Raincy. That arquebusier at Château Thierry fetched me a villain thwack on the cheek-bone, and on cold days one eye still weeps in sympathy with my misfortunes!"

"Ah, my good lord," said Raincy, "pray that before sundown this day many an eye in France may not have cause to weep!"

"Silence there, old croaker," cried the Duke; "my sword—my cloak! What, have you so forgot your business in prating of France, that you will not even do your office? Carry these things downstairs! A villain's day!—a dog's day! The cold the wolf-packs bring when they come down to harry the villages! Hold the stirrup, Raincy! Steady, lass! Wey there! Thou lovest not standing in the rain, eh? Wish me luck, Raincy. I carry the hope of France, you know—King Henry of Guise, and the throats of the Protestant dogs all cut—sleep on that sentiment, good Raincy."

And Raincy watched the Duke ride away towards the Castle of Blois. The last echo of his master's voice came back to him on the gusty December wind:

> "*The Guises are good men, good men,*
> *The Cardinal, and Henry, and Mayenne, Mayenne!*

For we'll fight till all be grey—
The Valois at our feet to-day—"

Raincy stood awhile motionless, the tears running down his face. He was about to shut the door, when, just where the Duke had sprung upon his horse, he caught the glimpse of something white on the black drip of the eaves. He stooped and picked it up. It was the handkerchief his master had bidden him fetch. It was adorned with the arms of Guise, the Lilies of France being in the centre. But now the *fleurs-de-lys* were red lilies. The blood of the Guise had stained them.

And Raincy stood long, long there in the open street, the sleety snow falling upon his grey head, the kerchief in his hand, marvelling at the portent.

CHAPTER XXI
THE TIGER IN THE FOX'S TRAP

Above, in the Château of Blois, there were two men waiting the coming of Henry, Duke of Guise. One was another Henry, he of Valois, King of France. He had many things to avenge—his own folly and imprudence most of all, though, indeed, these never troubled him. Only the matter of Coligny, and the sombre shades of the dead upon St. Bartholomew's Eve, haunted his repose.

At the private gathering of the conspirators, the King had found many who were willing to sympathise with him in his woes, but few who would drive the steel.

"The Parliament are to make Constable of France the man who is intent on pulling down my throne. I shudder with horror (he whined) to think that the nobles of France support the Guises in this—I speak not of fanatic bishops and loud-mouthed priests, who cry against me from every pulpit because I will not have more Colignys gibbering at my bed-foot, nor yet give them leave to burn Frenchmen by the score, as Philip does his Spaniards t'other side the mountains!"

The Marshal d'Aumont, D'O, and Lognac, the Captain of the Forty-Five Guardsmen, bowed respectful assent.

"What is the state of France, friends," the King cried, in a frenzy of rage, "I bid you tell me, when an alien disputes the throne of Francis First with the legitimate heir of Saint Louis? And what of Paris, my capital city, wherein I have lived like a bourgeois these many years, which receives him with shouts and caressings, but chases me without like a dog?—aye, like a dog!"

The comparison seemed to strike him.

"'Without are dogs,' I have heard the priests say. Well, as to heaven, it may be so. But as to Paris, be sure that if the dogs are without—within are wolves and serpents and all manner of unclean beasts! I would rather trust the Bearnais than any of them!"

There was some dismay at this. It stood out on the faces of the leaders at the council board. If His Majesty went to the King of Navarre, they knew well that their day would be over. However, they swore to do everything that the King required, but of them all, only Lognac meant to keep his word. He was a stout fighter. The killing of Guise was all in the way of business; and if the worst came to the worst, the Bearnais would not refuse a company to one who, in his time, had been Captain of the Forty-Five.

Henry of Valois had been up early that morning, called from his slumbers to bait the trap with his most secret cunning. He did not mean to take any part in the deed himself. For the soldier who had fought so well against Coligny now dodged out and in, like a rat behind the arras.

The Scots Guards were posted in the courtyard of the Château, to shut the entrances as soon as the Duke of Guise should have passed within. In the great hall were the Lords of the Council—the Cardinal of Guise, the Archbishop of Lyons, that clarion of the League, the Cardinal Vendôme, the Marshal d'Aumont, D'O, the Royal favourite, together with the usual clerks and secretaries.

But within, in the ancient chamber of audience, next to the cabinet of the King himself, stood in waiting certain Gascons, ready with their daggers only half-dissembled under their cloaks. They were men of no determined courage, and the King well knew that they might fail him at the last moment. So, by the advice of Hamilton and Larchant of the Scots Guard, he had placed nearest to the door one who would make no mistake—him whom the Man in the Black Cloak had sent, even Jean-aux-Choux, the Fool of the Three Henries.

But on that mask of a face there was now no sign of folly. Stern, grey, immovable was now the countenance of him who, by his mirth, had set many courts in a roar. He could hear, as he had heard it on the night of the Bartholomew, the voice of the Duke of Guise crying, "Haste ye—is the work not done yet?"

And now another "work" was to be done. The feet that had spurned Coligny were even now upon the stairs. He thanked God. Now he would perform his vow upon the man who had made him go through life hideous and a laughing-stock.

For in those days the New Law concerning the forgiveness of enemies was a dead letter. If you wished to live, you had better not forgive your enemy—till after you had slain him. And the dread "Remember the

Bartholomew," printed on all Huguenot hearts, was murmured behind the clenched teeth of Jean-aux-Choux. The Huguenots would be avenged. Innocent blood would no more cry unheeded from the ground. The hated League would fall with its chief. With Guise would perish the Guisards.

The princes of Lorraine had beheld their power grow through four reigns. It culminated on the day of the Barricades, when a king of France appealed to a subject to deliver him from the anger of the citizens of his own capital. So, secure in his power, Guise scorned all thought of harm to himself.

"They dare not," he repeated over and over, both to himself and to others; "the King—his kingdom—hangs upon a single hair, and that hair is my life!"

So he walked into the armed and defended fortress of his mortal enemy as freely as into his own house. Like perfect love, perfect contempt casteth out fear.

Yet when once he had saluted the company in the hall of audience, Guise sat him down by the fire and complained of being cold. He had, he said, lain down in his damp clothes, and had risen up hastily to obey the King's message.

"Soon you will be hot enough upon the branders of Tophet!" muttered D'O, the royal favourite, to Revol, the King's secretary, who went and came between the inner cabinet and the chamber where the council were sitting about a great table.

The superintendent of the finances, one Petremol, was reading a report. The Archbishop of Lyons bent over to the Duke of Guise, where he sat warming him by the fire.

"Where goes our royal Penitent so early—I mistrust his zeal? And specially," he added, as a furious burst of sleet battered like driven sea-spray on the leaded panes of the council room, "on such a morning; it were shame to turn out a dog."

"Oh, the dog goes of his own will—into retreat, as usual!" said the Duke carelessly; "in half-an-hour we shall see him set off with a dozen silken scourges and the softest down pillows in the castle. Our reverend Henry is of the excellent order of Saint Commode!"

Presently, leaving the fireside, the Duke returned to the table where the others sat. It was observed that he was still pale. But the qualm was physical only; no shade of fear mixed with it. He asked for a handkerchief from any of his people who might have followed him. As the greatest care had been taken to exclude these, he was supplied with one from the King's own wardrobe by St. Prix, the King's *valet de chambre*. Then he asked for comfits to stop his cold, but all that could be found within the castle was only a paper of prunes of Brignolles, with which Guise had to content himself, instead of the Smyrna raisins and rose conserves of Savoy which he asked for.

He chatted indifferently with one and another while the routine of the council unrolled itself monotonously.

"I think brother Henry might have let us sleep in our beds, if this be all," he said. "What is the use of bringing us here at this hour, to pronounce on the fate of rascals who have done no worse than hold a few Huguenots to ransom? Wait a while, and we will give the Huguenots something that will put ransoming them out of the question!"

The Cardinal smiled at his brother shrewdly.

"Aye," he murmured, "but we will have the ransoms also. For, you know, the earth belongeth to the Lord, and He has given it to the chosen of His Church."

A hand touched the Duke's shoulder; a voice murmured in his ear. A soft voice—a voice that trembled. It was that of Revol, the King's secretary, whom at first De Nambre, one of the Forty-Five on guard at the door, would not permit to pass. Whereupon the King popped his head out of the closet to give the necessary order, and seeing the young man pale, he called out, "Revol, what's the matter with you? Revol, you are as white as paper, man! Rub your cheeks, Revol. Else you will spoil all!"

Henry III. always liked handsome young men about him, and certainly the messenger of death never came in a prettier form to any than when young Revol tapped the Duke of Guise on the shoulder as he sat by the council board.

The chief of the League rose and, courteous to the last, he bowed graciously to the Cardinal Vendôme, to whom he had not yet had the opportunity of speaking that day. He threw his cloak carefully over one arm, and in the other hand he took his silver comfit-box (for he ever loved sweet things) containing the prunes of Brignolles. He entered into the little narrow passage. De Nambre shut the door behind him. The tiger was in the fox's trap.

Vaguely Guise saw stern faces about him, but as was usual with him, he paid no particular heed, only saluting them as he had done the shouting spice-merchants' 'prentices and general varletage of Paris, which followed everywhere on his heels.

The eight Gascons held back, though their hands were on their daggers. After all, the tiger was a tiger, and they were but hirelings. The curtain which hid the King's closet shook as in a gale of wind. But suddenly the terrible mask of Jean-aux-Choux surged up, so changed that the victim did not recognise the man who had often made sport before him.

"For Coligny—one!" cried the tragic fool.

And at that dread word the other traitor behind the arras might well have trembled also. Then Jean struck his first blow.

"Saint Bartholomew!" cried Jean-aux-Choux, and struck the second time.

The Duke fell on his knees. The eight Gascons precipitated themselves upon the man who had been deemed, and who had deemed himself, the most invincible of the sons of men.

So strong was he that, even in death, he dragged them all after him, like hounds tearing at the flanks of a dying tiger, till, with a cry of "Oh, my friends—oh, what treachery! My sins— —" the breath of life went from him. And he fell prone, still clutching in his agony the foot of the King's bed.

Then the turbaned, weasel face, pale and ghastly, jerked out of the royal closet, and the quavering voice of the King asked Guise's own question of sixteen years before—"Have you finished the work? Is he dead?"

Being assured that his enemy was indeed dead, Henry at last came out, standing over the body of the great Leaguer, holding back the skirts of his dressing-gown with his hand.

"Ah, but he is big!" he said, and spurned him with his foot. Then he put his hands on his brow, as if for a moment to hide the sight, or perhaps to commune with himself. Suddenly he thrust out an arm and called the man-slayers about him.

"Ye are my hands and arms," he said; "I shall not forget that you have done this for my sake."

"Not I!" said Jean-aux-Choux promptly. "I have done it for the sake of Coligny, whom he murdered even so. His blood—my master's blood—has called a long while from the ground. And so"—looking straight at the King—"perish all those who put their hands to the slaughter of the Bartholomew night."

Then King Henry of Valois abased his eyes, and men could hear his teeth chatter in his head. For, indeed, he and Catherine, his mother—the same who now lay a-dying in the chamber below—had guided, with foxy cunning and Italianate guile, that deadly conjuration.

He was, however, too much elated to be long subdued.

"At any rate," he said, "Guise is dead. I am avenged upon mine enemy. Guise is dead! But some others yet live."

CHAPTER XXII
BERÁK THE LIGHTNING AND TOÀH HIS DOG

The blue midland sea, the clear blue of heaven just turning to opal, and the glint of mother-of-pearl coming up with the gloaming! A beach, not flattened out and ribbed by the passage of daily tides, but with the sand and pebbles built steeply up by the lashing waves and the furious wind Euroclydon.

On different planes, far out at sea, were the sails of fishing-boats, set this way and that, for all the world like butterflies in the act of alighting. It was early spring—the spring of Roussillon, where it is never winter. Already the purple flowers of the wild Provençal mustard stood out from the white and yellow rocks, on which was perched a little town, flat-roofed and Moorish. Their leaves, grey-green like her own northern seas, of which she had all but lost the memory, drew Claire's attention. She bit absent-mindedly, and was immediately informed as to the species of the plant, without any previous knowledge of botany.

She kicked a strand of the long binding sea-grass, and then, after looking a moment resentfully at the wild mustard, she threw the plant pettishly away. Our once sedate Claire had begun to allow herself these ebullitions with the Professor. They annoyed the Abbé John so much—and it was practice. Also, they made the Professor spoil her. He had never watched from so near the sweet, semi-conscious coquetry of a pretty maid. So now he studied Claire like a newly-found fragment of Demosthenes, of which the Greek text has become a little fragmentary and wilful during the centuries.

"This will serve you better, if you must take to eating grass like an ox," said the Professor of Eloquence, reaching out his hand and plucking a sprig of sweet alison, which grew everywhere about.

Claire stretched out hers also and took the honey-scented plant, on which the tiny white flowers and the shining fruit were to be found together.

"Buzz-uzz-uzz!" said half-a-dozen indignant bees, following the sprig. For at that dead season of the year, sweet alison was almost their only joy.

"Ugh!" exclaimed Claire, letting it go. She loved none of the sting-accoutred tribe—unless it were the big, heavy, lurching bumble-bees, which entered a room with such blundering pomp that you had always time to get out before they made up their mind about you.

The Professor watched her with some pride. For in the quiet of Rousillon Claire had quickly recovered her peace of mind, and with it the light in the eye and the rose-flush on the cheek.

But quite suddenly she put her hands to her face and began to sob.

If it had been the Abbé John, he might have divined the reason, but the Professor was not a man advised upon such matters.

"What is it?" he said, stupidly enough; "are you ill?"

"Oh, no—no!" sobbed Claire; "it is so good to be here. It is so peaceful. You are so good to me—too good—your mother—your brothers—what have I done to deserve it?"

"Very likely nothing," said the Professor, meaning to be consoling; "I have always noticed that those who deserve least, are commonly best served!"

"That is not at all a nice thing to say," cried Claire; "they did not teach you polite speeches at your school—or else you have forgotten them at your dull old Sorbonne. Do you call that eloquence?"

"I only profess eloquence," said Doctor Anatole, with due meekness; "it is not required by any statute that I should also practise it!"

"Well," said Claire, "I can do without your sweet speeches. I cannot expect a Sorbonnist to have the sugared comfits of a king's mignon!"

"Who speaks so loud of sugared comfits?" said a voice from the other side of the weather-stained rock, beneath which the Professor and Claire Agnew were sitting looking out over the sea.

A tall shepherd appeared, wrapped in the cloak of the true Pyrenean herdsman, brown ochre striped with red, and fringed with the blue woollen tassels which here took the place of the silver bells of Bearn. A tiny shiver, not of distaste, but caused by some feeling of faint, instinctive aversion, ran through Claire.

Jean-aux-Choux did not notice. His eyes were far out on the sea, where, as in a vision, he seemed to see strange things. His countenance, once twisted and comical, now appeared somehow ennobled. A stern glory, as of an angry ocean seen in the twilight, gloating over the destruction it has wrought during the day, illumined his face. His bent back seemed somehow straighter. And, though he still halted in his gait, he could take the hills in his stride with any man. And none could better "wear the sheep" or call an erring ewe to heel than Jean-aux-Choux. For in these semi-eastern lands the sheep still follow the shepherd and are known of him.

"Who speaks of sugared comfits?" demanded Jean-aux-Choux for the second time.

"I did," said Claire, a little tremulously. "I only wished I had some, Jean, to while away the time. For this law-learned Professor will say nothing but rude things to me!"

Jean looked from one to the other, to make sure that the girl was jesting. His brow cleared. Then again a gleam of fierce joy passed momently over his face.

"*He* had comfits in his hand in a silver box," he said, "jeweller's work of a cunning artificer. And he entered among us like the Lord of All. But it was given to me—to me, Jean-aux-Choux, to bring low the haughty head. 'Guise, the good Guise!' Ha! ha! But I sent him to Hattil, the place of an howling for sin—he that had thought to walk in Ahara, the sweet savouring meadows!"

"I hated Guise and all his works," said the Professor, looking at the ex-fool boldly, "yet will I never call his death aught but a murder most foul."

"It may be—it may be," said Jean-aux-Choux indifferently; "I did my Lord's work for an unworthy master. I would as soon have set the steel to the throat of Henry of Valois himself. He and that mother of his, now also gone to the Place of Howling to hob-nob with her friend of Guise—they planned the killing. I did it. I give thanks! Michäiah—who is like the Lord? Jedaiah—the hand of the Lord hath wrought it. Jehoash-Berák—the fire of the Lord falls in the thunderbolt! Amen!"

The Professor started to his feet.

"What is that you say? The Queen-Mother dead? And you——?"

He looked at the long dagger Jean-aux-Choux carried at his side, which, every time he shifted his cloak, drew the unwilling gaze of Claire Agnew like a fascination.

"The Mother of Witchcrafts is indeed dead," said Jean-aux-Choux. "But that the world owes not to me. The hand of God, and not mine, sent her to her own place. Yet I saw in a vision the Woman drunken with the blood of saints, and with the blood of the martyrs of Jesus."

Then he, who had once been called the King's fool, became, as it were, transported. His eyes, directed at something unseen across the blue and sleeping sea, were terrible to behold. Faint greyish flecks of foam appeared on his lips. He cast his cloak on the ground and trod upon it, crying, "Even thus is it to-day with Great Babylon, the mystery, the mother of the abominations of the earth."

After a moment's pause he took up his prophecy.

"There was One who came and bade me listen, and I gave him no heed, for he blessed when I would have cursed; he cried 'Preserve' when I cried 'Cut off'; he cried 'Plant' when I would have burned up, root and branch. But when I heard that Catherine of the Medici was indeed dead, I shouted for joy; I said, 'She was arrayed in purple and scarlet, and gilded with gold and precious stones and pearls! I saw her glory. But now Babylon the Great is fallen—is fallen. And they that worshipped her throw dust on their heads—all they that have thriven on the abundance of her pleasures. For in one hour her judgment is come!'"

Then, all in a moment, he came down from the height of his vision. The light of satisfied vengeance faded from his face.

"But I forget—I must go to the herd. It is my duty—till the God, whose arm of flesh I am, finds fitter work for me to do. Then will I do it. I care not whether the reward be heaven or hell, so that the work be done. The cripple and the fool is not like other men. He is not holden by human laws or codes of honour, nor by the lust of land, nor wealth, nor power, nor the love of woman. He is free—free—free as Berák, the lightning of God is free—to strike where he wills—to fall where he is sent!"

The two watched him, and listened, marvelling.

And the Professor muttered to himself, "Before I lecture again, I must read that Genevan book of his. Our poor Vulgate is to that torrent as the waters of Siloah that flow softly!"

The voice of Jean-aux-Choux had ceased. That is, his lips moved without words. But presently he turned to Claire and said, almost in his old tones, "I am a fool. I fright you, that are but a child. I do great wrong. But now I will go to the flock. They await me. I am, you say, a careless shepherd to have left them so long. Not so! I have a dog in a thousand—Toàh the dart. And, indeed, I myself am no hireling—no Iscariot. For your good cousin, Don Raphael Llorient, of Collioure, hath as yet paid me no wages—neither gold Ferdinand nor silver Philip of the Indies. A good day to you, Professor! Sleep in peace, little Claire Agnew! For the sake of one Francis, late my master, we will watch over you—even I, Berák the lightning, and Toàh my dog!"

CHAPTER XXIII
THE THREE SONS OF MADAME AMÉLIE

They went back, keeping step together, tall Claire with hand fearlessly placed on the shoulder of her Professor, who straightened his bowed student-back at the light touch.

As he went he meditated deeply, and Claire waited for him to speak. Treading lightly by his side, she smelled the honeysuckle scent of the sweet alison which she had carried idly away in her hand.

"If the Queen-Mother be dead," said the Professor, "that is one more stone out of the path of the Bearnais. The Valois loves a strong man to lean upon. For that reason he clings to D'Epernon, but some day he will find out that Epernon is only a man of cardboard. There is but one in France—or, at least, one with the gift of drawing other strong men about him."

"The Bearnais?" queried Claire, playing with the sweet alison; "I wonder where he has his camp now?"

She asked the question in a carelessly meditative way, and quite evidently without any reference to the fact that a certain John d'Albret (once called in jest the Abbé John) was the youngest full captain in that enthusiastic, though ill-paid array. But the Professor did not hear her question. His mind was set on great matters of policy, while Claire wondered whether the Abbé John looked handsome in his accoutrements of captain. Then she thought of the enemy trying to kill him, and it seemed bitterly wicked. That John d'Albret was at the same time earnestly endeavouring to kill as many as possible of the enemy did not seem to matter nearly so much.

"Yes," said the Professor, "Henry of Valois has nothing else for it. The Leaguers are worse than ever, buzzing like a cloud of hornets about his head. They hold Paris and half the cities of France. He must go to the King of Navarre, and that humbly withal!"

"It will be well for him then," said Claire, "if our Jean-aux-Choux has no more visions, with 'Remember Saint Bartholomew' for an over-word!"

"Ah," said the Professor, "make no mistake. A man may be brave and politic as well. 'I am excellent at taking advice, when it is to my own liking,' said the Bearnais, and he will teach Master Jean to see visions also to his liking!"

At which Claire laughed merrily.

"I am with him there!" she cried; "so as you hope for influence with me, good sir, advise me in the line of my desires. But, ah! yonder is your mother."

And clapping her hands, she picked up her skirts and ran as hard as she could up the path towards a trellised white house with a wide balcony, over which the vines clambered in summer. It was the house of La Masane, which looks down upon Collioure.

Madame Amélie, or, more properly, the Señora, was a little, quick-moving, crisp-talking woman, with an eye that snapped, and a wealth of speech which left her son, the Professor of Eloquence, an infinite distance behind. She had with her in the house two other sons, the elder of whom was Alcalde of the little town of Collioure, and therefore intimately linked with the great house of the Llorients, whose turreted castle stood up grimly midway between St. Elne and La Masane. The Alcalde of Collioure was a staid man of grave aspect, a grinder of much corn during his hours of work, the master of six windmills which creaked and groaned on the windy slopes above the sea-village. In his broad hat-brim and in the folds of his attire there was always more or less of the faint grey-white dust which hall-marks the maker of the bread of men.

The Alcalde of Collioure thought in epigrams, explaining his views in wise saws, Catalan, Castilian, and Provençal. French also he had at call, though, as a good subject of King Philip, he thought, or affected to think, little of that language. His brother, the lawyer of Elne, attached to the bishopric by his position, was a politician, and never tired of foretelling that before long Roussillon would be, even as Bearn and Navarre, a part of a great and united France. The Bearnais would hold the Pyrenees from end to end.

These three old bachelors, each according to his ability, did their best to spoil Claire. And it was a nightly battle of words, to be settled only by the Señora, who should sit next her at supper. With a twinkle in his eye the Professor argued his seniority, the Mayor of Collioure his official position, while the notary brazenly declared that being the youngest and the best-looking, it was no less than right and just that he should be preferred.

Madame Amélie miscalled them all for foolish old bachelors, who had wasted their time cosseting themselves, till now no fair young maid like Claire would look at any one of them.

"For me," she would say, "I was married at sixteen, and now my Anatole owns to more than fifty years and is growing bald. Jean-Marie there waxes stout and is a corn-miller, while as for you, Monsieur the Notary, you are a fox who rises too late in the morning to catch many roosting fowls!"

Claire had now been a month in the quiet of the Mas of La Masane, yet she only now began to understand that Roussillon was a detached part of the dominions of King Philip of Spain—though it was nevertheless *tras los montes*, and under a good governor at Perpignan enjoyed for the moment a comparative immunity.

But dark shadows loomed upon the favoured province.

The Demon of the South wanted money. Moreover, he wanted his land cleansed of heresy. Rich men in Roussillon were heretics or the children of heretics. Philip was fighting the Church's quarrel abroad in all lands, on all waters—against Elizabeth of England, against the bold burghers of the Low Countries, the Protestant princes of Germany, against the Bearnais, and (but this secretly) against the King of France.

Far away where the hills of the Gaudarrama look down upon Madrid, and where in the cold wind-drift from their snows the life of a man goes out while the flame of a candle burns steadily, sat a little wizened figure, bent and seared, spinning spiders' webs in a wilderness of stone, in the midst of a desert wherein no man dwelt. He spun them to an accompaniment of monks' chanting and the tolling of bells, but every hour horsemen went and came at full gallop across the wild.

The palace in the wilderness was the Escurial, and the man Philip II. of Spain, known all over Europe by the terrible name of "The Demon of the South."

For him there was no truce in this war. He moved slowly, as he himself boasted, with a foot of lead, but hitherto surely. Of his own land he was absolutely secure, save perhaps in that far corner of ever-turbulent Catalonia which is called Roussillon.

The inhabitants considered that province almost a part of France. The Demon of the South, however, thought otherwise—that little man at the desk whose was the League, who moved Guise and all the rest as concealed clockwork moves the puppets when the great Strasburg horologe strikes twelve—whose was the Armada and the army of Parma, camped out on the Flemish dunes. He held that Roussillon was for him a kind of gold mine. And his black tax-gatherers were the familiars of the Holy Office, that mystery of mysteries, the Inquisition itself.

Nevertheless, for the moment, there was peace—peace on Collioure, peace on the towered feudalism of the castle thereof, peace on the alternate fish-tailed sapphire and turquoise of its sleeping sea, and most of all peace on La Masane, over against the high-perched fortress of St. Elne.

The Señora's two maidens served the evening meal in the wide, seaward-looking room, the windows of which opened like doors upon the covered terrace. Though the spring was not yet far advanced the air was already sweet and scented with juniper and romarin, lavender, myrtle, and lentisque—growths which, like the bog-myrtle of Scotland, smell sweet all the year.

The three men saluted their house-guest sedately by kissing Claire on the forehead. To the Professor, as to an older friend with additional privileges, she presented also her cheek. From the head of the table, which was hers by right, Madame Amélie surveyed tolerantly yet sharply this interchange of civilities.

"Have done, children," she said, "the soup waits."

And as of all things the soup of the Mas of Collioure must not be kept waiting, all made haste to bring themselves to their places. Then the Señora, glancing about to see that all were in a fit and reverent frame of mind, prepared to say grace. "*Bene——*Don Jordy!" she interrupted sharply, "you may be a good man of the law, and learned in Papal bulls and seals, but the Grace of God is scant in you. You are thinking more of that young maid than of your Maker! Cross yourself reverently, Don Jordy, or no spoonful of soup do you eat at my table to-night."

Don Jordy (which is, of course, to say George) did as his mother bade him. For the little black-eyed old lady was a strict disciplinarian, and none crossed her will in the Mas of Collioure. Yes, these three grey-headed men, each with a man's work in the world behind him, as soon as they crossed the threshold became again all of an age—the age their mother wished them to be, when she had them running like wild goats among the flocks and herds of La Masane. Happy that rare mother whose sons never quite grow up.

After the first deep breathings, and the sigh of satisfaction with which it was the custom to pay homage to the excellent pottage of Madame Amélie, the second brother, Jean-Marie, Alcalde of Collioure, a quiet smile defining the flour dust in the wrinkles of his grave countenance (it was not his day for shaving), looked across at Claire Agnew and said, "I thought mayhap you might have come to see me to-day. I was down at the Fanal Mill, and——"

"There are finer things to be seen at Elne," interrupted the Bishop's notary, "to wit, cloisters, an organ, and fine pictured books on vellum."

"Pshaw!" cried his brother, "it is better in the mills—what with whirling sails, the sleepy clatter of the wheels, and the grinding stones, with the meal pouring down its funnel like a mine of gold."

"Ah," sighed the lawyer, "but I wearied to-day among my parchments. The sight of you has spoilt us. A day without you is as long as one of Count Ugolino's!"

"What was that?" demanded the miller, interested.

"A day without bread!" said the notary.

"Silence, Don Jordy," cried the Señora to her favourite son, "that tongue of yours may plead well in a court, or for aught I know speak the best of Latin before the wise of the earth, but that is no reason why here, in this my house, it should go like the hopper of the Fanal Mill!"

"*Architæ crepitaculum!*" said the notary, "you are right, mother mine— the truly eloquent man, like our Sir Professor, keeps his eloquence to practise on young maids by the sea-beach! But I have not observed him fill his mouth with pebbles like his master."

"You are indeed but young things," said Claire, smiling at the Señora; "I would not take any one of you from your mother—no, not at a gift."

"They are slow—slow, my sons," said the Señora, well pleased; "I fear me they will be buried ere they be wed."

"Then we shall have small chance," cried the ruddy Don Jordy, "for according to what I hear my betters say over yonder at the Bishop's palace, in the place whither we are bound there is neither marrying nor giving in marriage!"

"Good brother," said the Professor of Eloquence sententiously, "if you do not mend your ways, you may find yourself where you will have little time and less inclination for such like gauds!"

Meanwhile, without heeding their persiflage, the Señora pursued the even tenor of her meditation. "Slow—slow," she said, "good lads all, but slow."

"It was not our fault, but yours, that we are Long," declared that hardened humorist, Don Jordy; "you married our father of your own free will, as is the good custom of Roussillon. Blame us not then that we are like Lambin."

"Lambin," cried his mother, "who was he? Some monkish rascal runagate over there at the palace?"

"Nay, no runagate; he goes too slow ever to run," said Don Jordy. "Have you never heard of Lambin our barber episcopal?

'Lambin, the barber, that model of gravity,
Shaving the chins of myself and my brother;
Handles his blade with such reverend suavity,
That ere one side is smooth—lo, 'tis rough on the other!'"

"And I," said the Mayor of Collioure, "have been this day with one who goes fast enough, though perhaps he goes to the devil."

They looked at the miller in astonishment. It was but seldom that he served himself with words so strong.

"A cousin of yours, my little lady," he added, looking at Claire.

"Raphael Llorient!" cried the remaining two brothers; "is he then home again?"

"Aye, indeed he is!" said a voice from the doorway. The figure they saw there was that of a man clad in black velvet, fitting his slender, almost girlish figure like a glove. Only a single decoration, but that the order of the Golden Fleece, hung at his neck from a red ribbon. He was lithe and apparently young, but Claire could not see his face clearly. He remained obstinately against the light, but she could see the points of a slender moustache, and distinguish that the young man's eyebrows met in a thick black bar on his forehead.

"Don Raphael," said the Mayor of Collioure, "you are welcome to this your house. This is my brother Anatole, Professor of Eloquence at the Sorbonne——"

"Ah, the Parisian!" said the young man, bowing slightly; "so you have killed King Guise after crowning him? We in Madrid ever thought him a man of straw for all his strutting and cock-crowing. He would have none of our great King Philip's advice. And so—and so—they used him for firewood in the guard-room at Blois! Well, every dog has his day. And who may this be—I ask as lord of the manor and feudal superior, while warming myself by your fire as a friend—this pretty maid with the downcast eyes?"

"I believe," said the Professor gravely, "that the lady is your own cousin-german. Her name is Claire Agnew, and that of her mother was Colette Llorient of Collioure."

CHAPTER XXIV
COUSIN RAPHAEL, LORD OF COLLIOURE

"Is this thing true?"

The young man in the velvet suit, with the order of the Golden Fleece on his breast, spoke hastily and haughtily, jerking his head back as if Doctor Anatole had made to strike him in the face.

"My friend Professor Anatole Long does not lie," said Claire firmly. "I am the daughter of Francis Agnew the Scot, and of his wife Colette Llorient."

"You are prepared to prove this?"

"I have neither wish nor need to prove it," said Claire. "I am content to be my father's daughter, and to have known him for an honest man. I trust not to shame his memory!"

The young man with the golden order at his throat stood biting his lip and frowning—with a frown so concentrated and deadly that Claire thought she had never seen the like.

"The daughter of Colette Llorient—to whom my grandfather——"

He broke off hastily, his sentence unachieved. Then all at once his mood appeared to alter. A smile broke upon his lips. Upon his forehead the bushy black brows disjoined, and he sat down near Claire, so that he could look in her face with the light of the sunset streaming upon it through the door, while his own was still in shadow.

"So you may be my cousin—my aunt Colette's daughter," he said meditatively. "Well, Don Jorge, you are a lawyer and learned, they say. I charge you to look at any papers the young lady may have, and report to your brother, this grinder of good meal and responsible civil authority of my town of Collioure. And pray tell me, little one," he continued, taking Claire's hand, as if he had been an old acquaintance, "how would you like me for a cousin? We have much need of one so young and fair in our dingy old castle. The stock of the Llorients of Collioure has worn itself away, till there remains only myself and—if there be no mistake—you, my kinswoman, fresh as the May morning! Why, you will redeem us all!"

It was then that the Señora found her tongue. Indeed, she had not lost it. But she did not approve of this too familiar and masterful young man, and she only waited an opportunity of telling him so.

"Raphael Llorient of Collioure, listen to me," she said. "I was your foster-mother—you and my Don Jordy there are of one age, and lay on my breast together. It is my right to speak to you, since, though they may owe you feudal obedience and service, I abide here in this house of La Masane for the term of my natural life. Let this maid stay with us. If I could bring up you and these children of my body, I am able to guide also this young maid, who has nor father nor mother."

"But we have gay company down yonder at the Castle," said Raphael Llorient, "ladies of the Court even—or rather, who would be of the Court if we had one, and not merely a monastery with a bureau attached for the Man-who-traffics-in-kingdoms!"

"I wish to stay here," said Claire, alarmed all at once by the strangeness of her kinsman's manner. "I am very happy, and Professor Anatole brought me from Paris!"

"Happy Professor," smiled the Lord of Collioure, somewhat sneeringly. "I presume he did not forget his office, but used his eloquence to some purpose by the way? But, all the same, though we will not compel you, sweet cousin, it would cheer us mightily if you would come. There are great ladies now doing the honours of my house—the Countess Livia, the Duchess of Err, and—Valentine la Niña."

"Raphael—little son," said the old lady, laying her withered hand on his lace wristband, "leave her with me. She is better and safer with old Mother Amélie than with all your great folk down there!"

"That for the great folk," cried the young man, snapping his fingers; "they are no greater than any daughter of the house of the Llorients of Collioure. Besides, they have seen her already. The duchess passed her yesterday with the Countess Livia on her way to the rock-fishing. But I will not tell what she reported of you to the duke, or it might make you vain!"

Claire moved uneasily. The man's eyes affected her curiously. She would now very gladly have sat as close to the Abbé John as even that encroaching youth could have wished.

"Do you know, little cousin," the lord of the manor continued, after a pause in which no one spoke, "you are not very gracious to your kinsfolk? Perhaps you have more of them than I—in Scotland, maybe?"

Claire shook her head sadly enough.

"Save these good friends here, I am alone in the world," she answered steadily. "I do not know my father's family in Scotland. I think they know as little of me as you did before entering that door!"

"Perhaps," Raphael went on courteously, "that is more than you think. We are a poor little village, a poverty-stricken countryside, in which such a pearl as you cannot long be hidden. Somebody will surely be wanting it for their crown!"

"Pearls mean tears and of those I have shed enough," said Claire simply; "also I have seen and heard much of crowns and those who wear them. I would rather stay at the Mas and take the goats to the mountains, and——"

"The learned Professor to the beach!" added Raphael, with a curl of his lip.

"Indeed, yes!" cried Claire, reaching out her hand to the Professor. "I am always happy with him. He teaches me so many things. My father was a wise man, but he lacked the time to talk much with me."

"And I dare say the learned Professor of the Sorbonne gives his time willingly," said the Lord of Collioure; "his tastes are not singular. And pray, of your courtesy, what might he teach you in your *tête-à-têtes*?"

"I have everything to learn," Claire answered with intent, "except fencing with the small-sword and how to shoot straight with a pistol! These my father taught me!"

"Ah," cried Raphael Llorient, clapping his hands, "this is a dangerous damsel to offend. Why, you could call us all out, and kill us one by one, if duelling were not forbidden in Spain!"

"I stand for peace," said the Professor, interrupting unexpectedly, for even after many years filled with learned labours and crowned with success, the feudal reverence was strong on him; "I am a man of peace, but there are many who would not let Mistress Claire go without a defender. Even I——"

The feudal superior laughed unpleasantly.

"Oh, yes," he cried, "you would defend her with a syllogism, draw your major and minor premises upon the insulter, and vanquish the lady's foes before a full meeting of the Sorbonne!"

"Indeed," returned the Professor shortly, "we have had some meetings of that body lately which came near to losing kings their thrones!"

The keen, dark features of the Lord of Collioure took on a graver expression.

"Where I come from," he said, "we live too near to the rack and the water-torture to air our opinions concerning such things. Our Philip has taught us to guard our thoughts for times when we find ourselves some distance outside the frontiers of Spain."

He cast a significant look around, on the dusking purplish sea, on the great mass of Estelle and the Canigou, standing out black against a saffron sky. The glance conveyed to those who knew Raphael Llorient, that they dwelt at present too far within the dangerous bounds of Spain, and that if they had once to do with the Demon of the South, it would be worse for them than many Holy Leagues and Bearnais war-levyings.

He rose to take his leave, kissing the Señora, and palpably hesitating between Claire's cheek and her hand, till something in the girl's manner decided him on the latter.

"*Au revoir*, sweet cousin newly found!" he cried, lifting his black velvet bonnet to his head with grace; "I hope you will like me better the next time you see me. I warn you I shall come with credentials!"

"I sha'n't—I won't—I never could!" Claire was affirming to herself behind her shut lips, even as he was speaking.

"I hate that man!" she burst out, as soon as the lithe slender figure in the black velvet suit was sufficiently far out of ear-shot down the mountain side.

"You mean," said the Professor soothingly, "that you are a little afraid of Don Raphael. I do not wonder. Perhaps I did wrong to bring you here. But I never thought to see him cross this doorstep. He has not done so much for years and years. For how long, mother?"

"For sixteen years—not since his father's death," said the old woman; "he was angry that the farm of La Masane was left to me burden-free for my lifetime, when he had so great need of the money to spend in Madrid!"

"I hate him! I cannot tell why—no," added Claire, recurring to the former speech of Professor Anatole, "I do not fear him—why should I? In the end, I am stronger than he!"

"Ah," said the Professor, "but it is always such a long way to the end!"

CHAPTER XXV
CLAIRE'S EMBARRASSMENT OF CHOICE

There could be no longer any doubt about it. Raphael Llorient, Lord of Collioure, was in love with his cousin. At least he made love to her, which, of course, is an entirely different thing. The Professor pointed this out. The grave Alcalde of Collioure showed the meal-dust in a new wrinkle, and said that, for a Doctor of a learned college which excluded women as unholy things, Anatole was strangely learned in matters which concerned them. Whereupon the Professor asked his brother who had placed a handful of early roses beside Claire's platter, in a tall green Venice glass, at the mid-day meal. He further remarked that these roses came from the castle gardens, and wished to be informed whether the miller of Collioure was grinding his own corn or another man's.

Don Jordy openly laughed at them both. One he declared to be bald and the other musty. He alone, owing to his handsome face and figure—considering also his semi-ecclesiastical prestige, a great thing with women in all ages—had a right to hope!

The Professor broke in more sharply than became his learned dignity.

"Tush—what is the use?" he said, not without a certain bitterness; "she is not for any of us. I have seen another. I have stood silently by, while she was thinking about him. I do as much every day. If we all died for her sake——"

Don Jordy clapped his elder brother on the shoulder with a more anxious face, crying, "What, man, surely this is not serious? Why, Anatole, I thought you had never looked on women—since—but that is better not spoken of. I was only jesting, lad. You know me better than that!"

But Jean-Marie, the Alcalde of Collioure, gravely shook his head. He knew Raphael Llorient was not a man to stick at trifles, and that the fact that his young cousin loved an unseen captain warring for the Bearnais would only whet his desires. So it happened that once in a way the service of defence broke down. The Señora, a brave worker about her house, could not pass the bounds of her garden without laying herself up for days. The Alcalde was down at his mills, the Notary Ecclesiastical had ridden over to

Elne on his white mule, by the path that zigzagged along the sea cliff, up among the rock-cystus and the romarin, twining and twisting like a dust-coloured snake striking from coil.

The Professor, called by a sudden summons to the castle to see a most learned man who had just arrived from Madrid, and was high in the favour of Philip of Spain, had betaken himself most unwillingly down to the town. It was a still day, and the sea without hardly moved on its fringe of pebbles, sucking a little with languid lip and sighing like an infant fallen asleep at the mother's breast. Claire Agnew wearied of the stillness of the house-place. In the base-court she could hear Madame Amélie calling *"Viénn-nè, viénn-nè!"* to her goats. For there was no milk like Madame Amélie's of the Mas of La Masane above Collioure, and no goats so well treated. Why, each day they had a great *pot-au-feu* of nettles, and carrots, and wild mustard leaves, just like Christians. So careless and wasteful are some people. As if goats were not made to find their own living among rocks and stone walls!

Such, at least, was the collated opinion of Collioure, jealous more than a little of the good hill-farm in free life-rent, the three well-doing sons, and smarting, too, after fifty years' experience of the Señora's tongue, which, when the mood was upon her, could crack like a wine-waggoner's whip about the ears of the forward or froward.

The house silence, broken only by the solemn pacing of the great seven-foot Provençal clock, ventrose, aldermanic, profusely gilded as to its body and floreated as to its face, presently grew too much for Claire. She was nervous to-day, at any rate.

She regarded the dial of the big clock. Half-past three! In a little while the goats would be coming home to be milked. That would be something. They generally kicked her when they did not butt. Still, that also was interesting. "Patience," said Claire to herself, though it is hard to be patient with an active goat in an unfriendly mood.

Then, round the corner of the sea-road Notary Don Jorge would be arriving presently, the westering sun shining on the white mule which the bishop had given him for his easier transport. They believed greatly in Don Jordy over at Elne. He it was who had pled their case as against big, grasping, brand-new Perpignan, which wanted to take away their bishopric, their relics, their prestige, and its ancient glory from their hill-set cathedral. Yes, Don Jordy would be coming. He always had a new jest each evening—a merry man and a loyal, Don Jordy. Claire liked him, his rosy monk's face, and twinkling light-blue eyes.

Then, presently, the Alcalde Jean-Marie would come climbing up, the abundantly-vowelled Provençal speech, sweet and slow, dropping like honey from his lips. It was fun to tease Jean-Marie. He took such a long time to get ready his retorts. He was like the big, blundering, good-natured humble-bees aforesaid—you could always be far away before he got ready to be angry. Then, like them, he would go muttering and grumbling away, large and dusty, and—not too clever.

The Professor also; he would not stay long, she knew, down at the castle with that very learned man from Madrid. Nor yet with the great ladies. He would rather be listening to his friend, little Claire Agnew, reading the Genevan Testament, while he compared Calvin's rendering with the original Greek, or perhaps merely sitting silent on their favourite knoll above the blue Mediterranean, watching the white town, the grey and gold castle walls, and the whirling sails of Jean-Marie's windmills.

Yes, they would all be coming back, some one of them at least; or, if not, there would at least be the Señora and the kicking goats. It was better to be kicked than to be bored, and *ennuyée*, and sickened with the measured immeasurable "tick-tack" of time, as it was doled emptily out by the big-bellied Provençal clock in the kitchen-corner.

At La Masane above Collioure, Claire suffered from the weariness of riches, the embarrassment of choice. In a little forsaken village, with her father busied about his affairs, she would have been well content all day with no more than her needlework and her Genevan Bible. There were maps in that, and a beautiful plan of the ark, so that she could discuss with herself where to put each of the animals. But at La Masane, with four people eager to do her pleasure, the maiden picked and chose as if culling flowers among the clover meadows.

So Claire went out, and stood a long minute. Her hand went up to her brow, and she looked abroad on her new world. She could hear where to find the Señora. She loved the Señora. But then the Señora and the goats she had always with her. On the whole, she preferred the men—any of the men—to amuse her, and, yes, of course, to instruct her also. Claire felt her need of instruction.

She looked down the steep zigzags of the path over the cliff to the towers of the Castle of Collioure. She saw no Professor, staff in hand, walking a little stiffly, his hat tilted on the back of his head, or carried in his hand, that he might the more easily look up at La Masane when he came in sight of his birthplace.

The Alcalde-miller's towers stood out dazzlingly white, the sails turning merrily as if at play. They made her giddy to look at long. But no sturdy Jean-Marie was to be seen, his bust thrown out, the stiff fuzz of his beard half a foot before him as he walked, every way a solid man, and worthy to be chief magistrate of a greater town than Collioure. Only, just at that moment, Claire could not see him.

The whip-lash path, running perilously along the cliff-edge towards Elne, was broken by no slowly-crawling white speck, the mule bestridden by Don Jordy, Notary Episcopal of the ancient See of the Bishops of Elne.

Remained for Claire—the Señora, the goats.

Now it chanced that the night before, the Alcalde Jean-Marie, grappling for small-talk in the dense medium of his brain, had thought to point out to Claire a little ravine far away to the left, beyond the pasture limits of La Masane. The Alcalde was strong on local topography. That, he said, was the famous sweet-water fountain and Chapel of the Consolation. You found your fate there. Young girls saw their husband that was to be, upon dropping a pin into its depths in the twilight. Good young women (imaginatively given) sometimes saw the Virgin, or thought they did. While bad men, stooping to drink, certainly saw the devil looking up at them—in the plain clear mirror of that sweet-water spring.

A most various spring—useful, too! She might see—but Claire did not anticipate even to herself what or whom she hoped to see. At any rate, pending the arrival of her three male servitors, she would go—there could be no harm in just going—to the Spring of the Consolation, hid deep in that bosky dell over which the willow and oleander cast so pleasant a shade.

Claire snatched a broad Navarrese bonnet and went.

"My sweet cousin, I bid you welcome," a voice spoke, mocking a little, but quiet and penetrating.

Hastily Claire let the laurel branch slip back, stood upright like a startled fawn, and—found herself in face of Raphael Llorient, who at the other side of the little brook which flowed from the Spring of Our Lady of the Consolation, leaned against a tree, tapping his knee with a switch and smiling triumphantly across at her.

"Ah, cousin," he said, "you did not give me any very pressing invitation to come again to see you at the Mas on the hillside yonder. All the more gracious of you, therefore, to have come so far to meet me at my favourite retreat!"

"But I—I did not know—I had no idea——" Claire stammered.

The Lord of Collioure waved his hand easily, as one who passed lightly from a childish indiscretion.

"Of course not—of course not," he agreed, as if humouring her mood, "how should you know? You had never even heard of the Spring of Our

Lady of the Consolation, or of its magic properties. Well, we have time—I will explain them to you, sweet cousin Claire!"

"Oh, pray do not," cried Claire breathlessly; "I know—what they say—what Jean-Marie says, that is. He pointed out the nest of bushes on the hillside last night—I should not have come!"

"And he told you, I doubt not—he would not be a Collioure man if he did not, and a good Catholic of Roussillon (which is to say a good pagan)—that you had but to look in the well at the gloaming to see the Predestined. Well, look!"

In spite of herself Claire glanced downwards. She stood on the opposite side of it from her cousin Raphael, and it was with a thrill of anger and fear that she saw his slender figure mirrored in the black pool.

"It looks like a betrothal—eh, cousin?" said Raphael, "even by your friend Jean-Marie's telling?"

"No, no!" cried Claire desperately, "I do not believe it. It is only because I found you standing there. Of course, you can also see me from where you stand! It is nothing!"

"It is everything—a double proof of our fate, yours and mine, my cousin," said Raphael softly. "The Well of the Consolation has betrothed us. Sweet cousin Claire, there remains for me only to leap the slight obstacle and take possession! So fair a bride goes not long a-begging!"

"No, no!" cried Claire, more emphatically, and making sure of her retreat in case of need, "I do not want to marry. I could not marry you, at any rate—you are my cousin!"

Inwardly she was saying to herself, "I must speak him fair to get away. When once I am back at La Masane I shall never wander away again from the Señora. I shall milk goats all my life—even if they butt me. I wish it were now." Her cousin Llorient smiled with subtlety. There was a flash in his eyes in the dusk of the wood like that of a wild animal seen in a cave.

"Because I am your cousin—is it that I must not marry you? Pshaw!" he said, "what of that? Am I not a servant of King Philip, and of some favour with him? Also he with the Pope, who, though he hates him, dares not refuse all his asking to the Right Hand of Holy Church."

Claire glanced behind her. The little path among the bushes was narrow, but beyond the primrose sky of evening peeped through. Two steps, one wild rush, and she would be out on the open brae-face, the heath and juniper under foot, springy and close-matted—perfect running right to the door of La Masane.

She launched her ultimatum.

"I will not wed you, whether you speak in jest or earnest. I would rather marry Don Jordy, or his white mule, or one of Jean-Marie's windmills. No, not if you got fifty dispensations from as many popes. I am of the religion oppressed and persecuted—Huguenot, Calvinist, Protestant. As my father was—as he lived and died, so will I live and die!"

With a backward step she was gone, the bushes swishing about her. In a moment she was out on the open slope, flying towards La Masane. There was the Professor laboriously climbing up from the castle, his hat on the back of his head, his staff in his hand, just as she had foreseen. Good kind Professor, how she loved him!

There, at the door of the Fanal Mill, making signs to her with his arms, signals as clumsy as the whirling of the great sails, now disconnected and anchored for the night, was the Miller-Alcalde Jean-Marie, the flour-dust doubtless in his beard and mapping the wrinkles of his honest face. She loved him, too—she loved the flour-dust also, so glad was she to get away from the Well of the Consolation.

But nearer even than Don Jordy, whose white mule disengaged itself from the rocky wimples of the road to Elne (Claire loved Don Jordy and the mule also, even more than she had said to Raphael, her cousin), there appeared a lonely sentinel, motionless on a rock. A mere black figure it was, wrapped in a great cloak, on his head the slouched hat of the Roussillon shepherds, looped up at the side, and a huge dog couchant at his feet.

"Jean-aux-Choux! Jean—Jean—Jean!" cried Claire. And she never could explain how it came to pass that her arms were about Jean's neck, or why there was a tear on her cheek. She did not know she had been weeping.

By the Fountain of the Consolation, Raphael Llorient remained alone. He did not even trouble to follow Claire in her wild flight. He had the girl, as he thought, under his hand, whenever he chose to lift her. Her anger did not displease him—on the contrary.

He laughed a little, and the lifting of the lip gave a momentary glimpse of white teeth, which, taken together with the greenish sub-glitter (like shot silk) of his eyes, was distinctly unpleasant in the twilight of the wood.

"The little vixen," he said to himself, changing his pose against the great olive for one yet more graceful, "the small fury! A little more and she would have bitten her lip through. I saw the tremble of the under one where the teeth were biting into it, when she was holding herself in. But I like her none the worse for that. Women are the poorest sort of wild cattle—unless you have to tame them!"

The night darkened down. The primrose of the sky changed to the saffron red of a mountain-gipsy's handkerchief, crimsoned to a deep welter of incarnadine, the "flurry" of the dying day. Still Raphael stood there, by the black pool. A little bluish glimmer, which might have been Will-o'-the-wisp, danced across the marisma. The trees sighed. The water muttered to itself.

In that place and time, simple shepherd-folk who had often seen Raphael, Lord of Collioure, pass into the haunted coppice, were entirely sure of the explanation. The devil spoke with him—else, why was he not afraid? They were right.

For Raphael Llorient took counsel there with his own heart. And as that was evil, it amounted to the same thing.

The Kingdom of God is within you, saith the Word. The other kingdom also, according to your choice.

CHAPTER XXVI
FIRST COUNCIL OF WAR

There was more than one council of war within the bounds of the circle of hills that closed in little Collioure that night.

First, that which was held within the kitchen-place of La Masane. The maids were busied with the cattle, but all three brothers were there. The Señora, sloe-eyed and vivid, continually interrupted, now by spoken word, now trotting to the steaming *casseroles* upon the fire, anon darting to the door to make sure that this time no unwelcome visitor should steal upon them at unawares.

When Claire had told her story, the three men sat grave and silent, each deep in his own thoughts. Only the Señora was voluble in her astonishment. She thought she knew her foster-child.

"He had, indeed, ever the grasping hand," she said, "therefore I had thought he would have married lands wide and rich with some dwarfish bride, or else a merchant's daughter of Barcelona, whose Peruvian dollars needed the gilding of his nobility. But Claire—and she is his cousin too——!"

"Also no Catholic—nor ever will be!" interrupted Claire hotly.

The old lady sighed. This was a sore subject with her. Had she not spent three reals every week in candles at the shrine of the Virgin in the Church of Collioure, sending down the money by one of her maidens, all to give effect to her prayers for the conversion of her guest? For Donna Amélie believed, as every Spanish woman does in her heart believe, that out of the fold of the Church is no salvation.

"Ah, well," she murmured on this occasion, "that was your father's teaching—on him be the sin."

For dying unconfessed, as Francis Agnew had done, she thought a little more would not matter.

"I have been too long away to guess his meaning, maybe," said the Professor at last; "for me—I would give—well, no matter—he is not the man, as I read him, to fall honestly in love even with the fairest girl that lives——!"

"You are not polite," said Claire defiantly; "surely the man may like me for myself as well as another? Allow him that, at least!"

But the Professor only put out his hand as if to quiet a fretting child. It was a serious question, that which was before them to settle. They must work it out with slow masculine persistence.

"Wait a little, Claire," he said tenderly; "what say my brothers?" The Alcalde in turn shook his head more gravely than usual.

"No," he said, "there is something rascally at the back of Don Raphael's brain. I will wager that he knew of his cousin being here the first night he came to La Masane!"

"I have it," cried Don Jordy; "I remember there was something in his grandfather's will (yours, too, my pretty lady!) about a portion to be laid aside for his daughter Colette. I have seen a copy of the deed in the episcopal registry. It was very properly drawn by one of my predecessors. Now, old Don Emmanuel-Stephane Llorient lived so long that all his sons died or got themselves killed before him—it never was a hard matter to pick a quarrel with a Llorient of Collioure. So this grandson Raphael had his grandfather's estates to play ducks and drakes with——"

"More ducks than drakes," put in the sententious miller.

"Also," the lawyer continued, without heeding, "I would wager that to-day there is but little left of the patrimony of little Colette, your mother, and——"

"He would marry you to hide his misuse of your money!" cried the miller, slapping his thigh, as if he had discovered the whole plot single-handed.

"Exactly," said Don Jordy, "he would cover his misappropriation with the cloak of marriage. I warrant also he has lied to the King as to the amount of the legacy, perhaps denying that there was any benefice at all—saying that he had paid the amount to your father—or what not! And our most catholic Philip can forgive all sins except those which lose him money—so Master Raphael finds himself in a tight place!"

The silence which followed Don Jordy's exposition was a solemn one—that is, to all except Claire, who only pouted a little with ostentatious discontent.

"I don't believe a word of it," she cried; "money or no money, will or no will, it is just as possible that he wants to marry me—because—because he wants to marry me! There!"

But the Señora knew better.

"True it is, my little lady," she said, nodding her head, "that any man might wisely and gladly crave your love and your hand—aye, any honest man, were he a king's son (here Claire thought of a certain son of Saint Louis, many times removed, now mending his shoes on the corner of a farrier's anvil in the camp of the Bearnais)—an honest man, I said. But not Raphael Llorient, your cousin, and my foster-son. He never had a thought but for himself since he was a babe, and even then he would thrust Don Jordy there aside, as if I had not been his mother. I was a strong woman in those days, and suckled twins—or what is harder, a foster-child and mine own, doing justice to both!"

And Claire, a little awed by the old lady's vehemence, jested no more.

There was little said till Donna Amélie took Claire up with her to her chamber, and the three men were left alone. The Professor sighed deeply.

"Women are kittle handling," he said. "I brought you a little orphan maid. I knew, indeed, that she was Colette Llorient's daughter, and that there was some risk in that. But with her cousin Raphael, wistful to marry her for a rich heiress, whose property he has squandered—that is more than I reckoned with!"

"There is no going back when a woman leads the way," slowly enunciated the Alcalde.

"Who spoke of going back?" cried the Professor indignantly. "I have taken the risk of bringing the maid here, thinking to place her in safety with my mother. Neither she nor I will fail. We will keep her with our lives—aye, and so will you, brothers!"

"So we will!" said Jean-Marie and Don Jordy together, "of course!"

"Pity it is for another man!" said the lawyer grimly—"that is, if what Anatole says be true."

"It is too true!" said the Professor bravely—"true and natural and right, that the young should seek the young and love the young and cleave to the young!"

"That, at least, is comforting for those who (like myself) are still young!" said Don Jordy, with some mockery in his tone; "for you and the Alcalde there, the comfort is somewhat chilly!"

And neither of his seniors could find it in their hearts to contradict Don Jordy.

The brothers conferred long together, and at last found nothing better than that Claire should remain at La Masane with their mother, while she should be solemnly charged not to leave the house except in company with one of the three brothers. They would mount guard one by one, and even the master of the Castle of Collioure would hardly venture to violate the sanctuary of the Mas of La Masane.

Curiously enough, in their arrangements, none of them thought once of Jean-aux-Choux. Yet, had they but looked out of the door, they would have seen Jean wrapped in his rough shepherd's cloak, leaning his chin on his five-foot staff, his great wolf-hound at attention, his flock clumped about his feet, but his eyes fixed on the lonely Mas where, in the twilight, these three brothers sat and discussed with knitted brows concerning the fate of Claire Agnew.

CHAPTER XXVII
SECOND COUNCIL OF WAR

"You are late, Count Raphael," said a tall lady, presiding over a little gathering of men and women in the upper hall of the Castle of Collioure. The Duchess of Err was a Spanish lady who had dwelt some time at the Court of Paris in the time of Francis II. and Mary of Scotland. And ever since she had posed as one who could innovate if she would, so that the ancient customs of Spain would not know themselves again when she had done with them. As, however, she took good care to keep this carefully from King Philip's ears, nothing very remarkable came of it.

But, nevertheless, the Duchess of Err had a certain repute for originality and daring, which served her as well then as at any other period of the world's history. Her husband accompanied her, but as that diplomatist "abode in his breeches" and confined his intercourse with those around to asking the major-domo once a day what there was for dinner, his influence on his wife was not great. His trouble was spoken of, leniently, as "a touch of the sun."

"Our host comes from a rendezvous, doubtless," put in the Countess Livia, with a bitter intention, glancing, as she did so, at a fair-haired girl with wide-open eyes who sat listless and very quiet at the seaward window. A priest, playing chess with a robust, country-faced man, looked up quickly from his ivory pieces. But the girl said nothing, and Raphael Llorient was left to answer for himself.

This he did by turning towards her who had not spoken, or even looked in his direction.

"Mademoiselle Valentine," he said, "will you not defend a poor man who, having but one vineyard, must needs sometimes trim and graft with his own hands?"

Momentarily, the girl rested her great eyes, of the greenish amber of pressed clover honey, full upon him. Her face was faintly flushed like the blonde of meadow-sweet, but quite without pink in the cheeks. Her lips, however, were full, red, and more than a little scornful.

"The Lord of Collioure can surely please himself as to his comings and goings," she said; "for the rest, is not my ghostly uncle here to confess him, if such be his need?"

"Valentine la Niña," cried the Duchess, "is there nothing in the world that will make you curious? Only twenty-five, and reputed the fairest woman in Europe. Yet you have outlived the sin of Eve, your mother! It is an insult against the laws of your sex. What shall we do to her?"

"Make her confess to her uncle," said the Countess Livia, who also never could forgive in any woman the offence-capital of beauty.

"My niece Valentine has her own spiritual adviser," said the priest, looking up from his game, with a smile which had enough of curiosity in it to make up for his niece's lack of it. "A Pope may, if he will, confess his nephews, but a poor Brother of the Society had better confide the cure of his relatives' souls to the nearest village priest. Otherwise he might be suspect of conspiring against the good of the state. The regular clergy may steal horses, while a Jesuit may not even look over the wall!"

The ladies rose to say good-night. Like a careful host, Raphael took from the table a tall candelabra of two branches, in order to conduct them severally to the doors of their apartments. The Duchess of Err conveyed away her husband with her, holding up her long silken train with one hand and giving the ex-diplomat a push on before her with the other, as often as he needed it. The Duke had forgotten that he had once already partaken of supper, and craved another. He even shed a few tears. Yet he had his good points. His emotion showed a sympathetic nature, and besides, the ladies were there under his escort and protection. The Duchess said so, so it must be true. Meantime, however, she propelled him to bed.

The Countess Livia gave Raphael her hand to kiss, saying at the same time, "To-morrow I will find your village maid for you!"

On the way the Duchess divided her attention between making sure that her husband took the right turning in the long corridors of the castle of Collioure, and reproaching Raphael for not building a new and elegant château "after the manner of Chenancieux or Cour Chevernay—light, dainty, fit for a lady's jewel-case."

At this Raphael laughed, and, holding the candelabra high in his hand, begged them to look up and mark upon the lintels of the narrow windows the splintering of the cannon shots and the grooves made by the inrush of the arbalast bolts.

"My Lady Duchess," he answered, "I would be glad to do your bidding—first, if I had the security; second, if I had the river; third, if I had the money. But I have no money, alas, save what I gather hardly enough from my vines and the flocks on the hillside yonder (see that faithful man guarding my interests—I never had a herder like him). Besides, I am here between three fires, or it may be four—our good King Philip, the step-father of his people, the King of France, the Bearnais, and, may be before long, the Holy League also. Bullets may soon be whistling again at Collioure, as they have whistled before, and I would rather that they encountered these ten-foot walls, and mortar of excellent shell-lime, than the moulded sugar and plaster of these ladies' toys along the Loire!"

"Ah, you will not move with the times!" cried the Duchess, propelling her husband severely into his dressing-room to make sure that he, at least, moved with the times—a little faster even—"if you had been as long in France as I—well, but there—I forgive you. You are a good Catholic, and a subject of King Philip. Therefore you cannot help it, and our lord the King sees to it that you have something else to do with your money than to build castles wherein to entertain ladies. Sea-castles for the English robber dogs to batter with shot, and land-castles to hold down the Hollander frontier, are much more to his liking!"

At this point the Duke of Err created a diversion by turning in his tracks at the sight of the dark sleeping-chamber, through the open window of which came the light sap and clatter of the sea on the beach far below.

"My supper—my supper!" he muttered; "I want to go to the supper-room!"

The Duchess was not a lady of lengthy patience, and domestic manners were simple in those days. She merely gave the ex-diplomatist a sound box on the ear, and bade him get into bed at once.

"It takes all his family just like that before the age of fifty," she said; "I am a woman much to be pitied, with such a babe on my hands. Good-night, Don Raphael; you must build me that château to comfort me as soon as the wars are over— —"

"When God wills, and the purse fills!" said the Lord of Collioure, bowing to the ground.

A little farther along the corridor they came to the chambers of the Countess Livia and the niece of the Jesuit doctor. The Countess, with her eyes on her companion, gave Raphael her fingers to kiss, but Valentine la Niña swept past both with the slightest bow.

"No man can serve two masters," said the Countess, smiling after her with meaning; "you must give up your shepherdess!"

"What do you mean?" Raphael demanded, in a low tone.

"My brother Paul will tell you to-morrow, when he comes back from Perpignan. He, too, was on the hillside to-day—near to the valley——"

She paused long enough to give him time to ask the question.

"What valley?" said Raphael, in complete apparent forgetfulness.

"The Valley of the Consolation! An excellent name!" answered the Countess Livia, with a low laugh of malice.

She turned and went within. She found Valentine la Niña standing by the open window looking out upon the sea. Her large, amber-coloured eyes were now black and mysterious. She did not show the least trace of emotion. She was as one walking in a dream, or perhaps, rather, like one upheld by a will not her own.

The Countess Livia looked at the girl awhile, and then, with a vexed stamp of her foot, she pulled Valentine round, so that the light of the lamp fell on her face.

"Oh!" she cried, "was there ever a woman like you? As the Duchess said, you care for nothing. You are the most beautiful girl in the world, and it is nothing to you. No wonder a dairy-maid can supplant you. Why, if I had a tenth of your beauty—I would have kings and emperors at my feet!"

Valentine la Niña looked at her without smiling, or the least show of feeling.

"It is likely," she said; "you are free, I am bound. When I receive my orders, I shall obey them."

"You are a strange creature," cried the Countess. "Orders—who is to command you? Bound—what chains are there that a suitable marriage will not break?"

"Those!" said Valentine la Niña, opening her robe at the throat, and showing to the astonished eyes of the Countess Livia the black crucifix and the hair shirt of discipline.

CHAPTER XXVIII
THIRD COUNCIL OF WAR

Raphael had not been long in his bedroom when a light knock came to the door. He looked about him with a startled air, as if there might be something to be concealed on some table or in some alcove. All seemed in order to his eye. Reassured, he went on tiptoe and opened the door very gently, just so far that whoever stood without might enter.

"You?" he said, in a tone of surprise.

And the Jesuit father came into the room, softly smiling at the young man's surprise.

"Ah," he said, with the most delicate touch of rebuke in his tone, "you perhaps expected your major-domo, your steward. I forgot that you were a bachelor and must attend to the morrow's provender, otherwise we should all starve."

"Ah, no," said the Master of Collioure, "I have a good housekeeper, in addition to Sebastian Tet, my major-domo. I can sleep on both ears and know that my guests will not go dinnerless to-morrow. We are poor, but there is always soup in the cabbage-garden, fish in the sea, mutton on the hills, and wine everywhere at Collioure—good and strong, the wine of Roussillon!"

"Faith," said the Jesuit, "but for the Order, a man might do worse than abide here. 'Tis Egypt and its fleshpots! No wonder you are so fond of it. And" (here he paused a little to give weight to his words) "Paul Morella told me to-day that there is even a Cleopatra of the Heavy Locks up there among the flocks of Goshen! You make your land of bondage complete indeed!"

The dark face of Raphael grew livid and unlovely, as the eyes of the smiling priest rested shrewdly upon him.

"Paul Morella meddles with what does not concern him," he answered brusquely; "that is no safe business in Roussillon, as he will find—especially when one has a sister of an unguarded tongue. I have seen a knife-point look out at the other side of a man for less!"

Father Mariana raised his plump hands in deprecation.

"No, no," he said. "'*Quoniam Deus mortem non fecit, nec laetatur in perditione vivorum!*' Neither must you, my son, and a son of Holy Church. Besides, there are always other ways. I am writing a book to show how the Church can best be served with the guile of the serpent, yet with the harmlessness of the dove."

The mood of the young man changed as he listened, as it always did with Father Mariana of Toledo.

"I spoke in haste," he said. "I wish no ill to Paul Morella, nor to his sister, the Countess Livia—only I would their tongues were stiller!"

The Jesuit patted Raphael's arm gently and soothingly.

"Be content," he murmured; "the Countess Livia is neither your sister nor your wife. 'As the climbing up of a sandy way is to the feet of the aged—so is a wife full of words to a quiet man.' So it is written, and all marriage is but a commentary upon that text."

"Hum, it may be, my father," said Raphael, "and to tell the truth, I am tempted to try. In which matter I shall be glad to have your advice, my father Mariana, since you have come all the way from your hermitage at Toledo to visit your old pupil——"

"And also to serve the Order and Holy Church," added the Jesuit gravely, like a preceptor making a necessary correction in an exercise. "Is it as spiritual director or as friend that you desire my counsel?"

"As a man of the world, rather," said Raphael, sitting down on the edge of his bed and nursing his knee between his joined fingers. The Jesuit had already installed himself in the great tapestried armchair, and put his small, neatly-shod feet close together on the footstool.

"Alas, my son," said the priest, when at last he was comfortable, "I have long ago lost all title to that name. And yet, I do not know; I have been chased from most countries, and openly condemned by the General of my own Order. Yet I serve in faith——"

"Oh," said Raphael, smiling, "all the world knows that the Order approves your doings. The General only condemns your words for the benefit of the vulgar and anointed kings. If I make not too bold, it seems to me that there is a certain king in France—I say not of France—who may well be interested in your presence so near his territories! If I were he, I should say my prayers!"

"If you speak of the Bearnais, you are mistaken," said Mariana; "he, at least, is an open enemy, and, who knows, may one day be reconciled, being at heart a good, fightful, eat-drink-and-be-merry pagan—indeed, Raphael

Llorient of Collioure, very much of your own religion, save that where he would wield a battle-axe you would drive a dagger, save that he makes love where you would make money, and he trolls a catch where you whisper a pass-word. But as to the advice—well, put your case. The night is young before us, and this wine of Burgundy, like myself—old, old, old!"

"My father," said Raphael, "just now you spoke of money. It is true I seek it—but to spend, not to hoard. Too often I hazard it on the turn of a dice-cube. I lose it. Money will not stay with me, neither the golden discs, nor the value of them. This trick of gaming I have inherited from my grandfather. Only he had the good sense to die before he had spent all his heritance. His sons, being given rather to sword-play and the war-game, died before him. To all appearance I was sole heir, and so for long I considered myself. But when my grandfather's will was found, half only was left to me—the other half to his only daughter Colette and to her children. The will is in the provincial archives at Perpignan. He had placed it there himself. A copy is in the registry of the bishop at Elne. Yet another copy was sent to the Huguenot whom my aunt Colette married."

"Ah," said the Jesuit, narrowing his eyes in deep thought, "and this heretic—has he never claimed the inheritance?"

"He is dead, they say—was killed in Paris, on the day of the Barricades. Yet he received the paper, and now his daughter has come to Collioure, and is abiding at the house of La Masane with the family there—emigrants from Provence—one of whom, by some trick of cunning or aptitude for flattery, has become a professor at the Sorbonne—Doctor Anatole Long, he styles himself."

"Ah," said the Jesuit, in a changed, caressing voice, "a learned man; he has written well upon the eloquence of Greece and Rome as applied to the purposes of the Church. I myself have ordered a translation of his books to be made for the use of our schools at Toledo. And yet—I heard something concerning him read from the Gazette of the Order at our last council meeting. Had he not to flee, because he alone of the Senatus withstood the Holy League?"

Raphael nodded slightly. The quarrels of philosophers were nothing to him.

"Aye, and brought my cousin Claire with him—Colette's daughter, as I suppose, to claim the property—the property which I have no longer—which is blown wantonly upon every wind, rattled in other men's pockets, paid out for laces and silks which I never wore——"

"You have been a foolish lad," said the Jesuit; "but one day, when you have spent all, you will make a very good prodigal son to the Gèsu. Perhaps the hour is not far distant. What, then, is your intention?"

"I see nothing for it but that I must marry the girl," said Raphael Llorient; "she is fair, and you—and the King—must help me to a dispensation. Then her portion shall be her dower, and there is only her husband to account to for it. I shall be that husband."

A subtle change passed over the Jesuit's face as his pupil was speaking. He smiled.

"Softly, softly," he murmured; "to eat an egg, it is not necessary to cook it in a silver vessel over a fire of sandalwood, and serve it upon a platter of gold. It tastes just as well boiled in an earthenware dish and eaten in the fingers."

"I have gone too far," said Raphael; "I cannot stand upon metaphors. My eggs are already sucked. I have deceived the King, paid neither duty to him nor tithes to the Church upon my cousin's portion. I must marry or burn!"

"That you have not paid your tithes to the Church is grave," said the Jesuit, "but the time is not too late. Perhaps you can pay in service. We of the Society need the willing hand, the far-seeing brain more than coined gold—though that, of course, we must have too."

"The King's arm is long," said Raphael, "and I fear he thinks I have not done enough for his Armada. This news would end me if it were to come to his ears."

"I judge that there will be no such need," purred the Jesuit; "is this cousin of yours by chance a heretic, even as was her father?"

Raphael started. His netted fingers let go his knee, which in its turn slowly relaxed and allowed the foot to sink to the ground, as through a dense medium.

"I do not understand you, my father," he said, breathing deeply, his eyes fixed on the priest's mild and smiling face.

"If your cousin be a Protestant, a heretic," continued the Jesuit, "I do not see that there is any difficulty——"

"You mean——?" said Raphael, his face now of a livid paleness.

The priest beckoned him a little nearer, placed his lips, still smiling, close to the young man's ear, and whispered two words.

"No—no—no!" gasped Raphael, starting back, "not that—anything but that! I cannot—I will not—anything but that!"

"Then there is, I fear greatly, no other way!"

"None?"

"Your soul is the Church's—your body the King's," said the Jesuit; "take care that you offend not both. For such there is no forgiveness, even in the grave. Besides, you could never get a dispensation to marry a heretic. Trust me, my way is the best."

"She would return to the Faith," said Raphael, who, though a man of no half measures in his own plottings, yet stood aghast and horrified at what the smiling priest proposed to him.

"Never," said Father Mariana; "I know the breed—'proud as a Scot,' say the French, your friends, who know them best. And in nothing prouder or more stubborn than in their heresy and hatred of the Wholesome Discipline of the Church."

"I cannot," said Raphael; "after all, she is my cousin—my near and only relative."

"If she were the mother who bore you," affirmed the priest, "your duty would be the same. And moreover (though, indeed, it becomes not me to press upon you that which should be your first happiness), has it struck you that you have passed your word to the Señorita Valentine, my niece——?"

"The Lady Valentine would have nothing to say to me," cried the young man sharply; "I wed none such!"

"But are you so sure of your Scottish heretic? As for Valentine, when was a gallant young man discouraged by a woman's first 'No'? You have much to learn, young man; Valentine la Niña has been well taught. Fear nothing. Where she gives her hand, her heart will go with it. I have schooled her myself. She has no will but that of the Gesù—think on it, my son, and deeply!"

And still smiling gently, the Jesuit went out, leaving Raphael to meditations singularly unhappy, even for a man who has to choose between the gallows and marriage with one of two women, neither of whom he loves.

CHAPTER XXIX
THE SHUT HOUSE IN MONEY STREET

There is a house in the city of Perpignan, in the street called "of the money," where on a time strange things were done and still stranger planned. It is the ancient House of the Holy Office, that is to say, of the Inquisition. In an upper room, after the fatigues of the day, three priests were seated. One was a dark, thin man, the type of Philip's new inquisitors, a Torquemada reborn; the second was a little grey-haired man, with watering reddish eyes, and a small mouth, as if it had been cut with one blow of a chisel; while in the only comfortable chair lounged a certain smiling Jesuit father, who, though under the open censure of his General, was yet the most powerful man in all their terrible Order—one Mariana, historian, pamphleteer, disputant, plotter, inquisitor, and chief firebrand of the new Society which had come to turn the world upside down.

These three men awaited a messenger who was to bring them momentous intelligence from a city far away.

Little was said, though it was supper-time, and wines and meat had been placed on the table. The two Fathers of the Holy Office ate sparingly, as became men whose eyes had seen their fellows endure many hours of torment that day, in order that their hearts and minds might be purified from heresy, and their money chink in the coffers of Holy Church. Only Mariana ate and drank heartily. For was it not his business to go about the world with soft compressive palm and a cheerful smile on his rosy face, a complete refutation of the idea that a Jesuit must of necessity be a dark and cunning plotter, or an inquisitor, merely an ecclesiastical executioner?

The Chief Surintendant Teruel was a grim Aragonese, a peasant brought up hardly, the humanity ground out of him by long years of noviciate, till now he knew no pity, no kindness, no faltering, while he carried out the will of God as interpreted to him by his hierarchical superiors.

Little Frey Tullio, on the contrary, was a Neapolitan, who had been sent over from Rome on purpose to familiarise himself with the best Spanish methods. For nowhere did the Holy Office thrive so congenially and root itself so deeply as in Catholic Spain. Frey Tullio did his work conscientiously, but without the stern joy of his Aragonese superior, and certainly wholly without the supple, subtle wit and smiling finesse of Mariana, the famous "outcast" of the Company of the Gesù.

"A man is waiting below," said a black-robed acolyte, who had handled certain confession-producing ropes and cords that day, and was now also resting from his labours. The prisoners who had been saved for the next *auto de fé* (except those who, being delicate, had succumbed to the Lesser and Greater Question) rested equally from theirs—in the cellars below, the blood stiffening in their unwashed wounds, and their rack-tormented bones setting into place a little so as to be ready for ten of the clock on the morrow.

"A man waiting below?" repeated the Chief Inquisitor; "what does he want?"

"To see the Fathers of the Holy Office," said the servitor, wondering if he had sufficiently wiped the wine from his mouth ere he came in—the Surintendant was regarding him so sternly.

"He looks like a shepherd of the hills," said the acolyte; "indeed, I have seen him before—at Collioure. He is a servant, so he says, of Don Raphael Llorient!"

"Ah," said Mariana quickly, "then I think I can guess his message. I have already spoken of it with Don Raphael."

"Bid three stout familiars of the Office stand unseen behind the curtain there, weapons in hand," commanded Surintendant Teruel; "then show the man up!"

Jean-aux-Choux entered, long-haired, wild-eyed, his cloak of rough frieze falling low about his ankles, and his hand upon the dagger-hilt which had once been red with the blood of the Guise.

The three looked silently at him, with that chill, pitiless gaze which made no difference between a man asked to speak his message and him who, by one word out of his own mouth, must deliver himself to torture and to death.

"Stand!" commanded the Chief Inquisitor, "speak your message briefly, and if all be well, you are at liberty to return as you came!"

The threat was hardly veiled, but Jean-aux-Choux stood undaunted.

"Death is my familiar friend," he said; "I am not afraid. God, who hath oft delivered me from the tooth of the lion and the claw of the bear, can deliver me also from this Philistine."

The two judges of men's souls looked at each other. This was perilously like fanaticism. They knew well how to deal with that. But Mariana only laughed and tapped his forehead covertly with his forefinger.

"He is harmless, but mad, this fellow," he murmured; "I have often spoken with him while I abode at the house of Don Raphael of Collioure. He hath had in his youth some smattering of letters, but now what little lear he had trots all skimble-skamble in his head. Yet, failing our young Dominican of Sens—well, we might go farther and fare worse."

Then he turned to Jean-aux-Choux.

"Your message, shepherd?" he said. "Fear nothing. We shall not harm you."

"Had I supposed so, you would not have found me here—out of the mouth of the lion, and out of——"

"That will do," said Mariana, cutting him short; "whence come you?"

"From the camp of two kings, a great and a little, a true and a false, the lion and the dog——"

"Speak plainly—we have little time to waste!"

"Plainly then, I have seen the meeting of Henry of Valois and Henry of Navarre! They fell each on the other's neck and kissed!"

The two inquisitors rose to their feet. For the first time emotion showed on their faces. The chief, tall, black, sombre, stood and threatened Jean-aux-Choux with comminatory forefinger.

"If you speak lies, beware!"

The little Italian, formerly so grey and still, nothing stirring about him save the restless, beady eyes common to all Neapolitans, stood up and vociferated.

"It is an open defiance of our Holy Father," he cried, "a shame of shames—the Valois shall be accursed! He has delivered his realm to the Huguenot. He shall be burnt alive, and I—I would refuse him the *viaticum*!"

"He may not have time even for that!" said Mariana softly—"that is, when his day comes. But haste you, man, tell us what befel—where, and how."

"On Sunday last," began Jean-aux-Choux, looking his three inquisitors in the face with the utmost calm, "I was, as Father Mariana knows, in a certain place upon the affairs of my master.

"It was in a park near a great city of many towers. A river ran near by and a bridge spanned it. At the bridge-head were three great nobles—dukes and peers of France, so they said. Many people were in the park and about the palace which stood within it. There seemed no fear. The place was open to all. About a chapel door they cried 'God save the King!' For within a man, splendidly arrayed, was hearing mass—I saw him enter."

The inquisitors looked at one another, nodding expressively.

"But I cared not for that. I was at the bridge-head, and almost at my elbow the three nobles conferred one with the other, doubtful if he for whom they waited would come.

"'I should not, if I were he,' said one of them; 'my father did the like, and died! Only he had a written promise.'"

"That was Chatillon, Coligny's son, I warrant," said Mariana, who seemed to know everything.

"And another said, 'He has my word—he will believe that, though he doubts that of the King!'"

"Epernon, for a wager!" cried the Jesuit, clapping his hands; "there spoke the man! And the third, what said he?"

"Oh, he—no great matter," answered Jean-aux-Choux, gently stroking his brow, as if to recall a matter long past. "Ah, I do remember—he only caused great swelling words to come from his mouth, and rattled his sword in his scabbard, declaring that if there was any treachery he would thrust the traitor through and through with 'Monsieur la Chose' (so he named his sword), which he declared to be the peer and overlord of any king in Christendie!"

"That would be the Marshal d'Aumont," said Mariana, after a pause. "Well, and so these three waited there, on the bridge, did they?"

"Ay, I warrant. I was at their elbow, as I say," quoth Jean-aux-Choux, "on the bridge called the 'Pont de la Motte.' And presently there came in sight a cloud of dust, and out of the cloud galloping horses, with one that rode in front. And there were spear-heads that glinted, and musket-barrels, and swords with dinted scabbards. And the armour of these men was all tashed, and their helms like to a piece of lead that one has smitten with a hammer long and long."

"Battered armour is the worn breviary of the soldier!" commented Mariana. "Had these horsemen white scarves belting them?"

"Each man of them!" Jean-aux-Choux answered. "But even he that rode at the head had his armour (so much of it as he wore) in a like state; but whereas all the others rode with plain steel helms, there was a white plume in his. Those who stood near called it his panache, and said it was miracle-working. Also he wore a cloak, like that of a night-sentinel, but underneath, his doublet and hose were of olive-green velvet. He was of a hearty countenance, robust of body, and rode gallantly, with his head thrown back, laughing at little things by the way—as when a court page-boy, all in cloth of gold, fell off the tree on which he had climbed to see the show, and had to be pulled out of the river, dripping and weeping, with a countryman's rake all tangled in the hinder breadths of his raiment."

"The Bearnais! To a hair!" cried the Jesuit. "Ah, what a man! What a man—if only he were on the side of Holy Church——"

"He is a heretic of heretics," said the Surintendant Temel, "and deserves only the flames and the yellow robe!"

"It is a pity," said Mariana, with a certain contempt for such intolerance of idea; "you would have found him an equally good man in your father's wheat-field, and I, at the King's council. One day he will give our Philip tit-for-tat—that is, if he live so long!"

"Which God forbid!" said the inquisitor.

"Amen!" assented Frey Tullio.

"Well," smiled Mariana, "there is no pleasing you. For me, there are many sorts of gallant men, but with you, a man must either swallow all the Council of Trent, or be food for flames."

The inquisitors were silent. Discussion was not their business. They worked honestly from ten in the morning till five in the afternoon. Therefore, they deserved their rest, and if Mariana persisted in talking they would not get it. Still, they were eager to hear what the servant of Raphael Llorient had to say.

Mariana made Jean a signal to go on with his tale. He continued:

"So being used to run on the mountains, I outstripped the crowd and came to the door of the chapel where the Other King, he in the cloak of blue and gold, was at his prayers. The crowd pressed and thronged—all looking the other way.

"And I waited. But not long. From very far away there came a crying of many people—a great soughing whisper first, then a sound like the strength of the wind among high trees, and last, loud as the roar of many waters—'The White Plume! The White Plume! Navarre! Navarre!'

"Then the Other King, whom no one cheered greatly nor took much heed of, came out from his mass and strove to meet the king of the brisk and smiling countenance. But for a long time they could not. For the crowd broke in and pressed them so tight that during a good quarter of an hour these two Kings, the White Plume, and the Man-all-covered-with-Lilies, stood within half-a-dozen paces of each other, unable to embrace or even to touch hands. Whereat the White Plume laughed and jested with those about, bidding them remember that he had come without his breakfast, and such-like. But the Man-with-the-Lilies was sullen and angry with the concourse."

"Ah, for a couple of good disciplined Leaguers with long knives!" muttered the Chief of the Inquisitors regretfully.

"And then," continued Jean-aux-Choux, "the angry Soldier-Man, who had stood on the bridge with sword and baton, thrust back the people, speaking many words hotly, which are not fit that I should repeat in your reverend ears. So finally the two Kings met and embraced, and the people shouted, so that none might know what his neighbour said. And presently I saw these two walk arm-in-arm through the press, and so up into the château, out of my sight. They abode there long time talking, and then after eating they came out. For it was time that the King-covered-with-Lilies should go back to his chapel, being a man apparently very devout."

The expression on the faces of the two inquisitors was dreadful to behold in its contempt and hate. But Mariana laughed.

"So he came out again, and the King with the White Plume still with him. Only he of the Plume entered not in to the chapel, but stayed without, playing at tennis with the strongest and bravest youths of the court, and laughing when they beat him, or when the ball took him in his face.

"And all the while the crowd cried, 'Long live the White Plume! Long live Navarre!' And sometimes from the back, one or two would raise a feeble cry 'Long live France! Long live Henry of Valois!'"

The Chief Inquisitor brought down his fist on the table with a crash, so that the wine-bottles tottered and a glass smashed.

"But he shall not—by the crucifix, he shall not!" he hissed, chill-white with anger. "He shall die—if there be poison in Italy, steel in France, or — —"

"Money in Spain!" said Mariana calmly, putting his hand on the arm of his coadjutor. "Well, there is not much—but this is the Street of the Money— and I judge we shall find enough for that!"

CHAPTER XXX
JEAN-AUX-CHOUX TAKES HIS WAGES

No sooner had Jean-aux-Choux departed from the terrible house in the Street of the Money at Perpignan, in which he had found the three inquisitors seated, than Mariana, with a sigh of relief, drew from his breast a document on cream-coloured vellum.

Before reading it he looked at the other two, and especially at Frey Tullio the Neapolitan.

"We are all good Spaniards," he was about to begin. But remembering in time the birthplace of the junior inquisitor, he altered his sentence into, "We are all good subjects of King Philip?"

Surintendant Teruel and Frey Tullio bowed their heads. They wondered what was coming, and Tullio was growing not a little sleepy. Even inquisitors must sleep. A pulley-wheel creaked overhead uneasily. Down in the Place of Pain the familiars were trying the ropes for the morrow. There was one that had not acted satisfactorily in the case of that Valencian Jew in the afternoon. They had been ordered to mend it. King Philip did not approve of paying for new ropes too often. Besides, the old were better. They did not stretch so much. Blood and tears had dropped upon them.

So ever and anon the pulley creaked complainingly between two rafters, in the pauses of the Jesuit's soft voice, as he read the Pope's condemnation of King Henry III. of France (called of Valois)—excommunicated, outcasted, delivered to Satan that he might learn not to offend—for the sin of alliance with the heretic, for the sin of schism and witchcraft—"ordered to be read from the chair of our cathedral-church of Meaux, and of all others occupied by faithful bishops——"

The face of the peasant-ecclesiastic Teruel lighted with a fierce joy as he listened.

"We shall yet be able to send the Valois before our tribunals. The Holy Office shall be set up in France. At last the Edicts of Trent shall be obeyed.

What glory! What joy—to judge a King of France, and send him to the stake as a heretic, a schismatic, a hater of Holy Church——"

"Softly—softly, Brother Teruel," said Mariana, smiling fixedly. "France is not our happy Spain. The people there are not accustomed to fires in the market-places and the smell of burned sacrifice—to the sight of their parents and children being fagoted for the glory of God. See what happened in England a few years ago, when our Philip's wife Mary, Queen of that country, tried to introduce a little—oh, such a very little—of her husband's methods."

"Here we have no difficulty," said Teruel, from his peasant-bigot's point of view. "It is God's good method with the world to extirpate the heretic!"

But the Jesuit answered him truly.

"Make no mistake," he said, tapping the Papal Bull with a plump forefinger, "you succeed here in Spain, my country and yours, because the Spaniard, ninety-nine out of a hundred, is wishful that you should succeed. Our good John Spaniard hates Jews—he despises heretics. To him they are a foolish remnant. They prosper abominably; they are patient, unwarlike, easily plundered. Yet they take it upon themselves to offend the eye by their unnecessary industry. A striped blanket in the shade, a little wine, a little gossip—and in these later times, since blessed Ferdinand, a good rollicking *auto de fé* once a week. These suffice him when the King does not call our Spaniard to war. They are the very 'bread-and-bull-fights' for which he cried when he was yet a Roman and a citizen. But in France and in England—even in Italy we must act otherwise. We attain our end just the same, but without noise. Only one man somewhere, with a clear brain and an arm that will not fail, drives a knife—or, when all backs are turned, inverts the bottom of a poison phial. He gains the martyr's crown, skips Purgatory with a bound, and finds himself in Paradise!"

The little grey Neapolitan blinked owlishly at Mariana. He was growing sleepy, and with all his soul he wished this too-wise man would be silent. But being applied to, he thought it was safer to agree.

"Certainly—certainly," he said, "it is the same in Italy."

"In Italy—not quite, my friend," said Mariana; "your needs are scarcely the same. With you, cup-and-dagger are as common as—fleas, and as little thought of. You have means (literally) to your hand! But here we have to manufacture them, put spirit into them, send them out on their mission as only we of the Gesù can do."

The Jesuit of Toledo paused a little in his argument, turning his eyes from one to the other.

"As to this little matter," he said, again tapping the Papal Bull with his finger-nail, "I have a man who will execute His Holiness's will—in your national manner, my good Tullio. Only first, he would have a mandate from the Holy Office, a sort of safe-conduct for his soul—the promise of absolution for breaking his vow against the shedding of blood. He is, I must tell you, a little Dominican of Sens, presently misbehaving himself in the mother-college of St. Jacques at Paris. But he is good material for all that, properly handled."

Teruel spoke with the natural caution of the peasant.

"But," said he, "we will be held responsible if aught goes amiss; our duty here is difficult enough! The King——"

"The King I will take in my own hand," said Mariana. "I warrant you his fullest protection, and approval. You shall have great favour—perhaps even be moved to Seville or Granada, or some other place where Jews, Moriscos, and heretics are frequent and rich. Write me the paper and seal it with the seal official!"

So with his Papal Bull and an order from the chiefs of the Holy Office, assembled in council at the nearest accessible point, Mariana withdrew to his bed, and none in all the Street of the Money slept sounder than he that night, though when he opened the window to let in a breath of the cool, moist air off the Tet, the prayers of the prisoners could be heard coming up in moaning gusts from the dungeons beneath.

The machinery set in motion by the Jesuit Mariana revolved stately, wheel within his wheel. The "young Dominican of Sens," delivering himself to a strange but not unusual mixture of fanaticism and debauch, misspent his days with the rabble of Paris, his evenings in listening to the fair speeches and yet fairer promises of Madame de Montpensier, the Duke of Guise's sister, while all night mysterious voices whispered in the darkness of his cell that he was the chosen of God, the approved, and that if he, Jacques Clement, would only kill the King, angels would immediately waft his body, safe and unseen, to the quiet of his convent.

Had he not heard the Bull of the Pope read by the Father Superior? Had the Holy Office not promised him immunity, nay, even canonisation—had not Madame de Montpensier——? But enough, Jacques Clement, riotous monk of Sens, sat him down and made his dagger like a needle for sharpness, like a mirror for polish. This he did when he should have been reading his breviary in the monastery of the Dominicans in the Rue Saint-Jacques.

So it came to pass that on the evening of the third day of August, 1589, Jean-aux-Choux, still wearing his great shepherd's cloak, though all Perpignan city panted in the fervent heat, and the cool water of the Tet reeked against the sun-heated banks, stood again at the door of that gloomy house in the Street of the Money.

Above, the three men waited as before. But this time there was no hesitation about admittance, not even a question asked. The three men who had done a great thing far away, without lifting one of their little fingers, now waited, tense with anxiety—not for themselves, for no one of them cared for his own safety, but to know that they had won the game for their Church and cause.

To them Jean-aux-Choux opened his mouth.

"He is dead!" he announced, solemnly—"Henry of Valois is dead! The siege of Paris is raised. Epernon and the great lords have refused to serve a Huguenot king. They have gone home——"

"And the Bearnais—the Bearnais?" interrupted Mariana hoarsely, "what of him?"

"I saw him ride sadly away—the White Scarves only following!"

Then for once, at the crowning moment of his life, Mariana, the smiling Jesuit, leaned face-forward on the table. His strength had gone from him.

"Enough," he said, "I have done the Society's will. But so great success even I had not hoped for!"

And he rocked himself to and fro in that terrible crisis of nervous emotion which comes only to the most self-restrained, while Teruel, the Surintendant of the Holy Inquisition, and Frey Tullio his second, were prodigal of their cares, lavishing restoratives, of which (in virtue of their office) they had great store in the Street of the Money.

None minded Jean-aux-Choux, or even thanked him. But he, seeing a parchment with a familiar name written upon it, the ink scarcely dry, and as a paper-weight the seal of the Holy Office ready to append to it, coolly pocketed both seal and mandate.

It was a warrant to the familiars of the Holy Office in the city of Perpignan to seize the body of one Claire Agnew, a known and warrantable heretic, presently residing at the house of La Massane near Collioure, and to bring her within the prisons of the aforesaid Inquisition in the Street of the Money, in the city above mentioned, within ten days at most from that date—upon peril of their several lives, and of the lives of all that should defend, aid, assist, or shelter the said Claire Agnew, heretic, daughter of François of that name, plotter, spy, and Calvinist.

Followed the signs and signatures of the two inquisitors in charge—to wit, Teruel and Tullio. The name of Mariana did not anywhere appear.

"Ten days," muttered Jean-aux-Choux, when he had read it over; "that gives us time. And there"—he heaved the seal of the Holy Office into the Tet—"they will have to get one made. That will be another length to our tether!"

CHAPTER XXXI
THE WAY OF THE SALT MARSHES

The shore road from Perpignan to Collioure is a pass, dark and perilous, even on an August night. But Jean-aux-Choux trod it with the assured foot of one to whom the night is as the day. He had, as the people of Collioure asserted, been assuredly witch-born. Now to be "witch-born" may induce spiritual penalties hereafter, but, from all purely earthly points of view, it is a good thing. For then you have cat's eyes and can walk through black night as though it were noonday. Concerning this, however, Jean did not trouble himself. He considered himself well-born, well-baptised, one of the elect, and, therefore, perfectly prepared—a great thing when it is your lot to walk in the midst of many sudden deaths—for whatever the future might bring. He was turning over in his mind ways and means of getting Claire across the frontier—not very greatly troubled, because, first of all, there was the ten days' grace, and though the Inquisition would doubtless have watchers posted about the house, he, Jean-aux-Choux, could easily outwit them.

So he traversed the desolate flats between Perpignan and Elne, across which wild bulls were then permitted to range. Indeed, they came at times right up to the verge of the vineyards, which cultivators were just beginning to hedge from their ravages with the strange spike-leaved plant called the Fig of the Moors. But Jean-aux-Choux had no fear of anything that walked upon four feet. He carried his long shepherd's staff with the steel point to it, trailing behind him like a pike. And though, rounding the salt marshes and *étangs* or "stanks," there came to his ears the crooning of the herds, muttering discontentedly in their sleep with bovine noises, the sharp click of horns that tossed and interlocked in their effort to dislodge the mosquitoes, the sludgy splash of broad hooves in the wallows, the crisp snap of the salt crust, like thin ice breaking—for all which things Jean-aux-Choux cared nothing. Of course, his trained ear took in all these noises, registering, classifying, and drawing deductions from them. But he never once even raised his pointed staff, nor changed his direction. Perhaps the shepherd's cloak deceived the animals, or more likely the darkness of the night. For ordinarily it is death to venture there, save on horseback, and armed with the trident of Camargue. Once or twice he shouldered two or three bulls this way and that, pushing them over as one who grooms horses in their stalls after the labours of the day.

But all the time his thoughts were on the paths by which he would carry off his master's daughter, Claire Agnew, and set her in safety on the soil of free, if stormy, France, where the Inquisition had no power—nor was likely to have so long as the Bearnais lived, and the old-time phalanx of the Calvinists, D'Aubigné, Rosny, Turenne, and the rest stood about him.

Once or twice he thought, with some exultation, of the dead Valois. For, if Guise had been the moving spirit and bloody executioner of Saint Bartholomew, this same Henry of Valois, who had died at St. Cloud, had been the chief plotter—rather, say, the second—for Catherine, his mother, the Medicean woman, had assuredly been the first. For all he had done personally, Jean had no care, no remorse. As to the deed of Jacques Clement, he himself would not have slain an ally of the Bearnais. But, after all, it was justice, that the priest should slay the priest-ridden, and that the fanatic monk should slay the founder of the Order of the Penitents.

Altogether, Jean-aux-Choux had a quiet mind as he went. Above him, and somewhat to his left hand, hung a black mass, which was the rock-set town of Elne on its look-out hill. Highest of all loomed the black, shadowy mass of its cathedral, with the towers cutting a fantastic pattern against the skies.

Then came again the cultivated fields, hedges, ditches, the spiked *agavé* dykes, over which he swung, using his long staff for a leaping-pole—again the salt marshes, and lastly, the steep shingle and blown sand of the sea.

Here the waves fell with a soft and cooling sound. Twenty miles of heavy, grey-black salt water, the water of the Midland sea, statedly said "Hush" to the stars.

Jean stopped and listened. There was no need for haste. Ten days, and the task would need thinking over—how to get her, by Salses, to Narbonne, where there was good French authority, and the protection of the great lords of his own party. But he would succeed. He knew it. He had never failed yet.

So Jean was at peace. The stars looked down, blinking sleepily through various coloured prisms. The sea said so. You heard the wavelet run along the shore, and the "Hush" dying out infinitesimally, as the world's clamour dies into the silence of space.

But Jean-aux-Choux would have been a little less at ease, and put a trifle more powder into his heels, had he known that the warrant of the Holy

Office which he carried in his pocket was only a first draft, and that the actual document was already in the hands of the familiars, to be executed at their peril. Also, that in this there was no question of days, either of ten or any other number. The acolytes of the Black Robe had a free hand.

The morning was coming up, all peach and primrose, out of the East, reddening the port-waters of Collioure, and causing the white house of La Masane, up on its hill, to blush, when Jean-aux-Choux leaped the wall of his own sheepfold, and came suddenly upon a figure he knew well.

He saw a young man, bare of head, his steel cap, velvet-covered and white-plumed, resting on a low turf dyke. He had laid aside his weapons, all except his dagger, and with that he was cultivating and cherishing his finger-nails. His heel was over the knee of his other leg, in that pose which the young male sex can only attain with grace between the ages of twenty and twenty-five.

"Hallo, Jean-aux-Choux!" he cried. "Here have I been waiting you for hours and hours unnumbered. Is this the way you keep your master's sheep? If I were that most scowling nobleman of the castle down there, I would soon bid you travel. If it had not been for me, your sheep would have been sore put to it for a mouthful, and the nursing ewes certainly dead of thirst. Where have you been all these three days?"

"The Abbé John—the little D'Albret!" cried Jean-aux-Choux, thoroughly surprised for once in his life; "how do you come here?"

"I have been on my master's business," answered the Abbé John carelessly, "and now I am waiting to do a little on my own account. But there have been so many suspicious gentry about, that I hesitated to go down till I had seen you. Now tell me all that has happened. That SHE is safe, I know; I have seen her every day—from a distance!"

"She—who?" asked Jean, though he knew very well.

"Who—why Claire, of course," said the cousin of the Bearnais; "you do not suppose I came so far to see the little old woman in the blue pinafore, who walks nodding her head and rattling her keys? Or you, you great, thick-skulled oaf of Geneva, or the Sorbonnist with the bald head and the eyes that look and see nothing? What should a young man come so far for, and risk his life to see, if not a fair young girl? Answer me. What did John Calvin teach you as to that?"

"Only this," said Jean-aux-Choux solemnly; "'From the lust of the flesh, from the lust of the eye, from the pride of life, good Lord deliver me!'"

The young man looked up from his nail-polishing, sharply and keenly.

"Aye—so," he said. "Well—and did He?"

For a moment, but only for a moment, Jean-aux-Choux stood nonplussed. Then he found his answer, and this time it was John Stirling, armiger, scholar in divinity, who spoke.

"The God of John Calvin has delivered me from all thought of self in the matter of this maid, my master's daughter. What might have grown up in my heart, or even what may once have been in my heart, had I been aught but a battered masque of humanity, an offence to the beauty of God's creation—that is not your business, nor that of any man!"

The young fellow dropped his knife, and rising, clasped Jean-aux-Choux frankly about the neck.

"Jean—Jean—old friend," he cried, "wherefore should I hurt you? Why should you think it of me? Not for the world—you know that well. Forgive an idle word."

But Jean-aux-Choux was moved, and having the large heart, when once the waves tossed it, the calm returned but slowly.

"Sir," he said, "it is only a few months since you first saw Claire Agnew. Yet you have, as I judge from your light words, admired her after your kind. But I—I have loved her as my own maid—my sole thought, my only—ever since her father gathered me up, a lame and bleeding boy, on the morning after the Bartholomew. And ever since that day I have loved much, showed little, and said nothing at all. Yet I have kept keen guard. Night and day I have gone about her house, like a faithful dog when the wolves are howling in the forests. Now, if you love this girl with any light love, take your way as you came—for you shall have to reckon with me!"

The Abbé John dropped back on the round stone which served equally as seat and rubbing-post in the sheepfold. The oil off many woolly backs had long since rendered it black and glistening. He resumed the polishing of his nails with his dagger-edge.

Grave and stem, Jean-aux-Choux stood before him, his hand on the weapon which had slain the Guise. The Abbé John rubbed each finger-nail carefully on the velvet of his cap as he finished it, breathed on it, rubbed again, and then held it up to the light.

"Ah, Jean," he said at last, "I may not go about her house howling like a wolf, nor yet do any great thing for her. As you say, our acquaintance has not been long. But if you can love her more than I, or serve her better, or are willing to give your life more lightly for her sake than I—why then, Jean, my friend, you are welcome to her!"

Jean-aux-Choux did not answer, but D'Albret took no heed. He went on:

"'By their deeds ye shall know them. They taught you that at Geneva, I warrant. Well, from what I have seen these past three days, Claire Agnew is far from safe down there. I have watched that black-browed master of yours conferring with certain other gentlemen of singularly evil physiognomy. There has been far too much dodging into coppices and popping heads round stone walls. And then, as often as the maid comes to the door with the little old woman in the stomacher of blue—click—they are all in their holes again, like a warren-full of rabbits when you look over the hedge and clap your hands! I do not like it, Jean-aux-Choux!"

Neither did Jean-aux-Choux—so little, indeed, that he decided to take this light-minded young gentleman, of good family and few ambitions, into his confidence—which, perhaps, was the wisest thing he could have done. From his blouse he drew the parchment he had lifted off the table of the Inquisition in the Street of the Money, and thrust it silently into the other's hand.

This was all Jean-aux-Choux's apology, but, for the Abbé John, it was perfectly sufficient.

CHAPTER XXXII
IN THEIR CLUTCHES

It was the night of the grand *coup* which was to ease Master Raphael Llorient of all his troubles financial, and also to put an acknowledged heretic within the clutches of these two faithful servants of the Holy Office, Dom Ambrose Teruel and his second, Frey Tullio the Neapolitan.

The affair had been carried out with the utmost zeal, and though at first success had seemed more than doubtful, the familiars of the Office had pounced upon their victim walking calmly towards them down a little hollow among the sand-dunes.

At La Masane, it appeared to them that an alarm had been given, and that, as little Andrés the ape expressed it, "the whole byre had broken halter and run for it."

The familiars were hard on the track, however, and the way from La Masane to the beach is no child's playground when the nights are dark as the inside of a wolf. Serra, Calbet, and Andrés Font were three sturdy rascals, condemned to long terms of imprisonment, who had obtained freedom from their penalties on condition of faithfully serving the Holy Inquisition. They were all nearly, though vaguely, related to prominent ecclesiastics, the warmth of whose family feelings had obtained this favour for them.

They had, therefore, every reason for satisfying their masters. For pardon frequently followed zeal, and the ex-culprit and ex-familiar was permitted to return in the halo of a terrible sanctity to his native village. There were not a few, however, whom the craft ended by fascinating. And after in vain trying the cultivation of crops and the pruning of vines, lo! they would be back again at the door of the Holy Office, begging to be taken in, if it were only to be hewers of wood and drawers of water for the *auto de fé* and the water-torture.

Of the present three, Serra, a Murcian from these half-depopulated villages where the Moors once dwelt, alone was of this type. A huge man with a low forehead, a great shapeless face like a clenched fist, with little twinkling pigs' eyes set deep under hairless brows, he did his work for the love of it. He it was who saw to it that no harm befel the prisoner on the long night-ride to Perpignan. It was a dainty capture, well carried out. Since the wholesale emigration of the Jews of Roussillon to Bayonne in the West, the *auto de fé* of the East was usually shamed for want of pretty young maids. These always attracted the crowd more than anything, and Serra the Murcian bared his teeth at the thought. In his way he admired Claire Agnew. From various hiding-places he had watched her many days ere his superiors judged that all was ready. Now he would do his best for her. She should have the highest, the middle pile, which is honour. Also, Serra the Murcian would see to it that her bonfire contained no sea-grass or juniper rootlets, which blazed indeed, but only scorched; neither any wet, sea-borne wood from wrecked ships, which smoked and sulked, but would not burn. No—he, Serra, would do the thing for her in gentlemanly fashion as became a hidalgo of Murcia. The pretty heretic should have clear dry birch, one year old, with olive roots aged several hundreds, all mixed with shavings and pine cones, and a good top-dressing of oil like a salad to finish all. And then (the Murcian showed his teeth and gums in a vast semi-African grin, like a trench slashed out of a melon), well—she would have reason to be proud of herself.

The pillar of clear flame would rise above Claire's head ten—nay, twenty feet, wrapping her about like a garment. She would have no long time to suffer. He was a kind-hearted man, this Serra the Murcian—that is, to those to whom he had taken a fancy, as was the case with Claire. If any torture was commanded, either the Lesser or the Greater Question, he would make it light. It would never do to spoil her beauty against the Great Day! What, after all, did they know, these two wise men in black who only sat on their chairs and watched? It was the familiars who made or marred in the House of Pain—indeed, Serra himself, for he could destroy the others with a word. They had accepted bribes from relatives—he never.

They mounted Claire on the notary's white mule, the sometime gift of the Bishop of Elne. Ah, Serra chuckled, Don Jordy would ride it no more. It would be his—Serra's. He would sell the beast and send the money to his old mother who lived in a disused oven cut out of the rocks near the Castle of the Moors, three leagues or so from Murcia city. She was an affectionate old lady—he the best of sons. It was a shame they should have miscalled her for a witch, when all she ever did was to provide those who desired a blank in their families, or in those of their neighbours, with a certain fine white powder.

Serra himself had been observed stirring a little in some soup at the mansion where he was employed as cook. So, only for that, they had sent him to work as a slave in the mines. But a certain powerful friend of his mother's, who lived in the lonely abbey out on the plain, near the great water-wheel (Serra remembered the dashing of the water in his babyhood before he could remember anything else), got him this good place with Dom Teruel, who had been his comrade of the seminary. And so now his mother was safe—aye, if she sold her fine white meal openly like so much salt. For who in all Murcia would touch the mother of a First Familiar of the Holy Office. They reverenced her more—much more—than the village priest who held the keys of heaven and hell—for, after all, these were far away things.

But the Holy Office—ah, that was another matter. None spake of that either above or below their breaths, from one end of Spain to the other.

So Serra the Murcian communed with himself, and with only an occasional tug at the ropes that bound his captive to the white mule of Don Jordy, he continued his way, rejoiced in heart.

But the other two, ordinary criminals with but little influence, contented themselves with hoping for the freedom of the broad champaign, the arid treeless plains of old Castile, the far-running sweeps of golden corn, the crowded *ventas* with their gay Bohemian company, the shouted songs, and above all, the cool gurgle of wine running down thirsty, dust-caked throats—ah! it would be good. And it might come soon, if only they served the Holy Office well!

Both of them hated and despised Serra, because of his place, his zeal, and especially because of his favour with the Surintendant.

The senior of the two underlings, Felieu Calbet, from the Llogrebrat (Espluga the name of the town, where they are always fighting and every one lives on the charity of the fathers of Poblet), was ill at ease, and said as much to Andrés Font, a little lithe creature with a monkey's hands and temper, treacherous and vile, as a snake that writhes and bites in the dust.

These two were trudging behind, their long Albacete knives in their hands, ready for any attempt to escape. But the tall young maid sat steady on the broad back of Don Jordy's white mule. She said no word. She uttered no plaint.

Said Felieu Calbet of Espluga, senior familiar, to little wizened Andrés, third of the band, "Our brave Serra is content. Hear him! He is humming his Moorish charms—the accursed wizard that he is! But for me, I am not so sure that all goes well. They let that lass go somewhat too easily—eh, Andrés?"

And the little ape-faced man, first sliding his dagger into its sheath as they emerged upon an open rocky bit of road with a few tall stone-pines all leaning back from the sea-winds, answered after his fashion, biting his words maliciously as he uttered them.

"Yea, belike," he muttered; "indeed, it was a strange thing that within five hundred yards of the sea, where they had their boat anchored ready, they should not turn and fight for the prisoner. How many were there of them, think you, Felieu?"

"Four I saw—and there might have been another. One cowered in the hood of a cloak, as if he feared that his face would be seen——"

"That makes five, and we but three! The thing smells of an ambush. Well, all we have to do is to be ready, and, if need be, fight like the Demon of the South himself. It is our prisoner or the stake for you and me, my lad!"

The little, ape-faced, bat-eared Andrés, who had never told any what he had been sent there for, was arguing the matter out by himself.

"There is something behind this," he said; "they have a card somewhere we have not seen the front of."

They marched a while, the silence only broken by the fall of the mule's feet on the stones.

"I have it," cried Andrés, suddenly elevating his thin voice above a whisper. It was only a squeak at best, but it aroused the First Familiar from his dreams of honour at the mule's bridle.

"Silence there, you Andrés," he commanded, "or by Saint Vincent I will wring your neck!"

"Wring my neck! He dares not," snarled the little wrinkled man, with an evil grin, in the darkness—"he dares not, big as he is, and he knows it. He would find a dozen inches of steel ensconced between his ribs. If I am no bigger than an ox-goad, I am burnt at the end, and can drive home a sharp point with any man."

"Do not mind the hog," said Felieu the Esplugan. "What was it you thought of?"

"That Don Raphael Llorient was out with a band of his lads from the Castle of Collioure. Doubtless he headed them off from the boat, and they had to save themselves as best they might. So they scattered among the sand-hills!"

"Hum, perhaps—we shall see," said Felieu the Esplugan. "At any rate, keep your eyes open and your knife ready to the five-finger grip. We must kill, rather than let her go. You know the rule."

Indeed, they all knew the rule. No relaxation of the Arm Spiritual till the culprit, arrayed in the flame-coloured robe of condemnation, was ready for the final relaxation to the Arm Secular.

All the same, there was no slightest attempt at rescue, and in the early hours of the morning the procession defiled into the city gates of Perpignan, which opened freely at all hours to the familiars of the Holy Office—the guard discreetly keeping their eyes on the ground. And so the four, in the same order as at first, turned sharply into the Street of the Money.

Serra, the huge, fist-faced Murcian, with the blood of Africa in him, carefully undid the bonds, and hoped, with a Spaniard's innate politeness, that they had not too greatly incommoded his guest. But the "guest" answered not a word.

"Sulky, eh?" muttered the Murcian, equally ready to take offence. "Very well, then, so much the worse!"

And he resolved to save the expense of the oil for Claire's funeral pyre. He had meant to go out of his way to do the thing in style. But with such a haughty dame—and she a Huguenot, one of the Accursed, no more a Christian than any Jew—why should she give herself airs? The thing was intolerable!

In this, Serra the Murcian, First Familiar of the Holy Inquisition, followed the Golden Rule. He did literally as he would be done by. If it had been his fate (and with a reliable witch for a mother it was no far-away conjecture)—if it had been his own fortune to die at the stake, he would have been grateful for the highest seat, the dryest wood, the tallest pillar of flame, the happiest despatch with all modern improvements. He resented it, therefore, when Claire Agnew showed herself ungrateful for the like.

Well, he had done his duty. The worse for her. Like Pilate, he washed his hands.

But such emotions as these he soon forgot. He had reason.

For above, in the accustomed bare room, with only the crucifix upon whitewashed walls, the same three men were waiting anxiously for the arrival of the prisoner.

The little band of familiars, having handed over the white mule to a trusty subordinate, came up the stairs, and after giving the customary knock, and being answered in the deep voice of Dom Teruel, they stood blinking in the glare of the lights, their prisoner in the midst.

There was silence in the room—a great fateful silence. Then the soft voice of Mariana the Jesuit broke the pause.

"And who, good Serra, may this be that you have brought us?"

"Why," said Serra, greatly astonished, "who but the lady I have been watching all these weeks, the Genevan heretic, the Señorita from the house of La Masane above Collioure. We overtook her in flight, and captured her among the sand-dunes on the very edge of the sea!"

"Ah, the Señorita?" purred the Jesuit; "then is the Señorita fitted with a nascent but very tolerable pair of moustacios!"

Serra stared a moment, tore off the cloak with its heavy hood, clutched at the lighter summer mantilla of dark lace and silk. It ripped and tore vertically, and lo! as a butterfly issues from the chrysalis, forth stepped the Abbé John, clad in pale blue velvet from head to knee, as for a court reception.

He bowed gracefully to the company, twisted his moustache, folded his arms, and waited.

CHAPTER XXXIII
AND ONE WAS NOT!

And this was how it chanced. All that was hidden from Serra, the fist-faced son of a Murcian witch, from Felieu, the querulous Esplugan, and from Andrés, the little ape with the bat's ears, shall be made clear.

With one exception, the family of La Masane was resolved to go back to France, where, if the country was still disturbed, at least there was no Inquisition.

"I," said the Professor, "know not whether I shall ever teach in my class-room again—not, at least, while the Leaguers bear rule in Paris. But I have a little money laid aside in a safe place, which will at least buy us a vineyard— —"

"And I," said the Miller-Alcalde, "have enough gold Henries, safe with Pereira, the Jew of Bayonne, to hire a mill or two. Good bread and well-ground wheat wherewith to make it, are the two things that man cannot do without. I can provide these, if no better."

"And what better can there be?" cried Don Jordy. "I—I am learned in canon law, which is the same all the world over. I grieve to leave my good Bishop Onuphre. But since he cannot protect me—nay, goes as much in fear of the Holy Office as I myself—Brother Anatole must e'en hire me by the day in his vigne, or Jean-Marie there make me as dusty as himself in his mills."

"And your mother, lads, have you forgotten her?" said Madame Amélie.

"You are coming with us, mother," they cried, in chorus, "you and Claire. It is for you that we go!"

"And pray you, who will care for my rabbits, my poultry, and the pigeons? All the *basse cour* of La Masane?" cried the Señora.

"That also will be arranged, mother," said Don Jordy. "I will put in a man who will care for all, till the better days come—a servant and favourite of Don Raphael. This inquisitioning and denouncing cannot last for ever—any more than Raphael our landlord or Philip our king."

"Ah," said his mother, "but both of them are like to last beyond my time. And the fair white house to which your father brought me, a bride! And the sea—on which, being weary, I have so often looked out and been refreshed—the cattle and the vines and the goats I tended—am I to see them no more?"

"Mother," said the Professor, taking her hand and drawing it away from her face, "here are we your three sons. We can neither stay nor leave you. They of the Inquisition would revenge on you all that we have cheated them of—taken out of their hands."

"They are welcome to my old bones," said the Señora, with a gesture of discouragement.

"No," interrupted Don Jordy, "listen, mother. You are none so ill off. Here are we, three sons, hale, willing, and unwed, all ready to stand by you, and to work for you—with our hands if need be. Are there many mothers who can say as much?"

"Besides," added the Alcalde-Miller, "after all, it is not so far to the frontier, and, in case of need, I have charged certain good lads I know of—accustomed to circumvent the King's revenue—to make a clean house of La Masane. So if aught goes awry—well, I do not promise, but it is possible that the cattle, and your household gods, mother, with Don Jordy's books and the Professor's green gown, may find themselves at Narbonne ere many weeks are over!"

"And for yourself?" said Don Jordy, "your mills, your property?"

The miller laughed and patted his two brothers on the back.

"The good God, who made all, perhaps did not give me so clever a head-piece as He gave you two. But He taught me, at least, to send every gold 'Henry' over the frontier as soon as I had another to clink against it. For the rest, ever as I ground the corn, I took my pay. The mills and the machinery down there are not mine. I am worth no more this side of the frontier than the clothes I stand up in. My ancient friend Pereira, the Israelite of Bayonne, has the rest."

So that is the reason why, when the three familiars of the Holy Office appeared hot on the trail, they found at La Masane nothing more human than Don Jordy's white mule, that knew no better than to resist friendly hands, break a head-stall, and set off after her master, to her own present undoing.

But what happened when the family of La Masane started for the shore, where Jean-Marie, on his way home from the Fanal Mill, had anchored the boat? As he worked his heart was more than a little sore that he should no more hear that musical song, the tremulous rush of the sails overhead, or the blithe pour of the rich meal through the funnel into the sack. Best of all he loved the Fanal Mill, both because the sea-water lashed up blue-green beneath, and because from the door he could see Claire's white dress moving about the garden of La Masane.

This was their plan.

To place Claire in safety was no difficulty. The light land-breezes would carry them swiftly along the shore towards the Narbonne coast. It was in Madame Amélie that the brothers found their stumbling-block. Not that the good old lady, so imperious upon her own ground of La Masane, meant in the least to be difficult. But she felt uprooted, degraded, fallen from her high estate, divorced from her own, and she trembled piteously as she tottered on stout Jean-Marie's arm down towards the beach.

Two days before Jean-aux-Choux had brought the Abbé John to La Masane. At first no one, certainly not Claire, appeared to make him particularly welcome. The Professor retrieved some of his old professorial authority. Don Jordy was frankly jealous. Old Madame Amélie found him finicking and fine. Only the burly Miller-Alcalde drew to the lad, and tried in his gruff, semi-articulate way to make the young Gascon understand that, in spite of his Bourbon birth and Paris manners, he had a friend in the house of La Masane. And this the young man understood very well, and repaid accordingly. He understood many things, the Abbé John—all, indeed, except Claire Agnew's coldness. But even that he took philosophically.

"He who stands below the cherry-tree with his mouth open, expecting the wind to blow the cherries into his mouth, waits a long time hungry," he meditated sententiously; "I will shake the trees and gather."

All the same, the rough grip and kindly "Come-and-help," or "Stand-out-of-the-way" manner of the miller went to his heart. Indeed, he could hardly have kept his ground at La Masane without it, and he was grateful in proportion.

"They think little of me because I look young and my hair curls," he muttered, as he tried in vain to smooth it out with abundant water, "but wait—I will show them!"

And the time for showing them came when Jean-aux-Choux, carefully scouting ahead, thrust his head over a bank of gravel and reported several men in possession of the boat which Jean-Marie had so carefully anchored in the little Fanal Bay just round the point out of sight of the Castle. Worst of all, one of the captors was Don Raphael Llorient himself.

Almost at the same moment, the last individual rear-guard of the little party, a slim young lad called in this chronicle the Abbé John, discovered that they were being tracked from behind. They had indeed walked into the sack without a hole at the other end. They stood between two fires. For they had on their hands good old Madame Amélie, ready at the first discouragement to sink down on the sand, and give up all for lost.

He dared not therefore speak openly. Cautiously the Abbé John called the miller to his side, and imparted his discovery.

"A quarter of an hour at the most, and they will have us!" he whispered.

"Umm!" said the Miller-Alcalde. "I suppose we could not—eh—you and I? What think you? I can strike a good buffet and you with your point! Are you ready?"

"Ready enough," said the Abbé John, "but they would call out at the first sight of us—indeed, either crack of pistol or clash of sword would bring up Don Raphael and his folk. We must think of something else. For men it might do, but there is your mother to consider—and Claire!"

"I wish it had been the bare steel—or else the cudgel," said the miller; "I am no hand at running and plotting!"

But the Abbé John was.

"Here," he said abruptly, stripping the silk-lined cloak from his shoulders, "take that. Get me Claire's lace mantilla and her wrapper with the capuchin hood. I have made a good enough maid before at the revels of carnival. They always chose me to act Joan of Domremy at the Sorbonne on Orleans Day. It is Claire they are after. Moreover, they are in a hurry. Be quick—bid her give them to you. But tell her nothing!"

And so the blunt Alcalde-Miller went up to Claire, who was busily supplying consolation to Madame Amélie.

"Your lace mantilla," he said, "your cloak and hood! Quick—we have need of them!" he said abruptly. "Take this."

Now Claire had served too long an apprenticeship to dangers and strange unexplained demands during her father's wanderings to show any surprise. She put them on the miller's arm without a single question. It was only when he added, "Now—put this on," and threw the silken court-cloak belonging to the Abbé John over her shoulders, that she stammered something.

"This—why this—is—is——"

"Never mind what it is," growled the Miller-Alcalde; "at any rate, it will not bite you, and you may need it before the night is out!"

And so without a good-bye—only just settling the lace mantilla as becomingly as possible upon his head and drawing the waist-ribbon of the girl's cloak close round his middle, the Abbé John, with a wave of his hand and a low-spoken "Take good care of her" to the miller, sauntered carelessly back through the maze of sand-hills in the direction of these three good and faithful bloodhounds of the Holy Inquisition, Felieu the Esplugan, Andrés the Ape, and the giant Serra of the African smile, who loved his work for his work's sake.

And between his teeth John d'Albret muttered these words, "I will show them."

Also once, just when he came within hearing of the stealthy creep of the pursuers, he added, "And I will show her!"

He did. For when next Claire Agnew looked back, the One for whom she looked was not.

CHAPTER XXXIV
BISHOP, ARCHBISHOP, AND
ANGELICAL DOCTOR

At sight of his master in the boat Jean-aux-Choux turned sharply to the left. Obviously they must try elsewhere. The way of the sea was shut to them in front; the enemy was clearly awake and waiting for them there. The net behind had not had time to be drawn tight, and if the Abbé John proved successful in deceiving the familiars of the Holy Office, it would not close. Still, there was every reason for haste. There was no disguising that fact.

Passing behind the town walls as swiftly as might be, with the burden of Madame Amélie in their arms, Jean-aux-Choux halted the brothers for a while in lee of a sheepfold with walls high enough for a fort. Then, passing within, he appeared presently with two poles and a piece of sacking, out of which he extemporised a carrying hammock. He and his comrades used it for carrying down to their huts and shelters such wounded sheep or weakly lambs as they found high up among the mountains, that they might be tended back to health again.

The Señora was a little woman—a mere "rickle of bones," in Jean's Scottish phrase, and hardly heavier than a stout six months' lamb. Indeed, so much had the flesh faded under the strain of her constant activity, that the restless spirit within seemed to pulse and throb under the frail envelope like a new-taken bird.

Jean-aux-Choux took the head. The brothers relieved each other at the feet—that is to say, the Miller-Alcalde and Don Jordy. After one attempt, the Professor acknowledged that the chair of the Sorbonne had unfitted him for such exercise upon the mountains.

They crossed the Elne road only a few minutes before the familiars, with the false maid mounted on Don Jordy's white mule, went past peaceably, trekking their way towards Perpignan and the Street of the Money.

It was clearly unsafe to continue. Yet what else to do? They crouched behind a pillar-rock (what in Celtic lands of Ker and Pol and Tre would have been a menhir) and listened. There came the sound of hoofs, the jingle of a bridle. A white shape skirted with well-accustomed feet the phosphorescent glimmer of the path, wet with dew, and wimpling upwards towards the summit of the cape.

"My mule—the bishop's mule," muttered Don Jordy. "Oh, the villains! Food for the *garrotte!*"

Then he comforted himself with thoughts of vengeance.

"Monseigneur will make them deliver," he growled to himself, "for White Chiquita's pretty sake if not for that of his poor notary. He does not greatly love the Inquisition at any time. He believes, and with justice, that it is they and the Jesuits who are striving to take the see-episcopal from ancient Elne, the Illiberris of the ancients, and give it to Perpignan— *champignon* rather, the mushroom growth of a night."

But Don Jordy's very anathema had given him an idea.

"What if it were possible—that Monseigneur would—yes, he has great power in what is hidden from the Holy Office. He could keep my mother safe in his palace till we have the girl in safety. I believe he would do it for me, his notary and registrar, who have always served both him and the see with fidelity."

In a low voice he made his proposition to his companions. They should all go to Elne. He, Don Jordy, would make his way into the palace of my Lord Bishop. He had the key to a door in the base of the rock, giving upon stairs that turned and turned till one was almost giddy.

There they would leave Madame Amélie till happier times. In a *tablier* of white, she might well and naturally bear rule in the episcopal kitchen, of which the waste and expense had long been a byword.

To this Jean-aux-Choux at first objected. It were best to hasten. All who were under the ban of the Holy Office must get out of Roussillon altogether. It was no place for them. For him it was different, of course. None suspected him. He had his sheep to attend to. For the present his comrade did what was necessary, believing him employed on his master's business. Also, if he were to succour and protect the abandoned bestial and poultry-yard, dear to the Señora, he must return as swiftly as possible.

Finally, however, he also was brought to see reason.

Indeed, the growing weakness of the old lady seriously disquieted every one. So much so, indeed, that Don Jordy went on ahead as soon as the black mass of Elne hunched itself up against the faint pearl-grey sheet which was hung behind the sand-dunes of Argelés, on the way of the sea.

Grey, pallid day was beginning to break when he returned, having seen and heard great things.

At first the night-watchman of the little palace had hesitated to intrude upon the Bishop, who, he said, had company—no other than the learned Doctor Ange de Pas, so learned that he scrupled not to enter into dispute with the Vatican itself, so holy that Sixtus V., at first angered by his stubbornness, finally made a saint of him before his time, because he was the only man who dared to withstand him face to face. "Also," said the watchman, "there was another, who had come from the south with a retinue, now lodged in the cells of the ancient monastery of the Cordeliers."

"His name?" Don Jordy demanded, fearing lest it should be some great missioner of the Inquisition on his rounds, in which case he was lost indeed—and most likely all those who were with him.

"He gave no name," said Leucate the watchman, "and his face was covered. But he knew this place well, and spoke of Fernand Doria, where certain of his chief men could put up, and also of the way to the ancient Convent of the Cordeliers."

This news somewhat reassured Don Jordy, and he bade Leucate carry up his message. He was immediately bidden to enter into the Bishop's private apartments. The good Onuphre de Réart, last Bishop of Elne, was a little smiling man, with a sweet obstinacy in his expression which was not belied by the good fight he had fought with the Inquisition for the privileges of the Church in Roussillon and in the diocese of Elne.

Doctor Ange de Pas was, of course, known to Don Jordy, and rose to give him greeting. But even the holy monk, his hand crisped, as about the quill with which he wrote his many books, showed certain signs of nervousness. The Bishop of Elne held up his hand as if to halt Don Jordy in what he was about to say. Then, going to the purple velvet curtain which divided his audience-chamber from the bedrooms, he announced in a clear, unmistakable voice, "My Lord Cardinal Archbishop!"

Upon which, with smiling dignity, there entered the famous Jean Téres Doria, now Archbishop of Tarragona and Viceroy of all Catalonia, whom the Infanta of Spain had caused to be thus advanced only four years ago, because of his treatment of her as Bishop of Elne when her ship was wrecked on the rocks of Collioure.

"Ah, Don Jorge!" said the great prelate, holding out his hand for the notary to kiss, "you serve early and late, as of yore. Though I think I never saw you in my house quite so belated as this."

Then all suddenly, finding himself in the company of three such good and holy men, all looking so kindly upon him, Don Jordy burst into tears.

The Archbishop Doria stepped quickly up to him, saying, "Don Jordy, friend of mine, you knew me and I knew you, when I was only your neighbour and fellow-student, Jean Téres Doria of Elne. Tell me your sorrow as you would have done, when we fought with burrs and pine-cones in the groves—I for Elne, and you for the honour of Collioure."

"My mother," said Don Jordy, controlling himself with an effort—"she is chased from her house by the familiars of the Holy Office. She and all of us! Only she is old, feeble, pushed beyond her strength. She cannot go farther, and must lie down and die, if the Bishop will not consent to receive her into his palace."

And he went on to tell all the story of the Professor's coming, Don Raphael's suit, and Claire's refusal—lastly, of the warning that had been given concerning the action of the Inquisition.

It could easily be observed how, at that dread name, even the Archbishop grew grave. There was no power comparable to that of the Holy Office in Spain—because the Holy Office was only the King working secretly, doing lawless things under cover of the ample robe of Mother Church.

But the quiet little Cordelier, the Doctor Ange, with his white skin and tremulous bird-like hands, only smiled the sweeter as he listened.

"I fear me," he said, "that the Bishop's palace is too public a place for your mother. Now, what think you? You have with her also your brother, that learned professor of the Sorbonne, with whom it would please me much to ravel out many a tangled web of high doctrine, according to the last interpretation of Paris—why, there is in our new House of the Cordeliers ample room and space for your mother—as well as for your brother, who can don our robe for once in a way. My friends here will doubtless make the matter easier for those of your party continuing their way to the north. Nay, do not thank me. I shall expect much joy from the acquaintance of so learned a man as your brother, though (as I have heard) he mingles too much earthly learning with the pure doctrine of Saint Thomas Aquinas!"

The Archbishop Doria and his successor in the see of Elne, Bishop Onuphre, looked at each other, one taking the other's mind.

"It is perhaps as good a solution as any," said the former meditatively; "however, I judge that you, Don Jorge, had better remain at your post. I see not wherein even the Holy Office can find matter against you. It is a pity that I have no control over its working. The King thinks little of the regular clergy" (at this the little Cordelier laughed). "So that My Lord Cardinal

Archbishop of Toledo, Primate of all Spain, is in the power of the meanest familiar of the Inquisition who may choose to lodge an information against him. Nevertheless, I possess something of the Secular Arm in this province, being for the moment Viceroy of the King. So that, I judge it will be as well—nay, more, it will look well—that you should go about your ordinary business, sending on your party with all speed to the frontier. I will give them a protection under my own hand and seal."

So by this fortunate intervention of the great Doria, Viceroy and Archbishop, our Claire's path was smoothed France-wards, and Madame Amélie rested securely in the newly-built annex of the Convent of the Cordeliers. As to the Professor, her son, he battled daily with Doctor Ange concerning the opinions of the Angelical Doctor—grace free and grace conditional, Arianism and Supra-lapsarianism, till Ange de Pas, who had friends all over the world, produced as a peace-offering the leaves of a certain curious plant, newly brought from the Western Indies, the smoke of which, being drunk through a tube and slowly expelled with the breath, proved a famous composer of quarrels. The plant was called, he said, nicotiana, but was so rare and expensive that, had he not had a friend Commander-in-chief of the forces in New Spain, their philosophic differences might have gone on for ever.

As for the Abbé John, no one knew what had become of him—except, that is, the Miller-Alcalde Jean-Marie, and he answered nothing to Claire's question. Because him also the devil tempted.

CHAPTER XXXV
THE PLACE OF EYES

Two systems were in force in the Street of the Money to convince, to convert, and to change the stubborn will.

One, the A B C of all inquisitors, consisted of the indispensable rack, the attractive pulley with the weights for the feet, the useful hooks, the thumbkins, the red-hot pincers, the oil-bath, and the water-torture. Dom Teruel and Frey Tullio, with the aid of Serra the Murcian, used these as a carpenter uses his tools, coldly, and with method.

But the finer mind of Mariana, working for political ends rather than controverting heresy by mere physical methods, had evolved a more purely moral torture. A chamber had been set apart, to which no least noise, either from the street or from the other guests of the Holy Office, could possibly penetrate. The walls had been specially doubled. Iron door after iron door had to be unlocked before even a familiar could enter. In the space between the walls in every side were spy-holes. Painted eyes looked down from the ceiling, up from the floor. The whole chamber was flooded day and night with the light of lamps set deep in niches, so that the prisoner could not reach them. All that he could ever see was the placing of another light as often as the old burned low.

"There is," Mariana explained the matter to his associates, "a compulsion working in the minds of the well-bred and well-born, of those who have always experienced only pleasantness and happy society, breathed the airs of wood and mountain, known the comradeship of street and class-room and *salle-d'armes*. Such cannot long be without someone to whom to tell their thoughts. For this unclipped gallant, two or three weeks will suffice. He has the gloss still on his wings. Wait a little. I have my own way with such. He will speak. He will tell us both who he is and all he knows! I will turn him inside out like a glove."

"I am not sure," said Teruel, shaking his head; "after the third fainting on the rack, when they see Serra oiling the great wheel—that is what few of them can stand. There is virtue in it. It has a persuasive force—yes, that is the word, a blessed persuasive force, to make the most stubborn abjure heresy and receive the truth!"

The Jesuit smiled, and waved a plump, womanish hand.

"I have a better means, and a surer!" he said, in gentle reproof.

They looked him in the face. But as often as it came to the tug of wills, this smooth, soft-spoken, smiling priest, with his caressing voice, was master. And well they knew it. He also.

"I have a niece," Mariana murmured, "one altogether devoted to the service of the Church and the society. I am, for the present, her nearest parent as well as her spiritual director — —"

"Valentine la Niña?" questioned Teruel. And Frey Tullio said nothing, only Mariana, ever on the watch, caught the oily southern glitter of his eyes, wicked little black pools, with scum on each, like cooling gravy.

"Ay, indeed, Valentine la Niña, even as you say," responded the Jesuit of Toledo calmly; "it is not fair that only men should labour for the good of Holy Church. Did not Mary, the wife of Herod's steward, and that other Mary, minister to the Son of the Holy Virgin? It is so written. If, then, sainted women followed Him in life, watched by His cross, and prepared His body for burial, surely in these evil times, when the Church of Peter trembles on its rock, we, who fight for the faith, have not the right to refuse the ministry of Valentine la Niña or another?"

And so, since Mariana was of Toledo and high in favour with Philip the King, and with the Archbishop Primate of all Spain, besides being more powerful than the General of his own Order, Dom Teruel and Frey Tullio bowed their heads and did as they were commanded.

"Give you the order," said Teruel to Mariana, with a faint, hateful smile, for he would have preferred Serra, a newly-wetted rope, and a slow fire.

But this was by no means Mariana's way.

"I but advise," he said. "How can I do otherwise, a poor Jesuit wanderer, dependent on your bounty for hospitality—I and my niece. I fear I must claim also a place for her here, when she leaves the house and protection of the Countess of Livia."

So into the chamber of light and silence went the Abbé John, after his first examination. He saw around him and above walls and ceilings painted all over with gigantic human eyes—the pupil of each being hollow—and watchers were set continually without, or, at least, the Abbé John thought they were. Within twelve hours he was raging madly about his cell, striving to reach and shiver those watching eyes everywhere about him. He kicked at the inlaid pavements. He tried to tear away from his bed-head and from the foot, those huge, open eyes with the dark, watchful pupils. But his riding-boots had been removed, and with his hempen *alpargatas* he could do nothing. No one took the least notice of his cries. Even the walls seemed echoless and dead, save for the watching eyes, which, after the first day, followed him about the room as he paced from end to end, restless as a wild creature newly caged.

He saw them in his sleep. He dreamed of eyes. They chased him across great smoking cities, over plains without mark or bound, save the brown circle of the horizon, through the thick coverts of virgin forests. He could not shut them out. He could not escape them. He covered his face with his hand, and they looked in between his fingers, parting them that they might look. He drew his cloak's hood about his brow, he heaped coverings on his head. It was all in vain. He began to babble to the walls, till he realised that these had ears as well as eyes. On the fourth day he wept aloud. He had long refused to eat, though he drank much. He began to go mad, and kept repeating the words to himself, "I am going mad! I am going mad!"

On the fifth night he tried to dash his head against the wall. He fainted, and lay a long time motionless on the cold floor, till suddenly, becoming aware that there was a painted eye underneath he sprang to his feet in that terrible place beset with eyes behind and before.

There came to him a noise of unbarring doors, the yellow lamp-light went out in niche after niche.

"Oh, the blessed dark!" cried the Abbé John, "they are going to leave me in the dark. I shall escape from the eyes."

But no; his tormentors had other purposes with him. A yet greater noise of rollers and the clang of iron machinery, and lo! on high the whole roof of the Place of Eyes fell into two parts (like huge eyelids, thought the Abbé John with a shudder). The sunshine flooded all the upper part of his cell, midway down the walls. The sweet morning air of Spain breathed about him. He felt a cool moisture on his lips, the scent of early flowers. A bee blundered in, boomed round, and went out again as he had come.

The Abbé John clutched his throat as if at the point of death. He thought he saw a vision, and prayed for deliverance, but no more eyes — for judgment, but no more eyes — for damnation even, but no more eyes!

Then he turned about, and close by the great iron door a woman was standing, the fairest he had ever seen — yes, fairer even than Claire Agnew, as fair as they make the pictured angels above the church altars — Valentine la Niña!

CHAPTER XXXVI
VALENTINE LA NIÑA

The girl stood smiling upon the young man, a spray of the great scarlet blossom of the pomegranate freshly plucked and held easily in her hand. She had broken it from the tree in the courtyard as she came in. The flowers showed like handfuls of blood splashed upon the bosom and neck of her white clinging robe.

"You are very beautiful," said the Abbé John, his voice no more than a hoarse gasp; "what are you doing here in this place? Tell me your name. I seem to have seen you long ago, in dreams. But I have forgotten—I forget everything!"

Then, without taking her eyes, mystically amber and gold, softly caressing as the sea and as changeful, from the young man's face, she beckoned him forward.

"We shall speak more at ease in another place," she said. And held out her hand to him, carelessly, palm downwards, as if he had been her brother, and they were playing some lightheart game, or taking positions for an old-time dance of woven hands and measured paces.

Valentine la Niña led John d'Albret into a summer parlour, equally secure from escape, being surrounded by the high fortress walls of the Hotel of the Inquisition, but full of rich twilight, of flowers, of broidery, and of faint wafted perfumes from forgotten shawl or dropped kerchief, which told of a woman's abiding there.

"Now," said Valentine la Niña, throwing herself back luxuriously on a wide divan of Seville, her hands clasped behind her head, "tell me all there is to tell—keep back nothing. Then we will take counsel what is best to be done! I have not forgotten, if you have!"

And John d'Albret, exhausted by the ceaseless searching of the Eyes into his soul, and the need of the dark which would not come, told her all. To which Valentine la Niña listened, and saw the fear fade out and the reasonable man return. But as John d'Albret spoke, something moved strangely in the depths of her own heart. Her face flushed; her temples throbbed; her hands grew chill.

"And you have done this for the sake of a woman—of a girl?" she said.

"For Claire Agnew's sake," the Abbé John answered, still uncertainly; "so would any one—any one who loved her!"

Valentine la Niña smiled, stirring uneasily on her divan, and as she smiled she sighed also, leaning forward, her great eyes on the youth.

"Any one?" she repeated, "any one who loved her! Aye, it may be so. She is a happy girl. I have found none such. I am fair—I should be loved. Yet I have only served and served and served all my life—ah!"

Suddenly, with a quick under-sob and an outward drive of the palm, as if to thrust away some hateful thing, she rose to her feet and caught John d'Albret by the wrist. So lithe was her body that it seemed one single gesture.

"If I had met you before she did," she whispered fiercely, "would you have loved me like that? Answer me! Answer me! I command you! It is life or death, I tell you!"

But the Abbé John, not yet himself, could only stare at her blindly. The girl's eyes, large and mystic, held him in that dim place, and some of his pain returned. He covered his face with both hands.

She shook him fiercely.

"Look at me—you are a man," she cried, "say—am I not beautiful? You have said it already. If you had not met this Huguenot—this daughter of Geneva, would you have loved me—not as men, ordinary men love, but as you have loved, with a love strong enough to brave prison, torture, and death for me—for me?"

The Abbé John, too greatly astonished to answer in words, gazed at the strange girl. Suddenly the anger dropped, the fierce curves faded from the lips that had been so haughty. Her eyes were soft and moist with unshed tears.

Valentine la Niña was pleading with him.

"Say it," she said, "oh, even if it be not true—say it! It would be such a good lie. It would comfort a torn heart, made ever to do the thing it hates. If I had been a fisher-girl spreading nets on the sands, a shepherdess on the hills, some brown sailor-lad or a bearded shepherd would have loved me for myself. Children would have played about my door. Like other women, I would have had the sweet bitterness of life on my lips. I would have sorrowed as others, rejoiced as others. And, when all was done, turned my face to the wall and died as others, my children about me, my man's hand in mine. But now—now—I am only poor Valentine la Niña, the tool of the League, the plaything of politics, the lure of the Jesuits, a thing to be used when bright, thrown away when rusted, but loved—never! No, not even by those who use me, and, in using, kill me!"

And the Abbé John, moved at sight of the pain, answered as best he might.

"A man can only love as the love comes to him," he murmured. "What might have been, I do not know. I have thought I loved many, but I never knew that I loved till I saw little Claire Agnew."

"But if you had not—tell me," she sobbed; "I will be content, if you will only tell me."

"I do not know," said John d'Albret, driven into a corner; "perhaps I might—if I had seen you first."

To the young man it seemed an easy thing to say—a necessary thing, indeed. For, coming fresh from the fear and the place of torment, he was glad to say anything not to be sent thither again.

"But say it," she cried, coming nearer and clasping his arm hard, "say it all—not that you might, but that you would—with the same love that goes easily to death, that I—I—I might escape. Oh, for me, I would go to a thousand deaths if only I knew—surely—surely, that one man in the world would do as much for me!"

But the Abbé John had reached his limit. Not even to escape the Place of the Eyes could he deny his love, or affirm that he could ever have loved to the death any but his little Claire.

"I saw her, and I loved!" he said simply—"that is all I know. Had I seen you, I might have loved—that also I do not know. More I cannot say. But be assured that, if I had loved you, not knowing the other, I should have counted, for your sake, my poor life but as a leaf, wind-blown, a petal fallen in the way."

Valentine la Niña nervously crumpled the glorious red and fleshy blossoms of the pomegranate clusters in her fingers, till they fell in blood-drops on the floor.

"You are noble," she said; "I knew it when I saw you at Collioure on the hillside—more, a prince in your own land, near to the throne even. So am I—and Philip the King himself would not deny me. He is your country's enemy. Yet at my request he would stay his hand. He must fight the English. He must subdue the Low Countries. That is his oath. But if you will—if you will—he would aid the Bearnais, or better still, you yourself to a throne, and give me—who can say what?—perhaps this very Roussillon for a dower. For I am close of kin to the King. He would acknowledge me as such. I have vowed a vow, but now it is almost paid; and if it were not I would go to the Pope himself, though I walked every step of the road to Rome!"

"I cannot—I cannot——" cried John d'Albret. "Thank God, I am not of the first-born of kings, whose hands are put up to the highest bidder. Where I have loved, there will I wed or not at all!"

"Ah, cruel!" cried Valentine la Niña, stamping her foot—"cruel, not only to me, but to her whom you say you love. Think you she will be safe from the Society, from the Holy Office in France? There is no rack or torture perhaps, no Place of Eyes. But was Henry of Valois safe, who slew the Duke of Guise? From whose bosom came forth Jacques Clement? My uncle put the knife in his hand and blessed him ere he went. For me he would do more. Think—this Claire of yours is condemned already. She is young. By your own telling she has many lovers. She will be happy. I know the heart of such maids. Besides, she has never promised you anything—never humbled herself to you as I—I, Valentine la Niña, who till now have been the proudest maid in Spain!"

"I am not worthy," cried the Abbé John. "I cannot; I dare not; I will not!"

"Ah," said Valentine la Niña, with a long rising inflection, and drawing herself back from him, "I have found it ever so with you heretics. You are willing to die—to suffer. Because then you would wear the martyr's crown, and have your name commemorated—in books, on tablets, and be lauded by the outcasts of Geneva. But for your own living folk you will do nothing. With all Roussillon, from Salses to the Pyrenees, for my dowry (Philip would be glad to be rid of it—and perhaps also of me—my friends of the Society are too strong for him), there would be an end to this prisoning and burning and torturing through the land. Teruel and Frey Tullio we would send to their own place. By a word you could save thousands. Yet you will not. You think only of one chit of a girl, who laughs at you, who cares not the snap of her finger for you!"

She stopped, panting with her own vehemence.

"Likely enough," said the Abbé John, "the more is the pity. But that cannot change my heart."

"Was her love for you like mine?" she cried; "did she love you from the first moment she saw you? NO! Has she done for you what I have done—risked my all—my uncle's anger—the Society's—that of the Holy Office even? No!—No!—*No!* She has done none of these things. She has only graciously permitted you to serve her on your knees—she, the daughter of a spy, a common go-between of your Huguenot and heretic princes! Shame on you, Jean d'Albret of Bourbon, you, a cousin of the King of France, thus to give yourself up to fanatics and haters of religion."

But by this time the Abbé John was completely master of himself. He could carry forward the interview much more successfully on these lines.

"I am no Huguenot," he said calmly, "more is the pity, indeed. I have no claim to be zealous for any religion. I have fought on the Barricades of Paris for the Guise, because I was but an idle fellow and there was much excitement and shouting. I have fought for the Bearnais, not because he is a Huguenot, but because he is my good cousin and a brave soldier—none like him."

Valentine la Niña waved her hand in contempt.

"None like him!" she exclaimed. "Have you never heard of my cousin Alexander of Parma? To him your Bearnais is no better than a ruffler, a banditti captain, a guerilla chief. If you must fight, why, we will go to him. It is a service worth a thousand of the other. Then you will learn the art of war indeed——"

"Aye, against my countrymen," said John d'Albret, with firmness. Bit by bit his courage was coming back to him. "I am but a poor idlish fellow, who have taken little thought of religion, Huguenot or Catholic. Once I had thought she would teach me, if life had been given me, and—and if she had been willing. But now I must take what Fate sends, and trust that if I die untimeously, the Judge I shall chance to meet may prove less stern than He of the Genevan's creed, and less cruel than the God of Dom Teruel and the Holy Inquisition!"

"Then you refuse?" She uttered the words in a low strained voice. "You refuse what I have offered? But I shall put it once more—honourable wedlock with an honourable maiden, of a house as good as your own, a province for your dower, the most Catholic King for sponsor of your vows, noble service, and it like you, with the greatest captain of the age, the safety of all your kin, free speech, free worship, the entrance of these thousands of French folk into France. Ah, and love—love such as the pale daughters of the north never dreamt of——"

She took a step towards him, her clasped hands pleading for her, her lips quivering, her head thrown back so far that the golden comb slipped, and a heavy drift of hair, the colour of ripe oats, fell in waves far below her shoulders.

"Do not let the chance go by," she said, "because you think you do not love me now. That will come in time. I know it will come. I would love you so that it could not help but come!"

"I cannot—ah, I cannot!" said John d'Albret, his eyes on the floor, so that he might not see the pain he could not cure.

The girl drew herself up, clenched her hands, and with a hissing indraw of the breath, she cried, "You cannot—you mean you will not, because you love—the other—the spy's daughter—of whom I will presently make an end, as a child kills a fly on a window-pane—for my pleasure!"

"No," said John d'Albret clearly, lifting his head and looking into the angry eyes, flashing murkily as the sunlight flashes in the deep water at a harbour mouth or in some estuary—"no, I will not do any of the things you ask of me. And the reason is, as you have said, because I love Claire Agnew until I die. I know not at all whether she loves me or not. And to me that makes no matter——"

"No, you say right," cried Valentine la Niña, "it will indeed make no difference. For by these words—they are printed on my heart—you have condemned her; the spy's daughter to the knife, and yourself——"

"To the fires of the Inquisition?" demanded the Abbé John. "I am ready!"

"Nay, not so fast," said Valentine la Niña, "that were far too easy a death—too quick. You shall go to the galleys among the lowest criminals, your feet in the rotting wash of the bilge, lingering out a slow death-in-life—slow—very slow, the lash on your back and—no, no—I cannot believe this is your answer. Here, here is yet one chance. Surely I have not humbled myself only for this?"

The Abbé John answered nothing, and after a pause the girl drew herself up to her height, and spoke to him through her clenched teeth.

"You shall go to the galleys and pray—ah, you say you have never learned to pray, but you will—you will on Philip's galleys. They make good theologians there; they practise. You will pray in vain for the death that will not come. And I, when I wake in the night, will turn me and sleep the sweeter on my pillow for the thought of you chained to your oar, which you will never quit alive. Ah, I will teach you, Jean d'Albret of the house of Bourbon, cousin of kings, what it is to love the spy's daughter, and to despise me—me—Valentine la Niña, a daughter of the King of Spain!"

CHAPTER XXXVII
THE WILD ANIMAL—WOMAN

Mariana the Jesuit rose, pen in hand, to embrace his "niece" as she entered his bureau. There was a laughing twinkle in his eye, and all his comfortable little pink-and-white figure shook with mirth.

"Bravo—oh! bravo!" he cried, "never—never did I suppose our little Valentine half so clever. Why, you turned yonder boastful cockerel outside in. Ha, they teach us something of dissimulation in our seminaries, but we are children to you, the best of us—the whole Gesù might sit at your feet and take lessons. Even Philip himself—were it not for semi-paternal authority! Never was the thing they call love better acted. I declare it was a great moral lesson to listen to you. You made the folly of it so apparent—so abject!"

The girl was still pale. The rich glow of health, without the least colour in her cheeks, had disappeared. But the eyes of Valentine la Niña were dangerously bright.

The Jesuit proceeded, without taking note of these symptoms of disorder. He was so accustomed to use the girl's beauty and cleverness to bait his hooks. By her father she had been vowed from infancy to the service of the Society. Her rank was known only to a few in the realm. Save on this condition of service, Philip would never have permitted her to remain in his kingdom of the Seven Spains. And, indeed, Valentine la Niña deserved well of Philip and the Gesù. She had served the Society faithfully.

For these reasons she was dear as anything in flesh and blood could be to Mariana the Jesuit. He laughed again, tasting the rare flavour of the jest.

"A rich prize indeed," he chuckled. "The cousin of the Bearnais—a candidate of the League for the crown of France. Ho, ho! Serving on the galleys as a Huguenot! You were right. There is no good fuel for Father Teruel's bonfires—he is meat for the masters of Tullio the Neapolitan and Serra his kinsman. Was there ever such sport? You do indeed deserve a province and a dower, were it not that you are too valuable where you are, aiding the Cause—and me, your poor loving 'uncle'! But what made me laugh as I listened, till the tears came into my old eyes, was to hear you—you, to whom a thousand men had paid court—begging for the love of that starved and terrified young braggart in his suit of silken bravery, tashed with prisons, and the fear of the Place of Eyes still white on his face!"

Then all unexpectedly Valentine la Niña spoke. Her tall figure seemed to overshadow that of her little, dimpling, winking kinsman, as the pouches under his eyes shook with merriment, while his mouth was one wreathed smile, and he pointed his beautiful, plump, white fingers together pyramidally, as if measuring one hand against the other.

"It was true," she said point-blank, "I was not pretending. I did love him—and I do!"

The dimples died out one by one on the face of the historian, Mariana of Toledo. The ripe colour faded from the cheek-bone. He glanced nervously over his shoulder with the air of a man who may be sheltering traitors under his roof-tree.

"Hush!" he whispered. "Enough—now you have carried the jest far enough. It was excellent with the springald D'Albret. You played him well, like a trout on an angle. But after all we are—where we are. And Teruel and Tullio are not the men to appreciate such a jest."

"I was never farther from jesting in my life," said Valentine la Niña; "I love him as I never thought to love man before. If he would have loved me, and forgotten that—that woman—I would have done for him all I said— aye, and more!"

"You—Valentine—a king's daughter?"

"Great good that has done me," cried the girl; "I must not show my face. My father (if, indeed, he is my father) would so gladly get rid of me that he would present me to the Grand Turk if he thought the secret would hold water. As it is, he keeps me doing hateful work, lying and smiling, smiling and lying, like—like a Jesuit!"

"Girl, you have taken leave of your senses—of your judgment!" said her "uncle" severely. "Do you not see that you are sealing the doom of the man for whom you profess a feeling as foolish as sudden?"

"Neither foolish nor sudden," retorted the girl sullenly, her hand on the back of a chair, gripping the top bar like a weapon. For a moment the little soft man with his eternal smile might have been her victim. She could have brained him with a blow—the angle of that solid oaken seat crashing down upon the shining bald head which harboured so many secrets and had worked out so many plots. Valentine la Niña let the moment pass, but while it lasted she might very well have done it.

"It is not foolish," she said, relaxing her grip for an instant. "I am a human creature with a heart that beats so many times a minute, and a skin that covers the same human needs and passions—just as if I were a free and happy girl—like—like that spy's daughter whom he loves. Neither is it sudden. For I saw him more than once on the hills above Collioure, when we stayed in the house of that cruel young monster Raphael Llorient. I wandered on the wastes covered with romarin and thyme—why, think you? 'A new-born passion for nature,' you said, laughing. 'To get away from our host, Don Raphael,' said Livia the countess. Neither, good people! It was, because, stretched at length on a bed of juniper and lavender, in the shadow of a rock, my eyes had seen the noblest youth the gods had put upon the earth. He was asleep."

"You are mad, girl," cried Mariana, as loudly as he dared. "These are not the words of the Valentine I knew!"

"Surely not," said the girl, her head thrown back, her breast forward, and breathing deep, "nor am I the Valentine I myself knew!"

"You dare to love this man—you—vowed to the Church and to the service of the Gesù, whose secrets you hold? You dare not!"

"I dare all," she answered calmly. "This is not a matter of daring. It comes! It is! I did not make it. It does not go at my bidding, nor at yours. Besides, I did not bid it go. For one blessed moment I had at least the sensation of a possible happiness!"

"Nevertheless, he shamed you, rejected you, like the meanest whining lap-dog your foot spurns aside out of your path. He has done this to you— Valentine la Niña, called the Most Beautiful—to you, the King's daughter an you liked, an Infanta of Spain! Have you thought of that?"

"Thought?" she said, tapping her little foot on the floor, and with her strong right hand swaying the chair to and fro like a feather—"have I thought of it? What else have I done for many days and weeks? But whether he will love me or cast me off—the die is thrown. I am his and not another's. I may take revenge—for that is in my blood. I may cause him to suffer as he has made me suffer—and the woman also—especially the woman, the spy's daughter! But that does not alter the fact. I am his, and if he would, even when chained to the oar of the galley, a slave among slaves—he could whistle me to his side like a fawning dog! For I am his slave—his slave!"

The last words were spoken almost inaudibly, as if to herself.

"And to the galleys he shall go!" said the Jesuit, "you have said it, and the idea is a good one. There he will be out of mischief. Yet he can be produced, if, in the time to come, his cousin the Bearnais, arrived at the crown of France, has time to make inquiries after him!"

A knife glittered suddenly before the eyes of the Jesuit. It was in the firm white hand of the girl vowed to the Society.

"See," she hissed, letting each word drop slowly from her lips, "see, Doctor Mariana, my uncle, you are not afraid of death—I know—but you do not wish to die now. There are so many things unfinished—so much yet to do. I know you, uncle! Now let me take my will of this young man. Afterwards I am at your service—for ever—for ever—more faithfully than before!"

"How can I trust you?" said the Jesuit; "to-morrow you might go mad again!"

"These things do not happen twice in a lifetime," said Valentine la Niña, "and as for Jean d'Albret, I shall put him beyond the reach of any second chance!"

Her uncle nodded his head. He knew when a woman has the bit between her teeth, and though he had a remedy even for such cases, he judged that the present was not the time to use it.

So Valentine la Niña went out, the knife still in her hand.

The Jesuit of Toledo threw himself back on his writing-chair and wiped his brow with a handkerchief.

"*Ouff!*" he cried, emptying his chest with a gust of relief, "this is what it is to have to do with that wild animal, Woman! In Madrid they tame the tiger, till it takes victual from its keeper's very hand. He is its master, almost its lover; I have seen the tiger arch its back like a cat under the caress. It sleeps with the arm of the keeper about its neck! Till one day—one day— the tiger that was tamed falls upon the tamer, the master, the lover, the friend! So with a woman. Have I not trained and nurtured, pruned and cared for this soul as for mine own. She was tame. She knew no will but mine. *Clack!* In a moment, at sight of a comely youth in a court suit asleep, as Endymion on some Latmian steep, she is wild again. Better to let her go than perish, keeping her."

Mariana listened a while, but the chamber of his work was as far from the lugubrious noises of the den of Dom Teruel as if it had been the Place of Eyes itself. Neither could he hear any sound from the little summer parlour which had been put at the service of his niece.

The old worldly-wise smile came back upon his lips.

"It is none of my business, of course," he murmured, "but it strikes me that the youth D'Albret had better say his prayers—such, that is, as he can remember. I, for one, would not care twice to anger Valentine la Niña!"

He thought a while, and then with a grave air he added, "If I were a man of the world I would wager ten golden ounces to one, that within five minutes Master D'Albret knows more about eternity than the Holy Father himself and all his College of Cardinals. Well, better so! Then she will come back to us. She has served us well, Valentine la Niña, and now, having drunk the cup—*now* she will serve us better than ever, or I know nothing of womankind!"

But Mariana, though he stood long with his ear glued to the crack of the door, could distinguish no sound within the summer parlour which Valentine la Niña had entered to look for the Abbé John.

CHAPTER XXXVIII
THE VENGEANCE OF VALENTINE LA NIÑA

When Valentine la Niña left him in the summer parlour where their interview had taken place, the Abbé John made no attempt to free himself. He seemed still half-unconscious, and, indeed, proceeded without rhyme or reason to make some repairs in the once gay court suit, exactly as if he had been seated in his tent in the camp of the Bearnais.

As yet he had no thought of escape. He was in the fortress of the Inquisition. The influence of the Place of Eyes was on him still. To escape appeared an impossibility to his weakened mind. Indeed, he thought only of the strange girl who had just talked with him. Was she indeed a king's daughter, with provinces to bring in dower, or——No, she could not lie. He was sure of that. She did *not* lie, certainly, decided the Abbé John, with natural masculine favour towards a beautiful woman. A girl like that could not have lied. Mad—perhaps, yes, a little—but to lie, impossible.

So in that quiet place, he watched the slow wheeling of the long checkered bars of the window *grille*, and the shadows made by the branches of the Judas tree in the courtyard move regularly across the carpet. One of the leaves boarded his foot as he looked, climbed up the instep, and made a pretty shifting pattern upon the silken toe.

The Abbé John had resumed his customary position of easy self-possession—one ankle perched upon the opposing knee, his head thrown far back, his dark hair in some disorder, but curling naturally and densely, none the less picturesque because of that—when Valentine la Niña re-entered.

He rose at once, and in some surprise. She held a knife in her hand, and her face carried something about it of wild and dangerous, a kind of storm-sunshine, as it seemed.

"Hum," thought the Abbé John, as he looked at her, "I had better have stayed in the Place of Eyes! I see not why all this should happen to me. I am an easy man, and have always done what I could to content a lady. But this one asks too much. And then, after all, now there is Claire! I told her so. It is very tiresome!"

Nevertheless he smiled his sweet, careless smile, and swept back his curls with his hand.

"If I am to die, a fellow may as well do it with some grace," he murmured; "I wish I had been more fit—if only Claire had had the time to make me a better man!"

Yet it is to be feared that even in that moment the Abbé John thought more of the process (as outlined in his mind with Claire as instructress) than of the very desirable result.

What the thoughts of Valentine la Niña were when she left the presence of her uncle could hardly be defined even to her own mind. But seeing this young man so easy, so debonair in spite of his dishevelled appearance, the girl only held out her left hand. A faint smile, like the sun breaking momentarily through the thunder-clouds, appeared on her lips.

"I was wrong," she said; "let me help you only—I ask no more. Come!"

And without another word she led him into a narrow passage, between two high walls. They passed door after door, all closed, one of them being the chamber of Mariana, in which he sat like a spider spinning webs for the Society of the Gesù. What might have happened if that door had been suddenly opened in their faces also remains a mystery. For Valentine's arm was strong, and the dagger her hand held was sharp.

However, as it chanced, the doors remained shut, so that when they came to a little wicket, of solid iron like all the rest, the steel blade of the dagger still shone bright.

Then Valentine la Niña snatched from a nail the long black mantle, with which any who left the House of the Holy Office by that door concealed from the curious their rank or errand. She flung it about John d'Albret's shoulders with a single movement of her arm.

"I do what I can," she said, "yield me the justice to allow that. I am giving you a chance to return to her. There—take it—now you are armed!"

She gave him the knife, and the sheath from which she had drawn it in her uncle's bureau.

"And now, bid me farewell—no thanks—I do not want them! You will not, I know, forget me, and I only ask you to pray that I may be able to forget you!"

The Abbé John stooped to kiss her hand, but she snatched it behind her quickly.

"I think I deserve so much," she said softly, holding up her face, "not even she would deny me!"

And the Abbé John, quieting his soul by the vow of necessity, future confession, and absolution, kissed Valentine la Niña.

She gave one little sobbing cry, and would have fallen, had he not caught her. But she shook him off, striking angrily at his wrist with her clenched hand.

"No! No! *No!*" she cried; "go—I bid you—go, do not heed me. I am well. They may be here any moment. They are ever on the watch. It cannot be long. Go. I am repaid. She has never risked as much for you! Lock the door without!"

And she pushed him into the street, shut the door, and fell in a white heap fainting behind it, as John d'Albret turned the key outside.

CHAPTER XXXIX
SAVED BY SULKS

When the so-called uncle of Valentine la Niña, Mariana the Jesuit, found that even his acute ears could distinguish no sound within the darkened parlour of his niece, he did what he had often done before. He opened the door with the skill of an evil-doer, and peered through the crack. The evening sun struck on a spray of scattered blooms which Valentine had thrown down in her haste—grenadine flowers, red as blood—upon a broidery frame, the needle stuck transversely, an open book of devotion, across which the shadows of the window bars slowly passed, following, as on a dial of illuminated capitals, the swift westering of the sun. But he heard no sound save the flick-flick of the leaves of the Judas tree against the window, in the light airs from the Canigou, already damp with the early mist of the foot-hills.

The Jesuit listened, carefully opened the door a little more widely, and listened again, holding his hand to his lips. Still only the stirring air and the leaves that tapped. Mariana drew a long breath and stepped within. The room was empty.

Then he brought his hand hard down on his thigh, and turned as if to cry a hasty order. He stopped, however, before the words found vent.

"She has freed him—fled with him, the jade," he murmured; "she was playing to me also—what a woman—ah, what a woman!"

Then admiration took and held possession of him—a kind of connoisseur's envy in the presence of a masterpiece of guile. The great Jesuit felt himself beaten at his own weapons.

"Used for sanctified ends," he murmured, "what a power she would be!" And again, "What a woman!"

But the order did not leave his lips. He felt that it were better to leave the matter as it was. If only he could find Valentine la Niña, no one would know of her part in the prisoner's escape. It could be put down to the carelessness of the watchers. The principal familiars were at their work deep in the caves of the Inquisition. The eyes in the prisoner's cell were painted eyes only— their effect merely moral. None had seen John d'Albret go into the summer parlour of Valentine. None had heard her interview, stormy as it was, with her uncle. They had other things to do in the House of the Street of the Money. If only, then, he could find La Niña. All turned on that.

"Ah," he thought suddenly, "the key! She has the key of the little door giving upon the ancient bed of the Tet."

And, hastening down the passage by which, a few minutes before, Valentine la Niña had led the Abbé John, he stumbled upon his niece, fallen by the gate, her white dress and white face sombre under the dusk of vine-leaves, which clambered over the porch as if it had been a lady's bower.

But the key was not in her hand. With the single flash of intuition he showed in the matter, John d'Albret had thrown it away, and it now reposed in the bed of the Tet, not half a mile from the lost seal of the Holy Office which, some time previously, his friend Jean-aux-Choux had so obligingly disposed of there.

The Jesuit, in order to keep up his credit in the house of his friends, was obliged to carry his niece to her summer bower, and leave her there to recover in the coolness and quiet. Then he put on his out-of-doors soutane, and passed calmly through the main portal to dispatch a messenger of his own Order to the frontier with a description of a certain John d'Albret, evaded from the prison of the Holy Office in the Street of the Money at Perpignan—who, if caught, was by no means to be returned thither, but to be held at the disposition of Father Mariana, chief of the Order of the Gesù in the North of Spain, and bearing letters mandatory to that effect from the King himself.

"For the present he is gone and lost," he murmured, as he went back; "the minx has outwitted me"—here he chuckled, and all the soft childish dimples came out—"yet why should I complain? It was I who taught her. Or, rather, to say the truth, I outwitted myself—I, and that incalculable something in women which wrecks the wisdom of the wisest men!"

And, comforting himself with these reflections, Mariana returned alone to the House of the Holy Office in the Street of the Money, which, of necessity, he entered by the main door.

Now that buzzed like a hive, which had been silent and deserted enough when he went out. The Jesuit stood in apparent bewilderment, his lips moving as if to ask a question. He could hear Dom Teruel storming that he would burn every assistant, every familiar in the building, from roof to cellar, while Frey Tullio and Serra, the huge Murcian, made tumultuary perquisition into every chamber in search of the runaway.

"Hold there—I will open for you," commanded Mariana, as he saw that they were approaching the door within which lay Valentine; "I will go in, and you can follow. But let no one dare to disturb the repose of the lady, my niece. Or—ye know well the seal and mandate of the King concerning her!"

Mariana went softly in, not closing the door, and having satisfied himself that all was well, he beckoned the inquisitors to approach. Valentine la Niña lay on the oaken settle, her head on the pillow, exactly as he had placed her, but thanks to the few drops from the phial which he had compelled her to swallow, she was now sleeping peacefully, her bosom rising and falling with her measured breathing.

The men stood a moment uncertain, perhaps a little awestruck. Serra would have retreated, but the suspicious Neapolitan walked softly across and tested the bars of the window. They were firmly and deeply enough sunk in the stone to convince even Frey Tullio.

So it chanced that while the messenger of the Gesù sped northward to the frontier with orders to arrest one Jean d'Albret, a near relative of the Bearnais, clad in frayed court-suit of pale blue, and even while the couriers of the Holy Office posted in the same direction seeking a criminal whom it was death to shelter or succour, the Abbé John, looking most abbatical in his decent black cloak, passed out of the city by the empty bed of the Tet, the same which it had occupied before the straight cut known as the Basse led it to southward of the town. Then—marvel of marvels—the hunted man turned to the south and made across the hills in the direction of the House of La Masane upon the slopes of the hills behind Collioure.

And as he went he communed with himself.

"I will show her!" affirmed the Abbé John grimly (for there was a hot and lasting temper under that light exterior, perhaps that of the aboriginal Bourbon, who to this day "never learns and never forgives"). "I will show her! If I loved her as an ordinary man, I would hasten to follow and overtake her! But she is safe and has no need of me. If she has any thought for me— any care (he did not say 'any love'), it will be none the worse for keeping.

I will go back to Jean-aux-Choux. He was to return and care for all that remained at La Masane. Well, surely he is no braver than I. What he does I can do. I will go and help him. Also, I shall be able to keep an eye on that rascal, Raphael Llorient!"

And so, with these excellent intentions he turned his face resolutely to the south—a determination which completely threw his pursuers off the scent. For it was a natural axiom in Spanish Roussillon, that whosoever embroiled himself with the powers-that-were in that province made instantly, by sea or by land, for the nearest French border.

Thus was John d'Albret saved by the Bourbon blood of his mother, or by his own native cross-grained temper. In short, he sulked. And for the time being, the sulking saved his neck.

CHAPTER XL
THE MAS OF THE MOUNTAIN

It was a day of "mistral" in the valley of the Rhone—high, brave, triumphant mistral, the wind of God sent to sweep out the foul odours of little tightly-packed towns with tortuous streets, to dry the good rich earth after the rain, and to call forth the corn from the corn-land, the grapes from the ranged vines, and to prove for the thousandth time the strength and endurance of the misty, dusty, grey-blue olive trees, that streamed away from the north-east like a faint-blown river of smoke.

A brave day it was for those who loved such days—of whom was not Claire Agnew—certainly a brave day for the whirling wheels, the vast bird-pinions of Jean-Marie's new windmills on the mountain of Barbentane.

Jean-Marie found his abode to his taste. At first he had installed Claire with a decent Provençal couple at the famous cross-roads called in folk-speech "Le Long le Chemin," till he should find some resting-place other than the ground-floor of the creaking and straining monsters where he himself spread his mattress, and slept, bearded and night-capped, among his rich farina dust and the pell-mell of bags of corn yet to be ground.

By the time, however, that Madame Amélie with Professor Anatole was able to reach France (thanks to the care of the good Bishop of Elne, and the benevolence of the more secular powers set in motion by the Viceroy of Catalonia), a new Mas had been bought. The gold laid carefully up with Pereira, the honest Hebrew of Bayonne, had been paid out, and the scattered wanderers had once more a home, secure and apart, in the fairest and quietest province of France.

Nay more, though the way was long, the cattle-tracks across the lower Canigou were so well known and so constantly followed, that Jean-aux-Choux had been able to bring forward the most part of Dame Amélie's bestial. Even her beloved goats bleated on the rocks round the Mas of the mountain. The fowls indeed were other, but to the common eye even they seemed unchanged, for Jean-Marie had been at some pains to match them before the arrival of his mother. Doves *roo-cooed* about the sheds and circled the tall pigeon-cote on its black pole with flapping wings.

The house mistress was coming home.

That day Madame Amélie was to arrive with her son, the Professor, and Jean-aux-Choux for an escort. And then at last Claire would learn—what she had been wilfully kept in ignorance of by Jean-Marie—the reason for the sudden desertion of the Abbé John on the sea-shore at Collioure.

There had been a struggle long and mighty within the stout breast of the Miller-Alcalde before he could bring himself to play the traitor. After all (so he argued with his conscience), he was only keeping his promise. John d'Albret had bidden him be silent. Nevertheless, when he saw Claire's wan and anxious face, he was often prompted to speak, even though by so doing he might lose all hope of securing a mistress for the new Mas of the Mountain, who in course of time would succeed Madame Amélie there.

The grave, strong, sententious ex-Alcalde had allowed no lines of meal dust to gather in the frosty curls of his beard since he had brought Claire Agnew to France. Busy all day, he had rejoiced in working for her. Then, spruce as any love-making youth, he had promenaded lengthily and silently with her in the twilight, looking towards the distant sea, across which from the southward his mother and his brothers were to come.

The Miller Jean-Marie loved—after a fashion, his own silent, dour, middle-aged fashion—the young girl Claire Agnew, whom he called his "niece" in that strange land. For in this he followed the example of his brother, judging that what was right for a learned professor of the Sorbonne could not be wrong for a rough miller, earning his bread (and his "niece's") by the turning of his grindstones and the gigantic whirl of his sails.

Still, he had never spoken his love, but on this final morning the miller had not gone forth. He was determined to speak at last. His mother and brother were soon to arrive. The mistral drave too strong for work. He had indeed little corn to grind—nothing that an hour earlier on the morrow could not put to rights. Then and there he would speak to Claire. At long and last he was sure of himself. His courage would not, as usual, ooze away from his finger nails. He and she were alone in the newly-furnished rooms of the Mas of the Mountain—for only a few portable items such as his mother's chair and the ancient pot-bellied horologe had been brought in a *tartana* from La Masane to the little harbour of Les Saintes Maries, where the big mosquitoes are.

"It is not good for man to be alone," began Jean-Marie, even more sententiously than usual; "I have heard you read that out of your Bible of Geneva—do you believe it, Claire?"

"Indeed I do," said the girl, looking up brightly; "I have longed—ah, how I have longed—all these weeks—for your mother!"

"I was thinking of myself!" said the miller heavily.

"Ah, well, that will soon be at an end," returned Claire; "I am sorry, but I did my best. I have often heard you sigh and sigh and sigh when you and I walked together of the evening. And I knew I was no company for you. I was too young and too foolish, was it not so? But now you will have your mother and your brother, the Professor, who is learned. He knows all about how to grow onions according to the methods of Virgil! He told me so himself!"

The big ex-Alcalde looked doubtfully sidelong at his little friend. He was not a suspicious man, and usually considered Claire as innocent as a frisking lambling. But now—no, it could not be. She was not making fun of him—of the man who had done all these things, who had brought her in safety by paths perilous to this new home!

So very wisely he decided to take Claire's words at their face value.

"My mother is my mother," he said, deciding that the time had come at last, and that nothing was to be gained by putting it off. "Doctor Anatole is my elder brother, and as for me, I have all the family affections. But a man of my age needs something else!"

"What, another windmill?" cried Claire; "well, I will help you. I saw such a splendid place for one yesterday, right at the top of the rocky ridge they call Frigolet. It is not too high, yet it catches every wind, and oh—you can see miles and miles all about—right to the white towers of Arles, and away to the twin turrets of Château Renard among the green vineyards. There is no such view in all the mountains. And I will go up there every day and knit my stocking!"

"Oh, if only it were *my* stocking!" groaned the miserable, tongue-tied miller, "then I might think about the matter of the windmill."

Foiled in a direct line, he was trying to arrive at his affair by a side-wind.

But Claire clapped her hands joyously, glad to get her own way on such easy terms.

"Of course, Jean-Marie, I will knit you a pair of hose—most gladly—winter woollen ones of the right Canigon fashion——"

"I did not mean one pair only," said the miller, with a slightly more brisk air, and an attempt at a knowing smile, "but—for all my life!"

"Come, you are greedy," cried Claire; "and must your mother go barefoot—and your brother the Professor, and Don Jordy, and — — "

She was about to add another name, which ought to have been that of Jean-aux-Choux, but was not. She stopped, however, the current of her gay words swiftly arrested by that unspoken name.

"Jean-Marie, answer me," she said, standing with her back resolutely to the door, "there is a thing I must know. Tell me, as you are an honest man, what became of Jean d'Albret that night on the sand-dunes at Collioure? It is in my mind that you know more than you have told me. You do know, my brave Alcalde! I am sure of it. For it was you who came to borrow my hood and mantle, also my long riding-cape to give to him. And I have never seen them since. If, then, this Abbé John is a thief and a robber, you are his accomplice. Nothing better. Come—out with it!"

Jean-Marie stood mumbling faintly words without order or significance.

Claire crossed her arms and set her back to the oaken panels. The miller would gladly have escaped by the window, but the sill was high. Moreover, he felt that escalade hardly became either his age or habit of body.

Therefore, like many another in a like difficulty, he took refuge in prevarication—to use which well requires, in a man, much practice and considerable solidity of treatment. Women are naturally gifted in this direction.

"He bade—I mean he forbade—me to reveal the matter to you!"

"Then it had to do with me," she cried, fixing the wretched man with her forefinger; "now I have a right—I demand to know. I will not stay a moment longer in the house if I am not told."

As she spoke Claire turned the key twice in the lock, extracted it, and slid it into her pocket. These are not the usual preliminaries for quitting a house for ever in hot indignation. But the ex-Alcalde was too flustered to notice the inconsistency.

"Speak!" she cried, stamping her foot. And the broad, serious-faced Jean-Marie found, among all his wise saws and instances, none wherewith to answer her. "Where did he go, and what did he do with my long cloak and lace mantilla?" she demanded. "Were they a disguise to provide only for his own safety—the coward?"

The miller flushed. Up till now he had sheltered himself behind the Abbé John's express command to say nothing. Now he must speak, and this proud girl must take that which she had brought on her own head. It was clear to Jean-Marie, as it had been to numerous others, that she had no heart. She was a block of ice, drifted from far northern seas.

"Well, since you will have it, I will tell you," he said, speaking slowly and sullenly, "but do not blame me if the news proves unwelcome. Jean d'Albret borrowed your cloak and mantilla so that he might let himself be taken in your place—so as to give you—you—*you*—he cared not for the others—time to escape from the familiars of the Inquisition sent to take you!"

He nodded his head almost at each word and opened his hand as if disengaging himself from further responsibility. He looked to see the girl overwhelmed. But instead she rose, as it were, to the stature of a goddess, her face flushed and glorious.

"Tell it me again," she said hoarsely, even as Valentine la Niña had once pleaded to be told, "tell me again—he did that for me?"

"Aye, for you! Who else?" said the miller scornfully—"for whom does a man do anything but for a silly girl not worth the trouble!"

She did not heed him.

"He went to the death for me—to save me—he did what none else could have done—saying nothing about it, bidding them keep it from me, lest I should know! Oh, oh!"

The miller turned away in disgust. He pronounced an anathema on the hearts of women. But she wheeled him round and, laying her hands on both his shoulders, flashed wet splendid eyes upon him, the like of which he had never seen.

"Oh, I am glad—I am glad!" she cried; "I could kiss you for your news, Jean-Marie!"

And she did so, her tears dropping on his hands.

"This thing I do not understand!" said the miller to himself, when, no longer a prisoner, he left Claire to sink her brow into a freshly-lavendered pillow in her own chamber.

And he never would know.

Yet Valentine la Niña would have done the same thing. For in their hearts all women wish to be loved "like that."

The word is their own—and the voice in which they say it.

CHAPTER XLI
"AND LAZARUS CAME FORTH!"

This was all of the most cheerful for John d'Albret. To be loved with wet glad eyes by the woman for whom you have done brave deeds is the joy of life. Only to taste its flavour, she herself must tell you of it. And John d'Albret was very far from the Mas of the Mountain of Barbentane. He did not feel the dry even rush of the high mistral, steady and broad as a great ocean current—yet how many times more swift. The wind that fanned his heated temples was the warm day wind of Africa, coming in stifling puffs as from an oven, causing the dust to whirl, and lifting the frilled leaves of the palms like a woman's garments. At night, on the contrary, the humid valley-winds stealing down from the Canigou made him shiver, as he crouched in the ancient sheepfolds and rude cane-built shelters where he had expected to find Jean-aux-Choux.

But these were deserted, the charge of his troop taken over by another. The house of La Masane had been put to sack—partly by those who had come to take away the more portable furniture for the *tartana* bound for Les Santes Maries, and also in part at a later date by the retainers of the Lord of Collioure. Several times, from his hiding-place on the mountain, John d'Albret had observed Raphael Llorient wandering idly about the abandoned house of La Masane, revolving new plots or brooding on the manner in which the old had been foiled.

As Jean-aux-Choux did not return, the Abbé John waxed quickly weary of the bare hillside, where also he was in constant danger of discovery from some of Jean-aux-Choux's late comrades. These, however, contented themselves chiefly with surveying their flocks from convenient hill-tops, or at most, in launching a couple of swift dogs in the tracks of any wanderers. But John knew that these very dogs might easily at any moment lead to his discovery, if they smelt out the reed-bed in which it was his habit to lie hid during the day.

Meantime the Abbé, with needle and thread drawn from Jean-aux-Choux's stores, had busied himself in repairing the ravages prison-life had made in his apparel. And with his habitual handiness, begun in the Bedouin tents of the Latin quarter, and continued in the camps of the Bearnais, he achieved, if not complete success, at least something which suggested rather a needy young soldier, a little battered by the wars, than a runaway prisoner from the dungeons of the Holy Office.

His aspect was rendered still more martial by Jean-aux-Choux's long Valaisian sword (with "Achille Serre, of Sion" engraved upon the blade), which hung from a plain black leather waist-belt, broad as the palm of the hand. The Abbé John, regarding himself at dawn in the spring near the chapel of the Hermitage, remarked with pleasure that during his sojourn upon the mountain his moustache had actually attained quite respectable proportions. As for his beard, it still tarried by the way, though he was pleased to say that in order to be respectable he must seek out a hostelry and find there refreshment and a razor—"If" he added, "mine host does not handle the blade himself"—an accomplishment which was not at all uncommon among the Bonifaces of Roussillon.

So leaving the town and castle of Collioure away to the left, and far below him, John d'Albret struck across the tumbled rocky country where the last bastions of the Pyrenees break down to meet the chafe of the Midland sea. He travelled by night, and as it was moonlight, made good enough going. It was pleasant and dry. The mountain wind cooled him, and many a time he paused to look down from the grey-white rocks upon the sweep of some little bay, pebbly-beached, its fringe of sand and surf dazzling white beneath the moon. He heard the sough and rattle as the water arched, foamed a moment, plashed heavily, and then retired, dragging the rounded stones downward in its suck.

John d'Albret meant to strike for Rosas, where he knew he might always hope to find some French boats come in from the pilchard and sardine fisheries about Ivitza and the Cape of Mallorca. He hoped for shelter on one of these. There would certainly be countrymen of his, drinking and running at large on the beach of Rosas. With them he would make his bargain in money or love, according to the province from which they hailed—the Norman for money, the Gascon for love, and the Provençal for a little of both.

There was also an inn at Rosas—the Parador of the Chevelure d'Or. Some few *ventas* were scattered along the sea-front, hard to be distinguished from the white fishermen's cottages, save for the evening noises which proceeded from them when the crews of the vessels in the bay came ashore to carouse. Altogether no better place for getting away from the realms of King Philip seemed possible to John d'Albret.

The Bay (or Gulf) of Rosas is one of the noblest harbours in the world—fifteen Spanish leagues from horn to horn, when you follow the indentations of the coast. So at least avers the Geographer-Royal. But it is to be suspected that his legs either wandered or that he measured some of the course twice over. The Bay of Rosas could contain all the navies of the world. A notable harbour in peace or war, with its watch-tower at either side, and its strong castle in the midst, it was no inconsiderable place in the reign of the Golden Philip.

Even in these last years when the gold was becoming dim, when its late array of war-ships had mostly found a resting-place on the rocky skerries of Ireland or the Hebrides, there were sometimes as many as six or eight king's ships in the bay—a fact which John d'Albret had omitted to reckon in his forecast of chances concerning the harbourage of Rosas.

The landlord of the Parador was a jovial, bustling man—a type not Spanish but purely Catalan. In the rest of Spain, your landlord shows himself little, if at all. Generally you serve yourself, and if you want anything you have not brought, you buy it in the town and descend to the kitchen to cook it. But the host of the Inn of Rosas was omnipresent, loquacious, insistent, not to be abashed or shaken off.

He met the Abbé John on the doorstep, and taking in at a glance his frayed court suit, his military bearing, and the long sword that swung at his heels, the landlord bowed low, yet with vigilant eyes aslant to measure the chances of this young ruffler having a well-filled purse.

"Your Excellency," he cried, "you do honour to yourself, whoever you may be, by coming to seek lodgings at the hostel of La Cabeladura d'Oro, as we say in our Catalan. Doubtless you have come seeking for a place and pay from Philip our king. A place you may have for the asking—the pay not so surely. It behooves me therefore to ask whether you desire to eat in my house at the Table Solvent or at the Table Expectant?"

"I do not gather your meaning, mine host," said John d'Albret haughtily.

"Nay, I am a plain man," said the landlord, "and you may read my name above my door—Sileno Lorent y Valvidia. That tells all about me. Therein, you see, you have the advantage of me. I know nothing about you, save that you arrive at my door with a cocked bonnet and a long sword."

John d'Albret felt that it was no time to resent this Catalan *brusquerie*. Indeed, he himself was enough of a Gascon to respect the man's aplomb. For what would be rudeness intentional in a Castilian, in a man of Catalonia is only the rough nature of the borderer coming out. So the Abbé John answered him in kind, using the Languedocean speech which runs like a kind of *Lingua Franca* from Bayonne to Barcelona.

"I am for the Table Solvent. Bite on that, Master Sileno, and the next time be not so suspicious of a soldier who has fought in many campaigns, and hopes to fight in many another! Now, by my beard which is yet to be, give me a razor and shaving-tackle, that I may make myself fit to call upon the Governor—while do you, Master Sileno, be off and get a good dinner ready!"

The landlord pocketed the coin as an asset towards the lengthy bill he saw unrolling in his mind's eye.

"Our Lord Governor the Count of Livia is at present with the King in Madrid," he said, "so I fear that you will be compelled to await his return, that is, if your business be with him, or has reference to any of the ships in the harbour, or is connected with supplies or stores military."

Señor Don Sileno, of the Chevelure d'Or, felt that he had given his guest quite sufficient latitude for entering into an explanation. But the Abbé John only thrust the hilt of his sword hard down, till the point cocked itself suggestively under the landlord's nose as he turned his back upon him.

"My business is with the Governor," he said shortly, "and if your house prove a good one and your table well supplied, I may indeed be content to await his return!"

"This bantling mayoral," muttered the landlord, "keeps his mask up. Very well—so much the better, so long as he pays. None gives himself airs in the house of Don Sileno Lorent y Valvidia, hosteller of Rosas, without paying for it! That is the barest justice. But, methinks this young boaster of many campaigns and the long sword, might have a new suit of clothes to go and see the Governor withal. Yet I am not sure—fighting is a curious trade. A good cook is not always known by the cleanliness of his apron."

At this moment the Abbé John roared down the stairs for the hot water.

"Coming, your Excellency!" answered the host, making a wry face; "all that you desire shall be in your chamber as fast as my scullions' legs can bring it."

Shaved, reorganised as to his inner man, daintied as to his outer, the Abbé John looked out of the window of the Golden Chevelure upon the sleeping sea. The Parador was a little house with a trellised flower-garden running down to the beach, and sheltered from the heat of the sun by vine-leaves and trembling acacias.

"That is a strange name you have given your inn," said the Abbé John, taking some oil from the salad-bowl and burnishing the hilt of his sword with a rag, as became a good cavalier. He had the sign of the Golden Tresses held by Sileno Lorent y Valvidia under his eyes as he spoke.

"You think so, sir?" said the landlord, his former *brusquerie* returning as soon as it was a question of property; "that shows you are unacquainted with the history of the country in which you desire to practise your trade of war!"

"I am none so entirely ignorant of it as you suppose," said John d'Albret.

"Yes, as ignorant as my carving-fork," said the landlord, pointing with that useful and newly-invented piece of cutlery to the sign below. "Now if you are a man of the pen as well as of the sword, what would you draw from that sign?"

"Why," said the Abbé John, smiling, "that you are named, curiously enough, Sileno—that your father's name was Lorent and your mother's Valvidia—that you are tenant of a well-provisioned inn called with equal curiosity the Golden Chevelure, and that you lodge (as you put it) both 'on horseback or on foot.' That is a good deal of printing to pay for at a penny a letter!"

"As I foretold, your Excellency knows nothing of the matter—and indeed, how should you? For by your tongue I would wager that you are from the Navarrese provinces—therefore a speaker of two languages and a wanderer over the face of the earth—your sword your bedfellow, a sack of fodder for your beast your best couch, and the loot of the last town taken by assault the only provender for your purse——"

"Let my purse alone," quoth the Abbé John, "you will find that there is enough therein to pay you, and—for a bottle of good wine on occasion for the pleasure of your company."

This mixture of hauteur and familiarity appeared to enchant the landlord, and he laid down on the bed the dishes he was carrying.

"I will explain," he said; "it is not every day that you can hear such a tale as mine for nothing."

"Bring a bottle of your best!" said John, who was disposed to talk, hoping that by-and-by he might receive also the best of informations as to the ships in the harbour, their incomings and outgoings, their captains and merchandises, together with the ports to which they sailed.

The wine was brought, and the host began his tale.

"This hostelry of mine was my father's also, and his father's before him for many generations. They were of noble blood—of the Llorients of Collioure, though the rolling of vulgar tongues has shortened it a little in these days. And my mother's name was Valvidia, being of one of the best houses of Spain. I am therefore of good blood on either side—you hear, Señor the Soldier?"

The Abbé John nodded. There was nothing remarkable in that. Every Spaniard counts himself so born, and it must be owned, so far at least as politeness is concerned, comports himself as such.

But the Chevelure d'Or, its carefully-mixed wine, and the tale thereto attached proved so soporific, that when John d'Albret awoke, he found himself chained to a bench in a long, low, evil-smelling place. A huge oar-handle was before him, upon which he was swaying drunkenly to and fro. He had on his left two companions who were doing the work of the rowing, and, erected upon a bench behind, a huge man with a fierce countenance walked to and fro with a whip in his hand.

"Where am I?" said John d'Albret feebly, his voice appearing to himself to come from an infinite distance, and sounding through the buzzing and racking of many windmills, like those of Jean-Marie the Miller-Alcalde when upon their beams and sails the mistral does its bitter worst.

"Hush!" whispered his neighbour, "the *comite* will flog you if you talk when at work. You are on the King of Spain's galley *Conquistador*, going south from Rosas to Barcelona. And as for me, I am a fellow-sufferer with you for the religion. I am Francis Agnew, the Scot!"

CHAPTER XLII
SECRETS OF THE PRISON HOUSE

"But Francis Agnew is dead! With my own eyes I saw him lie dead, in the robing-room of Professor Anatole——"

"*Row, you skulking 'Giffe'!*" cried the "comite," bringing down his whip upon the Abbé John's shoulders, which were bare, with a force that convinced him that he at least was both alive and awake.

So he kept silence and rowed in his place next the side of the vessel. And even his wonder in the matter of Claire's father could not prevent his cursing in his heart the man who had brought him to this pass—the talkative, hospitable, and far-descended Don Sileno Lorent y Valvidia, of the Parador of the Cabeledura d'Oro in the town of Rosas.

The galley of the first class, *Conquistador*, was one of the few which had been left behind in the Mediterranean at the time of the Great Armada. Most of the others had been carried northward for coast defence, and now lagged idly in port for lack of crews to navigate them. So that it became a quaint dilemma of King Philip's how to obtain sufficient heretics for his *autos de fé* without impoverishing too greatly his marine.

The *Conquistador* kept close company with the *Puerto Reale*, another of the same class, but with only two hundred slaves aboard to the three hundred and fifty of the *Conquistador*. The "comite," or master-in-charge of the slaves, walked up and down a long central bench. His whip was hardly ever idle, but it did not fall again upon John d'Albret—not from any pity for a newcomer, but because the ship's purser had let out the fact that a considerable sum in gold was in his hands to the credit of the newcomer. For King Philip, though he persecuted the heretic with fire and sword, fine, imprisonment, and the galleys, did not allow his subordinates to interfere with his monopoly. And indeed, as the Abbé John learned, more than one officer had swung from the forty-foot yard of his own mainmast for intromitting wrongfully with a prisoner's money.

As to the captains, they were for the most part impoverished grandees or younger sons of dukes and marquises. Most were knights of Malta and so apparent bachelors, whose money would go to the Order at their death.

In the meantime, therefore, they spent royally their revenues. The captain of the *Conquistador* was the young Duke of Err, recently succeeded to the ambassadorial title, and it was said of him that he counted the life of a galley-slave no more than that of a black-beetle beneath his seigneurial heel.

So long as the boat remained at sea, there was no sleep for any slave. Neither, indeed, for any of the "comites" or sub-officers, who consequently grew snappish and drove their slaves to the very limit of endurance, so that they might the sooner reach the harbour. Yet it was full morning before the awnings were spread within the roads of Barcelona, and the Abbé John could stretch his limbs—so far, that is, as the chain allowed. He had been placed, at the request of the senior oarsman of his mess, Francis Agnew, in the easiest place, that next to the side of the galley. Here not only was the stroke of the oar shortest, but at night, or in the intervals of sleep, the curve of the ship's side made a couch, if not luxurious, at least, comparatively speaking, tolerable.

The "comite" hoisted his hammock across the broad *coursier* or *estrada* which ran the length of the ship, overlooking and separating the two banks of oars, and formed the only passage from the high poop to the higher stern. It was also useful in rough seas, when the waves broke right across the ship, and (a mere detail) over the rowers also. For the only communication with the hold was by gangways descending from either end of the *coursier*.

The Abbé John heard the sound of the chief "comite's" whistle with astonishment—so varied were its tones, the quick succession of its notes, that the prompt understanding and obedience of the slaves and sailors, at whatever part of the deck they were placed, seemed as magic to him.

"Do as I do," said Francis Agnew, noticing his bewilderment. So the Abbé John halted and pulled, raised his oar level or backed water at the word of Claire's father. And all the while he kept looking sideways at the Dead-come-to-Life-again with speechless wonder and the sense of walking in a dream. Only the sound of the "comite's" lash on his comrades' backs kept him convinced of the general reality of things.

Francis Agnew was a strong and able-bodied rower, much remarked and approved by his chiefs. At various periods of an adventurous life he had served on the French and other galleys, even including those of Turkey. So that all the commands and disciplines came easily to him. He had even been charged with the provisioning of the rowers of the whole port side, and on occasion he could take the "comite's" whistle and pipe upon it, to the admiration of all.

Claire's father began his tale as soon as he had arranged his great grey cloak of woollen stuff commodiously, and laid the pillow (which he had by favour) close to the Abbé John's ear.

"The servants of the Sorbonne who were employed to carry my body to the vault were greedy rascals. It was their thought at first to sell my body to the younger surgeons for the purpose of their researching. But after stripping me of my apparel, it chanced that they cast a bucket of water over me to help me to 'keep'—the weather being hot in those Barricade Days in the city of Paris."

At this moment the tread of the night-sentinel approached along the *coursier* above their heads. The voices and whisperings ceased before him as by magic. It was full afternoon without, blazing under the chinked awnings. But officially it was night on board the galley. Day closed when the whistle of the "comite" blew. Mostly a careful captain, from motives of self-interest more than from any humanity, worked his men in the cool times of the night. For the Mediterranean is always so luminous of itself that the merest ripple of air is sufficient to stir the water and show the way. Moreover, in times of peace and on that safe coast galleys were rarely moored save in calm weather.

"It happened thus"—as the sentinel passed Francis Agnew took up the tale—"after the Sorbonne rascals had plashed the cool water over me, I sat up suddenly and looked about me for a sword. But, there being none, I was in their power. For ten days they kept me in hold in a secret place among firewood, deep underground, without any loophole whatever. Twice a day they brought me food, and by the light of a candle they dressed my wounds—one of them being expert at that business, having had practice in the hospitals. Then when I was recovered they gave me a candle which burned two hours only. And with it also a pile of brushwood to cut up into small pieces. This was the pleasantest part of the day to me. But they always took away the axe afterwards, bidding me push it through beneath the door, so that whoever came with my next meal might see it. Else I would get no dinner. For they feared lest I might brain one of them as he came in, and then make a rush for the passage-way. But I knew that the doors were shut behind, so that there was no chance. And besides, being a Christian man, I was covenanted to fight only when I could do so without sin, and with some chance of continuing the life so marvellously preserved to me!

"Then this Flamand, the chief of the servitors of the Sorbonne—Holtz was his name, a huge-handed animal of monkey breed, but with cunning under that sloping skull of his—made interest to find me a place in one of the slow waggons which carry the king's artillery to the port of Calais, where the new forts are. And me he laid, tied like a parcel between two brass guns for sieging, strapped down and gagged, feeding me at nights when the convoy halted. Also he paid the chief waggoner so much. For he meant to sell me for a slave to the Duke of Parma, who at that time was gathering a great fleet of galleys to destroy England. I had heard them arguing the matter somewhat thus:

"'Better kill him and be done,' said one; 'thus we are sure of a hundred shields for him from the lads of the beef barrel.' (So they spoke of the young surgeons of the Sorbonne.)

"However, the Flamand (a vantard and a bully, but very cunning) offered to fight any man there, or any two with fists or knives or any other weapon in their choice. And when no one took up his challenge, he cried out, 'Ho, stand back there, ye pack of cowards! This man is mine. A hundred silver shields! What is a hundred shields, when for such a wiry fellow, albeit a little old, we will get a hundred gold pieces from Parma, if only we can get him as far as Nieuport.'

"And so to Parma I was given, but the galley I was first placed in met with an English ship-of-war, and she ran us so close that we could not row. Her prow scraped us, breaking the oars and tossing the dead about, many being slain with the bounding fragments. And I—I was in the place next the port-hole, and I mind me I could lay my hand on the muzzle of a shotted gun. But that is the last I remember. For at that moment the Englishman fired a broadside and swept our decks. I alone was unhurt, and after a while in the lazar-house of Vigo, I came hither in a galleasse to teach the 'comites' of the Mediterranean side the newer practice of the fleets of the North."

He chuckled a little, his well-trained ear taking in the *diminuendo* and *crescendo* of the sentinel's footsteps on the wooden platform above his head.

"But from what I saw of the English," he murmured, "I judge that before long there will be no need of galleys to fight Spain's battles."

In a moment John d'Albret knew that his companion had not yet heard of the destruction of the Great Armada. He told him.

"Glory to the God of Battles," he said, hushed and low, "to Him the praise!"

Just then all the bells of the city began to ring, slow and measured. The sound came mellowed over the water and filtered through the striped awnings of yellow and red.

"Some great man is dead," he said, "perhaps the King—Philip, I mean. Or else a day of humiliation——"

"*Auto de fé!*" came along the benches in a thrilling whisper, for in spite of their fatigue few of the slaves were asleep. The afternoon was too hot, the glare from the water intolerable.

"Ah, well, the sooner to peace for some poor souls," said Francis the Scot. Then a thought seemed to strike him. "It is not possible—no, you cannot have heard. I dare not expect it. But I had a daughter, she was named Claire. They told me—that is, the Flamand Holtz, a not unkindly brute, though he had resolved to make money out of me, dead or alive—well, he told me that one of the wisest of the professors, a learned man, had taken her under his care. They escaped together to go to his mother's house with one of the students, a cousin of the Hope of Israel. You never heard—no, it is not possible. Why should I dream it?"

The Abbé John's throat became suddenly dry. He gasped for a moment, but could not speak.

"You do know—she is dead—tell me!" said Francis the Scot, shaking him roughly by the arm. And that was the single unkindness he used to the young man.

"No, no!" gasped John d'Albret. "She is well. I love her. I was that third who escaped in her company!"

"Where is she?"

"Nay, that I do not know exactly," said the Abbé John, "but it is in France, in a quiet province, with good folk who love her—though not as I love her. For I came hither for her sake!"

And he told the tale—how, in Jean-aux-Choux's secret *cache* behind the sheepfold on the hill, he had found a list of the articles for transport to Dame Amélie's new abode, with directions to the carriers, and one or two objects of price, evidently set aside for Jean to carry thither himself upon his next visit. So far, therefore, he was assured that all went well.

"God is great!" said Francis the Scot aloud; and the captive Turk who rowed outside oar, catching the well-known formula, added instantly, "And Mohammed is His prophet."

But on this occasion, at least, he was mistaken. For—like many a good proselyte who knows little of his master's doctrine yet draws converts notwithstanding—not Mohammed or Another, but plain, flippant, light-hearted John d'Albret was on this occasion the Prophet of the Lord.

CHAPTER XLIII
IN TARRAGONA BAY

Henceforth little personal was said. The two men spoke mostly of the work of the ship, the chances of escape (like all prisoners), and especially concerning the progress of the Holy War against ignorance and tyranny. But of Claire, nothing.

Something withheld them. A new thing was working in the heart of John d'Albret. Like many another he had been born a Catholic, and it had always seemed impossible to him to change. But the Place of Eyes, the Question Greater and Lesser in the Street of the Money, the comradeship of Rosny and D'Aubigné in the camps of the Bearnais, had shaken him. Now he listened, as often as he had time to listen, to the whispered arguments and explanations of his new friend. I do not know whether he was convinced. I am not sure even that he always heard aright. But, moved most of all by the transparent honesty of the man whose body had so suffered for that royal law of liberty which judges not by professions but by works, the Abbé John resolved no more to fight in the armies of the Huguenot Prince merely as a loyal Catholic, but to be even such a man as Francis Agnew, if it in him lay.

That it did not so lie within his compass detracts nothing from the excellence of his resolution. The flesh was weak and would ever remain so. This gay, careless spirit, bold and hardy in action, was much like that of Henry of Navarre in his earlier days. There were indeed two sorts of Huguenots in France in the days of the Wars of Religion. They divided upon the verse in James which says, "Is any among you afflicted? Let him pray. Is any merry? Let him sing."

The Puritans afterwards translated the verse, "Let him sing *psalms*." But the Genevan translators (whom in this book I follow in their first edition of 1560) more mercifully left out the "psalms": "*Is any merry, let him sing!*" say they.

Now such was the fashion of the men who fought for Henry IV. Even D'Aubigné, the greatest of all—historian, poet, and satirist—expelled from France for over-rigidity, found himself equally in danger in Geneva because of the liberty of his Muse's wing.

So, though the Abbé John became a suffering and warring Huguenot, on grounds good and sufficient to his own conscience, he remained ever the lad he was when he scuffled on the Barricades for the "Good Guise"—and the better fighting! A little added head-knowledge does not change men.

No motives are ever simple. No eye ever quite single. And I will not say what force, if any, the knowledge that Francis Agnew the Scot would never give his daughter in marriage to a Persecutor of the Brethren, had in bringing about the Abbé John's decision.

Perhaps none at all—I do not know. I am no man's judge. The weight which such an argument might have with oneself is all any man can know. And that is, after all, perhaps best left unstated.

At first John was all for revealing his name and quality; but against this Francis Agnew warned him At present he was treated as a pressed man, escaping the "hempen breakfasts of the heretic dogs"—which the captain, the young Duke d'Err, often commanded the "comite" to serve out to those condemned for their faith. Only the Turks, of whom there were a good many, captured during the Levantine wars, strong, grave, sturdy men, were better treated than he.

"If, then," said his companion, "they know that you are a cousin of the Bearnais, they will most likely send you to the Holy Bonfire, especially as you are of too light weight to row in the galley, at any rate."

The Abbé John cried out against this. He was as good as any man, in the galley or elsewhere.

"In intent, yes," said the Scot, "but your weight is as nothing to Hamal's or even mine, when it comes to pulling at fifty foot of oar on an upper deck!"

The Duke of Err was a young nobleman who had early ruined himself by evil life. The memory rankled, so that sometimes the very devil of cruelty seemed to ride him. He would order the most brutal acts for sport, and laugh afterwards as they threw the dead slaves over, hanging crucifixes, Korans, or Genevan Bibles about their necks in mockery according to their creed.

"My galley is lighter by so much carrion!" he would say on such occasions.

It chanced that in the late autumn, when the great heats were beginning to abate and the equinoctials had not yet begun to blow on that exposed eastern coast of Spain, that for a private reason the Duke-Captain desired to be at Tarragona by nightfall. So all that day the slaves were driven by the "executioners"—as the Duke invariably named his "comites"—till they prayed for death.

Although it was a known sea and a time of peace the slaves were allowed no quarter—that is, one half rowing while the other rested. All were forced most mercilessly through a long day's agony of heat and labour.

"Strike, *bourreau*—strike!" cried the captain incessantly; "what else are you paid the King's good money for? If we do not get to Tarragona by four o'clock this afternoon, I will have you hung from the yardarm. So you are warned. If you cannot animate, you can terrorise. Once I saw a 'comite' in the galleys of Malta cut off a slave's arm, and beat the other dogs about the head with it till they doubled their speed!"

It was in order to give a certain entertainment at Tarragona that the Duke of Err was so eager to get there. For hardly had the *Conquistador* anchored, before the great sail was down, the fore-rudder unshipped, the after part of the deck cleared, and a gay marquee spread, with tables set out underneath for a banquet.

By this time, what with the freshness of the sea and fear of missing a stroke occasionally—a crime always relentlessly punished—the men were so fatigued with the heat, the toil, and the bruising of their chests upon the oar-handles, that many would gladly have fallen asleep as they were— but the order came not. All were kept at their posts ready for the salute when the guests of the Duke should come on board—that is, the lifting of the huge oars out of the water all in a moment and holding them parallel and dripping, a thing which, when well performed, produces a very happy effect.

After dinner the Duke conducted his guests upon the *coursier*, or raised platform, to look down upon the strange and terrible spectacle beneath. It was full moon, and the guests, among them several ladies, gazed upon that mass of weary humanity as on a spectacle.

"God who made us all," murmured the Abbé John, "can woman born of woman be so cruel?"

The young Duke was laughing and talking to a lady whom he held cavalierly by the hand, to preserve her from slipping upon the narrow ledge of the *coursier*.

"I told you I had the secret of sleep," he said; "I will prove it. I will make three hundred and fifty men sleep with a motion of my hand."

He signed to one of the "comites," whom he was accustomed to call his "chief hangman," and the man blew a long modulated note. Instantly the whole of the men who had kept at attention dropped asleep—most of them being really so, because of their weariness. And others, like John d'Albret and Francis the Scot, only pretended to obey the order.

At the sight of the hundreds of miserable wretches beneath, crowded together, naked to the waist (for they had had no opportunity of dressing), their backs still bleeding from the blows of the *bourreau*, the lady shuddered and drew her arm hastily from that of the captain. But he, thinking that she was pleased, and only in fear of slipping among such a horrid gang, led her yet farther along the estrade, and continued his jesting in the same strain as before.

"My dear lady," he said, "you have now seen that I am possessed of the art of making men sleep. Now you will see that I know equally well how to awake them."

Again he signed to the "comites" to blow the *reveille*.

A terrible scene ensued as the men rose to resume their oars. The chains clanked and jingled. The riveted iron girdles about their waists glistened at the part where the back-pull of the oar catches it. Hardly one of the crew was fit to move. With the long strain of waiting their limbs had stiffened; their arms had become like branches of trees. Even the utmost efforts of "hangman" were hardly able to put into them a semblance of activity.

As the party looked from above upon that moving mass, the moon, which had been clouded over, began to draw clear. Above, was the white and sleeping town sprinkled with illuminated windows—beneath, many riding-lights of ships in harbour. The moon sprang from behind the cloud, sailing small and clear in the height of heaven, and Valentine la Niña found herself looking into a pallid, scarcely human face—that of John d'Albret, galley-slave.

He was—where she had vowed him. Her curse had held true. With a cry she slipped from the captain's arm, sprang from the *coursier*, and threw her arms about the neck of the worn and bleeding slave!

CHAPTER XLIV
VALENTINE AND HER VENGEANCE

But as he watched, a strange drawn look appeared on the countenance of Francis Agnew the Scot. And there came that set look to his mouth, which had enabled him to endure so many things.

"The lad also!" he muttered, "and I had begun to love him!"

For it was not given to Francis Agnew, more than to any other son of Adam, to divine the good when the appearance is evil. And with his elbows on his knees he thought of Claire, of her hope deferred, and of the waiting of the sick heart. She believed this man faithful. And now, would even her father's return (if ever he did return) make up to her for this most foul treachery?

To John d'Albret he spoke no further word. He asked no question, as they rested side by side during the night-watches. The stammered explanation which the Abbé John began after Valentine's departure was left unanswered. Francis Agnew had learned a great secret—how to keep silence. It is an excellent gift.

The ancient, high-piled town loomed up tier above tier, white and grey and purple under the splendours of the moon. The Abbé John took it in bit by bit—the black ledges and capes with the old Moorish castles, and later corsair watch-towers, the flaring *phare* at the mouth of the harbour, the huge double swell of the cathedral crowning all, the long lines of the arch-episcopal palace on the slope, the vineyards and oliveyards—all stood up blanched and, as it were, blotched in pen and ink under the silver flood of light and the steady milky blue arch of the sky. Such was Tarragona upon that night of sleepless silence.

The morning brought a new order, grateful to both.

The armourer of the *Conquistador* came down, and with file, and rasp, and pince-monseigneur, he speedily undid the iron belt which had not yet had time to eat into the flesh. The Abbé John was commanded to go on shore. During his short time aboard he had made himself a favourite. The Turk, Ben Hamal, hugged him to his hairy chest and stammered a blessing in the name of the Prophet. Others here and there wished him good speed, and looked wistfully at him, even though after John had departed they shook their heads, and with quick upward motions of their thumbs imitated the darting flames of the bi-weekly *auto de fé.*

They understood why he was sent for—and envied him.

Only Francis Agnew the Scot said no word, bade no adieu, wished no wish, gazing steadily at a post on the shore, which to his distorted imagination took on the shape of a woman dressed in white waiting for John d'Albret.

Had he only thought, he would have known that to be impossible. But he did not think—except of Claire, his daughter. And—as he had said—he had begun to love the lad. So much the worse for him and for all.

It was not upon the shore, but high in the city that the Abbé John found Valentine la Niña. She awaited him in that secular annex to the palace of the Archbishop which the great Terés Doria now occupied as Viceroy of Catalonia. The Archbishop-Governor had put his private cabinet at her service. One does not say no to the daughters of reigning sovereigns, when one has served both father and grandfather.

Doria had ordered his valet, a layman with mere servitor's vows to give him a standing, to assist John d'Albret in his toilet. So before long the Abbé John found himself in a suit of black velvet, severe and unbroidered, which fitted him better than it could ever have done the stouter Don Jacques Casas, for whom it had been made. A sword hung at his side—a feeble blade and blunt, as John d'Albret ascertained as soon as he was left a moment alone, but sheathed in a scabbard of price. He sat still and let the good valet perfume and lave, and comb out his love-locks, without thinking much of what was coming. His mind was benumbed and curiously oppressed. Fate planned above his head, shadowy but unseen. And somehow he was afraid—he knew not why.

Finally all was done. Even Jacques Casas was satisfied, and smiled. The galley-slave had become a man again.

The cabinet of the Cardinal-Viceroy of Catalonia looked over the city wall, very nearly at its highest seaward angle, in the place where now they have pierced a gate, where red-kerchiefed gipsies sit about on steps, and vagabonds in mauve caps sell snails by measure. But then a little vice-regal garden fronted the windows, and the ancient walls of Tarragona, older than the Romans or the Greeks, older than Carthage—older even than the galleys of Tyre—fell away beneath towards the sea verges, so solid that to the eye there was little difference between them and the living rock on which they were founded. The giants who were in the times before the flood built them, so the townsmen said. And as no one knows anything about the matter, that opinion is as good as any other.

The two young people stood regarding each other, silent. The blonde masses of the girl's hair seemed less full of living gold and fire than of yore. Perhaps there was a thread or two of grey mingling with the graciousness of those thick coils and curves. But the great eyes, coloured like clover-honey dropped from the comb, were moist and glorious as ever. They had manifestly gained in directness and nobility.

The Abbé John bowed low. Valentine la Niña did not respond. There was, however, a slight colour on her cheeks of clear ivory. Man born of woman had never seen that before.

"I have sent for you," said Valentine la Niña, in a low and thrilling contralto, "I would speak with you! Yet this one time more!"

She put her hand rapidly to her throat, as if something there impeded her utterance.

"Yes," she continued, swallowing down her emotion with difficulty, "I would speak with you—it may be for the last time."

After this she was silent a while, as if making up her mind what to say. Then with a single instinctive mechanical gesture she twitched her long robe of white and creamy lace behind her. It seemed as if she wanted all space wide and clear before her for what she had to say and do. Her eyes devoured those of John d'Albret.

"You—still—love her?" she said, forcing the words slowly from her lips.

"I love her!" John answered simply. He had nothing to add to that. It had been said before. Any apology would be an insult to Claire. Sympathy a deeper insult to the woman before him.

The carmine flush deepened on her cheek. But it was not anger. The girl was singularly mistress of herself—calm, resolved, clear-seeing.

"Ah," said Valentine la Niña softly, "I expected no other answer. But still, have you remembered that I once gave you your liberty? How you lost it a second time, I do not know. Now I am putting all my cards on the table. I play—hearts only. If I and my love are not worthy of yours, will you tell me why another, who has done nothing for you, is preferred to me, who has risked, and am willing to risk everything for you—life, death, the world, position, freedom, honour, all! Tell me! Answer me!"

"I loved her first!" said the Abbé John.

"Ah, that too you said before," she cried, with a kind of sigh, "and you have nothing more to say—I—nothing more to offer. Yet I cannot tell why it should be so. It seems, in all dispassion, that if I were a man, I should choose Valentine la Niña. Men—many men—ah, how many men, have craved for that which I have begged you to accept—not for your vague princedom, not for your vague hopes, not for your soldier's courage, which is no rare virtue. But for you—yourself! Because you are you—and have drawn me, I know not how—I see not where——"

"I do not ask you to obtain my release," said John d'Albret, somewhat uneasily, "I have no claim to that; but I have on board that ship a comrade"— here he hesitated—"yes, I will tell you his name, for you are noble. It is Francis Agnew, her father, he who was left for dead on the Street of the University by the Guisards of Paris on the Day of the Barricades. He is now at the same bench as I, in the *Conquistador*——"

"What!" cried Valentine, "not the old man with the white tangled beard I saw by your side when—when—I saw you?"

"The same," the Abbé John answered her softly.

Then came a kind of glory over the girl's face, like the first certainty of forgiveness breaking over a redeemed soul. She drew in her breath sharply. Her hands clasped themselves on her bosom. Then she smiled, but the bitterness was gone out of the smile now.

"I must see this Claire," she said, speaking shortly and somewhat sternly to herself; "I must know whether she is worthy. For to obtain from my father (who will not of his own goodwill call me daughter)—from Philip the King, I mean—pardon for two such heretics, one of them the cousin of his chief enemy—I must have a great thing to offer. And such I have indeed— something that he would almost expend another Armada to obtain. But, before I decide, I must see Claire Agnew. I must look in her eyes, and know if she be worthy. Then I will do it. Or, perhaps, she and I together."

The last words were murmured only.

The Abbé John, who knew not of what she was speaking, judged it prudent to say nothing.

"Yes—I must know," she went on, still brusquely, "you will tell me where she is. I will go there. And afterwards I will return to the Escorial to see my father—Philip the King. Meantime I will speak to the Duke of Err, and to his mother, as well as to the Viceroy Doria. You shall abide in Pilate's House down there, where is a prison garden——"

"And my friend?" said John d'Albret.

The girl hesitated a little, and then held out her hand. The young man took it.

"And your friend!" she said. "There in Pilate's House you must wait, you two, till I see—till I know that she is worth the sacrifice."

Once again she laughed a little, seeing a wave of joy or perhaps some more complex emotion sweep over John's face.

"Ah," she cried, with a returning trace of her first bitterness, "you are certain that she is worthy. Doubtless so for you! But as the sacrifice is mine—I also must be certain—ah, very certain. For there is no back-going. It is the end of all things for Valentine la Niña."

She laughed little and low, like one on the verge of hysterics. A nerve twitched irregularly in her throat under her chin to the right. The pink came out brighter to her cheek. It was a terrible laugh to hear in that still place. And the mirthlessness of it—it struck the Abbé John cold.

"This shall be my revenge," she said, fixing him, with flame in her honey-coloured eyes; "long after, long—oh, so—so long after"—she waved her arm—"you will know! And you will see that, however much she has loved you, hers was the love which takes. But mine—ah, mine is different. Mine is the love which gives—the only true woman's love—without scant, without measure, without bounds of good or evil, without thought of recompense, or hope of reward. Love net, unselfish, boundless, encompassing as the sea, and like a fountain sealed within the heart of a woman. And then—then you shall remember that when ye might—ye would not—ah, ye would not!"

A sob tore her throat.

"But one day, or it may be through all eternity, you shall know which is the greater love, and you shall wish—no, you are a man, you will be content with the lesser, the more comprehensible, the goodwife warming her feet by the fire over against yours. There is your ideal. While I—I—would have carried you beyond the stars!"

The Abbé John took a step nearer her. He had some vague notion of comforting—not knowing.

But she thrust her arms out furiously as if to strike him.

"Go—go!" she cried, "you are breaking my heart every instant you remain. Is it not enough, that which you have done? I would be quiet. They are waiting for you to take you to Pilate's House. But tell me first where to find this—this Claire Agnew!"

She pronounced the name with difficulty.

"Ah," Valentine continued, when John had told her how she was safe in Provence, "that is no great way. I shall go and soon return. Then to Madrid is farther, but easier. But if I suffer—what I must suffer—you can well abide here a little season. The hope—the future is with you. For me there is neither—save to do the greatest thing for you that ever woman did for man! That shall be my revenge."

CHAPTER XLV
VALENTINE FINDS CLAIRE WORTHY

The mornings are fair—yes, very sweet and very clear at the Mas of the Mountain well-nigh all the year round. However hot the day, however mosquito-tormented the nights for those who do not protect themselves, the morn is ever fresh, with deep draughts of air cool as long-cellared wine, and everywhere the scent of springy, low-growing plants—the thyme, the romarin, the juniper—making an undergrowth which supports the foot of the wanderer, and carries him on league after league almost without his knowledge.

There was great peace on the Valley of the Rhone. It was at peace even from the drive of the eternal mistral, which, from horizon to horizon, turns all things greyish-white, the trees and herbage heavy with dust, and the heavens hiding themselves away under a dry steely pall.

"Avenio ventoso,
Si non ventoso, venenoso,"

muttered the Professor, as he looked at the black mass to the north, which was the Palace of the Popes. "But I thank God it is windy, this Rhone Valley of ours, with its one great, sweeping, cleansing wind, so that no poison can lurk anywhere."

He had a book in his hand, and he was looking abroad over the wide valley between the grey ridges of the Mountain of Barbentane and the little splintered peaks of the Alpilles. As on the landscape, great peace was upon the Professor.

But all suddenly, without noise of approach, Jean-aux-Choux stood before him—changed, indeed, from him who had been called "The Fool of the Three Henries." The fire of a strange passion glowed in his eye. His great figure was hollowed and ghastly. His regard seemed to burn like a torch that smokes. On the back of his huge hand the muscles stood out like whipcords. His arms, bare beneath his shepherd's cape, were burned to brick colour.

"Jean-aux-Choux!" cried the Professor, clapping his hands, "come and see my mother—how content she will be."

The ex-fool made a sign of negation.

"No, I cannot enter," he said; "there is a woman down in the valley there who would see Claire Agnew. She hath somewhat to say to her, which it concerns her greatly to know."

"Who is the woman?" demanded the Professor.

"I will vouch for her," said Jean-aux-Choux; "her name is nothing to you or to any man."

"But Claire Agnew's name and life concern me greatly," said the Professor hotly. "Had it been otherwise, I should even now have been in my class-room with my students at the Sorbonne!"

"In your grave more like—with Catherine and Guise and Henry of Valois!"

"Possibly," said the Professor tranquilly, "all the same I must know!"

"I vouch for the woman. She has come with me from Collioure," said Jean-aux-Choux. "Nevertheless, do you come also, and we will stand apart and watch while these two speak the thing which is in their hearts!"

"But she may be a messenger of the Inquisition," the Professor protested, whom hard experience had rendered suspicious in these latter days. "A dagger under the cloak is easy to carry!"

"Did I not tell you I would vouch for her?" thundered Jean-aux-Choux, the face of the slayer of Guise showing for the first time; "is not that enough?"

It was enough. Notwithstanding, the Professor armed himself with his sword-cane, and prepared to be of the company. They called Claire. She came forth to them with the flour of the bread-baking on her hands, gowned in white with the cook's apron and cap, which Madame Amélie had made for her—a fair, gracious, household figure.

She had no suspicions. Someone wanted to speak with her. There—down by the olive plant! A woman—a single woman—come from far with tidings! Well, Jean-aux-Choux was with her. Good Jean—dear Jean!

Then, all suddenly, there sprang a vivid red to her cheek.

Could it be? News of the Abbé John. Ah, but why this woman? Why could not Jean-aux-Choux have brought the message himself?

And Claire quickened her step down towards the olives in the valley.

The two met, the girl and the woman—Claire, slender and dark, but with eyes young, and with colour bright—Valentine la Niña fuller and taller, in the mid-most flower of a superb beauty. Claire, fresh from the kitchen, showed an abounding energy in every limb. Sweet, gracious, happy, born to make others happy, the Woman of the Interior went to meet her Sister of the Exterior—of the life without a home. Valentine la Niña had her plans ready. She had thought deeply over what to say and what to do before she met Claire Agnew. She must look into the depths of the girl's soul.

"I am called Valentine la Niña," she said, speaking with slow distinctness, yet softly, "and I have come from very far to tell you that I love the Prince Jean d'Albret. I am of his rank, and I demand that you release him from any hasty bond or promise he may have made to you!"

The colour flushed to the cheek of Claire Agnew, a deep sustained flood of crimson, which, standing a moment at the full, ebbed slowly away.

"Did he send you to ask me that question—to make that request?" she demanded, her voice equally low and firm.

"I have come of my own accord," Valentine la Niña answered, "I speak for his sake and for yours. The release, which it is not fitting that he should ask—I, who am a king's daughter, laying aside my dignity, may well require!"

It was curious that Claire never questioned the truth of these statements. Had not the lady come with Jean-aux-Choux? Nevertheless, when she spoke, it was clearly and to the main issue.

"Jean d'Albret has made me no promise—I have given none to him. True, I know that he loved me. If he loves me no more, let him come himself and tell me so!"

"He cannot," said Valentine la Niña, "he is in prison. He has been on the Spanish galleys. He has suffered much——"

"It was for my sake, I know—all for my sake!" cried Claire, a burst of gladness triumphing in her voice. Valentine la Niña stopped and looked at her. If there had been only a light woman's satisfaction in one more proof of her power, she would never have gone on with what she came to do. But Valentine saw clearly, being one of the few who can judge their own sex. She watched Claire from under her long lashes, and the smile which hovered about the corners of her mouth was tender, sweet, and pitiful. Valentine la Niña was making up her mind.

"Well, let us agree that it was 'for your sake,'" she said. "Now it is your turn to do something for his. He is ill, in prison. If he is sent back to the galleys he will soon die of exposure, of torture, and of fatigue. If he, a prince of the House of France, weds with me, a daughter of the King of Spain, there will be peace. Great good will be done through all the world."

"I do not care—I do not care," cried Claire, "let him first come and tell me himself."

"But he cannot, I tell you," said the other quietly; "he is in the prison of Tarragona!"

"Well, then, let him write!" said Claire, "why does he not write?"

Valentine la Niña produced a piece of paper, and handed it to Claire without a word. It was in John d'Albret's clear, clerkly hand. Claire and he had capped verses too often together by the light of Madame Granier's pine-cones for any mistake. She knew it instantly.

> "Whatever this lady says is true, and if you have any
> feeling in your heart for your father, or love for me, do as
> she bids you!
> "Jean d'Albret de Bourbon."

Three times Claire read the message to make sure.

Then she spoke. "What do you wish me to do? I am ready!"

"You will give this man up to me?"

"He never was mine to give, but if he had been, he is free to go—because he wills it!"

"I put my life in danger for him now—every moment I stay here," said Valentine la Niña; "Jean-aux-Choux will tell you so. Will you walk to the gates of death with me to deliver him whom you love?"

"I will," said Claire, "I will obey you—that is, I will obey him through you!"

"This you do for the love you bear to the man whom you give up to me?"

"For what else?" cried Claire, the tears starting in her eyes. "Surely an honest girl may love a man? She may be ready even to give her life for him. But—she will not hold him against his will!"

"Then you will come with me to my father, the King of Spain?" Valentine persisted. "Perhaps—I do not know—he will pardon Jean d'Albret at our request—perhaps he will send us, all three, to the fires of the Inquisition. That also I do not know!"

"And I do not care!" cried Claire; "I will come!"

"For his sake alone?" queried Valentine, resolved to test the girl to the uttermost.

"For whose else?" cried Claire at last, exasperated; "not for yours, I suppose! Nor yet for mine own! I have been searched for by your Inquisition bloodhounds before now. He saved me from that!"

"And I—all of you!" said Valentine la Niña to herself. "But the price is somewhat heavy!"

Nevertheless, she had found Claire worthy.

CHAPTER XLVI
KING AND KING'S DAUGHTER

Upon the high, black, slaty ledges of the Sierra of Guadarrama, winter descends early. Indeed, Peñalara, looking down on the Escorial, keeps his snow-cap all the year. From the Dome of Philip the King, one may see in mid-August the snow-swirls greying his flanks and foot-hills almost to the limits of the convent domain.

It was now October, and along the splendid road which joins the little village of San Ildefonso to the Escorial, a sturdy cavalcade of horses and mules took its way—a carriers' convoy this, a muleteers' troop, not by any means a raffle of gay cavaliers.

"Ho, the Maragatos! Out of the way—the Maragatos!" shouted any that met them, over their shoulders. For that strange race from the flat lands of Astorga has the right of the highway—or rather, of the high, the low, and the middle way—wherever these exist in Spain. They are the carriers of all of value in the peninsula—assurance agents rather—stout-built men, curiously arrayed in leathern jerkins, belted broadly about the middle, and wearing white linen *bragas*—a sort of cross between "breeks" and "kilt," coming a little above the knee. Even bandits think twice before meddling with one of these affiliated Maragatos. For the whole bees' byke of them would hunt down the robber band. The King's troops let them alone. The Maragatos have always had the favour of kings, and as often as not carry the King's own goods from port to capital far more safely than his own troopers. Only they do not hurry. They do not often ride their horses, which carry—carry—only carry, while their masters stride alongside, with quarter-staff, a two-foot spring-knife, and a pair of holster-pistols all ready primed for any emergency.

But in the midst of this particular cavalcade were two women riding upon mules. They were dressed, so far as the eye of the passer-by could observe, in the costume of all the Maragatas—dresses square-cut in the bodice, with chains and half-moons of silver tinkling on neck and forehead, while a long petticoat, padded in small diamond squares, fell to the points of their red Cordovan shoes. These Maragatas sat sideways on their mules and were completely silent.

It was not a warlike party to look at. Nevertheless, gay young cavaliers of the capital on duty at La Granja, who might have sought adventure had the ladies been protected only by guards in mail and plume, drew aside and whispered behind their hands as the Maragatas went by.

Now these women were probably the two fairest in Spain at that moment—being by denomination Claire Agnew and Valentine la Niña. In the rear a huge, vaguely misshapen giant in shepherd's dress—fleece-coat and cap of wolf-skin, with the ears sticking out quaintly on either side, herded the entire party. He seemed to be assuring himself that it was not followed or spied upon.

Beneath them, in the grey of the mist, as they turned a corner of the blue-black Sierra, there suddenly loomed up the snow-sprinkled roofs of a vast building—palace, monastery, tomb—what not. It was the Escorial, built by Philip of Spain to commemorate the famous victory of St. Quentain, and completed just in time to receive, as a cold water baptism, the news of the defeat of his Great Armada.

The pile of the Escorial seemed too huge to be wrought by man—a part of the mountain rather, hewn by giant hands into domes and doors and fantastic pinnacles. Indeed, the grey snow-showers, mere scufflings of sleet and hail, drifting low and ponderous, treated it as part of the Sierra, one moment whitening it—then, the sun coming out with Spanish fierceness for a few minutes, lo! vast roofs of blue slate would show through, glistening like polished steel.

And a king dwelt there—not discrowned, but still the mightiest on the earth. In spite of his defeats, in spite of his solitude, his broken purposes, his doubtful future, his empty exchequer, his ruined health, and the Valley of the Shadow of Death opening before him, there was nothing on earth—not pope nor prelate, not unscrupulous queen nor victorious fleet, not even the tempests which had blown his great Armada upon the inhospitable rocks of Ireland—that could subdue his stubborn will. He warred for Holy Church against the Pope. He claimed the throne of France from the son of Saint Louis. Once King of England, he held the title to the last, and in defence of it broke his power against the oaken bulwarks of that stiff-necked isle.

In his youth a man of as many marriages, secret and open, as Henry VIII. himself, he had been compelled to imprison and perhaps to suppress his son Don Carlos. The English ambassadors found him a man of domestic virtues. Yet the sole daughter who cherished him he sacrificed in a moment to his dynastic projects. And the other? Well, there is something to be said concerning that other.

Philip II. dwelt in the Escorial as in a fenced city. But Valentine la Niña had a master-key to unlock all doors. The next morning very early—for the King rose and donned his monk's robe in the twilight, stealing to his place in the stalls like any of his Jeronomite fellows—the two found their way along the vast corridors to the tiny royal chambers, bare of comfort as monastic cells, but loaded with petitions, reports, and letters from the four corners of the earth.

"Tell the King that Valentine la Niña, Countess of Astorga, would see him!"

And at that word the royal confessor, who had come to interview them, grew suddenly ashen pale in the scant light of a covered morning, as if the granite of the court in which they stood had been reflected in his face.

He made a low reverence and withdrew without a word.

At last the two girls were at the door of the King's chamber—a closet rather than a room. Philip was seated at his desk, his gouty foot on the eternal leg-rest, a ghastly picture of St. Lawrence over his head, and a great crucifix in ivory and silver nailed upon the wall, just where the King's eyes would rest upon it each time he lifted his head.

Claire took in the outward appearance of the mighty monarch who had been but a name to her up to this moment. He looked not at all like the "Demon of the South" of her imagination.

A little fair man, in appearance all a Flamand of the very race he despised, a Flamand of the Flamands His blue eyes were already rheumy and filmed with age, and when he wished to see anything very clearly he had a trick of covering the right eye with his hand, thrusting his head forward, and peering short-sightedly with the other. His hair, though white, retained some of the saffron bloom which once had marked him in a crowd as the white *panache* served the Bearnais. His beard, dirty white also, was straggling and tufted, as if in secret hours of sorrow it had been plucked out, Oriental fashion, by the roots.

"My father," said Valentine la Niña, looking at him straight and fearlessly, "I have come to bid you a good morning. My uncle of Astorga would have come too, but he prays in his canon's stall in the cathedral of Leon for his near and dear 'parent,' your Majesty."

The King rose slowly from his chair. His glabrous face showed no emotion.

"Aid me, my daughter," he said, "I would look in your face."

As he rose, his short-sighted eyes caught the dim silhouette of Claire standing behind. All a-tremble from head to foot, he stopped short in what he was about to say.

"And who may that be?" he demanded, in the thick, half-articulate mumble which so many ambassadors found a difficulty in understanding.

"A maid of Scotland, for whom I have come to ask a favour," answered Valentine la Niña.

"Ah," said the King, as one who all his life had had knowledge of such requests. But without further question he took Valentine la Niña by the hand and led her to the window, so that the grey light, half-reflected from the clay-muddy sky, and half from the snowy courtyard, might strike directly upon her face.

"Isabel Osorio's daughter—yes!" he said very low, "herself indeed!"

"The lawful daughter of your lawful wife," said the girl, "also an obedient daughter. For I have done ever what you wished me—save only in one thing. And that—that—I am now ready to do, on one condition."

"Ah," said the King again, pulling at his beard, "now aid me to sit down again, my daughter. We will talk."

"Aye," the girl answered, "we will talk—you and I. You and I have not talked much in my life. I have always obeyed—you—my uncle of Astorga—Mariana of the Gesù. For that reason I am alive—I am free—there is still a place for me in the world. But I know—you have told me—Isabel Osorio's brother himself has told me, that I too must sacrifice myself for your other and younger children, the sons and daughters of princesses. You have often asked me—indeed bidden me to enter a nunnery. The Jesuits have made me great promises. For what? That I might leave the way clear for others—I, the King's eldest-born—I, whom you dare not deny of blood as good as your own, a daughter of the Osorio who fought at Clavijo shoulder to shoulder with Santiago himself."

"I do not deny," said the King softly, "you have done a good work. But the Faith hath need of you. To it you consecrate your mother's beauty as I have consecrated my life— —"

"Yes," said the girl, "but first you lived your life—you did not yield it up on the threshold—unlived."

Silently Philip crossed himself, raising his thick swollen fingers from the rosary which hung about his neck as low as his waist.

"Then why have you come," he said, again resuming the steady fingering of his beads, "when you have not thought it fitting to obey, save upon condition? One does not play the merchant with one's father."

"I have been too young—yes," she broke out, her voice hurrying in fear of interruption—"too like my mother—ah, even you cannot reproach me with that!—to bury myself under a veil, with eternal walls shutting me in on every side. I have served you well. I have served the Society—I have done your will, my father—save only in this."

"And now," said the King drily, "you have returned to a better mind?"

"I have," said Valentine, "on conditions!"

"Again I warn you I do not bargain," said the King, "my will is my will. Refuse or submit. I make no terms."

The girl flashed into fire at the word.

"Ah, but you must," she cried. "I am no daughter of Flanders—no Caterina de Lainez to be shut up with the Ursulines of Brussels against my will. I am an Osorio of the Osorios. The brother of my mother will protect me. And behind him all Astorga and Leon would rise to march upon Madrid if any harm befell me. I bargain because it is my right—because I can stand between your children and their princely thrones—because I can prove your marriage no marriage—because, without my consent and that of my brothers Pedro and Bernardino, you had never either been King of England nor left children to sit in the seat of Charles your father. But neither they nor I have asked for aught save life from your hands. We have effaced ourselves for the kingdom's good and yours. A king of Spain may not marry a subject, but you married my mother—your friend's sister. Now will you bargain or no?"

"I will listen," said Philip grimly; "place my foot-rest a little nearer me, my daughter."

The calmness of the King immediately reacted on Valentine la Niña.

"Listen, my father," she said, "there are in your galleys at Tarragona two men—one of them the father of this young Scottish girl—the other, her—her betrothed. Pardon them. Let them depart from the kingdom——"

"Their crime?" interrupted the King.

"They were delivered over by the fathers of the Inquisition," said Valentine, less certainly.

"Then it is heresy," said the King. "I can forgive anything but that!"

"For one and the other," said the girl, "their heresy consists in good honest fighting, outside of your Majesty's kingdom—against the Guisard League. They are not your subjects, and were found in your province of Roussillon only by chance."

"Ah, in Roussillon?" said Philip thoughtfully. And picking up a long pole like the butt of a fishing-rod furnished with a pair of steel nippers like a finger-and-thumb at the top, he turned half round to an open cabinet of many pigeon-holes, where were bundles innumerable of papers all arranged and neatly tied. The pincers clicked, and the King, with a smile of triumph at his little piece of dexterity, withdrew half-a-dozen folded sheets.

"Yes, I have heard," he said, "the men you commanded my Viceroy to remove from the galleys and to place in Pilate's House at Tarragona—a young Sorbonnist whom once before you allowed to escape at Perpignan, and the Scottish spy Francis Agnew."

"My father," began Claire, catching the name, but only imperfectly understanding the Castilian which they were speaking—"my father is——"

But Valentine la Niña stopped her with an imperious gesture of the hand. It was her affair, the movement said.

The King shook his head gravely and a little indulgently.

"My daughter," he said, "you have taken too much on yourself already. And my Viceroy in Catalonia is also to blame——"

"Pardon me," cried Valentine la Niña, "and listen. This is what I came to say. There is in your city of Madrid a convent of the Carmelites, the same which Theresa reformed. It is strictly cloistered, the rule serene, austere. Those who enter there have done with life. Give these two men their liberty, escort them to France, and I promise you I will enter it of my own free will. I will take the Black Veil, and trouble neither you nor your heirs more in this world."

The King did not answer immediately, but continued to turn over the sheaf of papers in his hand.

"And why," he said at last, "will you do for this maid—for the lives of these two men, what no persuasion of family or Church could previously persuade you to do?"

Valentine went hastily up to the King's side who, dwelling in perpetual fear of assassination, moved a little uneasily, watching her hand. But when she bent and whispered softly, none heard her words but himself. Yet they moved him.

"Yes, I loved her—the wife of my youth!" he answered aloud (and as if speaking involuntarily) the whispered question.

"And she loved you?" said Valentine la Niña.

"She loved me—yes—God be her judge!" said the King. "She died for me!"

"Then," continued Valentine la Niña slowly, "you understand why for this young man's sake I am willing to accept death in life! I desire that he shall wed the woman he loves—whom he has chosen—who loves him!"

But under her breath she added, "Though not as I!"

And Valentine la Niña took the King's hand in hers, and motioned to Claire to come near and kiss it.

But Claire, kneeling, kissed that of Valentine la Niña instead.

Then, for the first time in many years, a tear lay upon the cheek of the King of Spain, wondering mightily at itself.

CHAPTER XLVII
GREAT LOVE—AND GREATER

Now this is the explanation of these things.

In his hot youth, Philip, son of the great Emperor, had wedded in secret his comrade's sister, that comrade being one of the richest and most ancient nobles of his kingdom, Osorio, Marquis of Astorga. But by a miracle of abnegation, Isabel Osorio had stood aside, her brother and the full family council approving her act, in order that her husband, and the father of her three children, should add Portugal, and afterwards England, to his Spanish domains.

Therefore, from the point of view of dynasty, the Osorios of Astorga held the succession of the kingdom of Spain in their hands. At the least they could have produced a bloody war, which would have rent Spain from one end to the other, on behalf of the succession of Isabel Osorio's children. Therefore it had been the main purpose of Philip to keep them all unmarried. The sons, Pierre and Bernardino, he had severally made priors of great Flemish and Italian monasteries. Only Valentine la Niña he had never been able to dispose of according to his will. Now he had her word. No wonder that the King slept more soundly that night.

After all, what did it matter to him if a couple of heretics escaped— if only Valentine la Niña were once safely cloistered within the house of the Carmelites of El Parral. It cannot be denied, however, that a thought of treachery passed across the royal—oh, so little royal—mind.

"Afterwards?" he murmured "But no—that would not do. I must keep my word—a painful necessity, but a necessity. The Osorios of Astorga are too powerful. To spite me, Valentine might return to the world. And the Pope would be glad enough to embroil the succession of Spain, in the interests of the Milanais and his own Italian provinces."

After all, better to keep his word! So, satiated with well-doing and well-intending, the King said a prayer, clicked his beads, and as he turned towards the slit in his bedroom through which he could see the high altar, he thanked God that he was not as other men. He could forgive. He could fulfil. Nay, he would go himself and witness the ceremony of the Black Veil—to make sure that his daughter really became the bride of Holy Church. And to this end he sent certain orders to Tarragona.

Philip II. had a natural eye for artistic effect. He would, indeed, have preferred to send the inconvenient Valentine willy-nilly to a convent. He would have delighted to arrange the details of the funeral pyre of these two dangerous heretics, John d'Albret and Francis the Scot. It would have cost him nothing, even, to permit the piquant young beauty of Claire Agnew to perish with the rest.

But Valentine la Niña had posed her conditions most carefully. The Marquis, her near kinsman, had come specially from Leon, with many gentlemen of the province in his train. For, though never insisted on, the nativity of Valentine was no secret for the grandees of her own province.

The chapel of the Convent of the Carmelites on the Parral of Madrid had been arranged by Philip's orders for a great ceremonial. He attended to the matter in person, for nothing was too great or too little for him.

A sweet sound of chanting was heard, and from behind the tall iron bars of the *coro* the spectators, as they assembled, could dimly see the forms of the cloistered nuns—of that Carmelite Order, the most austere in Spain, no one of whom would ever again look upon the face of man.

There before an altar, dressed for the occasion, and in presence of the King, Claire and John d'Albret stood hand in hand. There they exchanged their vows, with many onlookers, but with one sole maid of honour. And when it was demanded, as is customary, "Who giveth this woman?" the tall figure of Francis Agnew, bent and bearded, took his daughter's hand and placed it in that of Valentine, who, herself arrayed like another bride, all in white, with lace and veil, stood by Claire's side. Valentine la Niña looked once, a long, holding look, into the eyes of John d'Albret. Then she took the hand of the bride and placed it in his. The officiating priest said no word.

For, indeed, it was she who had given this woman to this man—more, too, she had given him her own life.

King Philip looked on, sternly smiling, from the stall which, as a canon of Leon, was his right. Now, however, he had laid aside his monk's dress, and was arrayed royally, as became the first cavalier of Spain. What the King was really waiting for came later.

Valentine la Niña retired to a tiring-room where, the first ceremonies accomplished, her splendid hair was cut close, and she was attired in the white and brown of the Order of the Carmelites. Then the final black veil was thrown over her head. She came forth with her sponsors—two cardinal-archbishops in the splendid array of their rank as princes of the Church. The chant from the choir rose high and clear. Behind the black bars the cloistered nuns, their veils about their faces, clustered closer. The wedding-party had drawn back, John d'Albret standing in the midst, with Claire on his arm, clinging close and sobbing—for the debt which another had paid. The procession of priests passed slowly back down the aisle. Valentine was left kneeling before the altar with only her sponsors on either side.

"Sister Maria of the Renunciation!"

The Archbishop of Toledo proclaimed the new name of this latest bride of Holy Church. Claire whispered, "What is it? Oh, what does it mean? I do not understand!"

For the Protestant and foreigner can never understand the awfulness of that sacrifice. Even now it did not seem real to Claire. Surely, oh, surely she was walking in a vain show. Soon she must awake from this dream and find Valentine by her side, as she had been for weeks past.

But, in the midst of the solemn chant, the black gratings of iron opened. The nuns could be seen kneeling on either side, their heads bowed almost to the ground. Only the abbess came forward, a tall old woman, groping and tottering, her bony hand scarce able to find its way through the dense folds of her veil.

She stretched out her hand, feeling this way and that, like a creature of the dark blinded by the light. The two cardinals delivered the new sister of the Order into her charge. This was done silently. The sound of Claire's sobs could be heard distinctly.

But ere the tall iron gratings shut together, ere the interrupted chant lifted itself leisurely out of the silence, ere the groping hands of the old blind abbess could grasp hers, Valentine la Niña had turned once more to look her last on the world she was leaving.

Her eyes searched for and met those of John d'Albret. And if soul ever spoke to soul these were the words they said to him, "This I have done for you!"

The huge barred doors creaked and rasped their way back, shutting with a clank of jarring iron, not to be again opened till another sister entered that living tomb.

Dimly the files of phantom Carmelites could be seen receding farther and farther towards the high altar. The chant sank to a whisper. Valentine la Niña was no more for this world.

With a choking sob Claire fell into her husband's arms.

"God make me worthy!" she whispered, holding very close.

AFTER THE CURTAIN

In the Mas of the Mountain the olive logs were piled high. The mistral of November made rage outside. But those who gathered round were well content. Claire sat by Dame Amélie's knee, her hand in her father's, her husband watching her proudly.

There were the three brothers, to all appearance not a day older—the Professor with a huge Pliny on his knee, the miller with the lines of farina-dust back again in the crow's feet about his eyes, and Don Jordy, who had taken up the succession of a notary's office in Avignon, which is a great city for matters and quarrels ecclesiastical, being Papal territory of the strictest: he also throve.

The three were telling each other for the thousandth time how glad they were to be free and bachelors. Thus they had none to consider but themselves. The world was open and easy before them. Nothing was more light than the heart of a woman—nothing heavier than that of a man saddled with a wife. In short, the vine having been swept clean, the grapes had become very, very sour.

All this in natural pleasantry, while Dame Amélie interrupted them with her ever-new rejoinder.

"They are slow—slow, my sons," she murmured, patting the head of Claire which touched her side—"slow, but good lads. Only—they will be dead before they are married!"

Into the quietly merry circle came Jean-aux-Choux. He brought great news.

"The Bearnais has beaten Mayenne and bought the others!" he cried; "France will be a quiet land for many days—no place for Jean-aux-Choux. So I will hie me to the Prince of Orange, and there seek some good fighting for the Religion! Will you come with me, Francis Agnew, as in the days before the Bartholomew?"

But the worn man shook his head.

"I have been too long at the oar, Jean-aux-Choux!" he said. "Moreover, I am too old. When I see these young folk settled in that which the Bearnais hath promised them, I have a thought to win back and lay this tired tickle of bones in good Wigtonshire mould—somewhere within sough of the Back Shore of the Solway, where the waves will sing me to sleep at nights! Come back with me, John Stirling, and we will eat oaten cakes and tell old tales!"

"Not I," cried Jean-aux-Choux, "I go where the fighting is—where the weapon-work is to be done. I shall die on a battle-field—or on the scaffold. But on the shore of mine own land will I not set a foot, unless"—he paused a moment as if the more surely to launch his phrase of denunciation—"unless the Woman-clad-in-Scarlet, Mother of Abominations, returns thither in her power! Then and then alone will John Stirling (called Jean-aux-Choux) tread Scottish earth."

So, without a good-bye, Jean-aux-Choux went out into the night and the storm, his great piked staff thrust before him, and the firelight from the sparkling olive-roots gleaming red on the brass-bound sheath of the dagger which had been wet with the blood of Guise.

Then the Professor, looking across at the lovers, who had drawn together in the semi-obscurity, murmured to himself, "Which is better—to love or to go lonely? Which is happier—John d'Albret—or I? Who hath better served the Lord—Valentine the cloistered Carmelite, or Jean-aux-Choux the Calvinist, gone forth into the world to fight after his fashion the fight of faith?"

Then aloud he said, speaking so suddenly that every one in the comfortable kitchen started, "Who art thou that judgest another man's servant? To his own master he standeth or falleth!"

Without, Jean-aux-Choux faced the storm and was happy. Within, the lovers sat hand in hand in a great peace, and were happy also. And in her narrow cell, who shall say that Valentine la Niña had not also some happiness? She had given her life for another.